I0563999

1001 NIGHTS WITH THE LYCAN KING

RUBY K.

Copyright © 2024 by Ruby K

All rights reserved.

No portion of this book may be reproduced in any form without written permission from the publisher or author, except as permitted by U.S. copyright law. No part of this publication may be reproduced, distributed, or transmitted in any form or by any means, including photocopying, recording, or other electronic or mechanical methods, without the prior written permission of the publisher, except as permitted by U.S. copyright law.

The story, all names, characters, and incidents portrayed in this production are fictitious. No identification with actual persons (living or deceased), places, buildings, and products is intended or should be inferred.

Book Cover by Selkkie Designs

Illustrations by ArtbyHaadi

Proofreading/editing by Emily at Second Set of Eyes.

Proofreading by Chloe at BookwormsbyPr

Before you read...

This is a fairytale retelling of 1001 Arabian Nights (not to be confused with Aladdin!). The story goes that the Sultan of Persia executed his first wife for being unfaithful. Henceforth, fueled by betrayal and a broken heart, he would take a virgin bride every night and have her beheaded at dawn. Until one woman insisted on becoming the Sultan's new bride and told him captivating stories, always ending on a twist right before dawn which would lead to another story. The stories of Aladdin, Sinbad the Sailor, and even Alibaba and the forty thieves were all part of stories narrated by Queen Scherezade. After one thousand and one nights, Queen Scherezade, now the mother of the Sultan's children, finally completed her stories. The Sultan professed his love for her and admitted to the error of his ways. In a time where women had virtually no rights, Queen Scherezade was an inspiring figure who used her mind and determination to save the lives of countless young women. I can only hope my FMC can be as inspiring.

Please be forewarned that this story has certain tropes, explicit content, loss of life, depression, childhood trauma, and themes of noncon/dubcon which everyone might not be comfortable with. However, let me assure you that everything between Amara and the King is consensual. You have to read to find out what exactly happens. For a full list of warnings, please visit my social media. If at any time you feel the need to stop reading, please do so. Your mental health is most important to me.

Contents

Dedication

For the queens fighting unseen battles—you do not need to be invincible, you just need the courage to rise, to heal, and to keep moving forward. Turn your scars into crowns.

My FMC, Amara, is not a chosen one. She is not a princess but a peasant. She is not a destined mate, and she does not possess any magical powers. But she is determined and courageous, which is what we truly need to overcome the trials and tribulations that can often blindside us.

Know that there is strength in your vulnerability and power in your truth.

Glossary of Terms

The kingdom of Elamaria is a fictional land within a setting that pulls from Persian, Middle-eastern, and Subcontinental cultures. Therefore, some words and phrases might be unknown to the reader. I have attempted to display them in mostly self-explanatory manners. However, to avoid confusion, here is a list of words that will crop up throughout the story.

1. **Baba:** Father

2. **Choli**: A short blouse that is worn with a lehenga. Choli is also known as a blouse.

3. **Dupatta**: A long scarf or shawl that is worn over the head, shoulders, or both.

4. **Emir:** A chieftain or independant ruler who has power over a province or tribe.

5. **Henna:** A reddish-brown dye that is used especially on hair and in temporary tattoos and is obtained from the leaves of an Old World tropical shrub.

6. **Jan:** Term of endearment which means my life or my soul.

7. **Lehenga** A traditional Indian outfit consisting of a long skirt, a blouse, and a dupatta (scarf). Lehenga is also known as ghagra.

8. **Salwar Kameez:** A traditional Indian outfit that consists of a loose-fit-

ting shirt (kameez) and pants (salwar). The pants are tapered at the ankle and often gathered at the waist with a drawstring.

9. **Shehenshah:** A title which means 'King of Kings'. In the subcontinent, Mughal Emperors held this title as they reigned supreme over the lesser kings, tribal chieftains, and feudal landlords.

Playlist

1001 Nights Playlist

Prologue

I am a child of the desert, born from the fiery sands and relentless sun. A product of its volatility, of its vast expanse of shifting dunes and scorching winds. With every step I take, the grains of sand whisper ancient tales of the survival of my people.

My skin is kissed by the sun, tempered to a dusky honeyed glow by the unforgiving elements. My eyes, like the endless horizon, hold the secrets of a thousand sunsets. In the blistering heat, I dance with the desert winds, my movements fluid and graceful. My soul is one with the sand, my footsteps leaving imprints that vanish as quickly as they appear. As quickly as I will disappear.

He is the King of the desert. Master of the countless dangers that lurk beneath the surface, waiting to ensnare the unwary traveler. He possesses an unparalleled mastery over the desert's fury. Capable of taming the untamed, bending the desert to his will. Just as he has subdued my heart, trapping it in his web of lies and deceit.

I am his bride...fated to die by his hand.

Chapter 1

The sun beat down mercilessly, casting a blinding glare across the endless expanse of desert sand. Each grain shimmered like flecks of gold under its scorching touch. I stood, *talwar* in hand, feeling the weight of the blade against my palm, the metal singing with anticipation.

Across from me, he lunged, a formidable figure amidst the swirling sand. My opponent's eyes burned with a fierce intensity, matched only by the relentless sun overhead. The wind whipped at our clothes, carrying with it the faint scent of sweat and sand.

I dodged agilely, jumping back with a smirk. The hilt of my *talwar* cool against my sweaty palm. As we circled each other, the air crackled with tension, the only sound the soft hiss of shifting sand beneath our feet. With a sudden rush, he lunged forward again, his curved blade slicing through the air with deadly precision. This time, I met his attack head-on, the clash of our blades echoing across the desert's landscape. Our gazes locked as our blades fought for dominance. This time, I would not relent. My left hand clamped over my forearm as I struggled to exert pressure. Struggled to push my opponent back. There was too much at stake to lose today.

The heat bore down upon us, sapping our strength with every passing moment. Beads of sweat dripped from my brow, stinging my eyes as I fought to keep my strength from waning. The sand beneath my feet shifted and gave way, the ground seemingly ready to swallow me whole as I stumbled backwards.

I hissed in frustration, my body bending backwards in a graceful arch as my attacker's blade swiped, missing my neck by a hair's breadth. I let my back hit the scorching sand beneath me, grateful for my tunic and starched white pantaloons which served as a barrier against the abrasive sand.

My *talwar* flashed in the sunlight as I brought it up to parry his blow. And so it went on, blow after blow. With every strike, I could feel my opponent tiring. Such is the connection when two people fight. It is a connection forged in the heat of battle. We were two warriors, locked in a dance as old as time itself, each move a testament to our skill and determination.

The sun dipped low on the horizon, casting long shadows across the desert sands. My breathing was becoming labored, my mouth parched from thirst. With a swift, calculated strike, he suddenly disarmed me, sending my *talwar* spiraling through the air to land with a dull thud several feet away in the sand.

I looked at my adversary, anger sparking in my gaze. I could not lose. In the blink of an eye, I reached for my dagger which had been previously sheathed and secured at my waist.

"Surrender, Amara, it is nearly sunset."

His voice was hoarse, belying his fatigue. The hint of eagerness coating his words was not lost on me.

"Never," I spat, rushing at him as I brandished my tiny weapon.

This was not just any dagger. The silver, jagged edges were specifically designed to prevent a cool, clean cut. It left a scar so distinct that one could not deny being wounded by the weapon carried by every Blade-Caller throughout the kingdom.

He dodged my attack, his foot crashing into the back of my knee as I attempted to prevent myself from sliding across the grainy sand. I fell forward with an "oomph". Before I could turn to attack again, he reached for the veil covering my head and entire face, save for my dark midnight eyes, from the harsh elements of our surroundings.

I jumped to my feet, my dark tresses falling over one shoulder as I glowered at him.

"You cheat!" I spat.

A warrior could not fight without their veil, for the tempestuous winds of the desert made it nigh impossible to move forward when sand particles clogged one's throat and scratched at the tender skin on one's face.

"Amara...my love," he murmured, ignoring my anger. His hand reached to curve around my hip, gently pulling me into his embrace. "Do not be angry just because you lost, like always."

He let out an "oof" when I elbowed him angrily and moved out of his grasp. My almond-shaped eyes narrowed in ire before I turned to obtain my *talwar* with a defiant toss of my head. My waist-length hair moving riotously around me. I bent to grab my *talwar* and then turned to stare at him, hands on my hips.

I hated losing. Especially to him.

"In the name of the divine, you look like an angel of the desert marching into battle," he breathed, eyes on my form. "A true warrior princess."

"Flattery will get you nowhere, Ashad," I retorted, giving another toss of my head before reaching for the camel skin filled with water.

We often had our sword fights in the desert. As a woman training to be a Blade-Caller, an elite female soldier unit for the kingdom of Elamaria, this was practice for me.

For Ashad, it was a chance to spend time with me. Ashad was my oldest friend, my dearest confidant, and, as of recent times, my fiancé. Recently, Father had agreed to give him my hand in marriage. I had only just turned 21. Yet my mother had had my bridal gown ready since the first day I turned 16. It was customary to give one's daughter to the first suitor who asked for her hand. Especially when you were ruled by a bloodthirsty King who demanded one bride a year from his people. A bride who ended up mutilated, brutally murdered, and decapitated by the time the sun rose on her wedding night.

Ten queens had died so far, and our tyrant King showed no signs of stopping soon.

The water was all but drained from my camel skin by now. I eyed Ashad, who looked like an overly self-obsessed peacock as he strutted about, gathering our belongings to secure against the camel.

The deal had been that if he won today's fight, I would give him a kiss. I sorely missed the times he had asked for stories in place of kisses. When we had been young and feelings of affection had not gotten in the way. But only with him did I ever stand a chance of losing. Within my training cadre, I was the top warrior. No one could best me.

"Come here...Amara-jan." Ashad pulled me into him, his term of endearment (Jan) attached at the tail end of my name, catching me off guard.

It was the first time he had called me his soul.

I swallowed convulsively.

Ashad may be my future husband, but I knew beyond the shadow of a doubt that aside from an intimate level of companionship, I felt nothing for him. There was no burning physical attraction that I often spoke of in my stories. That I often dreamed of for myself.

I closed my eyes as his mouth slanted over mine, his hand curved into the nape of my neck. My hands bunched the front of his white loose tunic as I fought the urge to push him away. He would be my husband soon. I had to get used to this. I must.

Rejecting him was out of the question. Father had already delayed my marriage long enough. We would not test our luck. For word on the dirt-path streets of our capital, Ilm, was that the King was looking for a new bride.

I jerked back quickly as the trumpets of Ilm blared to life. The deafening roar reverberated through the vast expanse of the desert, so loud and terrifying that I felt as though my ears might bleed. It was the harbinger of doom for every female residing within the kingdom.

My body moved of its own accord, turning to stare at the city. The watch towers were ablaze with torches burning bright. My heart lodged in my throat. The announcement had been made. I watched from atop the sand dune with Ashad by my side as soldiers rode out into the setting sun to scour the land and bring back prospective brides within 24 hours.

Tomorrow evening, each unmarried female over the age of 18 would be rounded up and presented to the Grand Vizier. Of them, he would choose a bride for the King. She would be dragged away into the deepest recesses of the castle, her body would be stripped of hair and rubbed with a mixture of besan (chickpea flour) and turmeric for exfoliation. She would be adorned in the most beautiful of bridal attire, the most expensive, weightiest gold, the most exotic perfumes.

After an entire night spent in prayer to the divine spirits above, she would be married to our murderous king. The new queen would not see the dawn. I had heard stories of the women found completely mutilated come morning. One particularly gruesome story came to mind as the horizon of the desert flickered with the ominous fire of the setting sun. They say she had a gaping wound in her stomach with her intestines spread about the marital bed. Her blood had painted the walls crimson. Henceforth, many referred to her killer as the Crimson King. That was too kind a title. He was a bloodthirsty monster.

This King. This murderer of innocent women. His sadism knew no bounds. My mother, before she died, told me that the man had been betrayed by his first love. Ever since then, he had wanted to make all the women of his kingdom pay. A few years ago, there had been word of an uprising by the tribal chieftains and Bedouin tribes. But the Crimson King was powerful. He had crushed his adversaries, making sure to kill their offspring as well lest any come back for revenge. Whispers of a rebel faction often reached my ears. But I highly doubted it actually existed.

"Asya," I murmured, fear lodging itself firmly into the pit of my stomach.

The Crimson King rarely chose a young bride. We were pushing our luck. My sister and I were well over 18, yet unmarried. Asya, my sister, older by only one year, should have been married by now. Her betrothed, Salim, was a silk merchant, and he had not returned from his travels. They were madly in love with one another.

Though my father had pushed for Asya to marry the bevy of men who had come in Salim's absence with offers to marry the beautiful daughter of the city's recluse and retired palace scribe, Asya had vehemently remained steadfast. She would marry Salim, or marry no one.

"Better to die the Crimson King's bride than to chain myself to those lechers!" Asya had proclaimed with a defiant toss of her head.

She and I were so alike. Yet so different. She loved her betrothed. I did not love mine.

"All will be fine, Amara-jan," Ashad spoke softly, his hand reassuring on my shoulder.

I could not shake the feeling that he was wrong. Something was going to happen. And I was completely powerless to stop it. Like a star hurtling towards the earth, its brilliance fading the closer it got until finally it was nothing but a fleeting ember swallowed by the vast expanse of the sky, leaving only whispers of a celestial journey. As we made our journey back into the capital, I too felt like a shooting star hurtling closer and closer to my own demise. To my own death.

Chapter 2

We were awoken and pulled out of our beds at dawn. The guards were rounding up all the females, going door to door and physically forcing some of the women, caught hiding, out of their homes.

Asya and I got dressed, guards standing right outside our home waiting impatiently. Resistance was futile. It was only singling you out in their eyes if you fought. One thing a woman did not want on today of all days was to attract the attention of the crown. It is how we had gotten this far.

"May the spirit of the divine goddess be with you," my father murmured, placing a kiss on each of our brows.

"See you at sunset, *Baba* (father)," I assured him, giving him one last hug before finally throwing a scarf over my head.

It was another way my sister and I had remained inconspicuous. Dull, muted clothes, drab scarves/dupattas to cover our heads, hunched shoulders. Unlike some who were delusional enough to think they would be the one to change the King, we knew better. Remain as invisible as possible and live to see another day.

By the time we stepped into the opulent courtyard of the palace to meet the Grand Vizier, I was as tightly wound as a snake waiting to strike. All day we had been dragged from one end of the city to another, only to finally arrive and have our identities verified by the palace workers.

Every fiber of my being wanted to run. I had stood here twice before at the ages of eighteen and nineteen. When I was twenty, I had fallen extremely ill and had been exempt from this farce. Now I stood here again, hopefully for the last time, at the age of twenty-one. The noose of trepidation around my neck tightened with every second that ticked by.

My eyes flitted to the intricate calligraphy adorning the walls, whispering tales of bygone eras. What would the kings of old say, had their spirits been able to speak to us? Would they not be disgusted, be horrified, that one of them was brutally murdering innocent citizens of the kingdom? And for what? For revenge on a woman he had killed long ago? Why must all women pay for the betrayal of one? Though I could not blame her. Nobody could love someone as evil as the Crimson King.

My eyes darted to the guards stationed along the periphery, their imposing presence a reminder of the gravity of the occasion. They were here to make sure no one ran. Because many had tried. And failed. By now, everyone knew to remain stationary. Younger girls were admonished and guided by those older and much wiser. The first to run was always the one most likely to be picked.

I breathed deeply, trying to ignore the palpable tension rippling throughout the open courtyard. Tall, slender pillars adorned with intricate carvings rose majestically towards the heavens, their marble surfaces gleaming in the soft glow of evening's twilight. Ornate archways on all four sides, embellished with delicate gold filigree to create a latticework of swirling patterns, caged us in.

In the center of the courtyard stood a magnificent sparkling fountain, the cascading waters creating a soothing melody that echoed through the air. Jets of water danced joyfully from the fountain's center, propelled upwards in elegant arches before gracefully descending in shimmering curtains. I watched each droplet catch the fading golden and red hues of the setting sun, scattering it in a dazzling display of colors that danced across the clearing, bouncing off the mosaic-tiled blue walls.

If this had not been a place where the angel of death walked, I might have enjoyed the beauty surrounding me. I might have admired the clothes of the women standing next to me. Some of us were adorned in our finest attire. But none wore a smile. Some sobbed softly, while others trembled with fear. A few seemed eager yet apprehensive, whispering that just maybe they could be the special one. The anomaly who got to live to see another day. Maybe even be the woman to make the King fall in love.

Fools. Satan cannot love. And our King is Satan incarnate.

"Welcome!" The Grand Vizier's voice boomed as he stepped into the courtyard through a domed archway, his scarlet robes billowing behind him.

I could not help but notice, for the first time, the guards who trailed him. They were dressed in the distinctive garb of the Blade-Callers, their loose white tunics rippling in the breeze. The white facial covering which draped over their heads and mouth, leaving only the eyes free for sight told me all I needed to know. I wore this same garb, five days a week for my training. It was necessary to learn how to fight in the standard uniform.

My heart sank at the realization that becoming a Blade-Caller meant working for the Grand Vizier. A man who picked women to be killed like one picked flowers on a cool summer day after the rain. Maybe becoming a Blade-Caller was not the best course of action for me after all. I would sooner drive my *talwar* into the Grand Vizier's stomach than protect his person. The only reason I truly wanted to be one was because my mother had been one until she had my sister and I.

"You have all been chosen for the great honor of potentially becoming queen of the mighty Kingdom of Elamaria." The Grand Vizier raised his arms as if in supplication to the divine spirits, his bearded face tilting upwards to look at the sky painted in the coral hues of twilight.

"King Zayed, King of Kings, the master of the desert, the holder of the keys to the kingdom...has expressed a preference for older brides. Ones who can satisfy his...more baser desires...his worldly cravings," the Grand Vizier settled on saying, eyeing the women before him. "Who will we choose? Who will become the next queen? Possibly the mother of the next King? Who will become Walid Sultan?" the Grand Vizier ended pompously, giving women false hope that they might birth the next heir to the throne.

Walid Sultan: the title given to the mother of the king. She often held more power than even the queen consort herself. Of course people would cower in her presence. But no one would become Walid Sultan. Least of all any of us. Normal peasant girls dragged out of bed at the crack of dawn to be murdered by a mad king. There was a reason it was always us. Never a daughter of the "precious" nobility.

When our king finally satiated his bloodlust for innocent virginal women's heads on a pike, he would no doubt marry and sire children. They would not be the children of commoners. *Baba* had told me once that the King planned to take a neighboring kingdom's widowed queen for a bride eventually. *Baba* was a recluse, a commoner. But there had been a time where he had worked in the palace. He had been a scribe for the previous King.

I tried to make myself scarce, unconsciously stepping into Asya's personal bubble.

Asya smiled at me, a reassuring one as if this was all a joke.

"You there," the Grand Vizier barked.

My face paled. His sharp calculating shrewd eyes were on my sister.

"What is your name?" The Grand Vizier's voice was firm, cutting through the silence like a sharp blade.

"Asya, Your Excellency," she replied, meeting his gaze without flinching.

Quickly, a scroll was handed to the Vizier. He looked over the contents briefly, before his gaze travelled again to my sister. My hand itched to grab my dagger sheathed and securely hidden in the folds of my clothes. They had searched my person for weapons before entering the palace, but not very thoroughly. After all, who would suspect us poor defenseless women to ever strike out?

"Ahh...daughter of the retired scribe, Idris. Tell me...how is your father?" The Grand Vizier's tone suddenly became kind, almost parental.

Those scrolls he looked through were brimming with detailed records of our identities.

"He...is well, Your Excellency," Asya murmured demurely. "Though as of late, he is unable to get about due to his advancing age."

Asya remained silent, head bowed as she attempted to remain humble.

"One would think he would have the sense to see you married off."

It was an observation. And a question. I knew the underlying question this man wanted to ask. Why had Idris not married off his beautiful daughter yet to prevent her from being chosen and killed off?

"Is there something wrong with you?"

I cringed. How dare he speak to my sister in such a way! I hated this man more and more. In previous years, he had barely paid us a cursory glance. The Grand Vizier had always firmly remained fixated on women well over their twentieth year. I gulped audibly. Asya and I both fell into that category now.

"My betrothed is a silk trader. His caravan has been delayed due to the sandstorms. Once he returns from his trading expedition, we plan to marry."

"Unless you become the king's new bride," the Grand Vizier corrected, a snake-like smile marring his features.

There was nothing paternal about him any longer.

"Hobbies?" His question was abrupt, demanding a quick response.

Asya hesitated for a moment, gathering her thoughts before replying, "I enjoy reading, Your Excellency, and practicing archery."

I could not help but puff my chest out a little proudly. If I was deadly with a sword, my sister was absolutely lethal with a bow and arrow.

The Grand Vizier's sharp eyes narrowed slightly, as if assessing her sincerity. "Can you play any musical instruments?"

Asya shook her head slightly, "No, Your Excellency. My talents lie elsewhere."

The Grand Vizier's expression remained inscrutable as he nodded, filing away her responses. He finally moved past us, not even glancing my way, and we both let out a collective sigh of relief. Asya looked at me as if to say "I told you all would be well." The Grand Vizier strode down the lines of girls, asking questions and going over their respective scrolls to verify names as well as parentage.

I was impatient to return home, knowing that until we were safely under *Baba's* roof, we could not truly believe all was well. My eyes trailed the Grand Vizier as he finally made his way back to the entrance of the courtyard. I bunched my eyebrows together in confusion. He had not chosen a bride yet. The man seemed to pace the length of the floor before us, deep in thought before finally looking up. His eyes landed on Asya.

"Asya, daughter of Idris!" his voice echoed with authority. "You have been chosen to be the next Queen of Elamaria."

My breath caught in my throat as his words sank in. Chosen? The realization hit me like a thunderbolt, sending a shiver down my spine. Chosen to be the bride of the king; chosen to die.

Asya's expression was a mix of surprise and great heartbreak. I could not let this happen to her. She deserved more than this. The one who had always looked after me. The one who had managed to care for *Baba* and I after Mother passed away when I was eighteen.

She loved Salim. Her marriage was supposed to be the happiest day of her life. Resolve and bitter regret hardened my beautiful older sister's face. I watched her exhale deeply. Her chin tilted upwards, evidence that she had accepted her fate. When Asya took a step out of line, I placed my hand on her arm to restrain her, pushing her back into the row. No. Not her. Never her.

"What are you doing, Amara? I cannot defy an order of the Vizier," Asya whispered. "He will punish all of us. You know this."

"No." It was one word. One word spoken from my lips that sealed my fate.

There were surprised whispers amongst the crowd. Everyone was wondering if I had lost my senses.

"No?" the Grand Vizier repeated, a beguiling smile painting his features as he took in our uncanny resemblance. Asya might be the prettier sister, but we still looked quite alike. "My dear girl... Are you refusing to let your sister abide by a royal edict? It is tantamount to treason...foolish girl."

Asya tried to shrug my hand off her arm. I deftly moved in front of her, walking purposefully towards the front of the gathering. All eyes were on me as a lump of dread slowly settled into the pit of my stomach. However, not once did I hesitate. For I knew with acute clarity that this was what must be done.

Standing before the imposing figure of the Grand Vizier in the resplendent courtyard where long ago the kings of old had frolicked with their children, I squared my shoulders as I met death head-on. Determination burning bright within me, my gaze met his disdainful one. This man was odious. I would gladly become queen for even one night if it meant I could get rid of him. The idea burned itself into my brain with the intensity of the blazing sun on a hot summer's day. The vindictive thought evolved until a clear and very concise one burst forth. It settled at the forefront of all my thoughts. I could rid our kingdom of this plague. Of this evil.

"Well, girl? Are you going to just mutely stare at me until I order your beheading?" snapped the Grand Vizier after reviewing the scroll that held vital information regarding my person.

His presence demanded respect, but I refused to cower before him.

"Do you not fear the repercussions of your defiance?" He took in my form loftily, probably trying to decide the worst possible punishment to bring about a slow painful death for my insolence.

I met his gaze without flinching, my resolve unshakable. "I fear nothing," I declared, my voice ringing with conviction. "My sister... she deserves an opportunity for happiness. She cannot marry the king."

The Grand Vizier looked at me before his eyes flickered to Asya who, by now, stood right behind me. I did not have to look to know she was probably begging this bag of bones for mercy with her eyes. Mercy for me. For *Baba*. She would gladly die a thousand times over if it meant we would be safe. So like Asya to always worry about us and never about herself.

"It has been done and there is nothing you can do to revert the order. She will be our new queen by this time tomorrow. The kingdom requires a queen."

"You will have your queen," I hissed, balling my hands by my sides. "I volunteer in my sister's stead."

The hushed voices around us rose in a crescendo so great, I might have been swept away by its tide had the Vizier not raised his hand to silence everyone. I could see the confusion, the shock playing across his features. Never had a woman volunteered to die. Until me. He did not know what to do.

"You...would give yourself...in her stead?"

I inclined my head, hoping this horrendous man would agree, hoping my sister would stop trying to pull me behind her. I may have been younger, but my body had been honed through countless hours of wielding a *talwar*, imbibed with strength through strenuous activity which hers had not endured. She had the upper-body strength of an archer, but I had the might of a warrior. She was never a match for me in hand-to-hand combat.

"I would."

"NO, AMARA!" Asya cried out, falling to her knees. She shook her head, worry for me consuming her. "You cannot."

I refrained from turning to look at her because I knew that if I had, I would have collapsed beside her. Now was not the time to show weakness.

The Grand Vizier's expression softened, a hint of respect shining in his eyes. "Your loyalty to your sister is commendable," he conceded, "but I cannot accept your offer. Your skills as a Blade-Caller are too vital to the kingdom. The kingdom needs your skills."

A breath escaped my lips, a fire ignited in my soul.

"Your Excellency," I clipped out, eyes slanting in consternation. "I can assure you, if I am not chosen….a blade in my hand is the last thing the royal crown would benefit from."

For I would surely drive it into your king's heart.

The unspoken threat was not lost on anyone

Horrified exclamations reached my ears. The warriors standing guard across the expanse of the courtyard tensed, as if preparing for me to attack.

The Grand Vizier turned an unsightly shade of purple over the implications of my words. I had just threatened the crown.

"I could sentence you to death for such-such-such blatantly treasonous thoughts!" he spluttered out, left eye twitching as a vein throbbed in his temple.

The man looked as if he would be physically ill. No one had ever outright spoken this way to him. It was treason, punishable by death.

"Or you could choose me to be the next bride. The end result would be the exact one you desire, I can assure you." I looked at him coolly, my knees threatening to give way as my voice held firm.

Like a lone traveler in the vast desert, never divulge your fear to your adversary, for in doing so, you lay bare the oasis of your vulnerabilities amidst the arid expanse, leaving yourself susceptible to their predatory gaze.

Ashad's words rang true in my mind, as if he was here whispering them to me in my ear. He had spoken those words to me long ago, as he taught me how to wield a blade. My dearest friend…Oh, Ashad, forgive me for what I have done.

The imperceptible nod of the Vizier was all it took. Maids dressed in fine silk with gossamer veils covering their faces emerged like glimmers of light to whisk me away from the courtyard's ornate confines.

A bargain had been made. My life for the safety of Asya's. I smiled grimly to myself. Never underestimate a warrior.

For concealed within the sanctuary of my garments, my dagger lay nestled, a silent sentinel ready to be unsheathed in the pursuit of justice. With unwavering resolve, I vowed to become the harbinger of liberation, to cast aside the shackles of tyranny and reclaim the safety of our people from the grip of this murderous king. My life was forfeit regardless. I would go down fighting.

With a resolute click, the brass doors sealed shut behind me, muffling Asya's fervent pleas for my release.

Chapter 3

Richly embroidered tapestries woven in gold thread draped the walls, their vibrant colors a stark contrast to the turmoil churning within me. As I made my way further into the palace towards queen's chambers, the scent of exotic spices hung heavy in the air, mingling with the heady fragrance of perfumed oils. Dwindling rays of sunlight filtered through intricately latticed windows, casting dappled patterns of light which danced and pirouetted teasingly with the shadows and created a mesmerizing kaleidoscope of patterns on the smooth, reflective surface of the polished marble floors. My floors.

The great four-poster canopy bed rested on the far wall, its frame crafted from dark rich wood and carved with intricate designs. The silky deep red fabric of the canopy cascaded down, pooling onto the floor in elegant folds. Never had I seen such a luxurious room. My room.

My floors.

My room.

For tonight.

Beneath this facade of grandeur, I sensed the ominous presence of sinister intentions. The king's objectives were clear, his lust for blood palpable. The grandeur of this room, with its opulent furnishings and intricate carvings felt suffocating, akin to a gilded cage designed to ensnare me in the clutches of a murderer.

The maids pulled me every which way, exfoliating my body, harshly plucking my eyebrows until they were in two perfectly shaped arches, ridding me of every single strand of hair that grew on even an inch of skin other than my scalp. It was ridiculous.

"Does he demand a woman's privates be rid of pubic hair before killing them?" I mocked darkly as the women busily scrubbed away at my arms with the yellow paste more commonly known as *uptan*.

I sat in nothing but a white chemise so they could work on me, like I was some doll to be dressed up for playtime. I had never played with dolls. I had much preferred swords.

My arms, legs, and stomach felt raw from the abrasive mixture. I had never felt so exposed in my life. One would think a small mercy would be granted in the form of not being subjected to this farce if one were to die. One would be wrong.

My words made them all give pause, their hands going slack as they registered the barb. I raised an eyebrow, waiting for a response. All five of the maids looked as if they would rather be anywhere else but here, looking at me. The girl whose days were numbered. A flash of sympathy crossed their faces. That only made me angrier. I did not need their pity.

Once the maids had properly trussed me up in the finest silk, like a sacrificial lamb, an array of food was brought into the room. I watched as two women, the royal tasters, consumed the food to make sure it was not poisoned. The irony of this did not escape me.

The floor was adorned with cushions for comfortable seating, arranged around the wooden table situated in the middle of this behemoth of a room. It was too big for one person. It was too big to die in. The thought curdled my hunger and the lump of dread that had settled into the pit of my belly only became more pronounced.

My stomach heaved in protest despite the freshly cooked *lavash*. Steam rose out of the flatbread, beckoning me to dip it into the aromatic curry. But I was not hungry. I did not need a last meal. I wanted to figure out how to live. I did not want to die.

Candles were lit around the Queen's chambers and I was finally left alone to my own dark musings. Sherazi, the head maid, was a meek little thing. She was tiny, and entered once the previous five maids tasked with grooming me had left. With her head bowed, she asked if I had need of anything before they retired for the night.

A prayer mat was left at the foot of my bed. I was supposed to pray tonight. Pray so that my sins would be cleansed before I died tomorrow. Praying to the goddess above had not helped the ones before me. Prostrating myself on a prayer mat with my forehead touching the ground would get me nowhere tonight. Dismissing Sherazi, I stood, determined to not let those complicit in my impending murder dictate what I was to do.

Moving forward, I flung the latticed doors open that led out to my balcony. It was a beautiful night. The stars above seemed to twinkle happily, oblivious to my impending doom. The full moon was bright, casting a luminous glow across the green foliage below. Below me, the palace grounds were a splash of greenery amongst the honeyed sands and dirt paths of Ilm. Torches softly illuminated the ground below, torches that were slowly flickering out as servants moved about the grounds preparing to retire.

An entire fleet of servants worked tirelessly to maintain the gardens below, to ensure the palm trees and flowers remained vibrant for the King's pleasure. Beyond these gardens lay an expanse of farmland tilled to provide sustenance. Beyond that...lay freedom from these oppressive walls. A movement from afar caught my attention. Most likely an animal scavenging for food. But now, standing out here....a tiny flicker of hope niggled its way into my brain. I peered down from my balcony, into pitch-black darkness, wondering how much of a jump this actually might be. Not much apparently. My lithe body turned deftly to look at the golden doors that led out of this room and into the hallway.

There were guards posted right outside those doors. Not to protect, but to keep their victim from running away. But here...in the back lawns...there were no guards. I watched as the last of the servants below disappeared back inside the palace, the palace grounds now swathed in shadows. My heart thudded against my ribcage as the possibility began to form in the deep recesses of my brain.

I could escape, run home to my family. We could steal away in the middle of night. Ashad would get word to Salim for Asya on where to find us. It was a wild plan. But it was plausible. My heart thumped wildly as the possibilities raced through my head. My brain worked vigorously, all possible scenarios racing through it only to circle back to one thought as clear as the desert sky: I could do this.

Without further ado, my feet carried me back into the chambers that were supposed to serve as my tomb. I ripped the sheets from the bed before reaching for the luxurious tapestries that adorned the walls. With a violent jerk, I ripped those ancient priceless relics off the walls without a second thought. My hand shook as my dagger, which I had expertly hidden so no one could find it and take it away from me, tore into the handmade depictions of battles fought long before my time. Of queens who had ruled long before I. Queens that had lived to tell the tale. Queens that had lived to see many dawns come and go.

My hands were busy at work, viciously destroying centuries-old works of art more expensive than the mud house I lived in. I did not care. I was getting out of here.

Dividing the cloth into long thin strips was only the first part of my task. The next was tying them together, knotting the expensive fabric to create a long rope which I would tether to my balcony before using it to lower myself to the ground. In quick succession, I looped my haphazardly made creation around the railing of my veranda. Sending up a silent prayer for success, before closing my eyes, I jumped.

My hands gripped the soft fabric, legs slipping against the silken material as I clung to the slender rope for dear life. I remained suspended in the darkness like a spider dangling from a silken thread, looking down at the deep abyss before me. It seemed like a longer way down than I had anticipated. My heart skipped a beat as a wave of vertigo overtook me. My grip on the rope grew tighter, a fierce resolve pushing back against the encroaching panic. Now was the moment to stand firm, to refuse to surrender to fear. Slowly, I began to move downward, legs slipping over the knots, hands aiding my body's descent.

A sense of urgency pulsed through me with each passing second. Because with every downward movement, I could feel the makeshift rope groaning under the strain, the ominous creaking echoing in the stillness of the night. These fine threads had not been made to hold the weight of someone barreling towards escape from death. They had been made for beauty. My heart hammered against my ribs like a trapped bird, its frantic rhythm matching the cadence of my hastened descent. Almost there. The rope groaned in protest. It would not hold much longer.

With a solid, triumphant thud, my sandal-clad feet hit the ground, and I finally allowed myself to breathe a sigh of relief. Now, I had to get out. Freedom was within my grasp and I hastened my stride, completely lost but firm in the knowledge that at some point, I would encounter the palace walls indicating the border of the palace grounds.

That imbecile vizier would realize he had underestimated this 'girl' come morning. The murderous king would be denied his prey. The pit of my stomach dropped as I thought of what he might do. Would he find someone else to kill?

Guilt crept up my spine. I was escaping, only to leave a spot open for some other unsuspecting innocent female. Someone who might not be able to defend herself as well as I.

My steps began to falter as I looked every which way, wondering if I was making the right decision. A frustrated sigh escaped my lips, my conscience roaring to life. Should I turn back? My eyes tried to discern these unknown surroundings, but it was too dark. The moon had dipped behind the clouds, cloaking everything in the night's shadow.

With another sigh, more resigned than frustrated at this point, I realized that the border walls were still very far off. The back of my neck prickled with an eerie awareness as another thought struck. There were no guards for miles and miles. It seemed odd that the palace was teeming with them. But here, in this open endless space where enemies could easily infiltrate...not a single sentry was posted. The thought did not sit well in my mind. Were they overconfident? Careless? No. It was something else...

A delicate fragrance wafted through the air, drawing my attention to the night flowers blooming amidst the dark. The Queen of the Night only bloomed at this time amongst the prickly thorns of the cactus. It was my favorite flower, but rare on the barren lands of Ilm. Of course our king's lush gardens would carry them. I moved closer to look at the white flowers, their petals shimmering like silver pearls, beckoning me closer with an otherworldly allure. Without hesitation, I reached out to pluck one, inhaling the intoxicating scent in hopes that the familiarity of something I was partial to, might calm my nerves. It was imperative to ground myself and strategize.

The flower found its way behind my ear as I decided to stop second-guessing myself. Tonight, I was getting out of here and then my family and I would run away. We just had to make it to one of the neighboring kingdoms. The tribal chieftains inhabiting the far-off mountains which bordered our lands were constantly at odds with our kingdom. Maybe they would give us refuge? Or maybe we could even seek asylum in the land of Solaria, a beautiful tropical island ruled by a just king and his beautiful queen. The possibilities were endless.

But as I turned to continue on my way, a sharp crack shattered the silence behind me, jolting me from my reverie. My heart hammered against my ribs as I spun around, my senses on high alert.

"Who is there?" I called out, voice barely above a whisper, the words trembling with uncertainty.

What would they do if they found me out here trying to escape? Had I just sealed my impending doom a night early?

No answer came, only the eerie silence of the night enveloping me like a shroud. Panic clawed at the edges of my consciousness as I scanned the darkness for any sign of movement. I could hear the heavy breathing of...an animal. My chest constricted with a mix of relief—knowing a guard had not discovered me and trepidation over what exactly had. I braced for whatever unseen animal lurked, ready to pounce.

My hand moved to reach for my dagger, but then I stilled in complete shock. The moon peeked through the clouds, showing me exactly what had been stalking me.

Without warning, a great monstrous figure emerged from the shadows, its hulking form looming ominously before me. As the moonlight cast its eerie glow upon the creature before me, I beheld a sight that sent shivers down my spine. Towering above me on two powerful legs, the beast stood upright with an imposing stature that seemed to defy the laws of nature. The midnight black fur bristled with a primal intensity, every muscle rippling beneath the surface like coiled springs ready to unleash their fury.

But it was the creature's face that chilled me to the bone. A snout protruded forward, sniffing the air eagerly. A vicious, menacing snarl formed on the beast's face, sharp teeth gleaming in the dim light like daggers poised to strike. The pointy alert ears twitched with heightened senses, attuned to the slightest movement in the surrounding darkness.

Despite the humanoid form, there was no mistaking his wolfish visage that stared back at me with eyes that burned with an otherworldly intensity. They glowed with an unnatural red hue, reflecting the primal instincts that lurked within the depths of the creature's soul. Its claws, long and razor-sharp, flexed with lethal intent, poised to rend flesh from bone within a single swipe.

In that moment, I realized with a sinking dread that I stood face to face with a being that defied comprehension, a creature of myth and legend brought to life in the darkness of the night. And as it loomed over me with a predatory glare, I knew that I was utterly at its mercy, a mere mortal ensnared in the merciless grip of a beast that walked the line between man and monster. A creature that looked at me with the unmistakable gleam of a predator looking upon its prey.

Chapter 4

A scream tore from my throat as I stumbled backwards, my heart a wild drumbeat. For a moment, I thought it was a hallucination. Something so unnatural could not be real. But it was very real, and it was looking at me as if I was its next meal. Immediately, on pure instinct rather than conscious thought, my body turned and fled, footsteps echoing on the ground as I ran for my life.

Without thinking twice, I disappeared into the copse of trees nearby, zipping through the woods as I frantically realized that instead of escaping, I had brought myself directly into the face of doom.

A chilling howl reached my ears. A howl of a beast stalking prey. A howl that was too close for me to believe there was any chance of escaping. With a renewed zeal and motivation, I pushed myself harder, weaving through the trees easily with my tiny body, whereas his hulking form found it difficult. That was exactly what my quick mind had counted on. However, I doubted it was enough to slow him down or for me to escape with my life.

It was painfully obvious that no matter how fast I ran, the creature remained right behind, thunderous footsteps getting closer, like the approach of an unstoppable tempestuous storm. Branches whipped at my face, roots tangled beneath my feet. Though I had abandoned my sandals long ago, I persisted, motivated solely by the instinctual drive to survive.

A gasp left my lips, a tremor wracked my body when I felt it closing in...close enough that his hot breath fell upon my back.

The predator was toying with me. Like a cat toying with its quarry before delivering the final blow. I suppressed a defeated sob, berating myself internally. I did not come out here just to be killed by this beast. No!

With a scream, I pushed myself faster, this time jumping over the stones and fallen logs that I knew would rip open more scratches on the tender soles of my feet. My body had trained rigorously in the scorching sand; I could manage running barefoot in a forest. There was no other choice.

Up ahead to the far left, one low-lying branch caught my attention. A plan formed. My body took the sharp turn, and satisfaction pulsed through me when the beast behind was not able to do the same. It went barreling by the turn, unable to stop in time.

I heard the growl of frustration, the snarl of anger. There was a whoosh of hot angry breath as it closed in on me again. But I did not slow down. Only a little farther...

A tugging sensation indicated that claws had snagged onto the silk shirt I wore. I lunged forward, head bent, cloth ripping away from my lower right hip all the way up to my neck.

The threads unraveled with a soft rustling, almost like a whisper, as my shirt and loose trousers were pulled apart by the strong claws of the beast in a single lethal swipe. Cool air whipped against the newly bared skin as I was now left only in a flimsy chemise.

A thud and guttural roar of pain behind me indicated that this otherworldly creature hit the branch that had only been high enough for my form to get through. It was not enough to put it down. But it was enough to buy some time. Enough time to get back to my rooms. Running all night was nigh impossible for me.

Checking behind me, I could make out the hulking form growling in anger, sniffing the air to smell my body out. I cursed, looking down at my bleeding feet. At this rate...he would find me...unless...

The only option was to throw it off the trail. Throw its nose off my scent.

With a deep breath, I veered off the path I had been on, darting into the dense thicket of trees surrounding me. My feet were bleeding profusely, and I made sure to rub my blood against all the trees surrounding me intermittently. This creature, this demon...would need time to smell the path I took if the scent of my blood seemed to be everywhere. My body protested, begging for a break. But I kept racing forward with purpose.

Finally, satisfied that I could spare a few moments, my hands tore at the hem of what was left of my tattered chemise to bind my feet. I could hear the beast crashing through the foliage behind. His roars echoed through the night, sending shivers down my spine. This had to be quick, I had to be clever.

Standing, I looked up at the sky, trying to discern my position in this damned hell I found myself in. My eyes took in the heavens above, momentarily wishing I could simply float up and join them. Wishful thinking stemming from bed-time stories Mother would regale us with. I had to accept that fanciful notions of possessing my very own magic carpet, that could take me high enough to touch the stars, were a thing of the past. If only this life were so easy.

Stealthily, I began to move. A few times, I ended up going in the wrong direction, the stars above a sure sign that I was moving farther away rather than closer to the palace. The bone-chilling growls of frustration from my predator were still discernible, but they seemed to be getting farther and farther away the closer I got to the palace.

It seemed that the king had his own personal monster stalking the perimeter. It is why guards were not needed here. It is why any enemy who infiltrated the palace from behind was swiftly obliterated.

Finally, I broke through the trees and sighed in relief. The palace was in sight. I could see the very spot I had plucked my flower which now lay crumpled back in the copse of trees along with any hopes of escaping.

The distant howl of the beast behind me reminded me that now was not the time to mourn my failed plan of escape or my lost flower. Purposefully, I began to move forward, passing the beautiful white flowers in full bloom. With each step I took, I brought myself closer to at least another day of life. Another chance to figure out how to survive. Currently, my life would be forfeit if I remained out here.

However, in the next moment, a massive form crashed into me with bone-crushing force. The breath was knocked out of my lungs as I was thrown to the ground, the pain of the impact momentarily paralyzing me. Fur enveloped my body, warm yet dangerous, softer than feathers. The pain in my abdomen doubled and chaos reigned in my mind whilst the beast hurtled into my form and pinned me to the ground beneath its crushing power.

Panic surged through me like a tidal wave. My body writhed and struggled as I fought against the creature's relentless grip, but it was no use. I was trapped, helpless against the merciless monster.

As I lay trapped beneath the creature, its hot breath washing over my face, I braced myself for the inevitable.

There would be no escape from this monstrous creature that now held me captive in its powerful grasp. The stench of decay and blood filled my nostrils, mingling with the metallic tang of fear that coated my tongue.

Look death in the face when it is time, for a true warrior does not fear death, especially not when it arrives in the heat of battle.

Ashad's words resonated in my mind. I looked up to meet those otherworldly eyes, glowing red. They were locked on me with vicious intent. The vile monstrosity reared back, mouth wide open to feast on its next meal. My gaze stayed firm. I would look death straight in the eye. The beast faltered for a split second.

That was all I had needed.

My silver dagger came down hard over the hairy forearm pinning my body down, embedding itself deeply. I felt the sound of metal scraping bone. The creature reared back, howling in pain. In one deft move, I pulled out my weapon and wildly scrambled away, body groaning in protest. Gritting through the residual pain from being tackled viciously, I forced myself to stand. Turning to see the hulking beast's back was to me, I did not hesitate. Without thinking twice, I jumped, my legs straddling its waist from behind as I dug my dagger straight where a heart should have been if the humanoid form were any indication.

Another howl of pain. With one fierce jerk of his body, I was thrown off, like a pesky fly. Any triumph I felt over momentarily besting my predator was fleeting. The dagger was still in my hand. But I had felt the raw power rippling against my body. This beast was much too powerful. Quickly, I ran, leaving it hunched over in pain. Prayers were uttered with laboring breath that this thing would die after meeting the end of my blade.

But something told me I was not that fortunate.

My lungs felt as if they might burst. I forced myself to push forward.

With determination in my eyes, I reached for the rope still hanging from the veranda. The soft fibers stung my aching palms as I pulled myself up, ignoring the searing pain that shot through my arms and radiated outwards to every inch of my body. Every muscle strained and shook with effort, but I refused to give up. My fingers wrapped tightly around the rope, clenching with a fierce intensity as I continued to climb, driven by pure willpower. Sweat dripping down my face, each breath was a struggle against the weight of my own body as I pushed forward, determined to reach the safety of the veranda above.

As my hands moved up the rope, the fabric began to unravel beneath my fingertips. Panic rose in my chest as I struggled to find a secure holding. The cloth tore further with a deafening sound, and I knew I had to move quickly. My trembling fingers searched for stable purchase as I climbed higher and higher, determined to reach the top before it was too late.

I climbed faster and faster, limbs groaning in protest.

With a gasp, I saw the fabric give way beneath me, tearing from its delicate seams. The deafening sound of ripping rope echoed through the air as I struggled to hold on, my luck running out with each passing second. I pushed myself higher, but finally my lifeline gave way, ripping clean in two, and I felt myself falling.

Falling to my doom as a scream was rent from my throat, belying the fear of the monster waiting eagerly below for a chance to feast on the dead mangled body of a peasant girl who had been stupid enough to think she could make it out alive.

In a final bid to save myself, my hand reached out wildly and I successfully grasped the bottom half of the railing. Another scream tore from my mouth, searing through my throat with clawing pain. I dangled from one arm, feeling as if the rest of my body would simply break away from the limb that kept my body from plummeting to its eventual demise.

Every single nerve ending was crying out in protest, my body fatigued and in pain. I inhaled deeply. Warriors persevere. Agilely, I flung my feet forward, using the momentum to push myself forward and up. My other hand also managed to grasp the bottom railing. With one final grunt of pain, I pulled myself up, flipping over so that my back landed on the cool stone floor of the balcony. Never had I thought I would be glad to be in this goddess-forsaken place. But here I was. Grimly, I realized I would take the king over that monstrosity down below any day.

Exactly what was it?

Chapter 5

"By the goddess!"

Sherazi's exclamation of surprise woke me sooner than I was physically ready. I groaned; my body ached in a thousand different places. It hurt to move and if I had not broken a rib, surely I had bruised a few. The sensation throbbing across every inch of my body was akin to repeatedly being pummeled into the ground.

"What happened?!"

I raised my head from the massive bed that felt like it was swallowing me whole. She was eyeing the torn tapestries...the ripped sheets...

Her eyes rose to meet mine through the parted curtains and a curse issued from her lips.

"You are injured!" she exclaimed.

I looked down at my body, grimacing in pain over the slight movement. My own eyes widened as I recalled that I had been so exhausted, I had fallen asleep in the tattered silk chemise from last night. A chemise that, in its torn state, exposed my entire upper torso, which was now severely bruised. I moved my hand to reach for a sheet, only to recall I had ripped them all last night to make a rope. To escape. Except I had not escaped. Now they might just skewer me and place my head on a pike for all to see. I had ruined priceless works of art in my zeal last night. One tapestry alone was worth more than my entire hut.

"No...no...no." Sherazi shook her head, the tension on her face worsening with every passing moment.

Pursing her lips, with swift efficiency, she headed to the doors of the balcony. I had left them open last night. Truly, my body had been screaming in pain. It had taken every last vestige of my strength last night to drag myself into bed and fall asleep.

Her voice wafted inside, panic-stricken.

"Oh goddess, have mercy on us all. This does not bode well! You...you..."

She rushed back inside, the remains of my rope in her hands, face pale.

"You tried to escape last night," she rasped out, looking for all the world as if she was the one about to be sent to the dungeons.

"I came back," I retorted swiftly, praying that this tiny girl would prove useful.

Would she keep my secret? I moved off the bed, trying to stand but winced when my cut-up feet twinged in protest.

"You are injured," Sherazi gasped, eyes flitting to the bloodstained silk still wrapped around my feet.

Sherazi's eyes then went to the untouched prayer mat resting at the foot of the bed. Her lips pressed together, confusion flickering across her eyes.

"You did not even pray."

She made it sound like I had committed the gravest sin.

The doors flung open without warning. Sherazi froze. My eyes met a man who, for a minute, I thought might be our king. I had only ever seen the man from a distance when he addressed his people from the balcony of this palace. One time, I had watched him from afar when he travelled through the city of Ilm on his elephant.

The man had sat upon his makeshift throne, draped in thin gold fabric that fluttered in the breeze. The poor animal beneath him had borne the weight of a ruthless killer.

But the kind eyes that stared back at me could not be those of the king. They were smiling kind eyes that sought to reassure me. Brown eyes. The king's eyes were green.

"Ah, you are the one that has created such a ruckus." Amusement rather than anger colored his tone as his eyes took in my bruised and battered form. His lips tilted in amusement, eyes going to the torn rope held by Sherazi.

Sherazi took a step back, her eyes wide in fear.

"I had nothing to do with this, Your Grace," she murmured, her tone low and respectful.

"Of course you did not," he chuckled, walking forward towards me.

I took a cautious step back. Who was this man?

He wore a sword at his side. His chest was draped with a thin vest, revealing well-defined muscles. It seemed more like a decorative accessory than a practical article of clothing. On top of his head rested a turban accented by a single dark green jewel. Brute strength radiated from him. He was a warrior, like me.

I looked at his face again. This man seemed familiar...

"My name is Kadin," he said kindly, eyes on my face. "I am King Zayed's cousin and general of his army. You may have met my father yesterday. The Grand Vizier?" His eyes glinted in amusement, taking in the look of consternation that I made no attempt to hide. "I can assure you, I am nothing like him."

He again took a step closer to me. I took another back.

I was all too aware that my body was scantily clad before this man. There was a huge rip across the front of my chemise from ribs to abdomen. The side of my chemise was also frayed, exposing my left hip. My underclothes were the only articles of clothing effectively shielding parts of my body that I had never exposed to a man. When one is training to be a warrior, there is little time for love or even frivolous dalliances.

Kadin seemed to finally register my awkwardness and respectfully turned his back to me.

"Sherazi, draw her a bath. See that someone tends to her wounds. Your Highness, it was a pleasure to meet you. The goddess knows you are exactly what we have been waiting for."

And with that, Kadin blew out of the room as easily as he had entered. Taken aback by his cryptic message, I could only stand in my torn chemise, utterly confused.

"Come, we must prepare you...again," Sherazi muttered.

And so it began anew. The maids all collectively pushed, pulled, and trussed up my body. They treated the purple bruises by rubbing them with a healing salve. It alleviated the pain and made the discoloration less apparent.

By the time I was ready for my wedding, I could hardly recognise myself as the unsightly injured woman from this morning.

"It is time, my lady," Sherazi muttered respectfully, leading me towards the great hall where I would finally meet my killer.

"I do."

"I do."

"I do."

I spoke the words thrice, for making a vow thrice makes it binding. My head remained bent during the entire ceremony. I stood before long garlands of cascading fragrant jasmine flowers that formed a delicate curtain between the king and I.

It was customary for the vows to be said through the partition. My eyes lifted to look up through my golden gauzy veil only to see the figure of the King walk towards me, parting the long strands of white and red flowers hanging between us. He stepped closer, reaching for my veil.

My heart was now fluttering incessantly against my ribcage, frantic to be set free. Even it could sense we had been caged. We were in danger. I swallowed audibly, wondering frantically, '*Is this man going to kill me where I stand? In my bridal dress? In my mother's jewelry; my hands still red from henna?*'

He reached for the edge of my veil. My hands clenched at my sides, my eyes remained locked on his waist where a grand sword rested. I would never be able to reach his sword in time. Safely hidden within the draping of my skirts, the dagger was out of sight. I would never be able to reach for my dagger in time either.

If I was not so sure that his guards would kill me within the blink of an eye, I might have reached for my weapon. I might have buried it deep within his dark heart so that no more women died at his hands. I am not the first. Nor will I be the last if I fail.

King Zayed's hands gently trailed along the tiny pearls sewn into the hem of my veil with such love by my mother. Had she known she was preparing my burial dress, she might not have completed this task so ardently before her passing. The king stilled, a distinct deep exhale from him registering in the panicked recesses of my mind.

And then the veil was lifted whilst my eyes remained fixated on the floor, trailed on his gold sandal-clad feet mere inches from my long skirt.

I shut my eyes momentarily, feeling as if I were a helpless animal backed into a corner. Inhaling deeply, I hardened my heart with resolve. Finally, I tilted my chin to gaze defiantly into....

I blinked, taken aback momentarily.

Pools of dark hazel, more green than brown, stared back at me. His gaze was hard and firm. Resigned. Not cold and ruthless. Not the look of a man who wants to kill me. He stared at me for a minute that seemed more like an eternity, taking in my hair braided intricately with jasmine flowers. Those weary eyes swept over my features as if he was looking for something. Briefly, they dipped down to the rest of my form before turning to address his noblemen.

"I present to you....Queen Amara of the Kingdom of Elamaria!"

His voice was loud and commanding. Authoritative. It sent a shiver down my spine.

"I call upon you all to honor and protect her. She is the heart and soul of our realm. So mote it be, under the watchful gaze of the divine goddess, may our allegiance be steadfast and true; now and forevermore."

The words were repeated after King Zayed, spoken in hushed reverent murmurs.

"So mote it be, under the watchful gaze of the divine, may our allegiance be steadfast and true; now and forevermore."

A featherlight touch on my arm alerted me to the fact that the king beckoned for me to walk alongside him. Confused, I followed, nearly stuttering to a stop when his hand touched the small of my back, guiding me down the aisle. Away from the priest who made us recite our vows. Away from the nobles gathered around. The Grand Vizier stood at the doors. He bowed his head, though his eyes never left mine.

"Congratulations, King Zayed... Queen Amara."

My name was spoken ominously. As if he himself might be the harbinger of my death. Will he be? Because this man standing next to me did not seem inclined to kill me. Not yet anyway. Not in the way he touched me. Not in the way he looked at me...

"Take her to her rooms," King Zayed directed with another deep exhale, handing me off to one of my maids.

"Yes...My King," the maids respond collectively, heads bowed, eyes on the floor.

I was led away by them, wondering...when did he plan to kill me?

My hands shook, my breathing came hard and fast. Was he going to fulfill his marital rights and then kill me? A horrified laugh burst forth from my lips as I entered the queen's chambers, walking past the adjoining sitting room and into my bedroom.

"My Queen?" Sherazi queried in alarm. "Are you all right?"

"I...I...."

Words failed me. For how can one describe the abject horror of the absolute certainty that tonight will be their last? I was not fool enough to think I would survive the night unscathed. "Leave me!" I snapped angrily.

If I was going to die, they could at least allow me a few moments of peace. To think. To...figure out my next course of action. I was still alive. There had to be a reason I was still alive!

The dagger. I needed to use the dagger. Tonight when he came. If he came...

"We must prepare the marital bed," Sherazi whispered, helplessly gesturing towards the vast bed covered in decadent pillows and beige silk sheets.

New sheets. I also vaguely registered that new tapestries now adorned the walls.

"You must wait to receive the king in your marital bed," Sherazi whispered, eyes sad as she looked at me.

More like deathbed, I thought to myself darkly.

My hand unconsciously went to press against the side of my leg. The side where I had my dagger tucked away. I tensed. Were they going to make me change first?

"Come, My Queen..." Sherazi murmured soothingly, pulling the bedsheets back and motioning for me to sit on the bed.

I complied, huddling in on myself and clutching my legs to my chest.

He really was going to kill me in this bed.

"Would you like to eat anything while you wait?"

My stomach rolled in protest. It seemed as if they wanted to feed me to assuage their own guilt.

"No," I whispered, letting my head rest over my knees as my hands fisted in the fabric of my skirt.

The beads and pearls dug into the soft skin of my cheek. I embraced the pain. I needed it to anchor myself.

"All right, My Queen. Good...goodnight," Sherazi whispered before retreating out of the room.

I knew what she meant. She was telling me good-bye. Rose petals were spread around me, the deep red contrasting with the light gold accents of the bedsheets. Circling the canopy overhead were strings of blood-red flowers. Instinctively, my hand went to rest over the cool blade of my dagger hidden in my skirt. I breathed, letting the firm silver keep me grounded. Keep me from panicking. I rubbed my cheek harshly against the beads of my skirts, resting my head on my knees. There was no way out. Last night, I was nearly attacked by that monster that patrolled the perimeter.

"You will not panic, Amara," I scolded myself, my scared voice bouncing off the walls in the empty room. "You will not fail."

My grip tightened over the hilt of the blade.

I did my best to look vulnerable and scared. Always let the predator underestimate its prey. I waited with bated breath...the minutes turned into an hour. Then another hour. Was he not coming? Was I just supposed to sit here like a statue and die from hunger? Was that the—

My thoughts were interrupted when the door swung open slowly. King Zayed strode in, his face blank. His lips were set in a harsh scowl. I looked at him approaching the bed in the candlelight. The door creaked shut behind him, pulled closed by a guard. There was a guard waiting outside to take my dead body away once the deed was done. My heart thundered in my chest, begging me to run.

The bed dipped when the king sat down next to me.

"Have you no will to live any longer?"

His voice was rough, a deep timbre that carried the tone of a weary traveller.

"Why did you volunteer?" he pressed when I remained quiet and huddled in the middle of the bed

If he struck first, I would have to be ready to dodge his attack. My mind searched the room, looking for anything I could use to my advantage. I was looking everywhere but at him.

My hands shook but firmly remained clenched at my sides. I had to wait. Knuckles grazed against my cheek. I was momentarily taken aback by the unexpected gentle touch.

"It is a shame you will be dead by dawn," King Zayed muttered before pushing me down to lie on the bed.

Chapter 6

My back hit the mattress with a light thump, rose petals fluttering against the sheets due to the impact. My breath caught. I tensed, hand ready to pull my blade out. I just had to wait for an opening.

"Tell me, Amara...have you ever lain with a man before?" King Zayed breathed the question against my cheek, his hands on my shoulders as he pinned me to the bed.

Revulsion skittered through me. I would have to let him do this to me. His weight on the mattress shifted and he moved closer. I squirmed instinctively, despite my resolve to remain still.

My hands were not bound and I told myself I could do this. I could get rid of him for everyone. I might die in the process. But we would be rid of this monster who had been killing the daughters of Elamaria for the past decade.

"I have remained chaste for my husband," I muttered, speaking the words that were ingrained into every woman born in this kingdom since the day she was born.

Remain untouched. The pleasures of the body were only to be experienced with your husband. A woman who could not protect her virtue was a disgrace. It was as if our worth merely lay between our legs. Despicable.

The air in the chamber felt heavy with tension, the silence broken only by the crackling of the torches on the walls. I willed myself to remain composed despite the fear threatening to consume me. It was a horrible predicament I found myself in: praying to be raped rather than killed. Just so that I could find an opening to kill him.

"Ah... I am sure that is what they tell you. But have you really...remained chaste?" King Zayed queried, his voice dripping in acerbic disdain.

As if he did not believe me. As if he himself did not believe the words I spoke.

Without warning, his grip on my shoulders tightened and he shifted on the bed so that he no longer lay next to me. Now, he hovered over me, eyes boring into mine with an intensity I could not even begin to understand.

His hands trailed down my sides and I exhaled, fighting the urge to buck under him. To defend myself. He gripped my ankles quickly, pushing my legs into a bent position. I closed my eyes, tears gathering behind my eyelids.

He was going to use my body for his pleasure. He parted my legs, and positioned me so that my feet were flat on the mattress.

My chest heaved in fear, cold terror clawed up my spine. I itched to fight him and defend myself. But I could not. Not if I wanted to win. My hands twitched, and it was all I could do to force myself to keep them from scratching his eyes out. I just had to be patient. I had to be strong. Once he was buried deep inside of me, I would grab the dagger and plunge it into his murderous heart. I might die for murdering the king, but I would die a hero. For someone like me, there was no better way to leave this world.

His hands began to travel up the inside of my thighs, thumbs rubbing circles in an exploratory manner against my bareskin. Disgust and shame sneaked into my belly. I would have to allow this violation of my body. If things had been different, I would have fought him by now. But I only had one chance at this. One chance to dispose of this sorry excuse for a King. He could have any woman he wanted. He was a king. Yet he chose to rape and then kill his brides.

I resisted the urge to kick and bite. To fight. His hands were hot; his face was red. The searing violation of my body stopped when they reached my underclothes. I braced myself for his forced entry, unconsciously arching my back. I had never lain with a man, but I knew this would hurt.

His hand travelled over my womanhood, briefly cupping the soft mound of flesh in his palm before resuming his exploration. I dared to look at him to see his eyebrows furrowed in concentration.

In one deft move, he hooked his thumbs into the waistband of my long beaded skirt, pulling it off me abruptly.

"I am sorry," he grunted as the cool air hit my bare legs.

"Sorry for raping me? Or sorry for killing me? Or both?" I could not help but think darkly.

"But—" My eyes widened as he dug his hand into my skirt. NO! "I do not fancy being killed by my queen on my wedding night."

He extracted the dagger I had so cleverly hidden. I had *thought* I had so cleverly hidden. His hand firmly over the gold hilt of my silver dagger, he flung it across the room before looking at me, an amused expression on his face.

"If you were not queen, you would have been dead already for treason."

Red-hot anger surged inside of me. It flared to life, exploding like molten lava being spilled across my body.

I reared up and threw myself at him, rose petals swirling around me like a whirlwind of vengeance.

I did not need the dagger. I would kill him with my own two hands. I was not about to let him play with me. To toy with me before he killed me. We rolled off the bed in a flurry of gold silk, beaded gauzy net, and flowers.

I flailed against him, doing my best to get a hit in. To kick...to scratch...I would go down fighting. I would not cower in a corner while he had his way.

King Zayed finally managed to pin me under him, my legs trapped between his as he straddled my waist, my hands were pinned above my head as his huge hand gripped two of my wrists in his one big powerful one. He was more powerful than I. But still I struggled against him.

"Hold still," King Zayed admonished softly.

"So you can kill me?" I snarled.

I spat in his face. I did not care anymore. I was going to die anyway. A warrior does not die like a coward. I came from a long line of Blade-Callers. My mother had been one before me, as had my grandmother. I would have been one if I had not been chosen to be queen. To die.

"Nobody is killing you yet!" King Zayed's voice boomed at me sharply. "Though I am sorely tempted."

I stilled, shock coursing through my body at the statement whilst hope simultaneously sprang to life in my eyes.

"C-can I go home?" I asked, my eyes wide and hopeful.

His words had sparked a glimmer of hope within me, like a tiny flame struggling to find its way in the darkness.

The king looked down at me, his face red as he pinned me to the ground beneath his body. He looked at me in that same observant manner as he had done when he lifted my veil mere hours ago. My hair had come out of its braid, the flowers now strewn about the ground due to my attack. My chest was heaving from the exertion of the fight and remnants of anger coursing through me. I suddenly became acutely aware of the fact that I lay beneath him in nothing but a heavily embellished 'choli' and my underthings.

"No." King Zayed sighed, finally releasing my wrists. "If I get up, will you swear not to fight me? My guards will not hesitate to kill you if you try to harm their king."

"I will not fight you as long as you do not try to kill me," I countered right back.

Maybe I was imagining it, but I could have sworn I saw a smile flicker across his chiseled features. I might have thought him handsome, had I not known he was a cold-blooded killer. However, in the next moment, he had the same stern set to his mouth and scowling eyes staring down at me.

"You can fight all you want, little tigress, when the time comes," King Zayed finally acquiesced and released me.

He stood up and I released a great big exhale of relief. He was not going to kill me, yet. He most undoubtedly was not going to rape me...yet.

My mother had often called me her little tiger. Had he known?

"How did you know my mother called me 'little tigress'?" I queried, looking up at him as I still lay on the floor breathless.

The Crimson King tilted his head to stare down at me, the ghost of a bemused smile on his lips. Finally, he extended a hand, as if he wanted to help me up.

"I did not know. But you remind me of one." He finally stated this with an easy camaraderie that I had never known one could feel when in the presence of our mad king. "Come, get up. Let us not waste precious time."

Confused, I leapt up agilely, without taking the aid of his hand. The king raised an amused eyebrow, his hand dropping to his side.

"You are a Blade-Caller?" he queried, his broad shoulders and long muscular legs seeming even more imposing by candlelight. He walked purposefully towards the wooden closet in my room.

His comment gave me a momentary pause. How did he—?

"Those legs are not the legs of a pampered daughter; those are the legs of a warrior."

I could barely process the fact that he had been observing my legs, that he threw me a pair of loose white pantaloons. I caught them by instinct. A strangled gasp escaped my lips as I stared at them. This was my training outfit I wore when I did mock sword fights. It was the standard uniform of the Blade-Callers. How did they... Had all of my possessions been shifted here? As of last night, all my possessions had been back in my tiny hut with *Baba*. A dead girl did not need her worldly possessions.

"Get dressed. Let us see what you are capable of."

I stared at him, confused and completely at a loss for words.

I was supposed to be dead by now. At the very least, my body should have been defiled by the tyrant before me.

King Zayed turned to look at me with one eyebrow raised. The harsh lines etched into his face had eased somewhat, and my eyes trailed over his features. For the first time, I drank him in, letting myself observe him openly.

His sharp features were almost too perfect, with a strong jawline, chiseled cheek-bones, and a patrician nose that hinted at an arrogant air. My gaze was drawn upwards to meet his intense green eyes. He caught me staring and stared back pointedly, making it clear that he was aware of my keen observations.

I looked away, but his face remained seared in my mind's eye. It was a face made for ruling, for giving commands and making decisions. But it was not the face of a bloodthirsty king.

He was a man. Just like any other man. My fear of him lessened somewhat.

"I...please give me a moment of privacy," I finally stated evenly. "To change."

He gave me a curt nod and strode towards the door.

"I shall be waiting outside for you...my queen."

The King of Kings would be waiting for me.

I sagged against the bedpost, questioning everything that I previously believed to be true about this man.

Chapter 7

We walked in silence, King Zayed next to me and a guard trailing behind us. It was the same guard who had been standing outside my door since evening set in. He followed with one hand on the hilt of his *talwar*.

I wondered if it was to protect the king from outside enemies or from me.

Wordlessly, King Zayed threw open the doors to the training grounds. My steps faltered. We were not far from the back gardens, or the copse of trees where I nearly met my death.

As if sensing my hesitation, King Zayed turned with an expectant look. It spoke volumes, ordering me to follow him. My eyes went to the dirt courtyard beyond, surrounded by pillars of mud. I could not help my keen gaze from lingering on the blades resting on the far-right side of the training area.

My gaze darted to King Zayed. his back to me as he made his way towards the weapons, expertly grabbing one and tossing me another.

The sharp edge of the *talwar* sliced through the air with a fierce velocity, sending my heart racing and igniting every fiber of my body with enthusiasm. My hand reacted without conscious thought, closing over the hilt before it hit the ground. The metal felt cold and heavy in my grasp, its weight only adding to the surge of energy coursing through me. I experimentally lifted the blade, getting a feel for its weight.

The King's eyes tracked my movement, and I realized that this was more than just a light sparring match. He was carefully analyzing my skills, assessing me as an opponent. The arrogant part of me wanted to let loose. To unleash my fury on this man. To show him exactly what I could be capable of...

But the more rational and logical side wanted to proceed with caution. Let the enemy underestimate you. I could tell from his keen gaze that I could not expect him to miscalculate my skills just because I was a woman.

My eyes slowly took in his lazy stance, his muscular arms rippling with the palpable power stored within the corded muscles cloaked in a beige cotton shirt. I rested my gaze briefly on the deep V, taking in the corded muscles tensing in anticipation of a fight. On a deep exhale, I lifted my *talwar*, feigning a faltering swipe. Let him think I am a novice.

The clash of steel filled the air, I suppressed the urge to reveal the full extent of my skill. He blocked me easily, meeting me blow for blow. Our eyes momentarily met over crossed swords. I glared at him and pulled back to strike again.

With each strike, I feigned hesitation, allowing him to believe he possessed the upper hand. Let him think I am angry and throwing my all into this sham of a sword fight. It is all too blatantly obvious that his strength was formidable, but I also knew the power of deception. I took in his weaknesses, the slow movement of his feet, the lazy dip of his sword whenever he pulled back. I studied him closely, observing where he was lacking. My mind raced with strategizing on how to get one swift blow in. All I needed was one, straight to the heart. My aim must be true, for if I missed, I will have doomed more than myself. I am a daughter of Elamaria. I will be our salvation from him.

I raised my sword, but with a calculated slowness, meeting his with a deliberate clang. Our blades collided again and again, my arm trembling purposefully under his onslaught. I let him push me back, my movements betraying a hint of struggle, a facade carefully crafted to deceive.

Rarely has a man looked at me in the way the king is looking at me: as a formidable adversary. It did something to me. Made me think there might be some substance to him. I gave my head a firm shake. No. He kills innocent women. There was nothing good in this man. I could not let myself fall prey to such fanciful notions. Redemption? That is only for those who have a heart. The man before me did not possess one.

Sweat dripped down my face. I tasted the salty tang of it on my lips. Yet I kept going, ignoring the groaning of my limbs. The pain in my abdomen stung fiercely. My wounds are not fully recovered from last night's brush with the Grim Reaper.

The reminder of that monster disturbed me and I faltered so that I lost my footing, suddenly falling to my knees. The shadow of his blade arced over me as he brought it down. He was going to swipe my head off. I lifted my sword quickly, managing to block his attack.

The clash of metal on metal rang through the air, accompanied by vibrations sending reverberations through my fingertips and arm. I met his eyes from my position on the floor. He loomed over me, legs bent slightly, our blades still singing from the prolonged impact.

His stare felt like a physical weight, pressing down on me and causing my muscles to tense in response. I faintly felt the heat emanating from his body, the subtle tension in his muscles as he stood over me. My skin tingled and my hair stood on end as his gaze continued to linger on me, intensity and a sense of electricity emanating from his eyes.

The gaze of the king had the sharpness of a hunting falcon, the curiosity of a child, and the danger of a viper. It danced across my face, searching for any weakness to exploit.

My eyes hardened. Enough of this farce. I instinctively reached for my dagger, prepared to use my left hand to drive it into his heart. Foolish man left himself wide open. By the time the guard realized what I had done, his worthless king would be dead, bleeding out onto the ground. Yet right as I made up my mind, the most unpleasant deep rumbling sound emitted from the deep recesses of my belly.

Surprise flickered across the king's face, his sword fell away instantly, leaving me momentarily off-balance as he stepped away from me. I exhaled in frustration. I lost my chance. He was much stronger than I, and the element of surprise could no longer be used to my advantage.

"I believe I have won," he muttered, his lips tugging up in what must have been a faint smile. "You have not eaten?" he queried, tilting his head haughtily as he regarded me.

"When one has impending death on their agenda, food is the last thing on their mind," I rasped out, getting back to my feet.

I was looking down, brushing away dirt on my form. Therefore, it was rather startling when the king broke out into laughter. I looked up in surprise. He did not look as formidable with a smile on his lips. In fact, he did not look like a murderer. He was not. Because he had had his chance to kill me only moments before and did not. I regarded him curiously. Something...was not making sense.

"I suppose you are right," he mused.

Then again, laughing over my impending demise was rather dark. Was he just toying with his prey? Lulling me into a false sense of security? Who knew the full depth of his depraved mind?

The king beckoned to the guard who took our swords from us.

"Come...I wish to collect my winnings." He made his way to the door that led back into the main palace.

"Your winnings?" I echoed, walking behind him.

My eyes rested on his broad shoulders and muscular arms. He could have been done with me. Yet, he stopped.

"If I have bested you, I am to win something...no?"

"You are a king." Incredulity colored my words. "What could a man like you possibly want that you do not already have?"

The man walking next to me paused, his eyes closing for a brief moment.

"What indeed," he whispered, more to himself than me, before continuing his walk down the halls.

His tone wavered like a mirage in the scorching sun, betraying the torment of a soul akin to the desperate need of water in the arid wasteland of the desert. A heavy sigh left his lips, as if he might be carrying the weight of the world on his shoulders. It made me give pause, my feet stilling as I watched him walk purposefully further down the hall.

All was not what it seemed. I could feel it in my bones. There was a mystery here. And I was determined to find out and save my people.

Chapter 8

Apparently, the king was as obsessed with feeding me as his servants. By the time I had caught up to him, he had entered the great dining hall and instructed the cook to be awoken. Dried fruits were brought in as we waited for the food to arrive. He regarded me from the cushions he lounged upon, obsidian green peering at me as if I were some sort of mystery.

"Why did you volunteer?"

I regarded him with my own dark eyes, wondering if my answer would have any sway on whatever he planned to do with me. He was not going to kill me, of that I was becoming more certain with every passing moment.

"Did you think you could survive the night?" he challenged, eyes narrowing on me. "You could change the king? Perhaps seduction and love might save you?"

His arrogance really knew no bounds.

"If I were planning a seduction, we would not be sitting here after a sword fight," I responded coolly.

"Would we not?"

My eyes narrowed on him. The nerve of this man!

"Your vizier." My voice was bitter. I made no attempt to hide my disdain for the vile man. "He picked my sister. She was betrothed to a man she loved. I could not bear to see such a fate befall her. Not after all she has done for me."

I saw a flare of admiration in King Zayed's eyes. But just as quickly, it flickered out.

"For family..." He trailed off, eyes focused on something behind me.

He remained silent as the servants brought in food to set on the low-lying table.

The spread of dishes was an exotic display of color and scent, with the rich curries bubbling, their fragrant aroma making my stomach grumble louder in protest of being denied sustenance for so long. The chutney was a vibrant and tangy addition, and the rice was a mound of fluffy, perfectly cooked grains. Mouth watering, I realized I was famished and began to eat.

"What do I win for besting the little tigress?" King Zayed queried, taking in the way I practically inhaled the flatbread dipped in chutney. The hint of coriander and cumin on my tongue turned sour. What did this man want from me that he could not take by force?

"I—" I stopped short, a hacking cough working its way up my throat. The spice had gotten the best of me. The clatter of a goblet told me that one of the servants had poured me some of the king's wine. A wine only he was served.

"Drink," he commanded sharply from across the table, as if those words alone could cease my coughing fit.

However, I found that they did and I was able to take a few sips. Eyes watering, I watched King Zayed gesture for the servant to leave us.

"I used to challenge my friend to sword fights when we were little. If I lost, I had to tell a story," I ventured experimentally, deciding there was no reason to tell him that, as of late, Ashad asked me for a kiss rather than a story.

I briefly recalled the stories I would tell Ashad. They were stories my mother had told me of men who could shift into fierce animals. And amongst them all was the powerful wolf-shifter who ruled over everyone. Ashad would always listen with rapt attention when we were younger. But the older we grew, his interest waned in fanciful stories and became fixated on something else entirely—me.

King Zayed scoffed.

"Stories. Children's tales."

I raised a perfectly winged brow. "Do not underestimate the power of a well-crafted tale. It can transport one to far-off worlds and teach even mighty kings, such as yourself, lessons in humility."

There was a tense silence as my words hung between us. Dark green eyes stared at me, one finger circling the ring of his goblet.

"All right then. Let us hear your story." His voice dripped with acerbic disdain.

Searching my mind for a story that would be to King Zayed's liking, I settled on one of my personal favorites that Mother had quite often narrated to me in the past--the story of a wondrous magic carpet that could transport its riders to wherever they so wished. I speared a piece of veal with my fork, knowing that this might be exactly the opening I had been looking for.

"In the bustling kingdom of an ancient land, there lived a King named Farid. He was known far and wide for his cunning ways and insatiable greed. Farid's wealth seemed to grow with each passing day, but still, it was never enough. He always wanted more."

I watched King Zayed's lips turn downwards in a scowl, evidently expecting me to compare him to the man in the story. I held back a snort. King Farid wanted wealth. This man seemed to want innocent blood. He might not kill me, but it did not erase the fact that ten women had died in this very castle. Under this man's watch. Perhaps under his orders, if not by his own hand.

"One day, King Farid heard whispers of a legendary weaver who possessed the skill to create the most exquisite carpets imaginable. These were not just any carpets; they were said to possess magical properties. At once, King Farid decided that this weaver would weave for him a special carpet, capable of transporting its owner to distant lands upon one whispered command."

Intrigued, he leaned forward. I hid a smile. It seemed these childish tales had caught his interest. His goblet of wine was all but forgotten. I leaned back, taking a sip of my own wine. It was bitter yet sweet with a hint of tart. In my home, we had never had the luxury of anything like this. During my training as a Blade-Caller, drinking wine was frowned upon. It dulled the senses, and now that I had finally had a taste, I had to agree. I could feel myself becoming a little drowsy. Though it might also have to do with the fact that I had not had a good night's sleep in two days.

"*King Farid approached Yasmin with an air of arrogance, demanding that she weave him the finest magic carpet the world had ever seen. He promised her untold riches in return, but Yasmin was wary. She did not want riches. She merely wished for King Farid to use the carpet to do good in the world.*"

"Good," King Zayed snorted and rolled his eyes. "As if there really is still good left in the world." He shook his head tightly. I ignored him, plowing forward despite the urge to close my eyes and fall asleep.

"*Day and night, Yasmin toiled away at her loom, pouring her heart and soul into the creation of the magic carpet,*" I continued the story, my voice firm. "*With each stitch, she imbued it with the essence of her own kindness and compassion, hoping to temper the darkness that lurked within Farid's heart. As Yasmin delved deeper into her work, she discovered that the magic required for the carpet was not rooted in material wealth, but in the purity of intentions and selflessness. The more she understood the true nature of magic, the more she realized that it could not be harnessed for selfish gain.*"

King Zayed was scowling at me, his lips pressed together tightly. Something in the set of his eyes gave me pause. I took another sip of wine before proceeding.

"*When the carpet was finally complete, Yasmin presented it to the King. However, on that day, he could not hide his true nature and his voracious desire for riches and power became evident to Yasmin.*"

My voice was a mere whisper now, words slurring as I spoke. I blinked in confusion, wondering why I was not able to stay lucid.

"What did she do?" King Zayed queried when I did not immediately proceed with the story.

"She-she—" I tripped over my words, fighting to stay awake. "*Before King Farid could lay claim to the power of the magic carpet, Yasmin whisked it out of his reach and unraveled the intricate binds around it. King Farid was shocked to discover that the... the humble seamstress had...had...*"

I slumped over on the table, unable to keep my head up.

"Tired, little Tigress?" King Zayed queried, staring at me from across the table, a knife in his hand glinting in the candlelight.

I nodded sluggishly, my belly warm and limbs deliciously light. I was so tired from the strenuous activity of sparring against him. My stomach was full from the mouth-watering delicacies fed to me, and my limbs felt warm thanks to the wine in my system. As a Blade-Caller, our bodies had undergone rigorous training, but even my body had its limits.

"Was this your plan?" I murmured, my eyes drooping shut as the wine worked its magic on me. "Make me so tired that I will not be able to fight you?"

King Zayed's muted chuckle reverberated throughout the room. It did something to me. It was as if I could feel the vibrations of his laugh down to the very core of my heart.

"Maybe." His voice was amused.

"It is...so relieving to know you find the thought of my demise entertaining," I hummed, my head falling down against the table. I struggled to stay awake. But it was not possible. What was wrong with me? My mind felt fuzzy and I found it difficult to lift my hand. Panic filled my being. This was not just my body suffering from the effects of exhaustion.

"It really is not all that entertaining." King Zayed's voice was close to my ear now.

I realized he was next to me, hovering over me.

"Are you going to kill me now?" I asked, realizing that there was something mixed in the wine. Or the food. Or both. I guessed I would never know.

It took me a minute to realize that his knuckles were dragging gently against my jaw, trailing the contours of it before his cool fingers fluttered downwards across my neck...my collarbone. I exhaled deeply, only now realizing how shallow my breaths had been before. I should fight him. Had my gut been wrong? Had this man drugged me so he could have his way with me and then murder me before dawn?

"No, Tigress. I am not going to kill you. We have a deal...do not you recall?"

A deal? I tried to think back but found it rather difficult to think at all with his hands on my face and neck. With the drug imbibed into my system making my brain numb. Suddenly, I was lifted into his arms.

"Time to sleep, Amara," he whispered, his hands around me securely.

I let out a sigh of relief, believing his words. He did not hold me as if he would brutally murder me. He held me...carefully. As if he did not want to drop me.

I was jostled slightly when he walked out of the dining hall and unconsciously, I turned into him. At this moment, he did not feel dangerous. The prickling awareness of lethal intent has dissipated. Or maybe whatever was mixed in the wine completely dulled my sense of self-preservation.

I was not sure. All I knew was that my thoughts were muddled, my senses sluggish. The steady beat of his heart pounded against my ear. Like a lullaby it pushed me further under this blanket of drowsiness, and I was powerless to fight it.

"My King...please..." The words of the guards were muffled...garbled as my brain fails to register entire sentences. "We....take her back—"

In the recesses of my mind, I register a vicious snarl. It is primitive. It makes the back of my neck prickle uncomfortably. *"Run"* my brain screamed at me. But I could not.

I dream of the moon, its luminous glow casting a soft, ethereal light upon the lush green landscape so different from the vast expanse of desert and palm trees native to Elamaria. In the distance, a beautiful woman appears, her presence comforting yet enigmatic. She possesses an otherworldly grace, with flowing locks of midnight hair cascading around her gentle features like a veil of shadows. Her eyes, pools of warmth and compassion, radiate a serene light that seems to pierce through the darkness of the night. Her presence exudes an aura of tranquility and safety, wrapping me in a cocoon of contentment.

She glides towards me.

As she draws near, her voice, like a gentle breeze, whispers assurances.

"Fear not, Amara," she murmurs, her words a balm to my weary soul. "You possess the power to break free from the chains that bind you. Trust in yourself, and you will find the way forward."

In her presence, I feel a sense of peace enveloping me, dispelling the shadows of doubt and fear. Her words ignite a flicker of hope within me. With each word she speaks, a surge of courage and determination courses through my veins. I find peace, as if all the burdens weighing me down have been lifted.

But then, my dream takes a dark turn. I find myself falling...falling into a dark abyss until I land amongst the sand dunes. My throat is parched and I feel hot. As if I have been trekking through this dessert for eons. Suddenly, a primal growl echoes through the night. I look up in time to see a monstrous beast charging towards me, its snarling mouth filled with sharp teeth ready to rip my flesh open. It is the same creature that attacked me the night before my wedding. Panic sets in as I try to step back, to flee from its ferocity, but my efforts are futile. I trip on my nightgown and fall on my back.

The beast pounces, pinning me to the ground beneath its weight. Its eyes, glowing red with malice, bore into mine as I struggled. I reach for my dagger, my only means of defense, but it is gone, vanished into the darkness.

With a blood-thirsty growl, the beast sinks its sharp canines into my neck, sending searing pain coursing through my body. I awaken in a cold sweat, the echoes of my scream still lingering in the air, trapped in the grips of fear and desperation.

Chapter 9

My sweat-drenched body shivered as I shook off the final vestiges of the horrible, horrible nightmare. It was then that I realized with acute clarity that I was alive. My hands touched my form, trying to reassure myself that I *am* real...I *am* here...my heart beats! I pushed aside the curtains drawn across my bed, my eyes registering the sunlight streaming through.

I survived the night. A gasp of disbelief mixed pungently with relief overwhelmed me. I survived, I lived to see another day.

The doors to my room burst open. I stepped back instinctively. In walked an elderly woman, her lips pursed together.

"You are not the first," the woman hissed vindictively, her eyes narrowed on me. "Nor will you be the last," she ended cryptically.

Ire filled me at the way she stared me up and down. I was still in my Blade-Caller uniform from last night. My head covering however...A hand went to the crown of my head. Did the king remove my head covering when he brought me back into my room? The intimate gesture of removing a woman's headscarf...more often done by one's husband...The thought caused the pit of my stomach to drop. After giving myself a mental shake, my eyes went again to this stern, hateful woman.

Deep lines of sadness seemed to be etched into her face. Her eyes were cruel, but behind them there were faint traces of a woman who had once endured great pain. The permanent tilt of her eyes told me she might have spent many a night crying. However, the way she looked at me now, as if I were a bug she wanted to squash, made any sympathy I held for her dissipate. Did she really hate me for surviving?

She wore the clothes of a noble woman. But her hands were not the hands of a woman who had never worked a day in her life. They were the hands of a peasant woman who had spent many a night weaving baskets, scrubbing pewter dishes, and gathering gravel to mix into the mud cakes for creating mud houses. Our hands were the same. Our clothes were most definitely not. Neither were our dispositions with the way she was glaring at me.

Before I could begin to ask who she was, Kadin entered with a grin on his face.

"I knew it! I knew it," he chuckled, moving forward to greet me. He bowed his head. "My Queen," he murmured reverently.

Queen.

I am queen. Queen of Elamaria. Overcome by a surreal sense of awe and trepidation, my first thought was, "*this has to be a mistake.*"

"We will see if she is still queen tomorrow," the woman retorted, folding her arms.

Kadin barked out a laugh, "Dornia, you fear a mere slip of a girl?"

"Why would I?" Dornia grunted, raising her chin a notch. "She will not last another night."

With those words, Dornia turned on her heel in a flurry of expensive silk and exited the room. I was left with a pit of dread in my stomach. She was probably right. But I still had time to figure out my next move.

"Sherazi!" Kadin called.

At once, my head maid came scurrying into the room, head bowed and body trembling as if Kadin meant to strike her.

"Get the queen ready. We have much to do today."

When he said queen my eyes automatically searched the room only to realize I was looking for myself.

"Who is Dornia?" I asked Kadin as he placed the parchment before me, insisting that my signature was necessary.

Kadin was silent for a moment before speaking. "Dornia was his wet nurse."

The quill in my hand scratched against the parchment, and my head jerked up to look at Kadin in surprise. I had heard of nobility and royalty deeming nursing a child beneath their rank. However, I had never heard of any of the wet nurses remaining after the child was weaned, let alone having ever heard of a wet nurse who walked with the authority of the king himself. For a moment, I had thought she was Walid Sultan, mother of the king.

"His mother let the wet nurse remain even after King Zayed was weaned?" I asked, incredulity marring my tone.

Kadin's lips tugged downward. He scratched at his jaw, thinking for a moment before confessing, "The late queen died when our king was but a child of ten. Along with his younger brother who was still a suckling babe. Dornia was the babe's wet nurse as well. It was...a tragedy," Kadin ended mournfully.

Suddenly, the poignant flare in the king's eyes when he learned I had sacrificed myself for Asya made sense. It had been the briefest flash of pain, but it had been there. His brother had died? Did my sacrifice remind him of what he might have wished to be able to do for his younger brother?

"Dornia stayed on because a motherly figure was required. She raised His Majesty, under my own mother's supervision, of course. King Zayed had always been attached to her and...she has been here ever since," Kadin finally concluded.

I bristled, realizing that such a hateful woman raised our king. She was as much to blame as he was for his demand to kill innocent women.

Pensively, I scratched out my name with its lopsided 'r' and tried again.

Before I could affix my signature, the door burst open, and the Grand Vizier stormed in, his brow furrowed with anger.

"What is the meaning of this?" he demanded, his voice echoing off the chamber walls.

Kadin stepped forward, his demeanor calm yet resolute.

"She is queen," he declared, gesturing towards me. "In the absence of the king, her seal and signature are necessary for the governance of the realm. I am merely fulfilling the formalities that every queen must fulfill on the morn after her wedding."

The Grand Vizier's face reddened with fury, his hands clenched into fists at his sides. He opened his mouth to protest, but before he could speak, a hush fell over the room.

Awareness seeped into the atmosphere. Awareness and trepidation.

My gaze was drawn to him, his presence commanding the attention of all who stood before him.

King Zayed wore a shirt woven from the finest thread of light muslin cloth which was the color of his eyes; a striking green that seemed to shimmer in the sunlight spilling through the windows.

My dark brown eyes met his gold-flecked green ones, his gaze piercing and calculating.

The Grand Vizier turned to the king, his expression pleading, expecting him to intervene. But to my surprise, King Zayed remained silent, his eyes fixed upon me with a look of quiet intensity. Waiting...

Quickly, I placed my signature on the parchment. Kadin leaned forward, helping me with the wax seal that must be affixed next to my signature.

"Now that the queen's signature and seal have been documented, I will get these papers to the records keeper once the wax dries," Kadin finally stated, looking at me with a kind smile.

I gave a jerky nod, my eyes once again meeting piercing green.

Wordlessly, King Zayed motioned for me to join him. I stood on shaky legs.

Kadin bowed before me.

"My Queen," Kadin murmured respectfully. "I hope your wounds have healed."

King Zayed's eyebrows snapped together in confusion.

"What wounds?" His voice was stern, an underlying hint of concern evident.

"It is nothing," I hastened to state, shooting Kadin a severe look.

He merely smiled benignly at me.

"Her torso was bruised, it was quite unpleasant," Kadin informed the king.

I want to punch this man and his big mouth.

King Zayed's nostrils flared, his face turned a light shade of red.

"Is this true?" he asked, peering at me.

Lying to our king was punishable by death. But even if it were not, I am a terrible liar.

"It is," I acquiesced.

"And you sparred in such condition?" He tilted his head to the side, voice a low whisper.

"It is nothing I am not trained for. You know the training—"

"I am aware of the training you have undergone. I am also aware you were top of your class," King Zayed's voice interjected impatiently. "What I am not aware of is why the queen is injured. And why, and how, my general is aware of it?"

I inhaled sharply, realizing the implications of such words. If lying to the king was punishable by death, what must those endure who the king believes have been unfaithful to him? I recalled that he kills women because he does not trust them. Because his first love betrayed him.

Kadin's sharp crack of laughter reverberated through the room. I did not find anything humorous about this situation in the slightest. My eyes narrowed on Kadin.

"Breathe, my cousin. I merely visited her the morning after she tried to escape her first night here." Kadin was still chuckling.

My hands itched to hit him. He had just revealed to the king that I had tried to escape. Wonderful. If ever there was a way to dig someone a grave with mere words, Kadin should be the one to do it.

King Zayed's frown deepened. He turned to look at me.

"We must address the residents," King Zayed finally stated. "Come."

"N-Now?" I finally queried, wondering why we were doing this.

"Now," he countered, arm extended towards me, hand placed palm up.

He wanted me to put my hand in his. I complied, suppressing the shiver that coursed through me when his fingers clamped over mine.

The king of Ilm, a figure revered and feared amongst his people, walked beside me, his hand wrapped around mine. The weight of his gaze upon me was almost palpable, igniting a flurry of conflicting emotions within me.

His hand, warm against mine, sent tendrils of apprehension snaking through my being.

As we approached the balcony overlooking the main square of Ilm, the excited voices of the citizens below rose up to greet us. Women clutching their children stood in awe, their eyes wide with wonder at the sight of their new queen, a woman who should have been dead by now, by the king's side. Men raised their hands in salute, their faces filled with a mixture of respect and fear.

King Zayed stepped forward, his regal presence commanding attention as he raised his hand for silence. The crowd hushed immediately, awaiting his words with bated breath. His eyes flickered towards me briefly before he began to speak, his voice strong and authoritative as he addressed his people.

"Today, I stand before you with my queen by my side. Let it be known far and wide, do unto her as you would do unto me. For a threat against her, is a threat to your king."

The underlying message in those words was not lost on me. But he spoke as if someone would want to harm me. Why? And who?

His hand remained firmly over mine and we waved to the people below who seemed to be gazing at me in incredulous disbelief. Disbelief that I was actually alive. I could not help but smile. I was one of them. Surely they saw that this was not just my victory but theirs as well? Surely my survival gave them some hope that their daughters would be safe from this day forth. I would make sure of it. Even if it was the last thing I ever did.

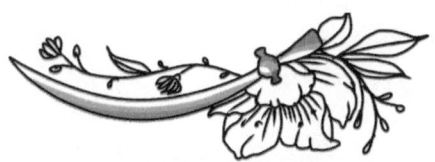

I walked in the gardens with Kadin, taking in the vast lawns in a part of the castle grounds I had not ventured before. He thought I was merely impressed by the grandiose nature of my surroundings. But really I was trying to learn the lay of the land. Trying to discern the best means of escape once the need arose.

"Quite the spectacle, was it not? The feared king of Ilm displaying his affection for his new queen for all to see." His tone was teasing, but I caught a glint of something else lurking in his gaze. Dare I say...hope? Does he hope that the king forms some sort of attachment to me? I surely hoped not.

"He was fulfilling a formality," I huffed out.

"A formality he has never fulfilled before."

"Because no one has survived long enough before," I could not help but shoot back.

Kadin's lips pressed into a scowl as we stopped near a rosebush. I could not help but turn every which way to see if a monster was going to jump out and attack me.

"The king is a good man, Amara." Kadin's voice was reproachful. Almost as if upbraiding a child.

I bristled under his censure. Good? I wanted to tell him exactly how wrong he was. But I could not. That would be treason.

"He is the king of kings. You do not realize how he is the only one stopping the Bedouin tribes from plundering the villages scattered across the deserts of Elamaria. It is because the emirs and chieftains have pledged allegiance to him that there is peace in our lands." Kadin shook his head in disgust. "I think we all know the dark times that plagued this land. Before a monarch ruled...women were kidnapped and sold as chattel by plundering raiders. There was no law. Only the mighty ruled and the weak were suppressed. The monarchy is important for us to flourish as a nation."

I snorted in derision.

"As is killing the daughters of Elamaria. Wonderful."

Kadin let out a deep mournful sigh that made me glance up at him from the roses I had been gazing at.

"It is much more complicated than you think," Kadin finally admitted in a whisper.

It was the tone of his voice more than anything, filled with sadness and bitter regret, that made me take a step forward. Just what did he mean? I opened my mouth to inquire further but was cut off by a loud, excited bark.

As I turned, my eyes fell upon a majestic creature unlike any other. A Tazi hound, with a long, flowing, light gold coat and regal features, bounded towards us with effortless grace. His paws seemed to hardly touch the ground as he approached, golden-white fur shimmering in the sunlight. His eyes gleamed with intelligence and curiosity, making him seem almost otherworldly. I could not help but feel a sense of awe at the sheer beauty of this magnificent animal.

"Hello, Baghel." Kadin bent to greet the dog, scratching him behind the ears, before looking at me. "This is the king's hunting dog. Or was. He is too old now. Now he just lazes about the castle grounds and is spoiled rotten by the palace cook."

I could not help but extend a hand, my fingers sinking into the softest fur I had ever had the pleasure of touching. Baghel let out a soft whine of appreciation, enjoying my touch.

"He is...magnificent," I murmured in awe.

"That he is," Kadin agreed. "Well...you are free to roam around these grounds. They make up the inner-sanctum of the castle grounds and if you keep walking down this path, you might find something of interest. This area is safer than the outer grounds. It is what should have been the harem if our king decided to constitute one."

My head snapped up to look at Kadin. Harem?

"Upon the death of the previous king, His Majesty disbanded it, making sure his father's concubines were well taken care of," Kadin added hastily. There was an unease in his eyes that I could not quite pinpoint the source of.

"It is none of my business what the king does," I swiftly responded.

Kadin cleared his throat.

"Well...I shall see you later? Hopefully tomorrow morning." He let out an optimistic laugh before leaving. As if he had made some sort of joke. Well, it was not a joke to me.

Baghel headbutted me, pushing me further down the path that Kadin had advised me to walk down. Behind me, Sherazi walked silently. Almost like a shadow. She appeared just as quietly as she seemed to disappear. I knew she was afraid of the king. I did not blame her. She also seemed to fear Kadin. But I did not want her to be afraid of me. I did not want to be a feared ruler. I wanted to be a respected one. There was a difference. And...I needed a friend in this death trap I found myself in.

"Where does this lead, Sherazi?" I asked.

"My Queen...do you wish to go back?" Sherazi's voice seemed eager. Too eager.

My eyebrows furrowed. I purposefully strode forward. There was something she did not want me to see here. I rounded a bend on the path and stopped short.

An explosion of color greeted me. There were flowers upon flowers in every direction.

Rich shades of purple, deep reds, delicate pinks and stunning violets filled the air with their sweet scents. The petals swayed gently in the breeze, like a symphony of dancers performing a delicate routine. Each flower was more beautiful than the last, a vibrant burst of life against the backdrop of greenery.

I blinked in confusion as I registered that there was a pattern to the perfectly placed flora. My eyes counted out ten headstones with names. And my heart nearly stuttered to a stop when my gaze fell upon a plot of empty land, completely flowerless, with the eleventh headstone that had my name on it.

Chapter 10

"We should not have gone there," squeaked Sherazi, wringing her hands as I sat in my room completely taken aback by what I had seen.

A beautifully kept cemetery of ten women gone before their time. As if they had mattered. As if they had been important. Not killed by someone in a bid to punish women in general.

"Who buried them there?" I queried, thoughts racing through my mind.

Baghel laid at my feet as I let my fingers absently sink into his luxurious fur. He seemed to sense my discomfort and licked my hand. I looked down at him. Ever since our walk in the gardens, Baghel had not left my side.

"Our king ordered it." Sherazi gulped, looking around as if anyone would barge in at any moment and punish her.

I breathed in deeply. So he killed them...and then gave them a proper burial? Not the actions of the Crimson King I had heard of.

"Were you the head maid to the queens who came before me?" My eyes bore into hers, hands fisted in my lap as I begged her for a straight answer.

She did that infuriating thing again. Where she looked around the room as if someone was eavesdropping on us.

"I was...for the last two. B-before that...my mother was..." Sherazi shuddered, as if recalling a horrible memory.

"Did any ever survive past the first night?" There was no time to be afraid. I had to get to the bottom of this.

"A f-few. According to my mother...th-the first one...she was queen for an entire week be-before..." Sherazi gulped, her voice the barest of whispers.

"Before the king found out she betrayed him and was in love with another man?" I challenged. "So he killed her in cold blood and doomed the daughters of Elamaria to the same fate? All women must now suffer for the heartache and embarrassment he endured?"

Sherazi let out a gasp, nearly jumping off the cushion she had been sitting on on the floor.

"These are all rumors," Sherazi argued meekly, crossing her legs. I did not miss the way her body practically trembled as she spoke. "He is our king. To talk in such a way is treason."

I scoffed, leaning back in my chair. He had his servants so afraid of him, they seemed to be afraid of their own shadows. They were afraid to even talk! And yet...my thoughts kept going back to the cemetery. To the tombstones. To the perfectly kept grounds and flowers. He killed them, and yet...it was all completely contradictory!

"What happened to the second one?" I asked brusquely.

Sherazi blinked and stared at me in confusion.

"The second one who survived the first night. You said there were two who lived to see dawn," I explained patiently.

Her eyes lightened in understanding.

"She was...was the third bride of the king." Sherazi spoke as if the king himself might come in here and skewer her alive for telling me this information. But I would wring as much information from her as I could.

"How long did she survive?" I pressed Sherazi, my eyes boring into hers and demanding an answer.

"Five days."

I sank back into my chair, closing my eyes in defeat. How long would I survive?

There were still so many questions I wanted to ask her but I needed to collect my thoughts first. I massaged my temples with the tips of my fingers, trying to decide what to ask next. I required information if I was going to strategize and figure out how to survive another night. How to survive the rest of the nights, too, if I were being honest. My mind went to Ashad. If he were here he would have guided me. Told me the best way to go about this. He had been my companion for so long. My friend and mentor. I squared my shoulders. No matter. He had trained me well.

Standing, I made my way towards the balcony. I needed fresh air. Inside these walls hung an aura of bleak hopelessness that I just could not seem to shake off. Sherazi coughed meekly into her hand.

"They..." Her cheeks colored pink and she suddenly shut her mouth as if she had spoken blasphemy and did not want anyone to find out.

"Speak out. What is it?" I urged, turning to face her.

This maid was my only source of true information. I gentled my tone. "Please, Sherazi, tell me so that I may figure out a way to survive. I do not want to die," I admitted in a low whisper, hanging my head. I did not often show my vulnerable side. But I was so frustrated with the entire situation.

"They say...the palace...is haunted. The ghost of the first dead queen..." Sherazi trailed off, lips trembling. "She seeks revenge."

My eyes widened in disbelief before I threw my head back and laughed. Ghosts. Child's tales. Oh, if they only knew what monster lurked not far from my balcony. Sherazi looked away, embarrassment written across her features.

"I...I am not laughing at you," I added hastily, suddenly contrite. Embarrassing her had not been my goal. "I just...it is a rather ludicrous tale," I murmured. "Ghosts," I scoffed.

Turning back to face my balcony, I pushed open the double doors and realized my palms were sweaty. My eyes went to the horizon, where dusk was setting in. It would be nightfall sooner rather than later. And dawn would come all too soon. I swallowed. Who knew that the dark of night would one day feel like a cocoon of safety and dawn would be something I came to dread?

Tonight, I paced the length of my room. My skin was bathed in aromatic scents and my hair open and flowing wildly down my back. The doors opened and I knew without looking up that it was King Zayed. Of their own accord, my eyes flitted to my empty bed swathed in gauzy curtains of the finest material. But just as quickly I looked away to meet the piercing gaze of the man who was now my husband.

Briefly, I wondered if he was aware of the spectral presence rumored to haunt these halls. Or was he merely consumed by his own desires and ambitions, oblivious to this unfounded fear amongst his servants?

He prowled closer, his steps deliberate and purposeful. Suddenly, he paused, eyes going to Baghel who was laying in a corner of my room.

"What is my hunting dog doing in your chambers?" Incredulity colored the king's tone.

I raised a brow. "He seems to like it here," I replied nonchalantly.

"Baghel does not like anyone, nor does he enjoy being indoors." King Zayed's eyes came back to rest on my form. He stepped closer to me. So close that our chests were almost touching now.

The air around us crackled with an unspoken tension, heavy with anticipation. I could sense the authority emanating from him, he commanded power, and I could not deny that he was a force to be reckoned with. Was he going to make me send Baghel away from my rooms?

"Amara." He spoke my name like a whispered command, his voice low and velvety. "Have you eaten?"

I stood frozen in shock, too stunned to speak. He was not upset that Baghel was here?

"You are asking me...if I am hungry?" I asked hollowly.

He had my headstone and grave dug up in the cemetery of queens. Yet he asked if I required sustenance.

"It is a simple yes or no answer," King Zayed ticked out, crossing his arms. "You cannot spar on an empty stomach."

Now my entire body stiffened and I stared at him as comical disbelief overtook me. Spar? Again?

"I...I have eaten," I finally spoke out.

"Good. Let us go. And when I win, you will continue the story," he added.

I suddenly understood what he had meant the other night when he said we had a deal. I had a story he wanted to hear. I did my best to hold back a sneer. Pompous man thought he could actually win against me. But if I had learned anything, it was to keep my strengths a closely guarded secret. The only way to ever defeat a man of his strength was to let him believe he would win. And when he grew overconfident and sloppy, I would strike. My lips curled up slightly as I recalled the story my mother would often tell me. The story of the tortoise and the hare. Slow and steady wins the race.

"Will you drug me again, like last night?" I challenged; my gaze stern as I put my hand on my hips in frustration.

King Zayed's lips quirked up in a smile.

"You would not have slept otherwise."

He was right. But I would not tell him that. I had been too afraid to sleep. Afraid that he would strangle me with the very bed sheets that covered my form. But he had not. Not yet. Would there be flowers on my tombstone too, once the deed was done? Shaking the thoughts from my mind, I gave him a nod of agreement and turned to reach for my Blade-Caller uniform.

"I will be out momentarily," I commented, conveying for him to leave the room while I dressed.

King Zayed complied, silently retreating after petting Baghel. Baghel, for his part, paid his master no mind. He trotted over to me, away from the king, and placed himself at my feet. For a minute, I thought the king was laughing silently as he exited the room. But it must have been a trick of the candle-light.

A quarter of an hour later, we faced each other over crossed blades. The head covering I donned as part of my uniform had long ago been discarded. My hair danced around my shoulders as I parried blow after blow. I did not miss the flicker of admiration in his gaze. It took all my self control to withhold my smirk. Fool. He did not know the true extent of my skill.

We circled each other, the air crackling with tension.

"You lean too heavily to the right. Even your stance," King Zayed instructed.

I pretended not to hear him. He thought he could teach me? What would he think, if he ever found out that I was purposefully making errors in my posture and footwork?

In the blink of an eye, he was behind me. The speed with which he moved gave me pause. A hand snaked out to touch my upper thigh, pulling my left leg further inward.

"Like this," he whispered, his lips close to the shell of my ear.

I had trained with men before. I had been instructed and touched, in a completely instructive manner, to help me achieve the correct stance. But never had another man's touch been so...possessive. Nor as insistent as his, bending me to his will with a mere tug. His long fingers remained wrapped around my thigh, the warmth of his hand seeping through the thin white cotton fabric. I swallowed when his other hand skittered over my shoulder, tracing a path to my elbow, over my forearm, and finally closing around my hand that gripped my sword.

"When you strike" —he applied pressure on my hand, making me swipe the air with my blade in a neat, precise arc— "you will be able to maintain your balance. And when you block" —our bodies moved together as he pulled me back, more firmly against his warm hard body, and lifted my arm to hold the blade up as if to block an incoming attack— "you will absorb the shock of impact more adequately."

I already knew all this. But even if I had not, his proximity made it near impossible to concentrate on his words.

I could feel his breath on my neck, his body pressed against mine in a way that sent shivers down my spine.

I pretended to try and listen, purposefully leaning too much to the left now.

King Zayed chuckled, the hand on my thigh trailing up over my lower abdomen and finally resting across my waist. He pulled me closer into him.

The pit of my stomach dropped. He was my husband. More importantly, he was the king. Could I even stop him from touching me like this? Did I even want to? His touch was possessive, his presence overwhelming, and my heart pounded loudly in my chest.

"When an enemy comes from the side, you will lose unless you can absorb the impact more effectively."

His breath ghosted over the skin on my cheek.

He slowly guided me through the motions of blocking an attack from different angles. All the while, one hand remained firmly around my waist while the other gripped my swordhand, his right arm pressed against mine.

With each precise movement, each subtle adjustment he made to my posture, my body molded more firmly into his in a strangely intimate dance. There was an unspoken undercurrent of something else at play. This was no longer just a sparring match.

Perspiration dripped down my forehead, and before I knew it, he was pulling back to a respectable distance and picking up his sword.

I blocked him easily, absorbing his impact just like he had taught me. King Zayed grinned down at me and it was a beautiful smile. His dark green eyes seemed to glow with warmth and...was it pride? Flecks of gold danced in his eyes as he gazed down at me. He stared down at me over our crossed swords as I blocked another swipe from him. Our bodies were close, our faces inches apart as our eyes connected amidst the clash of metal.

I could not help it. My gaze dropped to his lips, mind automatically going to the kisses from Ashad I had put up with. Something told me this would be different. Pulling back, he went again. A side attack this time. And so floored was I by the very disconcerting fact that I was thinking about my would-be killer kissing me so I could compare how the two men kissed, that I was not able to block him. The blade stopped a mere hairsbreadth from my waist.

I looked up at him, wondering if he was going to slice me in half. Instead, he lowered the blade, a smile playing across his full lips.

"I win again...time to collect my winnings."

It took me a moment to realize he did not want a kiss, but the rest of the story.

Chapter 11

"*Yasmin took the carpet, unraveling its threads that bound it. With a flourish, the carpet unraveled and whisked Yasmin away out of the castle. King Farid yelled for his guards to stop her. But the magic carpet was too fast, and Yasmin's intentions too pure. For magic is strengthened by the pure of heart—*"

King Zayed snorted, cutting me off and leaning back on the cushions of my bed. We had ended up back here, with me sitting on the edge of my bed whilst he stretched out as if this was his own room. In reality...it was. Because this was his palace. But...it felt odd seeing him here, sprawled across the bedding as if he belonged here.

"You find my tale funny?" I queried, tilting my head to the side to stare at him.

"I find it ludicrous how magic intertwines with purity in your tales." He spoke with disdain dripping from his words.

"You do not believe in the purity of magic, *Shehenshah*?" I queried respectfully, calling him by his title of 'King of Kings', inwardly seething at his statement. Of course a man like him would never see the good in anything.

And yet even as I thought those words, the beautiful flowers in the Cemetery of Queens rose up in my mind, as if to remind me that he might not be a complete monster.

"The reality is far harsher than any fairytale," he said dismissively, a hint of melancholy in his eyes. He studied me closely.

"Ah, but is that not the beauty of stories, *Shehenshah*? They allow us to escape the harsh realities and venture into a world where magic and purity can prevail," I retorted softly, meeting his gaze without flinching. Despite his tough exterior, there was a flicker of vulnerability in his eyes. Perhaps a hint of a longing for something more than the cruel world he was accustomed to ruling.

King Zayed's eyes bore into mine, searching for something I did not quite understand. "You have a way with words, Amara. Perhaps too much for your own good," he said cryptically before sitting up straighter on the bed, his demeanor changing as quickly as the shifting sands in a desert storm. Gone was the sad king and he was again the man with a stoic expression on his face. He waved a hand carelessly towards me, motioning for me to continue the story.

"Yasmin found herself whisked away on the magic carpet to far-off lands. She soared over ancient cities, their minarets reaching for the heavens, and visited bustling bazaars. Yasmin stayed only long enough to help those in need before going onto the next adventure. For hot on her trail was King Farid, intent on reclaiming the magic carpet for his own nefarious purposes. However, in every corner of every city he ventured, stories of Yasmin's kindness and the magic carpet that adorned her side echoed.

The more the king learned about her compassion and generosity, the more captivated he became. However, try as he might, Yasmin remained ever elusive. She managed to slip away undetected, leaving nothing but the tales of her good deeds for the king who found his heart slowly changing.

As King Farid continued his pursuit, he suddenly found himself torn between his lingering desire for power...for wealth...and for the growing admiration he felt for Yasmin."

I paused, taking in the way King Zayed was leaning forward, his eyes rapt with attention and interest. I took a deep breath, knowing this story was all that was most likely still keeping me alive. I deliberately stood up, slowly walking towards the far end of the room to pour myself a glass of water from the earthen pitcher.

"What happened when he found her?"

The question fell from the king's lips, more a demand than the query he posed it as. My back was to him, and my hand shook as I brought the glass of water to my lips. My eyes strayed to the balcony, every fiber of my being fearing the first crack of dawn. What had my life become? I absently looked at Baghel, laid out in the middle of the vast room, sleeping peacefully. Would he fight his master, if it came to it? Or would he help carry out the king's orders?

I cleared my throat and turned to face King Zayed who was now sitting at the edge of the bed, his arms crossed as he looked at me impatiently.

"City after city, King Farid witnessed the impact of Yasmin on the lives of the people she touched. Her acts of kindness brought hope to the hopeless...and joy to the sorrowful. Suddenly...he found himself wanting to change his own ways...and be deserving."

"Deserving of what?" King Zayed asked, brows furrowed in confusion.

I rubbed my sweaty palms against the fabric of my Blade-Caller uniform.

"Of her love, *Shehenshah*," I whispered pointedly.

There was a silence in the room, where nothing but the sounds of Baghel's peaceful snores could be heard. And then King Zayed threw his head back and laughed. He laughed and laughed until he fell back on the bed. Briefly, he was no longer the rough and stoic king. He was a man, laughing in his wife's room. His face was lit up with a grin that made a smile tug at my own lips. The lines on his face, the frown on his brow...they had all but disappeared momentarily.

"An enemies-to-lovers story. I should have known," he chortled into the cushions before lifting himself off the bed and walking over to me with purposeful strides. "And when he finds her...he makes her his queen. How very typical...and boring," he deadpanned, stepping closer to me.

I took an instinctive step back and hit the table behind me. The jug of water clattered to the floor. In an instant, Baghel was up and by my side. He let out an indignant yelp, eyes trained on his master.

"No, *Shehenshah*," I protested, hoping the title would diffuse the tension on his face. "My story is not as straightforward as that, but if you prefer not to know..."

He stepped closer to me, so close we were breathing the same air.

"Know what?" His hot breath tickled my cheek as he stared down at me curiously.

I swallowed, shaking inwardly. My chest grazed his slightly upon my deep inhale. He could not know my fear. I looked up at him, praying my calm facade did not crack.

"Yasmin made a friend upon her travels. Harun became the steadfast companion she had always yearned to have. However, what Yasmin did not know was that Harun was a mage, intent on stealing the carpet for himself. All he needed to do was gain her trust. And gain her trust he did. For one night...as the two sat together in front of a fire deep in the desert...Harun asked Yasmin to marry him. He gifted her with the most beautiful of rings which Yasmin immediately allowed him to slip onto her finger. And that is when the handsome young man in front of her transformed in an instant. His youthful handsome face gave way to one filled with deep frown lines. The loving smile became a grotesque smirk, and Yasmin....Yasmin found her body turning to stone before her very eyes. Horrified, Yasmin discovered that the ring was cursed to turn the wearer into a statue. She screamed in agony as she felt her body begin to calcify. Tears streamed down her face as her heart shattered, the first heartbreak of love, a pain beyond belief for the young woman. Laughing, Harun took the carpet and flew off. All the while, Yasmin's tears continued to stream down the statue, a never-ending river of pain."

"He betrayed her," King Zayed deduced with a frown.

I nodded, biting my lip to hide my triumphant smirk. He did not find the story boring now.

"The tale of the crying statue spread far and wide, as did the story of what befell Yasmin. When it reached King Farid's ears, he immediately made his way to Yasmin, every fiber of his being wanting nothing more than to somehow lift the curse."

"What happens when he finds her?" King Zayed demanded of me.

I sucked in a breath. He was too close. I could smell the cardamom on his breath, see the flecks of gold in his green eyes...

My eyes went to the balcony again. It was still dark. Dawn would not be for another few hours. My eyes hardened with resolve. I feigned a yawn.

"I am tired, My King. May we continue the story tomorrow?"

King Zayed looked at me with narrowed eyes. I tried to side-step him, my own eyes avoiding his calculating gaze. His hand clamped over my wrist like a vice, stopping me. My shoulder pressed against his chest, sending a jolt of awareness across every nerve ending. He was too strong. I would not be able to stop him if he tried to claim his husbandly rights. I closed my eyes, hating my weak body in that moment.

"Look at me," he demanded.

He looked down at me, and I, powerless to avoid a direct order, raised my defiant eyes to his. I would not cower in fear.

"You are purposely delaying the story," he summed up.

I could see now why he was a formidable king. It was nigh impossible to fool him.

Rather than outright lie or admit anything to his face, I tried to wrench my arm free. He only tightened his hold, his hand hot on the skin of my wrist.

Baghel let out a low warning growl. I looked down, wondering if he was ready to attack me for defying his king. But to my surprise, Baghel was tense and ready to pounce on the king.

Without breaking eye contact with me, King Zayed slowly raised his other hand, gesturing for Baghel to stand down. The tension in the room was palpable, the air heavy with unspoken threats. I could feel my heart pounding in my chest as I tried to maintain my composure under the king's piercing gaze. His eyes momentarily flickered down to my lips before raising back to meet my gaze.

"You are afraid?" he surmised.

Baghel growled in warning again, and I felt a little safer for some reason. If his hunting dog was on my side...maybe I stood a chance? Summoning all the courage I had left, I narrowed my eyes on the man before me. He was a man. Just like any other man. He would bleed, just like any other man.

"No," I stated, pulling my arm away from him successfully. Albeit, I had to admit it was because this time, he offered little resistance.

I stepped away, clearing my throat. My dagger. It was sheathed and inside the pocket of my uniform. Idly, I reached for it, wondering if Baghel would keep him preoccupied long enough for me to attack.

"Then why are you reaching for your dagger? I must warn you, Amara, should you try anything, the guard outside your door will not hesitate to end your life. And Baghel's as well. He is loyal to you, which is commendable. Do not waste precious life on a mere chance of ending mine."

I turned to him, only to see those stern green eyes filled with a cynical mirth.

"You think you are the only queen who has attempted to kill the king?" He sighed wearily. "I cannot say I blame them. However, their tactics veered towards the use of poison. But I must say...you...you are the first to actually have such an opening as this." He raised his hands, gesturing between us.

My eyebrows furrowed in confusion.

"I never sought out their company," he clarified.

"Then...how did you kill them?" I queried, completely forgetting myself and bluntly asking the question burning a hole in my skull.

King Zayed regarded me with an odd expression.

"I could tell you...but then I would have to kill you," he ended somberly, turning on his heel to leave the room. "You may continue your story tomorrow night. Sleep, or at least attempt to." With those parting words, he closed the door to my room.

I sank to the floor in disbelief. Baghel's head came to rest in my lap. I would live another night...see another dawn. Tears of relief streamed down my eyes. My hands absently went to rest over Baghel's head. He licked the palms of both my hands before nuzzling his nose into my side comfortingly.

The story...I had to keep the story interesting...

I woke up the next day and found myself idly wandering the halls of the palace with Baghel by my side. I knew there was a library here. If stories are what were keeping me alive, I needed inspiration. For indeed, I needed to craft something to keep him more interested in the plot than spilling the blood of innocent women.

Sherazi was busy changing out the bed linens and making sure the maids cleaned my room thoroughly. She warned me to stay inside and keep Baghel by my side at all times. Even my head maid could discern how loyal Baghel was. She had given me directions to the library, but I still found myself perplexed. Was I was walking in the correct direction?

Maybe that is why I found myself passing a room where familiar voices floated through the cracked door.

"What are you doing, *Shehenshah*? You put us all at risk. The Emirs expect a ruler in control—"

"I am in control, Uncle!" King Zayed's voice was a sharp reprimanding bark. His voice seemed strained however, laced with frustration.

"You know as well as I that you are hanging on by a thread. This cannot go on—" The Grand Vizier was cut off by a loud thump.

Unable to resist, I leaned forward, peering through the crack of the door.

King Zayed's fist rested over a table brimming with official scrolls and seals. The sound must have been the impact of his fist against the wooden table. My eyes widened in understanding. This was his office where he met with his advisors and nobles. It was strategically attached to the throne room, an antechamber of sorts for more private meetings.

"You do not order me on what can and cannot be done," King Zayed reprimanded sternly, eyes on the Grand Vizier. "I know what I am doing."

"I do not wish to see you suffer," another voice spoke up, softer and kinder than the Grand Vizier's. It took me a few moments to realize the voice belonged to Dornia, the wet nurse. "You have not slept, have you?"

King Zayed's eyes softened as they rested on Dornia who sat across from him in a seat next to the Vizier's. Their backs were to me, so I could not make out their faces. But I could see King Zayed's face as his seat was facing forward, giving me a direct line of sight to him. He seemed tired, haggard, and pale. Had the dark bruises under his eyes always been there and I was only noticing them after Dornia pointed them out? Uneasily, I had a feeling that was exactly the case. Why was he not sleeping?

"I will be fine. I just...need time..." King Zayed leaned back in his chair, his eyes on the parchment before him. "We must approve the work on the water storage system for the oncoming drought."

"There is no oncoming drought!" exploded the Grand Vizier. "Do you know how costly—"

"I said," King Zayed spoke authoritatively, his tone brokering zero argument, "we must approve the work for the oncoming drought. I will decide what cost the crown can bear and cannot. Cut your pay, increase the taxes on the nobles, they have fattened their coffers enough. We must protect the citizens of Ilm."

King Zayed's demeanor had shifted from tired to resolute, his eyes flashed with a determination that sent a shiver down my spine. He exuded power and control with every breath he took, looking exactly like the King of Kings he was meant to be.

Dornia's voice cut through the air like a soothing balm, her concern for the king evident in her gentle tone as she assured King Zayed that all would be well, but he must sleep first. The Grand Vizier seemed to bristle at King Zayed's orders, but there was an underlying sense of respect in his posture. It was clear that while the older man questioned the king's decisions, he had no choice but to comply.

"As you wish, my King," the Grand Vizier murmured, bowing his head in reverence.

It was then that King Zayed's eyes snapped straight ahead and fixed on me, my form visible through the small crack in the door. My heart plummeted to my knees. He knew I was here and eavesdropping.

Chapter 12

After King Zayed's eyes landed on me through the crack in the door, I quickly scurried away and found myself in the gardens.

The conversation I overheard was a jumbled mess, like pieces of a puzzle that did not quite fit together.

It was like trying to read a book in a foreign language without any context. A drought was coming? We had not had a drought in over ten years from what I could remember.

During the relentless drought and famine, our city was reduced to a desolate wasteland. Corpses littered the streets as people succumbed to starvation and thirst. My parents sacrificed their own meals so my sister and I could eat, but even then we had to ration every drop of water. It was a daily struggle just to stay alive in a world where death seemed to reign supreme.

People withered away in front of us, their eyes hollow as they pleaded for death as salvation from the constant pangs of hunger. It had been a dark time for the kingdom as a whole. I had been but a child of eleven at the time, if I recall correctly. My sister's emaciated form from back then came to mind. I shook off the horrible image, pausing at a rosebush. I had ended up too far away from the main palace.

My eyes searched the familiar territory. In my haste, I ended up where I had encountered that vile beast my first night here. But it was daytime. Surely he was locked away deep in the king's dungeon? I looked around, only to realize that Baghel was not here. Had he been distracted during my walk here? Or had he sensed the monster nearby and decided to hide?

Turning, I decided it was best to go back towards the palace. I had wandered too far.

"Well...well...well. What do we have here?" a voice spoke up in cold amusement.

I stopped in my tracks, my head snapping up to look in the direction of the voice. For a minute, I thought Ashad stood before me and my heart nearly burst through my chest in happiness. But I blinked and realized it was just wishful thinking. The man was tall and his coloring was similar to Ashad's, but he was not my friend. My eyes took in his expensive clothes and gold flashy sword at his hip. It took all of my self-restraint to prevent my lips from curling into a derisive sneer. The flashier the sword, the more useless the wielder. That was what Ashad had always said. As I stared at this stranger with the odd glint in his eye, I was inclined to agree.

How had I ever confused him for my friend? He was lanky, lacking the muscular build of a strong swordsman. The finely threaded cloth across his form told me this man spent more attention on his apparel than he should. He was vain. And...my eyes narrowed as I glanced at his hands. Even King Zayed had more calluses on his hands from practicing with the sword. This man's hands were unblemished, like a baby's. He was a man child.

"What is a beautiful maid such as yourself doing out here?" he queried, stepping closer.

My eyebrows rose in consternation. Maid? I looked down at my clothes, realizing I was dressed quite simply. I had not wanted to be trussed up today like a sacrificial lamb. Sherazi had been busy airing out my room. I had only meant to go to the library until Sherazi came to get me. I could see how my plain white clothes of simple cotton made him think I was a maid. Well...no matter.

I raised an eyebrow at him, wondering if he was going to order me to perform some menial task. He stepped even closer to me, and alarm rose within my consciousness. He was too close. And the way he gazed at me, in that predatory fashion...

"I am merely enjoying a walk in the gardens," I replied calmly, taking a step back to put some distance between us. His gaze lingered on me, assessing and calculating, as if weighing his options. I could feel my heart pounding in my chest, a sense of unease creeping up my spine.

"Well, a walk is always more enjoyable with company," he said with a smirk, reaching out to brush a strand of hair from my face. I instinctively recoiled at his touch, the hairs on the back of my neck standing on end. "Come now, I am sure I could make it worth your time, maid. A beautiful woman such as yourself..." His hand fell to my shoulder, a demanding squeeze that told me he would not take no for an answer. "You will make more money within the hour than you would make in an entire month."

I stared up at him, stunned. He...wanted to buy me? As the reality of his proposition sunk in, a fury like no other coiled up my belly, flames licking up my spine until rage exploded in my head.

Before I could stop myself, my hand fisted and flew out, hitting him hard across the face with a resounding crack that echoed through the quiet of the gardens. The noble stumbled back, his hand flying to his jaw in shock. His eyes blazed with fury as he recovered from the initial surprise of my reaction.

My knuckles were bleeding, the impact too great for my skin to bear. And if I had not broken a bone, I was pretty sure I had at least fractured one with the way my hand pounded in pain.

"How dare you lay a hand on me, you insolent wench!" he snarled, his voice filled with venom.

I stood my ground, clutching my now useless hand to my chest which heaved with a mixture of fear and anger. Never had a man been so bold! And to think...I was a queen and had to put up with this! What must the maids have to deal with when these bothersome nobles visited the castle? Despite the tremble in my hand, I lifted my chin defiantly and met his gaze head-on.

"I am not for sale," I spat out, my voice laced with anger. "And you will show me the respect I deserve."

The man's expression twisted into a dark scowl as he took a menacing step towards me, his hand reaching once again. But I was ready for him. My uninjured left hand snaked out, clamping over his wrist just as he grabbed onto my arm. I twisted his wrist, moving my body behind his forearm and grit through the pain as I reached my right injured hand out to exert pressure on his elbow joint. He crumpled to his knees, a surprised cry of pain on his lips.

"You do not get to touch me," I hissed out, leaning down close to his ear to warn him. All it would take was one firm twist to break his arm.

"Bitch!" he spat, but cried out in agony when I exerted more pressure on his elbow and wrist simultaneously with both my hands.

"I might be a bitch," I grit the words out, tears blurring my eyesight as the pain in my injured hand increased. I blinked them away, channeling all my rage into overpowering this despicable excuse for a human. "But at least I am not the one about to be thrown in jail for trying to force myself upon a woman."

He gave a dark chuckle. My eyes fell upon the guards making their way towards us. Kadin was at the front, his eyes taking in the entire situation.

"You must be delusional if you think I am going to jail over a lowly maid!"

"Men like you disgust me," I seethed. I twisted his arm so it was behind his back and pushed him down. His knees buckled and his face fell in the dirt. I wedged my knee between his shoulder blades for good measure.

"Kadin!" I barked out once he was within earshot. "Get this piece of filth out of my sight!"

"Help me! She must be hanged for attacking a noble," the man under me exclaimed, his voice muffled as a mouthful of dirt and grass found its way onto his tongue.

Once Kadin was close enough, I let up on the man, moving back to again nurse my injury. I could see the skin becoming blue and the blood crusting over.

"You are under arrest—" Kadin began sternly, eyes on the noble who was panting as he attempted to stand.

"For angering a maid?" he blustered in disbelief, eyes hardening. "Kadin, you have been known to be overly friendly with the maids. If she was your whore, I did not know. You cannot just arrest me! When the king hears of this—"

"When the king hears of this, he will have your head for assaulting the queen." Kadin's eyes sparked dangerously as he cut the poor fool off.

"Qu...queen?" He looked as if he had just seen a ghost.

"I said take him out of my sight!" I thundered, tears stinging the back of my eyes as the pain became near unbearable in my hand.

At once, my orders were carried out and the lecher was hauled away. Kadin looked at me, worry marring his features.

"My Queen...your..your hand..."

I could not protest, I did not have the energy left to do so. So I let Kadin lead me away, tears of pain finally free-falling down my cheeks.

I was in the antechamber to the throne room, my injured hand neatly obscured by the folds of my long *kameez*, the plain flowy shirt that went down to my knees. Kadin was dealing with the aftermath of the events outside, in the throne room beyond.

"You cannot just attack nobles!" the Grand Vizier reprimanded, standing across from me in the antechamber to the King's throne room.

King Zayed sat at a desk, eyes trained on me.

The Grand Vizier pointed an accusing finger at me. "You will be our downfall...our ruin!"

"Enough!" King Zayed barked out, making the Grand Vizier stop. He looked at me, eyes steady and keen. "You do not talk to your queen in that manner."

"My King," the Grand Vizier pleaded, eyes beseeching as he stared at his ruler. "You know as well as I, as the son of a noble from a neighboring kingdom, Shain was sent here as an emissary! He and his brother have proved valuable assets in negotiating trade between Elamaria and Kaizern. We need the trade, if a famine were to occur..." the Grand Vizier trailed off helplessly, shaking his head. "And the queen assaulted him!"

"I was defending myself!" I protested, unable to stay quiet a moment longer. "Is that not allowed in this country? Am I to...to take him up on his proposition just to please him?"

"Proposition?" King Zayed queried, eyes narrowed on me. Clear green eyes turned nearly black, and his voice became a deathly whisper. "What proposition?"

I shifted uncomfortably, feeling my face heat up. How exactly was I supposed to tell him?

"What proposition, Amara?" King Zayed repeated, eyes boring into mine ominously.

"He thought I was a servant...and that...I was...that my body was...for sale," I spoke haltingly, cheeks on fire as I averted my gaze.

There was a sharp crack that made me look up only to realize that King Zayed had stood up so fast that his chair fell back behind him. I blinked and he was suddenly at the door leading into the throne room.

"No, My King! This could mean war!" the Grand Vizier begged, attempting to stop King Zayed.

A ferocious growl ripped through the room, animalistic and primal. For a moment, I was back in the trees running for my life from the humanoid beast. It took me a moment to realize the growl came from the king.

He wrenched the door open, nearly ripping it off its hinges with the ferocity he employed. As the king disappeared into the throne room, the Grand Vizier turned to stare at me with contempt.

He crossed his arms, staring me down as if I was a cockroach that needed to be squashed. "You, young lady, are more trouble than I bargained for." With those parting words, he turned and disappeared to attempt to assuage the volatile situation he claimed I was the sole culprit of.

Through the crack in the door left open by the Vizier, I spotted the king holding my assaulter by the neck, slowly raising him off the ground with just the strength in one arm. My assaulter's eyes bulged and his feet flailed in the air as he gasped, trying to prevent himself from suffocating at the hands of the king.

"Touch my queen again, and I will tear your limbs off," I heard King Zayed snarl before flinging the lecher clear across the throne room as if he were a weightless rag doll.

My eyes widened at the display of ferocity and raw power. But I could not smother the satisfaction I felt as the pervert's body hit the far wall and lay crumpled in a heap, blood seeping from the back of his skull.

I winced as the doctor wrapped a poultice around my hand. King Zayed stood at the foot of my bed, watching the doctor keenly.

"Nothing is broken," the doctor assured. "She just requires rest and..." He lifted a cup to my lips. The unpleasant smell made me wrinkle my nose. Jerking my head away, I attempted to sink deeper into the pillows I was propped up against.

"It will dull the pain while you heal," he cajoled.

"Leave us," King Zayed demanded.

The doctor complied immediately, setting the cup down on the side table. He stood and bowed to the king before retreating.

I stared at King Zayed witheringly.

"This is your fault," I stated without preamble.

He looked at me, surprised.

"Because a man like that was on palace grounds? I must admit, you are right. Emissaries should be vetted thoroughly before being allowed to enter the kingdom."

"Because he thought he could do as he pleased since I was a maid! What does that say about you? About the importance you give your commoners? If a man thinks it is all right—"

"I give each and every citizen of my kingdom equal rights," King Zayed protested in a steely voice that brokered no argument.

Equal rights? Ha. Killing off the peasants' daughters was not "equal rights".

"Then why was he so sure I, a maid, would be punished and not him?" I shook my head in disgust. "I have a feeling if it had been Sherazi in my place, she would have been punished for defending herself."

The King looked at me in confusion for a moment.

"Who?"

I wanted to rip my hair out. The man did not even know the names of his servants!

"My maid!" I spat bitterly. "See...this is what I mean." I sighed in resignation. I looked at him, his gaze trained on the cup of medicine. "You do not even know the names of the palace servants," I pointed out bitterly.

"I know the names of all the servants within my palace," Zayed stated dismissively as he made his way to sit on the edge of my bed.

I could tell his mind was not on servants but on the medicine I was supposed to consume. Insufferable arrogant king!

"Do not make me drink it," I protested, realizing why he was still here and where his true attention was fixated.

"You must."

"And you will kill me if I do not?" I could not help but say the words bitterly as I stared down at my throbbing hand.

"I will force it down your throat if required," was his stern response.

My gaze shot to him in consternation.

"It smells...vile. It must be poison."

He held the cup to my lips a smile tugging his lips upward.

"No poison today. Maybe tomorrow."

I looked at him in consternation. I did not appreciate his jokes.

King Zayed sighed, still holding the cup. "It is medicine, Amara. He is my own personal physician. I would not allow anyone else to look after you."

Those words held an underlying meaning I could not decipher at the moment. Not when I was trying my damned best not to drink what was in that cup!

"It is a sedative as well as a painkiller. I will not be able to tell you the story tonight if I drink it."

The King glared at me. "I am willing to live with the consequences. I can wait one night. Now, as your king, I order you to drink."

With a scowl, I tried to take the cup from him. He moved it back so that I missed it by a hair's breadth.

"I must make sure you finish it." He looked at me as if I were a child who had to be force-fed.

"It smells disgusting!" I burst out, not wanting to drink it at all.

I needed my wits about me. This would dull my senses.

"You, a fierce Blade-Caller, afraid of a little medicine?"

I pressed my lips together into a thin scowl. He chose his words quite deliberately. To make me feel inadequate. I tipped my head, allowing him to bring the cup to my lips. I drank, holding back a gag as the foul-tasting concoction burned a path down my throat.

Several pauses were necessary, during which the king's steadfast gaze remained on my form, to completely finish emptying the cup. Finally, he set the cup down.

My eyes began to droop closed almost immediately. I felt his hands skate up my arms to rest on my shoulders. The cushions I had been propped against were removed so I could lay back.

The king's fingers gently traced the line of my jaw, and I could feel his breath against my skin as he spoke. "Sleep now, Amara. I promise you...you will awaken in the morning to a new dawn."

Letting those words reassure me that I would see another day, I finally succumbed to sleep.

Chapter 13

"Uncouth...barbaric!" Dornia screamed as I sat in my room where Sherazi tended to my hand by wrapping a new poultice around it.

The doctor had come earlier to check on me. The swelling had gone down considerably. However, he instructed me to keep my injured hand wrapped to prevent further swelling. Somehow, Dornia ended up in my chambers, without knocking, and was now screaming at me. The sound was like knives scraping against stones.

"What that noble did was even more barbaric," I retorted coolly, eyes on her. "He deserves death for trying to force himself upon me."

"It is your own mistake for wandering in the gardens alone! How was he to know that you were the queen?"

This woman had the audacity to blame me, the victim. Not the man who tried to harm me. Typical.

"Even if I were not the queen, he would still deserve death," I responded calmly, taking my hand away from Sherazi's hold. "You are disturbing my recuperation time period. Please leave me," I requested politely, knowing it was futile to ask this woman anything. But my head was pounding from the after effects of the sedative, and I just wanted to be left in peace.

Dornia's face turned red. A vein began to throb at her temple.

"You think you are royalty just because you are the king's wife? You are nothing but a commoner, a peasant girl whose fate was sealed the moment your hands were adorned with the ceremonial bridal henna. I will not stand by while you destroy this kingdom with your folly! You will destroy him in the process as well!" Dornia exclaimed vehemently, and I could have sworn I saw her frothing at the mouth in anger.

She looked like a rabid wild animal, nearly ready to pounce. "I have raised him since he was a newborn—" her voice cracked, and the emotion that suddenly marred her face was not one of an evil woman looking to kill me. It was almost akin to that of a lioness protecting her cub.

"I cannot lose him now...not him too..."

She trailed off, and I wondered exactly what she meant. Turning abruptly, the woman left in a flurry of silk and perfume.

"What did she mean, not him too?" I queried, looking at Sherazi.

"Perhaps she meant the king's younger brother?" Sherazi mused. "She was a wet nurse for him as well...before...he was killed."

That got my attention.

"The king's younger brother was killed?" I asked, completely aghast. Who would kill a royal? I had thought he had died. Maybe of an illness of some sort.

Sherazi turned beet red and stood up to start bowing out of the room.

"No, Sherazi, you cannot leave me after revealing such a vital piece of information!" I exclaimed in frustration.

"I...I am sorry, My Queen. But to discuss the matter is punishable by death," Sherazi whispered, already at the door of my room. She gave one last bow before scurrying off.

I wanted to run after her. But if she truly thought she might be beheaded there was no point in pressuring her. I would have to encourage another slip of tongue, like she had done just now. Slowly. I would wheedle the information from her slowly.

But in the next moment, I did not have much else time to strategize as King Zayed himself strode through the doors. At least he had the decency to knock first.

"The doctor says your swelling has gone down," he stated without preamble, walking over to where I sat on one of the floor cushions. He sat down next to me, taking my hand to look at it. His touch was gentle yet firm.

"It should be healed in a few days," King Zayed stated. He then looked at me closely. "I must leave to visit Kaizern and ensure that man receives his just deserts for what he did to you. It is an insult to the crown that I cannot let slide."

"How long will you be gone?" I briefly wondered if an escape would be possible.

"Two days. Do not go anywhere without Baghel or one of the guards Kadin himself assigns. Many would want to attempt to assassinate the queen. It is not safe, Amara." He dropped my hand from his hold, and the loss of the warmth of his touch was immediately noticeable.

"You are afraid someone might try to harm me?" I asked, marveling at his contradictory ways. This man had my headstone prepared and grave already dug up, yet he was telling me to stay safe?

"I am," he relented.

"Just like they harmed your younger brother?" I ventured.

King Zayed stiffened, lips pressing into a scowl.

"Who told you this?" he demanded.

If I told him the truth, Sherazi might be punished.

I remained quiet as his eyes bore into mine.

"There are many rumors floating about the palace," I finally settled on saying.

That piercing gaze of his narrowed on me and then, for a moment, the mask fell away to reveal a very sad man. A man who seemed burdened by a life of devastation and endless sorrow. But I blinked and that man was gone. In his place stood my king, face cold and stoic.

"My father killed him," he stated with zero emotion.

I gasped, recalling Kadin's words. He had never revealed that to me. I had thought it had been an accident, a tragedy, an illness. And after what Sherazi told me, I assumed it was an assassination attempt.

"He made me watch. Told me to look at what must be done when a woman is unfaithful..." King Zayed swallowed and looked away, eyes resting on a tapestry on the far wall.

He did not need to say more. Now, I finally understood. His father had killed his mother for being unfaithful and giving birth to another man's child.

The words spilled forth before I could stop myself.

"Kadin told me your brother died as a mere babe...not even weaned from the breast..." King Zayed looked at me now, his eyes unnaturally bright. "He made it sound like an accident occurred," I was quick to add, lest the king reprimand Kadin for revealing it to me. "How...how could your father be sure...the child was not his?" I could not help but ask the question. "It might have been a mistake," I offered feebly. "A misunderstanding?"

"The men born in our family possess certain qualities, qualities my younger brother did not possess." King Zayed sighed, the heels of his hands going to dig into his eyes. "My mother was a good woman, Amara," he whispered. "My father considered her act of infidelity a stain upon our lineage that could not be allowed to continue."

Nowhere in the words he had spoken had he said he believed in the same principles. It was so clear from the haunting sadness in his eyes that he did not agree with his father's actions. And yet...he felt duty bound to kill women?

"You are not your father." I said the words beseechingly, wishing they would claw their way past the walls he had built around himself. I willed them to break through these barriers he had constructed, and I realized...no longer did I wish to destroy him. I wanted to heal him. But if I could not, I would have to get rid of him to save the kingdom. However, now the deed made my stomach churn in protest.

"I am not," he agreed, hands falling from his face to look at me. His eyes were rimmed red, but unnaturally dry now. "However...his words haunt me to this day. I was told women can never be trusted." He leaned his head back, eyes now on the ceiling, lost in his own memories for the moment. "Betrayal is unacceptable and must never be tolerated. A cheating heart of a woman cannot be allowed to beat..." He trailed off, vulnerability and pain rolling off him in palpable waves.

I could not help but feel a surge of empathy for him. The weight of his family history, the tragedy that had befallen his mother and brother, all bore down on his shoulders like an unbreakable chain. The hypocrisy of his father's statements was also not lost on me. I recall Kadin telling me the previous king used to have a harem. A harem that King Zayed disbanded. So the king could do as he pleased, but his unloved queen was expected to just bear it? I hated such double standards.

Another thought then struck me. Was King Zayed emulating what he saw his father do? His first wife had loved another. Maybe his father's words and actions had twisted his mental state to an extent where he felt duty bound to kill his brides? Had they too loved other men when they were chosen? And that knowledge triggered King Zayed to kill the women? Or was something else at play entirely?

Our eyes met, and I saw a glimmer of something else beneath the sorrow and duty that weighed on him. It was a flicker of desperation, a silent plea for understanding and forgiveness. In that moment, all I wanted was to reach out and touch his hand, to offer him solace and reassurance that he was not condemned to repeat the sins of his father. He could be better.

But just as I opened my mouth to say so, there was a timid knock at my door before a servant entered. She bowed to the king, a vase of flowers in her hand.

"Queen of the Night," I stated, looking at my favorite flowers in the vase.

"They are your favorite, yes?" King Zayed asked, eyes steady on me.

I nodded, watching as the servant girl went to set them on my nightstand.

"Better to have them here than to go walking about the gardens at night," King Zayed said gently. "I ordered them to be picked before dawn to preserve their natural bloom."

I blinked in confusion. Had he asked for the flowers to be picked for me? The gesture was not lost on me. How did he know they were my favorite?

"I shall see you again in two days time, My Queen. And I expect the rest of my story upon my return."

The way he looked at me with those parting remarks created flickers of fire deep inside my belly, and a tugging sensation inside my heart. As if maybe I wanted to follow him. Or ask him to stay longer.

Later that night, as I sat alone in my room, with Baghel adamant on sleeping on the balcony, I looked at the flowers the king arranged for me. I wondered briefly if it really was the story that was keeping me alive, or something else entirely?

I nestled into my warm and cozy bed, ready to drift off into a peaceful slumber. A warmth spread through me as I recalled the way the king had looked at me, and bid me farewell before leaving. He was a mystery, like a puzzle. There were so many facets of the puzzle, so many parts of the mystery. But one thing I knew with absolute certainty now, he did not kill those women in blood lust. A man who held me so gently, who looked at me as if I was his oasis...a man who still left flowers at the graves of his ten dead brides. A man who had the forethought to have my favorite flowers picked. No. There was more to the story. Something I was unaware of.

The night was quiet, and the gentle lull of the wind outside my window whispered a sweet lullaby as the thoughts racing through my mind began to slow down to give way to a gentle sleep.

Slowly, I began to surrender to the embrace of sleep. However, I suddenly jolted awake, startled by a faint whisper that seemed to echo in the darkness.

"One bride was promised... One bride was promised," the words reverberated in the confines of my room, sending shivers down my spine.

Confusion and fear flooded my senses as I strained to comprehend the meaning behind the eerie chant.

A putrid odor invaded the air, assaulting my nostrils with the scent of decaying flowers. The sickly sweet aroma hung heavy, suffocating any hope of tranquility. Sitting up in bed, I looked at my night stand to see that the once fresh flowers were a rotting black now. How was this possible? Panic began to claw at my chest, urging me to investigate the source of this unsettling phenomenon.

The doors to my balcony flew open with a violent gust of wind, causing me to gasp in shock. The curtains billowed wildly around my bed, as if possessed by an unseen force. I brought a hand to my thumping heart, breathing deeply in an attempt to calm myself. The room became engulfed in a chilling draft, sending a shiver down my spine. It was as if the very essence of the night had come alive, taunting me with its presence.

Driven by a mixture of curiosity and sheer terror, I stumbled out of bed and rushed towards the open balcony door in a bid to close it and whatever malevolent force was seeping in. But my hand stilled as my eyes fell on the scene before me, illuminated by the moonlight. It was a sight that would forever haunt my dreams.

Lying on the ground was an unconscious Baghel, breathing labored, his once vibrant pure-white fur now matted and stained with blood. His mouth was wide open in a silent yelp of pain as blood seeped out in rivulets. The sight of his beautiful form, bleeding out onto the cold stone floor, sent a wave of alarm and despair crashing over me. Who could have done this to him? Or what? The beast that patrolled the perimeter? No. Something else! I needed to get help. But how did this happen?!

A primal fear gripped my heart as I realized that something sinister was unfolding around me.

Without a moment's hesitation, I fled from the balcony, my breath ragged and my mind racing. The echoes of the whispered chant continued to haunt my every step.

"One bride was promised... One bride was promised." The words were a constant mantra, chasing me through the room, a constant reminder of the malevolence that surrounded me. Could it be? Were the rumors Sherazi told me true? Did King Zayed's first bride truly haunt this castle?

As I stumbled upon the threshold of the front door of my bedroom, gasping for breath, I could feel the weight of the night's terrors pressing down upon me. The air was thick with an otherworldly presence, suffocating and suffused with an unrelenting darkness.

At that moment, I realized I was trapped in a nightmare from which there was no escape. My injured dog, the rotting flowers, and the chilling chant were all pieces of a terrifying mystery that I was powerless to solve. With a powerful tug, I wrenched open the door to see the guard standing sentry. He jerked awake, having nodded off whilst leaning against the wall.

"Get Kadin now," I demanded of him. "And we need a doctor. Baghel is injured."

He looked at me in alarm, suddenly wide awake. Complying, he ran off to do as I commanded of him whilst another guard who stood sentry at the corner of the hall made his way towards me to take up the post. They did not know the true threat was inside this room already.

Before I could even vocalize my thoughts, a sharp pain pierced through my head, and I fell to my knees. An eerie chilling voice seemed to whisper into the recesses of my brain, threatening to crack open the plates of my skull.

"Beware, Amara, of the shadows that dance in the dark, for they hold secrets that can shatter the fragile veil of reality. In the depths of the night, your nightmares will come alive. Your king cannot save you from the horrors that await."

Chapter 14

"Will he be alright?" I asked frantically whilst an animal doctor looked over Baghel.

My little protector opened his eyes feebly, letting out a little yelp, happy to see I was safe, before closing them again. I held back a sob.

Kadin put an arm around me comfortingly.

"Whatever was on that balcony, Baghel was able to fight it off. I shudder to think what would have happened if he had not been in your room. He will die an honorable death, My Queen, for protecting you is tantamount to protecting the king. The decree was passed before King Zayed left."

"But...will he survive?" I asked, needing the answer to be yes.

"If he dies because he was protecting me..." I trailed off and Kadin's arm around my shoulders tightened comfortingly.

"I cannot say for sure," the doctor finally said once he had finished bandaging up Baghel. "He will need to stay here with me in my clinic for a few days so that I may monitor him. It is odd though...you say you think a wolf attacked him? Yet there are no claw marks on his body. These wounds look like burns. Except for this here on his neck," —the doctor pointed to three thin lines running across Baghel's neck down to his flank— "these are not the claw marks of a wolf. But of a woman's fingernails."

"Not a wolf...a beast! A monster that is part-man part-beast!" I snarled vehemently.

I did not miss the way the doctor's eyes went to my own hands to look at my bluntly cut fingernails.

"You do not believe me," I said softly, realization sinking in. He was checking to see if it might have been my own fingernails that harmed my dear friend.

"My Queen, even if I were to believe a beast with claw-like fingernails had harmed him, the evidence is on the animal. These are strictly human-inflicted." He pointed to the three scratch marks. "This was done by a person...a woman judging from the sharp pointed tips."

"Do you dare to say the queen lies?" Kadin asked in an ominous whisper. "To doubt the crown's word is punishable by death!"

The doctor paled and shook his head fervently. I shot Kadin a glare. This was not what I wanted. I did not want to scare the man into giving me a diagnosis I wanted to hear. I wanted the truth.

"Please speak openly," I beseeched him, pushing Kadin's arm away from my shoulders and moving forward. "You are the doctor, not I. And if you claim this was inflicted by a human, it means someone was on my balcony..." I trailed off again, recalling the haunting voice.

Here in the light of day, it seemed preposterous that the voice had been inside my head. No. It made perfect sense that someone had most likely been on the balcony. An attempt to scare me most likely. Maybe they had hoped I would be too scared to fight back had they entered my room? But whoever this person was had not counted on Baghel laying in wait. I looked at the doctor, expecting an honest answer from him so I could understand exactly what I was dealing with.

The doctor hesitated, his gaze shifting between me and Kadin, before finally speaking, "My Queen, I cannot deny what I see before me. These wounds are indeed from a human assailant. But surely, it must be a mistake, a misunderstanding."

I shook my head, feeling a chill run down my spine at the realization that someone had been so close to me in the dead of night. Someone that Baghel tried to protect me from. Someone that might be human but not entirely alive.

Kadin's expression darkened at the doctor's words, his jaw clenching in anger. "We must investigate this further," he declared, his voice commanding.

As the doctor nodded in agreement, unease settled over me.

My mind raced with questions, and a deep sense of foreboding crept into my heart as I realized that danger lurked closer than I thought.

As we left the animal clinic, my thoughts were consumed by the events from last night. The chilling voice...

"Come, My Queen." Kadin held his hand out to me to assist me onto the elephant that I had traveled here upon to check on Baghel. I placed my hands in his but stilled when a voice caught my attention.

"Amara!" I turned, my heart leaping into my throat and a joy like no other bursting forth.

"Asya!" I exclaimed, running towards her.

We met in the middle of the bustling street, hugging each other as tears streamed down our eyes. She kissed my cheeks, then my forehead, smothering me with kisses like a mother would. My beautiful sister who had always loved me unconditionally. Oh how I missed her!

"When I heard the queen left the palace to traverse the city, I had to come." Her grip around me grew tighter as she pulled me to the other side of the street. I heard Kadin calling for us. "I have you, Amara. I have been waiting for this opportunity. Oh sister, I am so glad you managed to survive. *Baba* was right, our little tiger would find a way to live."

Surprise filled me as Asya brought me into a side alley. I could hear Kadin barking out orders to the guards. His voice was tinged with borderline panic.

"We know this city like the back of our hands. Losing a few guards will not be a difficult task for us. There is no time to lose, Amara. We escape this city now. Baba is waiting—"

I pulled free of Asya, looking at her with wide eyes. Leave? Now? My thoughts went to Baghel who had risked his life for me. If he recovered, he would look for me in the palace. And then my thoughts went to King Zayed, returning to hear the end of the story only to find me gone. What would he do to Kadin? I would have been lost on his watch.

Asya gave me a harsh tug.

"We cannot waste time!" she whispered fiercely, but I dug my slippered feet into the ground, refusing to budge.

"Asya...wait—" I began.

But my moment's hesitation had been all the king's men needed. At once we were surrounded and a flash of metal had me drawing my dagger. I stopped Kadin's blade from coming down on Asya's head just in time.

I glared up at him, angry he had tried to harm Asya and I faltered. For before me did not stand the kind smiling man, but a face twisted into a mutinous scowl, eyes dark and sinister. He would have killed Asya if I had not blocked him. He might still.

Without a moment's hesitation, I took advantage of his surprise when I blocked him deftly. Side stepping, I used my dagger to exert enough pressure to make his blade veer to the right and away from my sister. In one swift turn, my back was to his chest, my hand on his wrist. I twisted it and he cried out in pain, the blade falling from his hand. I grabbed it before it hit the ground and turned once more protectively in front of Asya, the blade pointed at Kadin's throat.

"Do not touch my sister," I spat angrily, my furious gaze going to Kadin's men that surrounded us with their own *talwars* pointed straight at her. "Drop your weapons!"

As one, they complied, lowering their blades.

"I said drop them!"

My eyes did not leave Kadin's but the clattering of metal hitting the dirt was confirmation enough that my orders had been followed.

"If attacking the queen is tantamount to attacking the king, then attacking her family is just as unlawful," I hissed out, raising the blade up a notch so it was level with Kadin's throat.

He held his hands up defensively.

"What was I to do? We assumed someone was attempting to kidnap our queen. I acted accordingly. Any threat to you must be obliterated swiftly. My Queen...the king...he would not survive your loss," Kadin was quick to point out.

"And what if I wanted to go with her?" I challenged, my eyes narrowing in defiance. "Would you try to kill me?"

Kadin's eyes lightened with understanding and he exchanged a look with his men.

"I would never threaten the crown," he stated solemnly, taking a step back. "If that is what you truly wish..." he trailed off, uncertainty tingeing his tone, signaling for his men to also fall back. They cleared a path for our escape.

"Go, Asya," I sighed, my own blade staying firm in case I had to defend her. "Take *Baba* and leave the city. It is not safe here for you any longer." For whoever had tried to harm me on my balcony might try to harm my family. It might be a malevolent spirit, or an angry noble. Regardless, I would not leave anything to chance. My family could not come to harm.

Kadin inclined his head obediently, eyes flitting to Asya. The fool actually smiled at her.

"I apologize for my impulsive behavior. The king would have had my head if something had happened to his queen, especially on my watch."

Asya looked at him insolently before pulling on my arm.

"Amara, go with me...please."

"No, Asya. I am needed here," I murmured. My hand tightened on the hilt, letting the cool brass metal of Kadin's sword ground me. "Tell *Baba*...I love him." Tears filled my eyes. I missed my family. Seeing Asya today was as rejuvenating as a cool breeze. If only I could bask in it a while longer. "Now go!"

Asya gave a few last tugs at my arm but I would not let up. Realizing that it was futile, my beautiful sister let out an angry sob and retreated.

"I will save you, Amara, I promise!" were her final parting words as she left.

"No one is to follow her," I growled out, looking at Kadin's men. I could not trust anyone. My sixth sense was screaming it at me.

Something or someone was out to harm me. My family could be used as leverage.

"She is your family and under the protection of the crown henceforth," Kadin assured, looking at the blade in my hand warily.

I turned to make sure Asya was no longer within sight. No longer trackable.

Finally, I sagged, letting the sword fall from my fingers and the tears stream down my eyes as Asya's final parting words repeated in my mind. Oh, Asya...if only you knew...I was not the one that needed saving.

I had opted to go on horseback to the palace rather than sit on the elephant again. My eyes remained alert as I took in my surroundings. I hoped Asya was not foolish enough to follow me. As I approached the towering gates of the palace, their intricate carvings glinted under the midday sun. The air was heavy with the scent of polished stone and freshly cut flowers from the gardens beyond. But as I crossed the threshold and agilely jumped off my stead, no easy feat in the light blue silks embellished with intricate beadwork that adorned my form, a sight struck me like a cold wind: a woman, her face streaked with tears, was being dragged backwards, by the fabric of her tunic, by two guards, her cries echoing against the marble walls.

In her arms, she held a small bundle, a baby swaddled tightly who was sleeping peacefully, oblivious to the chaos. The guards, clad in their imposing armor, seemed indifferent to her pleas, their expressions hard and unyielding.

"Please! I just wanted to care for my child!" she cried, her voice breaking in anguish. With a desperate pull, she tugged herself out of their arms and fell to her side, cradling the baby in her secure hold.

I felt a stirring of compassion within me, compelling me to step closer. "What is happening here?" I asked, my heart racing. The guards paused, one glancing at me with a mixture of annoyance and duty.

"My Queen, do not bother yourself with such trivial issues. She is being arrested for breaching her agreement with a prominent noble," one of them explained, his tone clipped. "She is a wet nurse for a noble family and smuggled her own child into their home. She was feeding both newborns, which is strictly forbidden."

The woman's eyes locked onto mine, filled with a mix of fear and hope. "Please, M-My Queen...h-have mercy. I did not mean any harm," she pleaded, her grip tightening around the baby. "I just wanted to feed them both. They both needed me."

I felt a wave of anger rise within me at the injustice of it all. How could they treat a mother this way? "She is being punished for caring for her own baby? Is there nothing you can do?" I asked the guards, my voice rising with indignation.

But they remained stoic, their duty blinding them to the humanity of the situation.

"It is pointless, My Queen. The Grand Vizier will not risk angering the nobles," one guard warned with a weary sigh.

But I stood firm, my body between them and the poor woman sobbing as she clutched her baby to her bosom. My heart raced as I weighed my options. I could feel the weight of the palace around me, the opulence of its walls contrasting sharply with the heart-wrenching scene before me. I had to make a choice.

"Where is this noble heartless enough to punish a mother for nursing her child?" I demanded, my voice steady despite the tumult of emotions swirling inside me. The guard shifted uncomfortably, glancing at his partner before answering.

"They are in the king's throne room," he said, his voice lacking any warmth. "The vizier will conduct the trial and decide her punishment."

A surge of determination coursed through me. In the king's absence, I realized I had the power to intervene. "Then let us go," I stated firmly, stepping toward the distraught woman and offering her my hand. "I will not let them treat you this way."

With a gentle but assertive touch, I helped her to her feet, her eyes wide with surprise and gratitude.

"Thank you," she whispered, as the baby cooed sleepily in her arms and shifted slightly.

I could feel the weight of her fear and desperation; it mirrored the injustice I had a feeling these palace walls had witnessed far too often.

We made our way toward the throne room, the guards standing watch reluctantly parting as we approached. They exchanged a look and stared at me uneasily. I ignored them and pushed through the heavy doors, the grand space opening up before me, adorned with lavish tapestries and golden accents that felt surreal against the gravity of the situation. The last time I was here was on my wedding day. I had thought I would not survive the night. Now, I stood here ready to stand before these people as their queen.

The Grand Vizier stood at the foot of the throne, his expression smug and self-assured as he prepared to pass judgment. But as I entered, all eyes turned toward me, the atmosphere shifting abruptly. I strode forward, my heart pounding, and without hesitation, I ascended the steps to the throne, walking past the odious man whom I hated more intensely than I had probably hated anyone in my entire life.

"Your authority is noted, my lady," the Grand Vizier sneered, attempting to regain control by blocking my path to the throne. "But this is a matter for the king—"

"In his absence," I interrupted, my voice unwavering, "I am the one in power here." I gestured for him to move aside, and he hesitated, his surprise evident. The court watched in hushed silence, the tension palpable. "If you have any doubts, Kadin can provide you with the legal documents stating that Queen Amara has the authority to handle matters as they pertain to the kingdom when the king is away."

With a firm hand, I pushed him aside, moving towards the throne next to the king's. It was the one meant for the queen and I knew it had remained empty for a very long time. I settled into the throne; it felt both foreign and empowering. The weight of what I was about to do was heavy on my shoulders. I took a steadying breath, filled with the responsibility of the moment.

"This woman is a mother, and her actions stem from love and desperation. We will not punish her for caring for her child." My voice rang out clear and true.

Indignant whispers arose from the nobles around me. I paid them no heed, my gaze going to the vizier.

The Grand Vizier's face hardened, but I held his gaze, challenging him to oppose me.

"We will hear her story, and I will decide what justice looks like today."

The murmurs of the court echoed around me, a mix of shock and intrigue filling the air. I had taken control, and now it was time to fight for this woman and her child. The question was...could I maintain the control I had just wrested away?

Chapter 15

"Tell me what happened," I said kindly to the peasant woman.

Tears streamed down her face as she looked around hesitantly, eyes landing on one of the nobles standing close to the Grand Vizier.

"Yo-your Majesty, protocol dictates that you hear the noble out firs—"

"Silence!" I snapped, cutting off the Grand Vizier. "I will decide whose testimony to hear first."

The sobs of the poor woman echoed softly against the stone walls.

"Thank you...Your Majesty," she choked out, the baby stirring against her momentarily before cuddling further into his mother's bosom. "I...I am being punished unfairly."

"Why are you being punished?" I asked gently, my voice barely above a whisper as I tried to be mindful of not waking the infant.

She hesitated before speaking, her voice quivering with fear.

"I was fired, Your Majesty," she said, wiping her eyes. "Without even being given my rightful pay for the days I did work. I was told I would be thrown in the dungeons for violating my contract."

"Violating the contract?" I echoed, asking for her to expound upon the statement.

The peasant woman looked at me beseechingly. "We wet nurses are not allowed to breastfeed our own children. His Grace said it was an act of defiance, that my milk was meant for his heir alone."

Anger flared within me, hot and fierce. How dare he! I nearly jumped out of my throne in my fury.

"No one can dismiss you for feeding your own child."

"Your Majesty," implored the Grand Vizier. I wanted to throw him in the dungeons. My gaze cut to him, sharp and indignant. "Actually..." He trailed off, beckoning the noble who had been hovering close to him forward. "If you look at these papers...she signed them herself. She agreed to exclusively nurse her employer's heir."

There was a distinct rustling of parchment as the Vizier drew forth a scroll from the noble next to him. I snatched it out of his hand, reading the stomach-churning contents. This was sickening!

"Barbaric. You expect a woman to deny her child nourishment just to make sure another child can survive? Her child will perish without the proper care of his mother!" My tone belied the disgust I was feeling.

"This is not a novel practice," the Grand Vizier explained patiently. "Children of nobles are far superior in rank than the children of peasants."

I could hardly contain my anger at the vizier's callous words. "Superior in rank?" I repeated, my voice sharp and cutting through the tension in the room. "Is this what we have come to? Valuing one life over another based on their birthright?" The weight of injustice settled heavily upon my shoulders as I gazed at the trembling woman before me, her only crime being a mother's love for her own child.

"This is a blatant disregard for human life! Her child will not survive according to this contract." I held up the offending scroll, my eyes finally landing on the noble who I knew was the main culprit here.

"Is this how you treat your servants? Forcing them to choose between their own child's life and your heir's well-being?"

The nobleman shifted uncomfortably under my intense gaze, but his arrogance still shone through. "It is the way things have always been done, Your Majesty. The peasants exist to serve us, not to question our traditions. Her duty, in exchange for the money I was to pay her, was to my family. Not to her own. No one forced her to sign the contract."

"I have no other means of earning coin to survive!" the peasant woman cried out. "My husband is permanently disabled. What am I to do?"

I stood from my throne now, looking at all the nobles standing before me. Their faces were emotionless save for a few who looked at the peasant woman with pity. How could so many people be so heartless and blind to the suffering of those less fortunate?

My eyes locked on the Grand Vizier. "Her duty, as a mother, comes before any obligation to anyone else. I will not tolerate such cruelty in my kingdom." My words were final, carrying the weight of my authority.

"Release her at once and ensure she receives every coin owed to her. This nobleman and such archaic practices have no place here."

The noble seethed, his fists clenched, but he could not defy me. His anger was palpable, yet he knew better than to challenge a queen. He left in a storm of silent rage, and I sank back into my throne, satisfied that justice had been served. But as I stared at the faces of the nobles around me, I knew that the battle had only begun. Some looked at me warily, others with downright disdain. I was not one of their own. Only a few looked at me with respect and admiration.

"What are you doing, Sherazi?" I queried, when I entered my chambers.

Incense burned everywhere and Sherazi was hanging garlands of flowers in corners of the room.

As I glanced around, I caught sight of a lesser maid with a wooden pail filled to the brim with crystal-clear water. Her lips moved in a quiet chant as she carefully dipped her hand into the cool liquid, flicking droplets over the stone-cold walls that surrounded us. The water sparkled in the sunlight that filtered through the lattice doors of my balcony.

"Wards," Sherazi croaked out. "To keep the malevolent spirit of the dead queen away from you."

If she had said this a day ago, I would have laughed in her face. Baghel's wounds and the haunting voice from last night came back to me. Wards were a splendid idea.

I wearily sank down into my chair right as the doors flew open and Dornia marched in in a flurry of expensive silk.

"Your verdict was in favor of the wet nurse," she stated, dark beady eyes on me.

It struck me that Dornia did not look angry. But she did not look happy either.

"It was," I replied coolly, meeting her stoic gaze.

I saw something flicker in her eyes. It was brief. A flash of immense pain. But I blinked and it was gone, replaced by the emotionless stare from before.

"When I came to work at the palace, I left my six-month-old son behind," Dornia said seriously, looking at me with that same emotionless expression. "It is the way of the world. Noblewomen and royalty cannot breastfeed as they are expected to regain fertility and give birth to more heirs. Every wet nurse is expected to leave her child behind and serve a greater cause. Those children left behind, they often...do not live on."

"No one has a right to decide if one life is worth more than the other, Dornia," I scoffed. "I would expect you of all people to agree."

"My son died," Dornia whispered, closing her eyes and hiding her pain. "He died, and I was not even informed. It was not until much later that I discovered his passing."

I sat there, stunned into silence as Dornia's words hung heavy in the air. The revelation tore through her facade of stoicism, revealing the raw anguish and grief she had buried deep within herself. My heart ached for her, for the pain she must have endured in silence.

"I am sorry for your loss. No mother should ever have to endure such heartbreak alone," I whispered softly, for once I truly felt sorry for her. Is that what she had meant when she said she could not lose the king too?

"It is...the way. He died, so the king could live," Dornia whispered, opening her eyes and throwing up the walls she always had in place. She took in a long ragged breath. "I do not like you, Amara. Not even a little bit. Because you are not good for him. He is all I have left. But I would like to thank you for giving a mother a voice."

With that, she left just as quickly as she had entered.

I gazed at the incense wafting in the air, feeling the weight of Dornia's words settle upon my shoulders. It seemed as if the palace was a labyrinth of secrets and sorrow, each person carrying their own burdens hidden beneath masks of duty.

Sherazi moved to stand before me, her wise eyes searching mine. "You have a pure heart, My Queen. It is a rare thing in this place of shadows and whispers."

I reached out to touch her hand in gratitude for her support and understanding. "We must bring light to these shadows, Sherazi. We must stand against that which is wrong and give a voice to the oppressed."

A sound from my balcony caused me to turn my head, and I saw a lone raven perched on the railing, its black eyes staring directly at me. Before I could react, it let out a shrill cry that echoed through the room, sending shivers down my spine. Sherazi gasped in alarm, recognizing the omen for what it was.

"A messenger of death," she whispered, her voice trembling. "Beware, My Queen, for dark times lie ahead."

The raven took flight, disappearing into the dusky sky. But that was not what caused a chill to run up my spine. I did not believe in omens. Not yet. Sherazi did not see what I saw. For the sound on my balcony had not been caused by the raven at all.

Wordlessly, I stood and walked to pick up the scroll tied to a stone that rested a few feet from the balustrade of my balcony.

There was only one person who had ever passed messages to me in this manner. Had Asya told him to contact me? I opened the scroll to see Ashad's familiar loopy handwriting that could make wise scholars envious of his penmanship.

Meet me in the old harem gardens at midnight.

"My Queen...it is not safe to wander these parts at night," Sherazi hissed.

I knew that. I also knew that I should not be here. For if the king ever got wind of the fact that I was meeting my former betrothed ...I shuddered to think of what fate might befall me.

I stood at the edge of the lush green gardens, debating whether to leave her here as a lookout or take her with me deeper into the fragrant landscape. The air was saturated with the sweet aroma of flowers and freshly cut grass. The vibrant colors of the flora danced in the moonlight, beckoning me further in.

I turned to her, weighing my options, as a gentle breeze rustled through the leaves and carried the scents of nature toward us. Would she betray me, if she discovered who I came to meet? Given all I had come to glean regarding the king, he would not hesitate to cut me down should he ever discover that I met Ashad here. It would not matter that I did not love Ashad. What would matter was that I was still in touch with a man I had intended to marry.

I could not put my dear friend's life at risk. For Sherazi might break under pressure.

"Stay here," I commanded sternly. "I shall be back."

Sherazi's eyes became round as saucers and she looked at me as if I had told her it was time for her beheading.

"M-my Queen." Her voice trembled as she looked at me beseechingly.

"I shall be back soon." With those final words, I turned my back to her and walked deeper into the gardens. "Ashad," I whispered, once I was sure that Sherazi was not following. "Ash—"

An arm wrapped around my waist, a hand came over my mouth, muffling my surprised scream.

"Shhh," he whispered into my ear and I relaxed immediately. It was Ashad. I allowed him to pull me behind a stone statue. It depicted a wolf kneeling in front of a man. Not just any man. A king. A king who looked eerily similar to...

My stomach lurched as I realized the statue was King Zayed. I could not keep my eyes off his face, my own cheeks heating up as I realized that Ashad was holding me against him in an intimate embrace.

"Are you all right, Amara?" he queried, turning me to face him and embracing me.

My head rested on his shoulder, yet my eyes remained fixed on the statue of my husband.

It was almost as if King Zayed could see me hugging Ashad. Why did I feel guilty for meeting my dearest friend? I should not!

Ashad pulled back, looking down at me, his face filled with worry.

"Did he hurt you?"

I shook my head, registering the anxious look on Ashad's face. He looked like he had not slept in days. Worry for me was etched into every line of his visage.

"I...I am fine," I assured, moving back slightly to put some space between us and to show him that I was unharmed and adorned in the finest silks. "Look at me. Treated like a queen," I responded with a half-smile, feebly attempting to make a joke.

In the next moment, Ashad was on me, his lips claiming mine in a fiercely possessive kiss. I gasped in surprise as something cold and ugly slithered its way up my spine. Where there had been indifference to his kisses before, now there existed...revulsion. I pushed him away, my heart thudding with shock and confusion.

"Ashad, what are you doing?" I demanded, my voice tinged with anger. "He will have your head if anyone were to find out! You cannot—"

"You are mine, Amara! My betrothed! My love. You do not belong to him. Please—" he reached out, taking my hand in his "—leave with me. Tonight. Right now. Do not doubt my ability to keep you safe from him. A caravan waits to whisk us in secret to the neighboring kingdom."

I pulled my hand out of his grasp, my head spinning. He wanted me to run away with him? I shook my head.

"I cannot," I whispered and winced when his face became that of a man absolutely shattered.

The moonlight illuminated his features, casting shadows across his face that made him appear almost unrecognizable to me in that moment. He looked as if someone had ripped out pieces of his soul as his face twisted in anguish.

"Amara, there is much you do not know. You cannot change him. Listen to me," he pleaded, reaching out to touch my arm. But I recoiled from his touch, realizing that I did not want him to touch me like a lover would.

Of their own accord, my eyes went to the statue of my king as I realized exactly why meeting Ashad like this felt wrong. Because it almost seemed as if I was betraying my king. If King Zayed met a woman who loved him in the middle of the night in this manner, it would seem like a betrayal to me too.

"No, Ashad, I cannot...I must not do this. Leave. I am your queen now. I cannot run away with you," I ended in a firm tone, taking another step back.

Ashad's eyes darkened with a mix of emotions I could not decipher. Hurt, anger, and desperation played across his face like shadows dancing in the moonlight. For a moment, we stood there in tense silence, the statue of King Zayed looming over us like an ominous specter.

"This is our only chance. He will return tomorrow and I will not be able to save you. Amara, you will not survive! Do you understand me? You cannot change your fate. Many have tried before you—"

"It is not about me anymore," I retorted coolly. My mind went to the peasant woman I had helped today. "It is about doing what is best for the kingdom."

"No kingdom is worth your life!" Ashad barked out. Suddenly, his hand clamped over my arm. "I will take you by force if I have to."

He hauled me to his chest as I struggled to break free. The strength in his grip was unyielding, but I had fought him too many times to be bested by just his brute strength.

I brought my knee up swiftly, catching him in the abdomen. As he doubled over in pain, I pushed him away with all my might, sending him stumbling backward. My heart raced as I stood there, panting, outrage coursing through my veins. Did he not realize I wanted to stay here?

"Leave now, Ashad," I commanded, standing before him regally.

"Amara," he wheezed out, eyes burning with desperation as he stared up at me while on his knees. "He is a tyrant! He will fall. The rebel factions are preparing—"

He was cut off by a sound behind us. My eyes widened in alarm.

"My Queen, where are you? We must leave this place at once." Sherazi's urgent whispered plea reached my ears.

I looked at Ashad, holding a finger to my lips.

Carefully, I walked out from behind the statue, stopping Sherazi from moving further and spotting Ashad. He was still my friend. I still cared for him. Just not in the manner he wished for me to care.

"I am here. What is wrong, Sherazi?" I asked calmly.

"I-I do not know why you are here. But I do not think you want anyone to see and if we do not leave now, we will be caught." She spoke in a panic, her whispered tone growing more frantic with each syllable she spoke.

Quickly, I grabbed her hand, to make sure she did not go searching behind the statue, and began walking with her back to the palace.

However, right at the entrance to the gardens, I discovered exactly who Sherazi was afraid of catching us. Dornia. She stood there, staring at me as if she had been waiting for me to emerge from the gardens. I blinked, momentarily caught off guard. What was she doing out here at this hour?

Her voice was cold as she regarded me stonily.

"Trouble sleeping, Queen Amara?"

"I was just taking a walk," I replied, lifting my chin up defiantly. "A queen is allowed to take a leisurely stroll."

My voice was measured as I reminded her of my rank.

Dornia was quiet, her eyes flitting to the grounds behind me. I prayed Ashad had the good sense to leave. For if he had not, he had just signed my death warrant.

Dornia did not reply to me. Merely stepping aside to let me pass.

"Goodnight, Queen Amara." She said the words with distaste. As if they tasted bitter on her tongue.

I walked past her, not sparing her another glance. It was as we approached my rooms that Sherazi finally spoke up timidly.

"My Queen. Might I retire to my rooms if you have no need of me?"

I looked at her sympathetically. She must be tired. I gave her a node of assent and bid her goodnight. She scurried off. However, my heart nearly stuttered to a stop when I looked at the guards standing in front of the entrance to my room. There were two. One was King Zayed's personal guard.

And standing with the door open, just inside the threshold of my room, was King Zayed himself. My steps faltered momentarily. King Zayed was back early. He was not due back for another two days!

His eyes were narrowed on my approaching form, a flash of anger passing through his eyes.

"Amara." His voice shook with barely contained fury. "Do you take me for a fool?"

The pit of my stomach dropped.

He knows where I have been.

And as the king pulled me roughly into my room, shutting the door behind us firmly, I wondered if his angry face was going to be the last thing I saw before departing this world. But I was taken completely off guard when, instead of pushing me against the wall to attack me, he kissed me.

Chapter 16

His lips were warm, his body caging me and pinning me against the cool stone wall. But it was over in the blink of an eye and he pulled away from me as if I were on fire, eyebrows drawn together in suspicion. His fingers digging harshly into my hips.

"Where have you been?" he asked quietly, something akin to hurt marring his tone.

My lips still tingled from the memory of his on them.

"I could not sleep," I lied, feeling guilt pierce my heart over the lie. "I was out for a walk."

His penetrating stare locked onto me as if he could see right through my facade. I held his gaze, trying to appear calm and collected despite the storm raging within me.

King Zayed's grip on my hips tightened, and his eyes dropped to my lips before briefly flickering down to my form.

His touch was possessive, his fingers slowly splaying across my waist with a sense of ownership. His thumbs traced delicate circles over my hip bones, igniting a trail of shivers down my spine.

The pit of my stomach dropped as I wondered if he intended to exercise his husbandly rights on me tonight. Is that why he was here? My gaze went to the door he had shut firmly behind us. No one would try to stop him if he tried. As if sensing my trepidation, he took a few steps back from me, hands finally dropping from my waist.

"I apologize," he murmured breathlessly, running a hand through his hair. "I...I was upset...angry...worried." His tone was laced with sadness.

I pulled away from the wall, smoothing down my silk shirt in an attempt to calm my nerves. Two men had kissed me in the span of an hour. One was my former betrothed, the other was my husband.

"Do you often kiss women you are upset with?" I queried, tilting my head to the side.

"I was worried, Amara," King Zayed said harshly, eyes narrowing on me. "You were nearly attacked the other night and my most trusted men did not inform me. On top of that, when I rushed back to the palace, I discovered you were not in your rooms despite the fact I expressly asked you to avoid roaming the grounds after nightfall." He ran a frustrated hand through his hair. "Did you think I would not find out about the attack? Is that why you and Kadin decided to keep it a secret from me?"

I froze as I realized why he had come back early. The Grand Vizier and Kadin had agreed to not inform him. I had seconded the decision, signing off on the required papers that expressly forbade any messenger from leaving the palace to deliver the news to the king.

"Who told you?"

The Grand Vizier was a cunning man. He obtained my signature to shield him, professing that he was helpless to contradict a royal decree.

"I have other ways of keeping an eye on you," he replied honestly.

Sighing wearily, he lowered himself into a chair, sinking his head into his hands. At that moment, King Zayed did not look like a king. He looked like an utterly exhausted man.

I hesitated for a moment, then slowly approached him, my heart softening at the sight of his weariness. He must have traveled all day to reach here.

"How was your 'walk'," he asked, sarcasm tingeing his tone, head tilting to look up at me.

I paused, wondering if he could somehow read my mind and tell I had not been on a walk. He was merely tired after the arduous journey.

"Fine," I said dismissively."Did you even manage to complete the purpose of your visit?" I asked, tacitly changing the subject.

King Zayed chuckled, shaking his head. I did not miss the look of disappointment in his eyes. I felt as if, somehow, I had failed him. Done something disapproving.

"It has been taken care of. The odious noble's younger brother will begin negotiations for trade. He was previously a ward of the crown." King Zayed looked at me, scrutinizing my reaction to those words.

"I will try not to anger him. I did not mean for my actions to be detrimental to the kingdom."

King Zayed leaned back and looked at me, observing me closely as I stood before him.

"If any man ever touches you without your permission, damn the kingdom and protect yourself. Do you understand?"

It was on the tip of my tongue to ask him what if that man was him? But I did not. Instead, very cautiously, I sank down at his feet, settling onto one of the cushions. Looking up, I saw his face etched with lines of worry and exhaustion. All because of me. I was causing him to run himself ragged. And, in that moment, all I wanted was to do something for him to ease the immense burdens he carried.

"Shehanshah," I murmured respectfully, looking up at him in earnest.

King Zayed looked down at me, closing his eyes briefly with a look of utter desolation on his face.

"Let us continue the story," I murmured, hoping it would help him.

I reached out to squeeze his hand reassuringly, unable to control the rush of warmth that flooded my body. On a deep, sad exhale, he nodded and opened his eyes to look at me, his green gaze nearly swallowing me whole. His hand gave mine a wane squeeze before dropping it.

"When King Farid finally reached the statue of Yasmin, all he was able to think about was how to break the spell. But he was no magician.

He stood there, gazing at the beautiful stone figure before him, her expression frozen in eternal sadness. The moonlight bathed her in its silvery glow, casting shadows that seemed to dance around her delicate features. King Farid's heart ached to free her of the spell. Utilizing the vast amount of influence he possessed as king, mages from far and wide were called to come try and undo the spell, but to no avail."

"A spell can only be undone by the one who cast it, unless one knows the exact incantation," King Zayed pointed out as he leaned forward attentively, elbows resting on his knees and hands clasped together.

I nodded my assent.

"When a spell is cast, the incantation carries the way to break it. But no one knew the exact incantation cast on Yasmin," I stated in agreement and continued my story.

"Thus, King Farid attempted to track down the evil man who had tricked Yasmin. But he was elusive, and thanks to the magic carpet, nearly untrackable.

How he wished he could turn back time and undo the mistakes that had led to this moment. If only he had been a better man.

As he stood there one night in front of Yasmin's statue, lost in his thoughts, a gentle breeze stirred around them, carrying with it a faint hint of jasmine which King Farid learned during his travels was Yasmin's favorite flower. It was as if the very air itself mourned her fate and longed for her release.

Suddenly, a voice spoke from the darkness behind him.

'If you wish to break the curse, seek the Mirror of Truth,' the voice whispered, sending a shiver down King Farid's spine. 'Only by having the statue reflected within the mirror can the curse be broken, for the mirror of truth reveals the true essence of a person.'

King Farid turned around swiftly, his hand reaching for the hilt of his sword out of instinct. But there was no one there. Confusion clouded his mind as he scanned the area, searching for any signs of life in the desert.

'Who is there?' he called out, his voice echoing in the stillness of the night.

No response came, only the soft rustling of sand in the gentle breeze. King Farid felt a sense of unease creeping up his spine, unsure if it was a trick of his mind or something more mystical at play.

As he turned back to face Yasmin's statue, he noticed a single jasmine flower had materialized at the base of the stone pedestal. Its pristine white petals seemed to glow in the moonlight, drawing his attention like a beacon in the darkness.

Without hesitation, King Farid picked up the flower, inhaling the scent.

The sweet fragrance of the jasmine enveloped him, and a sense of calm washed over King Farid. It was as if the flower held a secret, a message waiting to be revealed. Clutching it tightly in his hand, he looked up at Yasmin's statue, her stony eyes seeming to glimmer with a faint light.

Determined, King Farid made a decision. He would find this Mirror of Truth, whatever it may be. With Yasmin's statue as his silent witness, he vowed to break the curse that bound her and restore her to life. With the jasmine flower clutched tightly in his hand, he set out on a quest that would test not only his courage and determination but also his understanding of what true love and sacrifice meant.

The journey to find the Mirror of Truth was fraught with challenges and dangers that tested King Farid's resolve at every turn. He traveled through dense forests and treacherous mountains, seeking guidance from wise sages and ancient spirits rumored to hold the key to unlocking the mystery of the mirror.

As he ventured deeper into unknown lands, the jasmine flower he carried never wilted, its fragrance a constant reminder of his purpose and the enchantment that held Yasmin captive. Each night by the campfire, King Farid would gaze at the flower, lost in contemplation as he searched for clues hidden within its delicate petals.

After many long weeks of travel, King Farid finally reached the fabled Valley of Reflection where the Mirror of Truth was said to reside.

The valley was shrouded in mist, the air heavy with anticipation as King Farid made his way through the lush greenery that thrived in the mystical realm. The sound of water trickling reached his ears, guiding him towards a shimmering lake that lay at the heart of the valley.

As he stood at the water's edge, King Farid beheld his reflection rippling on the surface of the lake. But it was no ordinary reflection that stared back at him. The features were distorted, twisted with shadows and half-truths that danced across the water like phantoms.

Realization dawned on King Farid as he understood the nature of the Mirror of Truth. It was not a physical object to be obtained, but a metaphysical concept embodied by the serene lake before him. The mirror showed not one's physical appearance, but one's innermost self, laid bare.

Every moment of doubt, anger, and of hope played out before him, showing him his most vulnerable moments like a painting come to life.

King Farid felt a pang of vulnerability as he confronted his inner self, stripped bare of royal titles and noble trappings. The mirror of truth demanded honesty, laying out his flaws and strengths in equal measure. He was just a man, like any other man, attempting to carry the burden of his crown. Attempting to make amends for previous misdeeds. And with a heavy heart, he realized that there was no way to take the mirror to Yasmin's statue. He had failed in his quest to free her."

"He failed?" King Zayed looked at me indignantly. "This is not a good story, Amara."

By now, we had ended up sitting across from each other on the low-lying table. His guard had brought him his wine which he sipped from lazily as he listened to my story with eyes closed. The shadows under his eyes seemed more pronounced tonight.

I gave my king a wan smile, holding a hand up to silence him so that I could continue.

"With a heavy heart, King Farid made his way back to Yasmin's statue with nothing but the jasmine flower at his side. He could not break the curse. But as he stood there, tears slipping down his cheeks, he fell to his knees before the statue of the woman who had once been his adversary. Suddenly, something strange began to occur.

The jasmine flower in King Farid's hand started to glow with a soft, ethereal light, casting a warm aura around him. The air shimmered with magic, and a gentle hum filled the night as the flower transformed before his eyes. Petal by petal, it unraveled and dissolved into a fine mist that enveloped Yasmin's statue in a swirling embrace.

King Farid watched in awe as the stone figure slowly came to life before him. The once lifeless eyes now sparkled with vitality, and a soft smile graced Yasmin's lips as she turned to face him. Tears of joy welled up in King Farid's eyes as he beheld the miracle unfolding before him.

'Thank you, My King,' Yasmin whispered, her voice like music on the wind. 'Your love and sacrifice have broken the curse that bound me. I am free because of you.'"

There was a clattering as King Zayed set the goblet of wine down and stood up abruptly.

"Love and sacrifice to break the curse," he scoffed, eyes hard as he stared down at me. I was completely taken aback by this turn of events. He had been vested in the story and now looked at me with disdain. "As if such things ever existed. Your story is nothing but fantastical nonsense."

With a swish of his voluminous royal robes, he turned and left the room, slamming the door behind him in anger.

"What do you mean by this?" I asked incredulously, sitting in King Zayed's antechamber. I held the petition before me and looked at the Grand Vizier in ire.

"The nobles have petitioned that your marriage is invalid," the Grand Vizier repeated patiently, eyes going to King Zayed. "She is not queen. She has no authority. Her rulings are null and void."

King Zayed looked at the Grand Vizier with a hard expression.

"I have never heard of something this preposterous in the history of the kingdom," he intoned sharply. "She is my queen. What is the meaning of this?"

"With all due respect," the Grand Vizier said kindly, a humorless smile on his face. "There has never been an instance such as this one in the history of the kingdom either. Royal law dictates that if the marriage has not been consummated between the king and queen, it is null and void. You must send her away, My King."

A lump of dread settled into the pit of my stomach.

King Zayed cursed.

"Sending her away is not an option," he bit out meaningfully. His eyes went to me. And then he looked at the Grand Vizier again. "We have consummated the marriage," he said abruptly, lying baldly to his most trusted advisor.

Dread mixed with trepidation, curling up my spine and freezing me in the chair I sat in across from King Zayed's vast desk filled with important decrees. My hands tightened over the petition meant to banish me from the palace.

The Grand Vizier looked at King Zayed with a wan smile.

"There was no blood on the sheets, My King. The maids have checked the morning of each time you have visited her chambers."

At that moment, I realized that even the Grand Vizier had his spies, keeping an eye on me. If only I had known. My eyes met King Zayed's from across his desk and he looked at the Grand Vizier angrily. He was the king. Surely, he could do something about this that did not involve sending me away or...

A shiver raked up my spine over the thought of what we might have to do.

Chapter 17

"There must be another way. Surely, a handful of nobles cannot dictate such terms," King Zayed countered, crossing his arms.

"Nobles cannot, but the law is the law. The law clearly defines what a valid marriage requires to secure the monarchy. A king who breaks the law is inviting anarchy into his kingdom." There were a few beats of pindrop silence as the Grand Vizier's words slowly sunk in.

Suddenly a curse elicited from King Zayed's lips as he stood from his desk, fists clenched at his sides.

"Is that the definition of a valid marriage?" he grunted, eyes narrowed and anger permeating off of him in waves. "Blood on the sheets?"

"Well, the blood would not be sufficient evidence of a consummated marriage any longer," the Grand Vizier pointed out brusquely. "Too much time has passed. If you intend to consummate the marriage now, we must have three nobles as witnesses. I do not make the laws, My King. They were made long before you and I were brought into this world. And the law clearly states that if the marriage is not consummated within the first week, witnesses chosen from amongst the nobles must be brought in to ensure the royal monarchy lives on and legal heirs are conceived."

This was a nightmare. There was a ringing in my ears as the words registered in my mind, embedding themselves inside the recesses of my brain. Witnesses...legal heirs...conception.

"If I send her away, she is as good as dead, Uncle," King Zayed grunted, his eyes imploringly looking at the Grand Vizier.

I realized he was now not looking at his advisor as the king, but as a nephew. Asking for advice from a family member. King Zayed had a point. I had too many enemies inside these castle walls now. If I were to be sent away, there would undoubtedly be a target on my back. Not to mention that many foreign spies who might wish to learn the secrets of the castle might try to pry me for information.

"She is as good as dead either way, Zayed," the Grand Vizier replied heavily. "We cannot continue this farce much longer. You know what must be done."

The king's voice was like a whip cracking through the air. Loud, sharp, slicing at everything in its wake. Destructive.

"Call your witnesses!" Zayed barked out, before determinedly stalking towards me like a predator hunting its prey.

In the blink of an eye, he scooped me up, throwing me over his shoulder like I was a sack of weightless potatoes.

"Unhand me!" I screamed, hand shooting out to resist. I flailed in his arms but his grip on me only tightened, one hand on my waist, the other splayed out to hold my calves against his hard unyielding torso.

I tried to kick out but to no avail.

"Yes...fight me," he muttered in a low voice, hands now firmly holding my legs together to keep me from kicking.

He walked stoically, almost robotically, with my body in his strong grip.

My legs attempted to pump up and down, trying to make it difficult for him to keep carrying me. But he paid me no heed, restraining my legs with a strength I had never encountered before.

"The witnesses will assemble." I heard the Grand Vizier mutter.

If I made it out of this, my next order would be to kill the man. To my horror, I realized that people were going to watch the king force himself on me.

"STOP!" I cried out angrily, my hand fisting to hit the man holding me captive. I beat against his back with all my might.

But I was just a pesky fly, barely even a bother as the guards flung open the doors to his room. Spice and leather assailed my senses. His room. I was in the king's bedchamber. I was going to be raped in here.

"You brute!" I screamed, my struggles increasing ten-fold.

He unceremoniously threw me on the bed. When he turned to draw the gauzy curtains, translucent enough for everyone to see exactly what would happen, I tackled him from behind, my arm wrapping around his neck.

"I will fight you until my last breath, King Zayed," I hissed into his ear, tightening my arm in an attempt to block his air. "Make no mistake—"

I was cut off when he leaned forward and flipped me so that I was thrown over him and landed with a thud on the feathered mattress. This was not the same man I had crossed swords with. This strength, this speed, was unheard of. He had been hiding his true skills from me the entire time...

My hand shot out to punch him. He grabbed it in his palm, forcing it down over my head before finally straddling my waist with his body. Pinning me under him effectively.

"Fight," he hissed, eyes dark as jade onyx.

I bucked under him. The creaking sound of the door opening into his bedroom fueled my panic. Whispering voices told me that the 'witnesses' had assembled.

"NO! I AM THE QUEEN!" My voice was hoarse and scratchy, belying none of the authority I had attempted to instill.

"Your position is tenable at best," Zayed muttered, reaching to rip open the front of my beaded bodice. I had dressed formally, in a *lehenga* (skirt) and *choli* (shirt), expecting to sit in the throne room alongside King Zayed. Instead, I was being raped. I gasped when the dagger nestled between my breasts fell out. "Ahhh there it is," he murmured. His warm hands trailed up my bare torso, grabbing the bronze hilt. "Silver..." he trailed off and met my eyes that were shimmering with unshed tears.

How could I have ever thought this man was not as ruthless as they all said? He had me pinned beneath his strong body, ready to force himself on me. All because the Grand Vizier had said it was necessary. My dagger now rested in his hand as he stared down at my bare torso while he was still fully clothed. I choked back a sob. He leaned down and whispered into my ear, breath hot.

"Where is that fire, Amara? I told you to fight me."

"Bastard!" I hissed out, realizing that he was probably one of those men that enjoyed forcing themselves on an unwilling woman.

My palm hit his cheek, nails raking down and causing scratches down the left side of his face. The tyrant king only grinned. He pinned my other hand above my head too, securing both my wrists with one hand and began to wedge open my legs with his knees.

"Please do not do this," I choked out, hating myself for begging.

His eyes briefly met mine before flickering back down to my legs. The long skirt I wore was, by now, unceremoniously hiked up to my waist. He must have done it when I hit him. It seemed as if everything around me was happening faster than my brain could process.

I may have imagined it but his hold on my wrists slackened imperceptibly. I closed my eyes when I saw him reach into the folds of his loose trousers. I was not a naive little girl. I knew what happened between a man and woman in the marital bed. But I had never...I had never actually participated in the act. In a land where a woman's virtue was her most prized possession, I had known that the man who became my husband would be the first to ever lay with me.

I just had not expected him to force himself on me.

I let out a cry of pain when I felt a sharp pinch on the inside of my thigh. I bucked under him instinctively, my body thudding against the mattress in helpless frustration. His hand came down hard over my lower abdomen, pushing me down into the mattress effectively.

I continued to struggle. This was it. He was going to violate me. My eyes remained shut but then a surprised gasp of pain left my lips when I felt the cool blade of my dagger swipe on the inside of my bare thigh and spill blood.

And then he began to move against me, simulating a copulation that was not taking place. If his grunts and the jerky movements above me were any indication, he was pleasuring himself. A king. The king of kings...a man that could have a harem filled with women at his beck and call if he so wished it, had no need for such an act. Unless...

My eyes flew open to meet his stormy green. My pupils dilated in sudden comprehension, fixing my gaze upon him, unwavering even as his breaths became more labored, the rhythmic motion of his arm palpable. A sob of relief caught in my throat, breaths coming in ragged bursts. Any lingering animosity, any vestige of resentment I harbored toward the king, vanished in that singular moment. The sob of relief finally escaped my lips. He would not force himself on me. Zayed's eyes narrowed in warning. They could not know. This would only work if he imitated an assault on my person. By now everyone knew I was not the docile lamb.

Hot wet sticky liquid spilled across my thighs and onto the bed. I watched as his breathing pattern normalized. Eyes on me the entire time.

"Call for the maid!" Zayed barked out, his voice ragged and rough. "It is done!"

Finally, he released his hold on me and I took the opportunity to instinctively pull away and huddle close to the foot of the bed. My shirt had been ripped and I was completely bare from the waist up. I glanced at the mixture of his seed and my blood staining the sheets. My body trembled, trying to come down from the panicked state it had been in earlier. Zayed reached a hand towards me and I flinched instinctively, hugging my upper torso. His hand faltered before determinedly moving to pull the bed sheet over my trembling upper body. The dagger, now sheathed, was placed in my lap. I swallowed. Nothing had happened. And yet I still felt as if something had.

"Take the queen to her rooms," Zayed commanded.

The gauzy curtains were moved aside.

Gentle hands wrapped a robe around my body. A maid carefully led me past the three men standing near the entrance. The witnesses. I cringed. One of them I recognized as the same noble I had ruled against and in favor of the wet nurse just yesterday.

"Amara."

Zayed's voice was a soft whisper, beckoning me to turn to face him. Blood had congealed on the three scratches drawn down the side of his face. Dark eyes stared at me, the emotions in their unfathomable depths completely a mystery. I turned to face him robotically, not entirely sure how I felt about what had just occurred.

"No one can challenge your position as queen now."

Queen. Lower in rank only to the King. I reigned supreme. Yet it had required the ultimate submission on my end to get there. And Zayed had made sure that did not occur.

Chapter 18

Two days. For two days and nights I remained in my rooms, neither going out, nor anyone coming in. I felt disturbed, distraught, and completely lost in my thoughts. The events of what occurred in King Zayed's room replayed over and over in my mind like a twisted dance, each step leading me further into a dark abyss. I could still hear his voice echoing in the hollow chambers of my mind, telling me to fight him. The memory of the witnesses, their faces grimly satisfied as I walked by them were like poison seeping into my veins.

Baghel had been released from the clinic, bandages wrapped around his shoulders and neck until his wounds healed. I was told King Zayed went personally to retrieve him and ensure he was brought to my rooms. Why King Zayed had not visited me himself was a mystery.

Baghel burrowed deeper into the bedding with me, his comforting licks on my hand doing nothing to stem the tumult of emotions rising within me. Nothing had happened. Yet it felt like everything had. A few times, I had woken up drenched in sweat, the remnants of a nightmare fading away. A nightmare in which I had actually been assaulted. Because even if a violation had not really occurred, it still troubled me deeply.

But as the hours stretched on, a new emotion began to bloom within me—a simmering anger that refused to be ignored. How could it be acceptable for a husband to treat his wife this way? They believed I had been assaulted, a copulation forced upon me. They had done it to teach me a lesson no doubt. To show me, a woman, that my value was in the heirs I could provide.

But if a woman who was queen had to endure this, what must other women face? Was it possible men forced themselves on their wives often and it was overlooked?

In this world, the rules had been made by men, for men.

But Zayed had given me the power to change that.

I rose from my bed, the weight of my realization settling on my shoulders like a cloak of defiance. With each step I took, a sense of purpose coursed through my veins, pushing me forward toward a future where my voice would not be silenced, where a woman's worth would not be determined by the whims of men.

I flung open my closet, looking for something suitable to wear. I would go to court today and sit in on the hearings King Zayed conducted.

The doors to my room were thrown open with a deafening thud. I turned to see the Grand Vizier stroll in, a bevy of Blade-Callers behind him, all dressed in pure white.

"Your Majesty—" he began, rather disdainfully. I cut him off without a moment's hesitation.

"The next person who enters my quarters without permission will be hanged." I stared at him stonily, my eyes full of challenge.

His face turned red, as incredulous disbelief marred his visage.

"You dare to threaten the Grand Vizier!" A vein now throbbed in his left temple. "I will come and go as I please! I am the royal advisor to the king!"

I stood tall, shoulders thrown back confidently. My icy gaze met his furious one with a steely determination. "You dare defy a royal edict?" My voice was strong and unwavering. "I will not be a pawn in this game of power and control. I am a queen, and my voice will be heard. My wishes will be respected."

His left eye twitched in response to my statement, before flashing with fury.

But he said nothing, his anger mirrored in the set jaw and tight fists at his sides. I knew this was just the beginning of the battle, but I was determined to fight. And win. I watched the man get his breathing under control and school his features. The gleam of triumph in his eye made me give pause.

"I came here to inform you that the doctor will be arriving shortly to perform a medical exam," the Grand Vizier finally stated emphatically.

Those words made me pause. Medical exam? Whatever for?

"I am not sick."

"It is a medical exam not to ascertain your health, but to ascertain the successful consummation of your marriage. Only then will your 'decrees' truly be of any worth." He scoffed out the word "decrees" as if they held very little worth in his eyes.

A hot flush of anger coursed through me, and I could taste bile in the back of my throat. The very thought of that examination, a cruel reminder of the cruel winds of power, made my stomach churn.

"I will not consent to such a barbaric examination," I spat out, my voice echoing with defiance. The Grand Vizier's lips tightened into a thin, derisive line.

"Your refusal is of no consequence, Your Majesty. It is a procedure every queen must endure. You are most definitely not the exception." His words dripped with venom. "Tonight, the doctor will arrive, and the examination will be conducted whether you consent or not."

A storm of resentment and fear surged within me, threatening to consume me whole. I was not a fool though. I knew the gravity of the situation, the stakes far more than just my personal dignity. What would happen if they found out King Zayed had tried to defy the law?

"An examination will not be possible," I retorted, crossing my arms firmly.

"I knew it!" the Grand Vizier crowed, his eyes filled with malice. "You may have used your wiles on my nephew, tricking him into believing you are worth keeping alive. Mark my words, you are not worth an entire kingdom! It is because of you we will fall into chaos, and he will be labeled as an unstable ruler. All because of you!" The Grand Vizier pointed his finger at me as he raved on and on, not making even a bit of sense.

"I will not let him jeopardize the kingdom over one silly girl! Now, if you are willing to admit to your duplicity, we will end this farce here and now. I will allow you time with your family, one week to say your good-byes." The Grand Vizier now held up one finger to signify a week's time. "After that, you will return to the palace and meet your fate. Your family will be looked after. As the late queen's relatives, they will be given enough gold coin to live like nobles for the rest of their days. Do we have a deal?" He folded his arms, eager to cement this new proposition.

I had never met a more delusional man in my entire life.

"There can be no examination because I am on my monthly," I lied baldly.

Men did not take well to being bested by a woman. And the Grand Vizier, who had thought victory was in his grasp, responded with a thunderous exclamation of a curse. His face turned an alarming shade of purple as his mouth remained open in a silent scream.

The Blade-Callers behind him shifted uneasily, their white garments like beacons of assurance for me. I was one of them. It was not lost on me how this entire exchange was affecting the women who stood behind him. They were not puppets. But living breathing people who had opinions. And something told me they did not appreciate the concept of a woman being forcibly examined to check if she was still a virgin.

The Vizier, however, was so angry that for a moment I thought he would lunge at me. Instead, his dark gaze remained fixated on me as a sneer formed on his lips.

"You think you can outsmart me, little queen? You think you can defy the will of the kingdom and get away with it?" He let out a harsh laugh. "You are not the first to think so. Bleeding will not hinder the physician. However, to show that I am a reasonable man, willing to humor your delusions, I give you three days. And then you must submit to the examination."

With those final words, he left. And I knew I had only three days to figure out what to do next. Zayed...I had to speak to King Zayed. But how much longer could we ever keep this farce up? Our lies would eventually come to light.

Sighing, I moved without conscious thought, dressing for court. I would not be bested by that Grand Vizier.

And once I was truly queen, I would get rid of these vile customs once and for all.

"What are you doing here?" King Zayed looked at me in surprise. He looked very stately in his beige tunic, sitting behind the desk in his antechamber.

I could faintly discern the outline of his muscular body and briefly recalled the raw strength that rested within him. How easily he could have overpowered me in his room. But he had not.

Those deep green eyes rested on me curiously, a paper in his hand with a complex depiction of what looked to be wells for storing water.

I raised my chin defiantly.

"As queen. I am here to sit in court with you today." I looked at him, hoping he understood how important it was for me to show the nobles that they had not broken me.

King Zayed leaned back in his chair, staring at me warily.

"There is no need to face them today," he said slowly. "I mean," he cleared his throat awkwardly, "you can wait...for a day where I am not present to be my stand-in."

My gaze cut to him, eyebrows furrowed in confusion. "Why would I want to wait for a day where you are not present?"

He ran a hand through his hair, eyes not studying me across from where he sat, but rather on the wooden grains of his large desk.

"I assumed...given previous events...you would rather choose a day where our interaction would be limited."

I saw the imperceptible clench of his jaw. Realization burned into me like the blinding sun on a hot summer's day. That is why I had not seen him in two days. Why he had not come to spar with me or listen to my stories. He thought I wanted to avoid him.

I had to check the impulse to step closer to him, feelings of warmth and safety encompassing me. I had not thought it possible to feel this way in his presence. But I did.

"I have been through much since I became...your bride," I spoke carefully. "But never once have I considered avoiding your presence." My voice filled with emotion as his gaze flicked up to me in surprise. "I would like to think we are in this together."

King Zayed stood abruptly, the softness in his gaze indecipherable. His eyes searched for the truth in my words and I looked back at him sincerely.

Finally, he stepped around the desk, offering me his hand.

"Then let us face them...together." His voice was soft and boyishly hopeful. It made butterflies erupt in the pit of my stomach.

I knew then that if I told him of the medical exam the Grand Vizier planned, he would help me find a way out of it. This man did not want to see me suffer. It drove home my previous inclinations to think that something must have triggered the killings of his previous brides.

Maybe they had betrayed him. It did not make their murders forgivable. But if a boy had grown up believing there was no other way, maybe I could show him there was?

Was I being a fool for thinking I could change his bloodthirsty nature?

Those thoughts swirled through my head as we stepped through the door leading to the throne room together.

"The King and Queen of Elamaria!" a booming voice intoned, announcing our arrival.

We stepped forward together, his fingers intertwined with mine.

In the grandeur of the throne room, the air was charged with anticipation and discernible whispers as we settled into our respective thrones, his hand still clasping mine.

We sat before them as united monarchs of Elamaria. His eyes locked on mine for a fleeting moment, showing concern, worry, and strength all at once. He was worried about how I might be feeling, facing everyone after what had happened. But they could not break me. Not so easily.

I gave him a reassuring smile and watched him visibly relax into his throne. A sharp barking sound made me look to the left only to spot Baghel making his way, rather authoritatively towards me. A servant rushed after him, trying to catch up. Baghel gave another bark of indignation, bounding towards me in an attempt to be free of his pursuer. I smiled, holding up a hand to stop anyone who tried to capture my little protector.

"Your Majesty—" began the Grand Vizier plaintively.

I turned to look at the sniveling advisor bent over King Zayed's throne, looking at him beseechingly as he motioned to Baghel making his way up the steps towards me. I rolled my eyes, not even bothering to hide my disdain. Was he going to show us a law that forbade animals in the throne room?

"Uncle, let it be." King Zayed's voice was quiet yet firm. He squeezed my hand reassuringly.

Baghel reached me, giving my free hand a lick. I smiled, scratching him behind the ears. Suddenly, I felt at ease as if the weight of everything that had happened had been lifted from my shoulders. I sat here with King Zayed by my side, holding my hand in front of the very nobles who had wished to see my downfall, and Baghel now settled comfortably at my feet. It was as if everything I needed was here before me.

"But, Your Majesty, this has never—"

"I said let it be," King Zayed now growled out in warning.

I looked up to see the Grand Vizier take a step back. Biting the inside of my cheek to keep from smirking, I looked triumphantly at the sea of nobles. And then my smile fell. For at the very front, where the most important nobles stood, was Ashad. No longer in commoner's garb. No, he stood before me in the most luxurious of silks, a red sash tied around his person that denoted his status of diplomatic immunity from the crown.

Do not doubt my ability to keep you safe from him. A caravan waits to take us to the neighboring kingdom.

His words spoken that night in the gardens held a new meaning now. He had not meant to hide me in a neighboring kingdom he was a commoner in. No, it was a kingdom he was a noble of.

Chapter 19

My mind was reeling from this revelation. I did not realize I was squeezing Zayed's hand until he leaned in imperceptibly and whispered if all was fine with me.

I closed my eyes, breathing in deeply, trying to make sense of everything before me. Ashad was a noble? No. He was a commoner. We had grown up together! I had met his parents. They lived in a small hut on the outskirts of the city of Ilm. We had been engaged!

"My Queen?" King Zayed's concerned voice from my left made me force my eyes open. My breath hitched when his free hand came to gently move a lock of my hair aside. "Would you like to retire?" His anxious face made me realize I had to maintain my composure. I could not fall apart here.

I feigned a smile.

"All is well. I...I am parched," I lied easily, too shocked to even think of revealing the reality of it all.

If the king truly was a jealous man, I did not want to risk any suspicion on his end. I did not want to reveal Ashad as my former betrothed. I shuddered to think what King Zayed might do if he ever found out I had met my ex-fiance' alone in the gardens.

King Zayed's sharp commanding tone did not brook any argument as he called for water. Almost immediately, a goblet of water was brought over on a gold tray, ice clinking rather ominously, as if heralding an impending disaster.

Before I could reach out for the drink, King Zayed's hand deftly plucked it from the tray and held it to my lips. Our eyes met over the rim.

"I-I am capable of drinking my own water," I murmured.

He still held my left hand in his right one and gave it a stern squeeze.

"I would like to do this for you," he whispered.

His eyes flickered to my lips and I took a slow, deliberate sip, letting the water trickle down my throat and soothe my raging emotions.

Once I had taken my fill, I let out a shaky breath. The discernible clink as he set the goblet back down in the tray a servant held was the only thing I could hear over the wild drum beat of my heart.

King Zayed's eyes seemed to bore into me, filled with concern. I forced a smile.

"I am fine, My King," I whispered.

I blinked in surprise when his thumb ran lazy circles across the palm of my hand which he held in his large warm one.

"Then let us return to our subjects and show them we are united?" he queried in a low whisper.

I nodded my assent, but as my eyes went out to the sea of nobles, I could not help my gaze being drawn back to Ashad. He was looking between us, a look of incredulous disbelief plastered on his face. Those eyes of his met mine. Eyes that implored me to listen to him.

But soon, I was distracted when the introductions of the nobles began. I learned that the noble who I had ruled against was one of the crown's most staunch supporters. His name was Arin, and he had been a loyal servant to the crown for many years. An emir by the name of Raja Darien greeted me with warm, kind eyes. He was an elderly man and commanded a tribe of Bedouins. And finally, I was introduced to Ashad. The son of a noble from a neighboring kingdom. He had been a ward of the crown from a young age and had grown up in Ilm under the crown's protection. I blinked, absorbing this news, realizing Ashad had lied to me all those years. The commoners who I had thought were his parents, had actually been his caretakers. A nanny and her husband, employed by his parents to look after him while he lived as a ward.

It was not uncommon for monarchies to exchange wards of their children for strategic alliance or political gain. Ashad's presence in Ilm, as a ward of the crown, was a testament to the bond between his parents and the ruling family.

"Pleased to make your acquaintance, Your Highness," Ashad murmured, inclining his head before me in respect. "I can assure you, you will find me much more agreeable than my older brother."

I blinked, straightening in my throne as his words sunk into me.

"The man I defended myself against was your older brother," I whispered in disbelief, realizing that that was exactly why I had thought he had been Ashad.

Because they looked alike in so many ways! How could Ashad be related to someone so foul?!

Zayed glanced at me before looking back at Ashad with a stern expression.

"I trust you to be a man of honor. Upon your father's word, I have agreed to let you take up your brother's role as mediator of the trade agreements."

I took in the imperceptible clench of Ashad's jaw. And it dawned on me. He was here to smuggle me away. That was all. Ashad had no desire to broker any agreements. My mind raced with plausible scenarios on how to convince the man before me to fulfill the role he had been selected for. My kingdom was at stake.

Ashad stepped back respectfully. However, I did not miss the way his gaze settled on our joined hands, a flicker of envy or jealousy that made my heart beat a little faster, but the look disappeared quickly, replaced by a mask of decorum.

With great effort, I tore my gaze away from Ashad and fixed it on King Zayed. His hand never left mine the entire time we held court. His grip was strong, steadfast, but there was a gentleness to him that I found myself drawn to. I felt safe beside him. Protected.

But when we retired to the antechamber, his hand dropped from mine immediately. His gaze, apologetic.

"I am sorry if I was too forward," he murmured, eyes boring into mine as we stood inside the antechamber, so close our chests nearly touched.

Forward? For holding my hand?

"They need to know you are important," he stressed, taking a few steps back and walking over to his desk, eyes on piles of papers pertaining to water storage.

I wanted to tell him it was all right. More than all right, really. But Baghel scratching at the door to be let out interrupted me. He was probably getting restless and yearning for a walk in the gardens. I did not blame him. I, too, needed air. Especially after the revelation regarding Ashad.

And it was while I walked aimlessly in the gardens with Baghel, recalling all the childhood adventures I had with Ashad and the dreams we once shared that I realized this entire time...my dearest friend had been lying to me.

A cold wind swept through the garden, causing the leaves to rustle and the flowers to sway. My heart pounded in my chest, drowning out the distant sound of the castle, as I tried to wrap my mind around it all. Had I known him at all? Or had I merely known the character he had allowed me to see?

Baghel, sensing my distress, nuzzled my hand, and I leaned down to stroke his sleek fur. In the dim light of twilight, I walked back to my rooms. There, Sherazi waited for me, a distressed look on her face.

"M-my qu-queen...I do not know what to make of this," she murmured, holding up a piece of parchment tied to a stone. "I f-found this on your balcony."

My heart skittered to a stop before beating wildly against my ribs. So Ashad had sent me another message. Opening the parchment, away from Sherazi's eyes, I read the contents. He wanted to meet me tonight in the same place as last time.

I knew it was not a good idea. But I wanted answers. And I would get them tonight.

"Amara, my love," Ashad murmured once I turned the corner and ended up behind the statue of my husband.

It was the exact same spot we had met last time.

He gathered me up in his arms and I immediately pushed him away with all my strength.

"All this time—" I spat angrily. "You lied to me, Ashad! You let me think you were a commoner! A peasant like me!"

"And why, Amara, would I do that?" he asked, his voice low and filled with an emotion that I could not quite place. "I did it for you."

I looked at him, the dim light from the moon casting his features in shadows. The only time I could see his face clearly was when the light from the full moon reflected off the statue behind us.

"For me?" I asked, incredulous. The idea was preposterous.

"Yes, my love," he said, taking a step towards me. His hand reached for mine, but stopped mid-air as if remembering the broken trust between us. "I wanted us to be married. What does it matter if I am of noble birth? If I revealed my true parentage, your father would have never agreed as readily. He would have been wary of sending his daughter to live in another kingdom."

It struck me that Ashad had not once thought how I would feel about leaving my homeland. He should have asked me! Had he always been so presumptuous and I was only seeing it now?

"I did intend to reveal everything before our wedding. You must believe me. There were approvals to be had from my kingdom to marry a citizen of another. Approvals pending in your kingdom, too. However, I knew that our love was strong. We are meant to be with each other."

Before I could stop him, he pulled me into his embrace. I was struck dumb by the realization that all this time, he had been playing me for a fool. How could he ever think to even look my father in the eye and lie? How could he even think it was acceptable to lie to me?

"Come with me, Amara," he pleaded, burying his face into my shoulder, arms tightly wrapped around my waist. "I will keep you safe. Trust in me."

How could I ever trust a man who had lied to me?

"Ashad," I whispered, squirming under his hold. "How can you say you love me, when you kept everything from me? When you lied to me all these years?" I leveraged myself against him, placing my palms flat against his chest to push him away. "Were we ever really even friends?" I blinked back tears. Friends did not lie to each other like he had!

"No, no, no, Amara, please believe me when I tell you that I was not allowed to tell you the truth. My identity was a closely guarded secret," Ashad pleaded, holding me even tighter. "I have loved you since the first day I met you. I had no one...except you growing up. Please, my love—" His voice cracked and I froze when I saw the tears leaking down his eyes. "I am nothing without you, Amara. I love you! I will always love you endlessly. You are my everything."

I could feel his breath on my neck as he whispered his feelings, voice trembling with vulnerability. This man was near tears because of me. He had always been strong and steady. The one who knew what he wanted and how to get it. To see him like this, broken and with tears in his eyes, was a sight I never thought I would see.

All because of me. My heart softened, and I stopped trying to push him away. Instead, I let my arms travel up the expanse of his chest and wrap around his shoulders. Because I felt guilty. He loved me. But I did not love him. Before, I had been complacent. Indifferent. Maybe even a little relieved that if I were to rush into a marriage, at least it was with a man who I had known my entire life. A man I called my friend. But now... my heart called out to another. A man with deep green eyes and a scowl that only seemed to relax when in my presence.

It took a few moments to realize that as I stood hugging Ashad and trying to console him, I was not looking at an image of Zayed in my mind's eye. No. I was looking at King Zayed in the flesh, walking purposefully towards us with Dornia by his side.

My blood chilled and dread settled into the pit of my stomach. I watched him draw his sword and, in the blink of an eye, I was pushing Ashad behind me.

"NO!" I cried, shielding my dear friend as the blade came down in a graceful arc, Zayed's eyes flashing dangerously.

Chapter 20

I braced myself for the kill, fully prepared to feel the edge of his blade cut through my feeble dagger and slice me in two. Hopefully, it would give Ashad enough time to get away.

But it never came. It was as if everything moved in slow motion. His sword landed at my feet with a resounding thud. King Zayed looked at me, his jaw clenched and body trembling from...rage? Or was it something else.

"Take it," he rasped hoarsely, eyes on me. And I realized that what I had taken for rage was not rage at all. It was bitter regret and frustration. Maybe even a hint of sadness. "Take it and run away with the man you love."

I could scarcely believe my ears as the words rang through the air.

"My King," Dornia gasped behind him. "I told you she was not to be trusted. But you would let her go?"

"Silence!" King Zayed barked out as I stood before him, the sword between us, along with an ever widening chasm.

I shook my head. He had not killed me over an assumed betrayal.

"What are you waiting for, Amara?" King Zayed hissed out.

There was an anguish in his eyes that made my heart yearn to assuage his mistaken assumptions.

"Go with your betrothed and be free. You deserve to be happy."

That statement nearly brought me to my knees in shock. He knew Ashad was my betrothed!

"You...knew?" I asked hesitantly.

King Zayed gave a cynical bark of laughter.

"You think I could unearth that you were top of your class, but not that you were betrothed? Especially when I was the one who approved the betrothal of a citizen from my country to a citizen of another?"

I took a few steps back, realizing that I had everything wrong. So utterly completely wrong.

"You informed me you volunteered because your sister was promised to a man she loved." His shoulders sagged under an unseen burden. "I assumed you volunteered because you did not love your betrothed." He sighed in resignation, turning his back to me. "Go, Amara."

"No! She must be captured and punished!" Dornia wailed.

"She must escape for surely, with me, only death awaits her," King Zayed responded crisply to Dornia. "Leave, Dornia. And speak not of this to a single soul."

Dornia stood there, hesitant to follow his orders.

"Leave now," King Zayed commanded sternly again of the elderly woman.

Finally, she retreated but not before saying, "My King, you are making a grave mistake in letting her go."

Then she was gone, disappearing into the shadows as quickly as she had appeared.

I felt an incessant tug on my elbow.

"Amara, we must go now! It is time to make good on our escape," Ashad urged.

"Go. I will not sound the alarm. However, once you are far enough away, I must make a show of looking for you. No one can know I allowed you to leave. My advisors would riot," King Zayed spoke, his back to me. "Go, Amara. Before I change my mind."

I wrenched my elbow free of Ashad's grip and took a hesitant step towards Zayed.

"Tell me," I implored, staring at his broad back as taut as a bow. He knew what I meant, even though I did not fully voice my question.

"It is of no concern of yours," he replied, not even turning to face me as he spoke. "This is my kingdom. I will ensure the survival of my people. Hurry and leave."

"Amara, please," Ashad pleaded, his voice soft as he placed a hand on my shoulder. "We do not have a moment to spare for such frivolous questions. We need to escape now."

But I could not let it go. There was something about King Zayed that stirred emotions in me. Emotions that seemed to be growing stronger by the second. He did not want to kill me. He did not want to kill anyone. A husband who believed that his wife loved another and let her go, would not kill innocent women in cold blood.

"Leave, Ashad," I whispered, taking the final steps and closing the distance between the king and myself.

"Amara! Have you lost your mind?!" Ashad yelled in disbelief. "You would stay with him? Rather than the man who loves you unconditionally?"

"I belong here, with my people," I responded evenly. I could not bring myself to state the obvious. I did not love Ashad, no matter how much he loved me. I was not beholden to him for his unconditional love. I never asked him to love me. And he could not guilt me into loving him!

"Amara, you are making a mistake!" Ashad yelled frantically. "Your sister is waiting for you! What am I to tell her?"

"Tell her..." I took a deep breath, tentatively placing a hand on Zayed's back. I felt the tension radiating from his form, his warmth seeping through the cloth and meeting the palm of my hand. I resisted the urge to pull him closer to me. "Tell her this is my kingdom." I felt King Zayed's back stiffen at my touch or maybe my words. I was not sure. "Th-these are my people," I choked out, holding back a sob. If I was wrong, I would surely not survive. But it would not be by my husband's hand that I died. Of that I was now certain. "And we will ensure their survival." My voice rang out clear as a ringing bell.

The great king before me let out a shuddering breath, as if he had been holding it in the entire time.

"Amara!" King Zayed's voice cracked through the air like a whip. It was full of censure. "He is right. There is nothing here for you with a monster like me except death. I do not know how long I can continue to keep you alive. Nothing is certain. Leave with him if you value your safety."

There was a silence that hung heavy in the air as I replayed Zayed's words.

"You are not the monster, King Zayed," I finally whispered, my voice barely audible even above the deafening silence that enveloped us.

"That is where you are wrong. Please." His voice trembled as he took a determined stride forward, breaking our contact. I missed his warmth. "Go."

Yet I stood firm.

"No," I responded, loud enough for my voice to carry in this clearing.

I heard the retreating steps of Ashad.

"This is not over, Amara. I will not give up," I heard Ashad mutter as he left. "Once you see him for the monster he truly is, I will be here to save you and take you away."

I paid Ashad's words no heed. Just because he loved me, did not mean I had to love him back. I did not want to go with Ashad. I wanted to stay here. Maybe because I felt something for my husband. Something I had never felt for Ashad.

But it was mainly because if I had survived thus far, I could continue to do so. I could help save the daughters of my kingdom. If I left, I was saving myself. But I was dooming another in my place. That was something I could not bring myself to do.

"Zayed," I whispered, taking a step towards him. "Tell me, why must they die?"

Zayed let out a heavy sigh and closed his eyes, letting his body slump slightly as if the weight of the world was suddenly too much to bear. I reached up again, this time gently letting my arms encircle his waist from behind, feeling the soft texture of his cotton shirt beneath my fingertips.

"I can help you," I whispered, laying my cheek against his strong back as I let my head rest on him from behind.

I felt his hands come to rest over mine, now clasped loosely just below his navel. I was so exhausted. Tired of strategizing, of trying to out maneuver the nobles all while trying to figure out how to live. So fed up with wondering if each day was going to be my last. I let myself lean against him. Against the man I thought responsible for all my woes. But it was becoming more and more apparent that something else was at play.

"If only you would let me help." I closed my eyes, feeling as if I was so close to learning the truth.

"It is my burden to bear, Amara. You should not have stayed," he rasped out in the dark of night, his hands resting over mine in a possessive manner. His demeanor was a direct contrast to his words.

"I could never leave you to bear this alone." I sighed, my voice breaking into the stillness. "Tell me, My King. Help me understand."

Zayed let out a shuddering breath, the tension in his body seemingly pouring out with each exhale. "You would not understand, Amara," he whispered, his voice full of sorrow. "You cannot imagine the darkness I carry within me."

I pressed closer to him, feeling the weight of his burden as if it were my own. "I may not know what it is like to be you, but I know what it is like to carry a burden that feels insurmountable." I carried the burden of being queen daily. Did I not? I carried the burden of saving my kingdom from more senseless deaths. And yet his burdens seemed far heavier than mine at this moment. "And I want to help you carry yours."

At first, there was only silence – a heavy, pregnant pause that seemed to stretch on for eons. But then he turned to face me, his fingers coming to gently tilt my chin up. I stared up at him earnestly, his eyes were soft and vulnerable as he looked down at me.

"You did not leave with the man you love?" he queried, a hint of anxiousness flickering in those eyes of his. Along with something else. Something that seemed like...was it jealousy?

"I never loved him," I replied sincerely. "Ashad was, and will always be, my dear friend. But there was no love between us." I admitted those words warily on an exhale.

Zayed's expression softened at my words, the hint of jealousy now replaced with a look of understanding. His free arm wrapped around my waist, pulling me closer to him. His eyes never left my gaze, searching for something. My compliance perhaps? I raised myself onto my toes, meeting his lips halfway in an earth-shattering kiss.

His strong arms held me close, as if I were the missing piece he never knew he needed. Or maybe he was the missing piece I never knew I needed. I could not be too certain in the warmth of his embrace, in the feel of his soft lips on mine, as we kissed under the moonlight.

Chapter 21

I woke up the next morning to Sherazi pulling the curtains back from my windows and veranda.

"My Queen, I was so worried!" Sherazi gasped, coming to sit beside me on the bed with a glass of cool water on a golden tray.

I sat up, throat parched and head still heavy from the restless sleep I had last night. Images of my own headstone and freshly dug grave had danced around my brain every time I closed my eyes. And when I finally succumbed to sleep, dreams of being chased by the beast I encountered my first night here had plagued me. After we had kissed, King Zayed had silently escorted me to my room. I tried asking him again for the truth. The truth on why his brides had to die. But he remained tight-lipped, bidding me good night rather than following me into my chambers. I had attempted to bribe him with promises of a story. He had merely shook his head, before retreating to his room. The shadows of exhaustion under his eyes had been quite pronounced.

"I hope you did not get in trouble on my account," I finally said after taking a few sips of water.

"Dornia dismissed me. Told me to leave if I wished to remain a servant in the palace. She said it was unseemly for me to witness what was to happen between the queen and king here," Sherazi confessed. "B-but I watched from afar, hoping there was a way I could aid you if required. If I could follow you..." she trailed off sheepishly.

My eyes widened in surprise.

"You would have left with me, Sherazi? Gone with me to a new kingdom if I had gone with Ashad?"

Sherazi looked at me surprised.

"I did not know that was what the noble had asked of you," she revealed carefully. "For I was too far away to hear. But it did seem as if the king were trying to send you away. You will always be my queen. Where you go, I will always follow," she ended solemnly, placing a hand over her heart as if making a vow.

My gaze softened. She might be a servant, a person who held no power, but she was an ally. A friend. Someone I could trust.

In quiet contemplation, I gazed out the window at the sprawling gardens bathed in the soft morning light. As I went over everything that had happened since my wedding to the king, a sense of resolve washed over me. I would uncover the mysteries of this place, confront the beast that haunted my dreams, and herald a rule of equality and justice for my people. It was time for the daughters of our kingdom to stop worrying if they would be picked to die.

"Sherazi, I was taken aback when he did not kill me last night when he assumed I had not been faithful," I finally revealed. "I realize now that my initial assumptions were incorrect. I need to find the truth regarding who is killing his brides. And why. It is not the king."

For some reason, I had a feeling that the Grand Vizier was the one who had a hand in all of this. Was he manipulating King Zayed? It was a possibility. I recalled King Zayed's words from long ago about how he never sought his brides out like he had me. Maybe it was someone...or something else that killed his brides.

"Will you help me?" I finally asked, a determined glint in my eye.

Sherazi looked taken aback by my question but gave an abrupt nod. "I will do as you ask, My Queen. But please be cautious. The walls have ears in this palace."

I reached out and took her hand. It was cold and trembled slightly in my grip. Her worry for me was palpable. She also looked surprised at my gesture. "Thank you, Sherazi. Your loyalty means more to me than you know." It truly did. For in the walls of the palace, it seemed she was my only ally. "Together, we will defy fate. Now, I must go speak with the king. Do you know where he is?"

"He is in a meeting with the Grand Vizier. Perhaps it is wise to see him once the Grand Vizier is gone?"

Sherazi made a valid point. I did not want to see the Grand Vizier, and that reminded me of another problem at hand. I slowly explained to Sherazi that the Grand Vizier planned to call in a doctor to perform a medical examination.

Sherazi reddened.

"I...My Queen...I am but a maid. I do not hold any power to stop the examination."

"But you can corroborate my story that I am bleeding," I pressed, standing to don my robe and looking at her with beseeching eyes. "For when he comes to examine me, he will surely be able to tell I lied. Who knows what the Grand Vizier might do if he is told of my falsehood?"

Sherazi nodded dutifully. She suddenly moved swiftly, gathering my sheets.

"I will not let the other maids clean them, stating that your monthly created stains on your bedding. Many women bleed merely for three days. No one shall know the truth."

I sagged in relief, glad I had trusted her. She would take care of any spies the Grand Vizier had amongst the servants.

"You are the only one allowed in my room from this day forth," I added, deciding it was best to stay safe rather than sorry. "If it is absolutely necessary for someone else to be in here, you must be present at all times. Else, the queen's room is off limits."

Sherazi gave another nod, eager to fulfill my instructions.

"As you say, so shall it be."

"Now," I resolutely tightened the sash on my silk robe, "there is only one thing left to do."

I met her eyes with determination.

"What is that, My Queen?" Sherazi queried, tightening her grip on the bed sheets in her arms.

"Sleep with my husband," I replied deftly, jutting my chin out defiantly as if I were preparing for war.

Nervously, I approached King Zayed's chambers, my heart pounding with anxiety. I knew I had to speak with him about the impending gynecological examination, a daunting prospect that filled me with dread. As I entered, the opulence of the room momentarily distracted me, but the weight of my concern quickly brought my focus back.

It was a vast room with a four-post canopy bed on one side, beautiful tapestries adorning the walls and a huge veranda on the far side of the room. In one corner was his desk, brimming with even more parchments than the desk in his antechamber.

"Your Majesty," I greeted, my voice quivering slightly.

Zayed looked up from his desk, his expression shifting from concentration to concern as he noticed my distress. "Amara, what are you doing here? I was surprised when I heard you wished to call upon me here," he revealed. He took in my features, watching me closely as I walked towards him. "What troubles you?" he asked, gesturing for me to take a seat across from him.

Taking a deep breath to steady myself, I settled into the chair, my hands clasped tightly in my lap. "It is about...the Grand Vizier has said a gynecological examination is required," I began, my words faltering. "I fear they will discover... that we have not consummated our marriage." My hands went to rest on his desk, trembling slightly as my nerves got the best of me.

I knew what I had to do. But did I have the courage to follow through? The fear of the unknown was daunting.

Zayed's brow furrowed, understanding evident in his eyes as he comprehended the gravity of my fear. He reached across the desk, gently taking my hand in his. "Amara, you need not worry," he reassured me, his tone gentle yet resolute. "I will speak to the physician. Nobody will be examining you. There is no need for it."

Relief flooded through me at his words, gratitude shining in my eyes as I squeezed his hand gratefully. I appreciated the lengths he was willing to go to make sure I was comfortable. However, I knew that the Grand Vizier was relentless in his pursuit to see me gone. How long could King Zayed keep doing this? How long could we keep lying?

As I looked into Zayed's eyes, a swell of conflicting emotions raged within me. Gratitude for his protection warred with the burden of our own deceit. How long could we continue this charade, dancing on a knife's edge between truth and deception? One lie away from everything I was trying to work towards crumbling beneath my feet?

Taking a deep breath, I mustered the courage to broach the delicate topic with King Zayed.

"My King," I began, my voice trembling slightly, "we cannot keep lying. We...must consummate our marriage."

Zayed's eyes widened in surprise, his brows furrowing in concern. "It is not necessary to do something you are not ready to."

I closed my eyes briefly, steeling myself against the discomfort of the conversation. "It is necessary to dispel any doubts that may arise during the examination," I explained, my voice firm despite my inner turmoil. "For while I appreciate your dedication and efforts to evade the nobles and Grand Vizier's attempts to dethrone me, each time we try, more suspicion will be cast upon me. The more we try, the more questions will arise about my validity as queen."

Zayed sighed, his expression conflicted as he considered my words. "I understand," he said finally, his voice tinged with resignation. "You want to cement your position as queen. It is at stake."

Despite his words of acceptance, a lingering sense of unease coiled in the pit of my stomach. His words dripped with bitterness, as if he had been expecting a different reaction from me. The tension between us hung thick in the air, like a storm brewing on the horizon. I could not shake off the feeling that something was amiss.

Nevertheless, I did not have time to ponder over his thoughts. I knew that this was a necessary step to protect both our reputations and the stability of our union. With a silent nod of agreement, I braced myself for what lay ahead.

Taking a deep breath, my eyes flitted to the bed where days ago he had pretended to copulate with me. Images of him throwing me over his back and onto the mattress invaded my brain. I blinked them away quickly as I felt my palms become sweaty.

I glanced back at him, his eyes were warily on me. This man. He did not kill his queens in cold blood. He would be kind to me. Hopefully gentle too.

I stood and walked to the bed slowly. Cautiously.

"Stop. We can delay—"

He stopped speaking when I dropped my robes to reveal my bare body underneath. I heard his sharp intake of breath as I stood with the curtains of his bed parted, my back to him and heart thundering against my ribcage.

Chapter 22

I reached to push the curtains further aside surrounding his bed, lifting myself onto the toes of my feet as the bed was on a raised dais. I heard a sharp intake of breath from behind.

Turning to look at him, I realized his gaze was resting...I blushed. It was resting much lower than my face, squarely on my backside. His eyes flitted up to meet mine and I saw molten-green pools of want staring back at me. He was a man. And I was a woman. It was a natural response.

"I-I should like it if you...you kissed me during the deed," I stuttered out, recalling that his kisses did not feel painful. "Sherazi told me it is dreadfully painful, but I promise I–"

"It will not be painful," King Zayed snapped, shaking his head in disbelief as he walked over to me, stopping a mere hairsbreadth away from me. "I will not let you feel pain, if you follow my lead."

And then he was pushing me gently down onto the very bed he had thrown me on brutally mere days ago. I sank down in the plush cushions. The silk soft against my skin but not softer than his featherlight touch as his hand slid up my bare leg. I felt my breathing speed up, heart drumming faster than a sparrow's wings.

"You tell me if you wish for me to stop," he whispered, his hand now resting over my abdomen, fingers splayed across the expanse of my entire waist. Long fingers that brushed against my skin oh so gently. My gaze went back to his green stormy eyes that were peering at me.

I lifted a hand hesitantly. He did not move, did not blink. Merely watched my hand slowly reach to cover his.

"I trust you."

A long shuddering breath escaped his lips as the implication of my words slammed into him. Trust. Trusted him to be good to me. Trusted him to not kill me. Trusted him to not hurt me.

For a fleeting moment, a hint of vulnerability broke through his stoic facade before he regained his composure.

Time itself seemed to hold its breath as he hovered over me, his hand still resting lightly on my abdomen. My pulse quickened with anticipation, uncertainty swirling in the air around us. But in that moment, as I lay beneath him with unspoken promises hanging in the balance, I knew that I had made a choice. A choice to believe in him, to believe that maybe, just maybe, there was more to him than the rumours I had heard.

Slowly, he leaned closer, smooth lips skimming the expanse of my throat. Such soft lips, such gentle hands.

I closed my eyes, feeling the weight of his touch as his hand inched ever-upward...across my stomach... over my ribs...the underside of my breasts.

As his fingers grazed my skin, a spark ignited within me and spread like wildfire, consuming every inch of my body. The heat radiating from his touch was almost unbearable, yet I could not pull away. It was as if every nerve in my being had come alive, pulsing with an intense energy that I never knew existed. This fire burned deep within me, fueling a desire that I never knew I had. And in that moment, nothing else in the world mattered except for the two of us and the flames that continued to dance between us.

His lips moved up, skimming across my jaw, one hand traced lazy circles at my hip while the other gently cupped my breast. These sensations were entirely new, yet not unwelcome. His touch was no longer hesitant but purposeful, trailing my body with a reverence that sent shivers down my spine. His lips claimed mine in a sweet slow kiss. The hand cupping my breast moved to roll my nipple between his thumb and forefinger. I gasped in pleasure against his mouth. But he did not deepen the kiss. Instead, his hand continued to massage my breast, more insistently this time.

But I held my breath when the hand drawing circles across my hip inched closer to the apex of my thighs. He pulled his soft lips from mine to observe me.

"Tell me if you like it," he muttered against my cheek.

I bucked when his hand went over a bundle of nerves I had only ever hesitantly touched while alone. His dark chuckle only made the flames licking across my skin increase in intensity.

He touched me again there and I bit my lip to keep from crying out. An insistent thumb grazed my bottom lip, tugging it free of the hold my teeth had over it, a look of reproach in his eyes. Eyes so close to me that I could see the flecks of gold shining within their depths.

"Let me hear you," he murmured, pushing down again only for me to cry out in pleasure.

Satisfaction glinted in those eyes of his I could get lost in.

He shifted above me, divesting himself of his white linen pants. I breathed deeply, knowing what was to come next.

His erection, pulsing and hard, pressed against my thigh, a testament to his arousal. I looked up at him, my eyes wide with anticipation and fear mingling within the maelstrom of emotions surging through me. He leaned down, his lips brushing against mine, and I felt that beautiful jolt of electricity course through me. There was the warmth of his lips and desire in his eyes that seemed to cocoon me in a feeling of security.

"Are you scared?" he asked, his voice husky.

"Yes," I whispered, truthfully.

"Do you wish for me to stop?"

"No."

His nostrils flared and his body was as taut as a newly strung bow. He positioned himself between my legs.

"Do not be afraid." Oddly enough, it seemed like a beseeching request more than a command.

I closed my eyes as I felt him begin to enter me slowly.

"Breathe," he commanded, sinking deeper into me.

A sharp pain shot through me. My body instinctively tensed, but I willed myself to relax, taking deep breaths as instructed.

Ever so slowly, he pulled out and pushed back in, deeper each time, creating a building pressure of heat pooling in my belly. My pleasure mounted.

I found my hips thrusting upwards instinctively to match his rhythm, to meet him and take him in deeper. With every undulation of my hips, a new wave of pleasure washed over me.

The feeling of his hands on my skin was like the soft caress of fine velvet, sending shivers down my spine with each tender touch. It was as if he was charting every curve and contour of my body with his fingertips, memorizing me as if he never wanted to forget a single moment of this.

I felt like I was flying, soaring through the heavens with him as my guide.

The pleasure building inside my core was overwhelming, a tide of ecstasy that threatened to consume me whole. I threw my head back, moaning in pleasure and arching further into him.

His fingers curled around my jaw in an almost tender caress.

"Look at me."

I did. His forehead was beaded with sweat, his body tense as if he was holding himself back. Was he?

"Is it pleasurable?"

"Yesss," I hissed out breathily, lifting my hips to meet his more forcefully this time.

"Do you want to find your release?"

I blinked, confused for a moment. Release?

His knowing gaze took in my deliriously perplexed expression.

"Let me show you."

My mouth fell open in a silent scream when he gave a particularly harsh jerk of his hips into me, bottoming out completely. Of their own accord, my hands went to bunch fistfuls of his cotton shirt. I tugged on the material, hands itching to touch him in the same way he was touching my body. I wanted to let my fingers run across the muscles rippling with power just beneath this hindersome cloth. I felt the cloth give way under the force of my hands, shirt ripping down the side. Zayed was momentarily caught off-guard, not expecting that.

"I want to touch you," I gasped out, hands slipping between the ripped seams to run over his smooth, taut muscles.

The beautiful man before me looked down at me with a solemn expression. "Whatever my queen wants, she shall get."

His queen.

He had called me that many, many times. But this time, I heard it. Finally heard it. His. I was his. And I wanted to be his.

He reared back, hands gently going over mine that were clutching fistfuls of his ripped shirt. We removed the offending material together. The cumbersome cotton shirt whispered to the floor. My eyes drank him in, greedily. This was all so new, yet so perfect.

"Touch me," he urged softly, the words silken in the air between us.

I hesitantly traced the lines of his body, as if touching him would imprint the moment forever in my memory. The muscles of his chest were firm and sculpted, his abs hard and defined. Growing bolder, my fingers danced over the rippling muscles of his abdomen, then lower, down to where our bodies were joined.

He watched me like a hawk, much like he had watched me the first time we had sparred against one another. But this time, we were not enemies. We were lovers. And together we soaked in every moment, every touch, every gesture.

His gaze was hot and intense, speaking volumes. In one deft move, his hands wrapped around my waist, holding me firmly against him and lifting me so that I now straddled him in a sitting position.

I wrapped my arms around his neck, my nails digging into his skin in my need for him to be closer, to bring me higher. And he did, his thrusts becoming more frenzied, his breath hot against my skin.

His tongue teased the sensitive skin at the hollow of my throat, and I gasped. My breaths came in short pants. His mouth then moved lower, peppering kisses across my collarbone before moving even lower.

When his lips closed over my nipple, gently sucking, the sensation made me moan louder.

I had heard the whispered words of the pleasures that could be derived in the marital bed. But nothing could have prepared me for this inferno of desire I was experiencing.

I was lost in the lustful haze of our lovemaking, feeling him inside me, moving deep and hard.

Our bodies moved in rhythm, each thrust sending pleasure coursing through my veins. The fire within me was burning brighter, its heat pulsating in unison with my heart. I was lost to the world around us, consumed by the desire that was tearing me apart, yet binding me to him in the most inexplicable way.

His hands roamed over my body with purpose, no longer hesitant but possessive. He was awakening a hunger that was so primal, it was almost feral. I arched my back, reaching for him, my hands fisting into his hair, pulling him closer. Our eyes met as he thrust into me so deeply, I felt as if he had become embedded deep within my soul. In that moment, it was as if we had become submerged in each other and nothing mattered outside of these four walls. We were merely a man and a woman. A husband and wife. There was no kingdom, no nobles, no threat of impending death.

My breath came out harsher, faster...a needy whine making its way up my throat.

But what I wanted, even I did not know. We moved as one, in perfect harmony, his body sinking into mine with each thrust, sending waves of bliss coursing through me. My eyes fell to his lips, and I realized.... I wanted to taste him, to feel him not just against my lips but inside my mouth. His eyes lit up in understanding. One arm still leveraging me against his hard body as I straddled him, gyrating to an unknown tempo, he let his other arm trail up my side, over my shoulders. His hand buried in my dark tresses and he brought his lips forward to capture mine. I gasped in sweet relief, and he deepened the kiss. Cardamom and spice invaded my tastebuds. I knew he would taste divine. I moved against him more ardently than before, reaching for...more.

The world around us began to spin. The air grew thicker with the scent of our rapture, and our bodies twined together like two halves of a single whole. It felt as though we were floating, suspended in mid-air, with nothing but our desire for each other to ground us.

Each movement built upon the last, until the pleasure between us became too much to bear. I cried out his name, breaking the kiss, my body tensing and then releasing as a wave of ecstasy crashed over me. All the while, his hand remained buried in my hair, making sure my eyes remained on his as pleasure coursed through me and I felt my entire body trembling from an approaching...*release*.

He groaned, eyes on me, his hips pumping harder and faster, it seemed his own release was drawing near. With a final, wild cry, he thrust deep inside me, and the pleasure that exploded between us was like nothing I had ever experienced before.

I was hurtling upwards into the endless sky, stars dancing across my vision. Who needed a magic carpet when Zayed could take me to heaven?

My body was convulsing, wave after wave of delirious pleasure washing over me as I grappled with the realization that this was the release he had spoken of. His seed filled me, bringing with it a wave of warmth and completeness, my body clenching around him in response. He cried out my name upon one final powerful thrust, before falling back onto the bed, my body atop his.

His eyes locked with mine, pools of green rich with emotion, and I could see the desire that mirrored my own reflected back at me. His hands went to my waist, pulling out of me gradually, my walls throbbing with each inch of him leaving me. I felt a pang of emptiness.

I reached for him, pulling him towards me in an embrace, the connection between us as electric as ever. His lips met mine, soft and tender, his body melding with mine once more. Tonight there was only us, and this beautiful moment.

"Are you all right?" he queried, lips soft against my temple.

My eyes were closed as I basked in the afterglow of what we had just done.

"Yes, My King," I murmured, opening my eyes to look at him.

He hovered over me, a look of frustration crossing his features.

"Amara, my name is Zayed. Here..." he trailed off, bringing his forehead down to meet mine. "Here, Amara, I am your husband. There is no king. There is only a man who wants to please his wife."

The words were simple, ordinary, spoken by many a man in the marital bed. Yet here, between us, the weight they carried was immense. Beneath their surface lay a profound depth of devotion I had not ever fathomed him capable of.

As the moonlight filtered through the curtains, casting a soft glow over us, I realized that in the delicate dance of our intertwined fates, I had found an unexpected solace in the arms of the very man who I had once considered my captor. The man who was supposed to be my undoing.

After endless hours of what Zayed termed as "love-making" in the throes of passion, I found myself curled up on my side, my back pressed against his chest as he placed gentle kisses along the length of my neck before letting his lips go down to my shoulder.

"Do you require anything?" he murmured huskily against my shoulder blade, lightly nipping at the area with his teeth.

"Mmmm...a long sleep?" I murmured into the bedding.

He chuckled, his hand gently moving strands of my long hair aside to give him better access to my spine. Smooth cool lips kissed the spot between my shoulder blades. I shivered.

"Sleep, My Queen," he whispered, an arm going around my waist.

My eyes began to flutter closed as he continued his lazy kisses across my back. My gaze absently dropped to the left arm slung over my waist, his hand boldly trailing up to cup my breast. The King of Kings...was holding me to him as if I was the most precious thing in the world. I mattered to him. As if maybe he...my thoughts drifted into oblivion, the last sight I took in was his strong muscular bare arm wrapping around my body possessively, a single lone jagged scar across his forearm....

Something pricked my brain. A jagged scar, like one from...but I fell asleep before I could even complete the thought.

Hot breath against my neck, soft feathers brushed against my bare body.

"Mmmmm," I murmured, turning into him and burrowing into his soft chest of fur.

He responded with a low, deep, chilling growl. An animalistic growl that I had only heard once before and it had sent the palpable taste of impending death crashing through me. It did so then. And it did now.

My eyes flew open in horror and I immediately jumped back, landing on my feet with knees bent, ready to run, as I took in the great hulking beast before me, in bed where my husband had lain previously. His lips were pulled back into a snarl, eyes a deep red. He was crouched low on the bed, eyes trained on me like a predator stalking his prey because...I gulped. I was his prey.

Chapter 23

I screamed, my hand immediately going for my dagger. My fingers hit against my bare skin and I cursed, remembering I was naked...my dagger amongst our pile of clothes. I had taken off my robes and left them in a heap on the floor at the foot of the bed. My mind was reeling. There was no time to think.

The beast pounced and I ducked. He hit the wall behind me. Quickly, I ran, my hand going down to scoop up the robes I had worn, exhaling in success when I felt the weight of the dagger inside a pocket. My eyes trained on the balcony, similar to mine. But his room was on a lower floor. I could make it. A clattering and an angry howl behind me told me I had to be fast. My bare feet slapped against the stone floor as I ran naked through the room, the first rays of dawn creeping onto the horizon and leaking through the lattice windows.

The monster behind me let out a blood-curdling howl. I broke through the doors, eyes taking stock of where I was. The back gardens facing the farmlands. Another chilling howl ripped through the room behind me. But as I reached the ledge, dagger in hand now, I registered the howl morphing into something less primal and more human. More familiar. Blankly, I turned, dagger still in hand, to see the beast bent over, on the floor of the balcony, fur receding from his body and giving way to smooth bronze skin.

"No," I whispered brokenly, hand shaking as I gripped the dagger tighter. "No, no, no...it cannot be! No!"

Claws retracted and fingernails formed, limbs elongated and now, before me, was the King of Elamaria, hunched over on his knees as he screamed in pain. My eyes went to the ledge, and then back to him. Then my eyes went to the dagger in my hand. He was disoriented. I could kill him and be rid of this beast. This beast that killed the women of my country. Because now it had all made so much sense though it defied the laws of science. The king morphed into a beast! However, the proof before me was undeniable.

I had sworn to kill him. I could do it. I took a step forward, hand shaking as I raised the dagger high above my head, eyes on his hunched form. But something inside me broke at the thought of angling the dagger just so with the intent to pierce his heart from behind. Tears filled my eyes. Did I have it in me to kill him?

Finally, he raised his head and looked up at me, eyes trained fearfully on my form.

He extended a hand as if he was reaching for me. My eyes fell on the jagged scar on his arm, then went to the dagger raised in my hand, poised to attack. The scar was from the dagger. The dagger I had buried into his arm my first night here when he had taken on his beastly form.

"Did...did...I hurt you?" He trembled out the question, lips shaking, face pale and torment reflected in his eyes. He was not afraid of me killing him. He was afraid of hurting me.

My husband was not aware of what he did when he shifted. I dropped the dagger, running to him without a second thought.

"How often does this happen?" I queried.

We sat in his room; him, clad in a new set of clothes. Me, wearing the same garb I had worn to his room the day before. My head was pounding from the realization of everything. King Zayed changed into a monster every night? But then...how had he managed to stay in his human form when he would spar with me or visit me for stories? My mind went to the stories my mother had told me when I was a child. Stories of men who could shift into animals at will. Had they really just been stories or her warning my sister and I of what lurked in the shadows of this realm? Being a Blade-Caller, she must have known such people existed...

"It only happens if I fall asleep," he finally relented on a deep apologetic breath.

"You have not been sleeping," I spoke in realization, all those conversations finally making sense.

"I have not," he relented, passing a tired hand over his face.

"This is why they die," I whispered. "Because your...monster" —he flinched as I spoke the word— "demands blood."

King Zayed's nostrils flared.

"My 'monster'," he scoffed, "is the only thing keeping the Bedouin tribes and emirs in check. Why do you think they pledge allegiance to me?"

"They know what you are?" I asked aghast.

King Zayed looked at me grimly.

"They know what I am," he relented. He stared down at his hands helplessly. "It is the fear of what I am that keeps them in check. The chieftains of the tribes in the mountains and the emirs with lands deep in the desert...they are shape shifters as well, though their forms are not as strong as mine."

I recalled the statue in the gardens. A wolf kneeling to King Zayed. Shifters. Exactly what my mother called them in her stories.

"They can shift into animals," I deduced. King Zayed gave a curt nod. I chose my next words carefully. "So, you were not sleeping...because you did not want to kill me," I stated, staring at Zayed curiously, my heart thudding against my ribcage.

"It is...not as simple as that," the King replied solemnly.

"Then tell me. Enough secrets," I spat angrily.

"I am cursed, Amara," King Zayed said, looking at me mournfully. "My Lycan—"

My head jerked up at the name. Lycan? Is that what his beast was called?

"—requires a sacrifice. One bride...one queen a year to satisfy the bloodlust. Or else....the curse states...'your Lycan form will rage.'"

My eyebrows furrowed in concentration, taking in this news.

"What happens after you give in to the bloodlust? Do you no longer turn?" I asked, tilting my head to the side.

King Zayed swallowed.

"I am able to control my Lycan after the kill. The curse only renders me powerless until I give in. Until I kill."

His shoulders slumped and he buried his head in his hands.

"The chieftains expect a king who can control his Lycan..." I trailed off, recalling the conversation I had overheard in his study.

It all made sense now. If he could not control his Lycan, he was an unstable ruler. He could be overthrown.

"And you...do not want to kill me," I ended, staring at him stonily.

"I have never wanted to kill anyone, Amara. I have tried...Oh how I have tried—" His voice broke and he looked up at me, a man shattered. The mask melted away to show me not a king, but a young man guilt-ridden for his past deeds. "I have tried to stop myself...to let them live..." Tears gathered in his eyes. He let out a frustrated huff of breath, digging the heels of his hands into his eyes. "It is no use. The curse is too strong, my Lycan...too bloodthirsty until the kill is done." He expelled a defeated breath.

"You faltered," I informed him patiently.

King Zayed looked up at me in confusion.

"The first night...before our wedding." I pointed to the wound on his arm. "When I gave you that. You went in for the kill, I was your prey. And yet you stopped. Long enough for me to do that."

His eyes went to the jagged scar on his arm.

"This dagger—" I held it up "—is the dagger of a Blade-Caller. It leaves a jagged scar to mark any man wounded by one of us. Since no Blade-Caller is foolish enough to wound the king...it can only mean I did it to you in your Lycan form."

The word fell from my lips on a shudder. Lycan. A half-human half-wolf beast. Who wanted me dead.

"Your eyes...I remember your eyes," he admitted quietly, staring at me. "Deep brown, reflecting the midnight sky...filled with courage. I thought it was but a dream. And yet, the scar on my arm stated otherwise. You looked at me on our wedding with courage. Knowing, or rather, expecting me to kill you. Yet you looked at me without fear...with defiance." He paused, reminiscing about that time. "No one has ever done that before," he confessed quietly. "They cower, they beg, they resign themselves to their fate. But not you." He looked at me earnestly, moving to kneel between my legs. His hand came to cup my cheek. And I was a fool because I let him. "Amara...I cannot bear to see that will to live die out. With you, every night I promised myself that tomorrow would be your last." He stared at me. "Until I realized, I would sooner take my life than end you—"

I placed a finger over his lips.

"You are the king. The one who keeps the kingdom from fracturing. The one who protects us. If you cannot control your Lycan, we will fall into chaos."

I remembered the words of the Grand Vizier. And I wondered, what was the death of one peasant in the grand scheme of things? I was one woman. "If that is what it takes to protect our kingdom—" I began.

He jerked back, cutting my words off with a firm shake of his head in alarm as he realized where my thoughts were going.

"I would willingly sacrifice a thousand kingdoms for you, Amara. I will not let you go. If ever there is one thing in which I am selfish...let it be this...let it be you."

My heart swirled with conflicting emotions as I gazed into King Zayed's torment-ed eyes. The weight of his curse, the burden he carried each night as he battled the monster within him, was almost suffocating. And yet, there was a tenderness in his words, a vulnerability that reached out to me in ways I could not fully comprehend.

I looked down at him, his hands in my lap, realizing with acute clarity that the king was kneeling before me. I blinked, disconcerted. His head slowly pressed against my stomach and arms wound around my waist in a hug as he remained on his knees before me.

"I cannot give you up. I will not," he whispered into my abdomen. I felt the wetness of his tears there.

These were not the words of a man who felt nothing for me. He cared for me. He had come to care for me.

My own hands went to bury in his deep, luxurious, soft locks. His voice was overflowing with an emotion that scared me. I was here to end the killings. To kill the king if that is what it took. I had not expected feelings to develop between us. But they had.

"A curse," I whispered to myself. "A curse..." My hands dropped down to his broad muscular shoulders as he held me to him. "A curse can be broken."

"It cannot," he murmured against my stomach.

I tugged at his hair, forcing him to look up at me.

"It can," I pressed, staring down at him with conviction. "Tell me."

His eyes told me I was right.

"If a bride shall survive the beast's rage one thousand and one nights, the curse will be lifted," he explained heavily. "No one can survive my Lycan form, Amara. It might as well be unbreakable."

"I survived one," I pointed out crossly.

"You were not my bride then," Zayed pointed out. He shook his head. "This is madness. Stop thinking—"

"Does this count? You did shift momentarily...I survived..."

"Amara," King Zayed said sternly, looking every bit the king he was despite the fact that he was on his knees before me. "This is not up for discussion. I will not risk your well-being."

"You will just never sleep?" I challenged.

He sighed, finally standing. His hands found mine, pulling me to stand and leading me towards a door on the far side of the room. It was barely discernible because it blended so well into the cool brown stone wall.

"When...it gets too much to bear." He opened the door.

My eyes widened in horror as I took in the room coated in silver. Silver chains attached to four silver cuffs crusted with blood were attached to the wall.

"This room was created when I first tried to resist the curse," he admitted in a low whisper. "I ask Kadin to restrain me. Silver is the only thing that can weaken a Lycan." My eyes flitted to the dagger in my robe pocket. The blade was made of silver. So that explained why the jagged scar remained. "He locks me away within these walls and stands guard. Kadin has picked up a pattern. I sleep for some odd hours, my body recuperating before shifting in the final hours of the night. Much like I did earlier." He looked back at me apologetically. "I did not expect to fall asleep, Amara. I put you at risk and for that...I will forever repent and regret shifting in front of you."

"I do not," I replied evenly, stepping into the room and taking in the scent of rusty, metallic, dried blood. What was he putting himself through? How long could a man go on like this? "If you had not fallen asleep and shifted, I would have never known. You surely would have never told me."

His silent reply was confirmation enough. I required a plan. And the wheels in my head were already turning. Magic could be used for good. If my mother's stories were any indication, curses could be broken. We just had to find a way.

Zayed pulled me slowly towards the bed.

"You must be tired. Sleep a while longer before it is time to hold court with the nobles. Come...unless you would rather sleep in your own bed?" he ventured, looking at me closely.

Sleep was the last thing on my mind. I wanted to figure out a way to break the curse. Listlessly, my eyes went to the bed and I noted one glaring fact.

"I did not bleed," I whispered.

King Zayed scoffed.

"Not every woman bleeds, Amara. It is a common misconception. One merely spread to perpetuate man's dominance over a woman." His eyes filled with revulsion as he guided me to sit on the bed and then sat next to me. "I did not expect you to bleed, My Queen." His hand came to cup my cheek gently. "I would have been surprised if you had, considering your vigorous physical training in the academy for Blade-Callers."

It was there in that moment that I realized the laws of our kingdom might be oppressive when it came to women, but Zayed's personal beliefs were very different from the laws. The spark of awareness in me was burning brighter as I realized that there was so much we could change together to help those who were oppressed. If only we could break this curse first.

Chapter 24

I was decked out in the finest silk, my body doused in the most expensive lavender and jasmine perfume available. The dress I wore was a beautiful deep pink with gold sequined flowers embroidered onto it. A gauzy net cape of the same color as my silk dress fluttered in the wind behind me. The gold beads on my cape glinted in the sunlight spilling into the hallways from the windows, casting an almost ethereal glow around my form. Sherazi said I looked every bit the queen I was meant to be. I sorely hoped she was right. The grand throne room loomed ahead. I could see through the crack in the partially opened double doors that the nobles and courtiers had gathered.

In a week's time, the emirs and chieftains of the Bedouin tribes would arrive for the annual feast celebrating the alliance that brought everyone under our rule. Before then, we had to make sure Zayed could control his Lycan. My thoughts briefly went to last night, cheeks pinkening as I briefly recalled our first time together. It had been beautiful. Zayed had shown me a tenderness and passion that I had not expected from the man I had once thought to be the bloodthirsty king. He was anything but.

And as I stood outside the antechamber, adorned in finery, my heart raced at the thought of seeing him once more. Earlier this morning, I had excused myself to go bathe and gather my thoughts. It was obvious not many knew of this curse. And I would not spill my husband's secrets to Sherazi. But Kadin knew. And it was a fervent hope of mine that Kadin could help me in my attempts to free my king of this wretched curse. Zayed was tight-lipped, not delving further into the history behind why the curse was placed upon him. But Kadin might be willing to provide the information I required. I paused at the side entrance to the antechamber that was attached to the throne room.

I knew my king was waiting for me beyond these doors. We would enter the throne room together. Taking a deep breath, I stepped through to see Dornia and the Grand Vizier sitting across from King Zayed as he sat behind his desk. He had a scowl on his face and it seemed as if they had been arguing.

But the moment I entered, the scowl vanished from Zayed's face. He stood, a smile breaking out onto his features. I blinked, realizing this was the first time I had seen him smile in this manner. I had seen his polite smiles, his sarcastic smiles, his bitter smiles. I had never seen a genuine smile of pure joy on his face.

All because I entered the room.

He looked at me as if I was the only person that mattered.

His eyes were alight with an emotion I could not quite place.

"My Queen," he murmured, inclining his head and motioning for me to join him. He extended his hand, offering it to me so we could enter the throne room with each other.

As I reached out to take his hand, a sudden realization washed over me. I could not deny the feelings that stirred within me any longer. This was not just about breaking a curse or fulfilling a duty as queen. It was about the connection between us, one that had grown stronger with each passing day. I wanted to help him because I cared for him.

"Leave," King Zayed demanded sharply, his stern cool voice contrasting with how he had spoken to me only moments before.

"But, My King," pleaded the Grand Vizier. "We still have to discuss the—"

"I would like a few words in private with my queen before we must hold court. Leave," King Zayed repeated, his voice even chillier than before.

My eyes slid to the Grand Vizier and Dornia as they silently retreated, looks of displeasure on their faces. Once the doors to the antechamber had shut firmly behind them, I looked at King Zayed with curious eyes.

"What is it you wish to speak of, My King?" I asked politely, curious.

"I have a name, Amara," he whispered, his hand reaching out to cup my cheek gently. "I like hearing it on your lips. "

My cheeks heated as I looked up at him.

"You are the king," I said cautiously, looking towards the doors that led to his throne room.

"I am not a king here as I stand before you, but a man who cares for you deeply. First, I am your husband. Then I am your king," he murmured, looking down at me intently.

"Zayed," I corrected softly, my gaze locked onto the intense deep green of his eyes, golden flecks dancing in their depths and hypnotizing me.

"Are you all right....after last night?"

I blinked, realizing he was worried about whether I was still sore after our activities the night before.

"I am fine," I assured him, enjoying the way the pad of his thumb brushed across my cheekbone tenderly.

"You are not afraid of me?" he ventured.

"I could no more fear you than the sky fears the storm—it may rage, but it is what brings the rain and breathes life into the earth," I breathed, awash with foreign emotions raging inside of me.

His thumb grazing over my cheek stilled, and the hand holding mine tightened its grip. His face became solemn as he took in my words.

"Is that all of what you wished to talk to me about?" I pressed, feeling I had given too much away with such a sincere expression of my feelings.

Zayed got a mischievous smile on his face. Another smile I had never seen before. And one that made my heartbeat stutter.

"I asked them to leave because I wanted to do this," he admitted, using the hand grasping mine to pull me into him so that I was now firmly pressed against his hard muscular body. And then he brought his lips down over mine in a kiss that started off gentle and sweet. But it transformed into something else entirely. His tongue delved through my parted lips, exploring every inch of my mouth with a fervor that sent shivers down my spine. My arms wound their way around his neck, pulling him closer as if I could never get enough of him.

Zayed's hands roamed over the silk fabric of my dress, his touch igniting a trail of desire in its wake. I felt the hard planes of his body pressed against mine; the strength and warmth of him enveloping me completely.

Zayed's touch sent waves of electricity through me, igniting a fire deep within my soul that I had never experienced before.

When we finally broke apart, my chest heaved with each ragged breath. Zayed's gaze bore into mine, filled with a hunger that mirrored my own.

He cursed, turning from me and clearing his desk with one fell swoop of his arm. Scrolls fell to the floor, a glass paperweight shattered into countless tiny pieces. But he paid the mess no mind, lifting me so that now I sat on the cleared space of his desk.

"My restraint is non-existent when it comes to you," he growled, hands tugging at the bodice of my gown.

I helped him by lifting my dress so that it was now hiked up to my waist, silk petticoats tumbling around me and spilling onto his desk. His lips trailed down my neck, finally closing over one exposed breast. I gasped softly, my fingers tangling in his dark locks as I pulled him closer to me. This passion between us was like a wildfire consuming us both. All rhyme and reason had fled. I felt his finger delve between my folds as I reached for the tie on his beige silk trousers interwoven with gold thread. But his hand clamped over my wrist, preventing me from freeing him so he could enter me. I gazed at him, wondering if I had overstepped. And then I saw his eyes trained on my womanhood, wet with arousal.

Desire burned in his gaze as he released my wrist and backed away slightly. I opened my mouth to ask if we should stop. But then froze when the man before me who held the title of *"the king of kings"* dropped to his knees before me and pulled me to the edge of the desk.

"You are the only woman I will ever kneel for," he grunted and gripped my thighs, draping my legs over his shoulders.

He brought his mouth to my core. The sensation of his warm breath against my womanhood caused me to arch my back and grip the edge of the desk. His tongue darted out and gave one slow, torturous swirl between my folds.

"Zayed!" I cried out as he sent lightning bolts of pleasure shooting through me.

"I need to taste you," he murmured from between my legs, hands digging into my thighs. "I need to know what your release tastes like on my tongue."

I bit my lip to stifle a moan at his words, but it escaped in a soft whimper

He chuckled, placing a kiss on my inner thigh before he traced slow circles with his tongue, dipping inside my folds, then over the tiny nub of nerves and then down the length of my seam, sending a surge of pleasure coursing through me.

Zayed's hands now gripped my hips firmly, anchoring me as his tongue continued its sensual assault. Waves of ecstasy crashed over me, the intensity building with each flick and caress. My hands fisted, fingers crumpling a piece of paper left remaining on his desk. In the recesses of my brain I realized it was a document about building granaries to store food. They were being constructed close to the Blade-Caller training arena. The training arena where the impending Blade-Caller trials would take place, trials to ascertain who would be worthy of joining the ranks as an official warrior. Trials I was also supposed to be part of. But granaries and trials were the furthest thing on my mind with Zayed's head between my legs and his tongue stroking me in the most intimate and exquisite of ways. My head fell back on the desk with a resounding thud as the king's tongue moved in circles between my folds, sending toe-curling pleasure through my body.

My release was building quickly, and I knew it would not take much to send me over the edge. Zayed sensed this too, his fingers digging into my hips as he increased the pace of his ministrations. My breath hitched, and I knew I was about to scream. A wave of pure pleasure crashed over me as Zayed's tongue found just the right spot, and I cried out in ecstasy.

As the waves of pleasure subsided, I fell back against the cool wood of the desk, gasping for breath. Zayed rose, his eyes dark with passion as he pulled me into an embrace. He kissed me deeply, finally freeing himself to slowly enter me. I whimpered into his mouth, enjoying the sensation of how he stretched and filled me. He pulled back to watch my reaction when he thrust against me.

"It does not hurt, does it?" he queried.

I shook my head. The intensity of our connection was overwhelming; it felt as if we were becoming one being.

"Feel me, Amara," he said, his voice low and raspy. "Feel me inside you. Just as surely as I feel you inside me. Just as I have felt your light illuminate the deepest shadows of my heart from the moment I first met you."

With one swift thrust, he entered me completely, filling me in a way that seemed to fill even the void in my soul.

I wrapped my arms around his neck, pulling him closer as we both began to move as one.

The king had his cock inside of me while his nobles were in the next room waiting for us to hold court. Did they know why our arrival had been delayed?

But I could not ponder on this for longer than a moment as the intensity of our movements grew, and the air between us thickened with passion and longing. Zayed's dark eyes locked onto mine, the corners of his mouth turning up in a half-smile as he watched me lose myself in our connection. I was being pulled deeper into this world of pleasure and pain; it was an indescribable mind-altering experience.

As our bodies continued to move against each other, I could feel the pleasurable coil building up within me. A wave of euphoria washed over me, and I let out a loud cry as I reached my peak for the second time. Zayed's thrusts matched my rapid breaths, his own breathing hitching as he continued to thrust against me. I could feel his body tense before he groaned my name, releasing within me.

We stayed like that, embracing each other and relishing this moment together, both trying to regain our composure.

Finally, he pulled out of me and my eyes went to my thighs sticky from his seed. And that was when a thought occurred to me.

"I do not want to conceive!" I exclaimed, the words spilling out of my mouth before I could stop them.

I realized too late that, as queen, that was most likely something I should not have told the king. What king wanted to know that his queen did not want to carry his heir? And the look on Zayed's face told me he was no different. Every monarch required an heir.

"You realize those words alone could be considered treason?" he grunted, eyes shuttered and staring at me as if I had committed a sin far worse than murder.

Chapter 25

"I—"

His hand went over my mouth, preventing me from speaking.

"Shhhh," he hissed, eyes sparking ominously. He leaned in close to my ear. "Amara, I cannot protect you if you keep digging a hole for yourself. Never speak the words out loud again," he whispered vehemently into my ear, his voice panic tinged. "A queen who does not wish to conceive can be hanged. Do you understand? Even the walls have ears."

I gave a jerky nod, realizing he was angry because I had said the words too loudly. He did not speak more to me, merely moving me into an adjoined room where a wash basin was present. He helped me clean up, playfully splashing water towards my face during the process.

"Your nobles will wonder why we took so long," I chuckled, urging him to hurry.

He reached out, moving a strand of hair away from my face.

"They will know I was enjoying time with my wife," he murmured gently. "A much better pastime than dealing with those stiff fools."

I could not agree more. I would rather be here, where it was just us. Rather than out there in the throne room trying to outmaneuver a bunch of nobles who most likely wanted me gone. And I could not blame them. For it was seemingly the only way to appease the cursed Lycan inside of him. And as we finally made our way towards the throne room, my mind was awash again with ways to break the curse.

Blade-Callers did not train within the castle grounds. Their training arena was further, closer to the perimeter of the city of Ilm where a grand training center had been developed for the elite female warriors. I had not wanted to become a Blade-Caller to protect the crown. I had always hated the mad tyrant king who killed innocent women. I had wanted to become a Blade-Caller to protect the citizens of my country. We were charged with protecting the borders, overseeing the streets of the city and ensuring that the weak were not preyed upon.

And I had nearly completed my training before I became queen. Baghel trotted happily next to me as I made my way with Kadin to the training academy.

"Are you sure you want to do this, My Queen?" Kadin asked.

I shot him a hard glare.

"Positive," I responded coolly. I turned to look at him.

I was cross with him, because the entire journey through the city, he had remained tight-lipped about the curse. I had poked, I had prodded. And he only repeated that it was not his secret to tell. Finally, and quite sullenly, I had given up. Kadin seemed on edge today. Maybe it was because I was venturing out into the city alone with him. King Zayed had wanted me to take an entire battalion of guards. But that was out of the question. I could defend myself, and Kadin was also a superb swordsman. So here we were, with him quite frustrated and peering around every corner as if someone might jump out to strangle me, while I kept poking him with questions.

"I spoke with the head trainer. She will not reveal who I really am. But if you follow me inside, I will be found out." Hence the entire reason I had refused a formal royal escort. We came here dressed as commoners.

"None of your old peers will recognize you?" Kadin pointed out with a roll of his eyes.

"Blade-Callers are divided into groups of twenty to train. There are three groups in every year. This is a group I have not previously trained with."

With those words, I turned and walked through the familiar double doors that opened into the circular arena where the final test was to be held. I just had to pass the preliminary obstacle course before being cleared to partake in the final test.

Greeting the Head Trainer, a retired formidable Blade-Caller in her own right, I was then guided towards the obstacle course where other women were already standing and waiting.

The course was designed to test agility, strength, and quick thinking—essential skills for any Blade-Caller. As I observed the different women standing next to me, a sense of familiarity washed over me. These were my sisters in arms, my comrades in the fight against injustice.

The Head Trainer blew a sharp whistle, signaling the start of the obstacle course. Without hesitation, I took off, feeling the drive to succeed coursing through my veins.

The obstacles were a series of climbing walls, dodging arrows, and navigating through a maze of swinging ropes that potentially lead to multiple dead-ends. Only ten women of the twenty here today would qualify for the final test. The rest would be sent home. I had to be amongst the first ten to complete this course. I pushed myself to the limit, determined to prove my worth not as a queen, but as a Blade-Caller.

My heart sank as I reached a dead-end whilst swinging from the ropes. I turned back, determined to maneuver myself to the other end successfully. But a commotion caught my attention. One of the women had lost her footing and was dangling precariously above the ground. It took me a moment to realize this woman had her arm in a sling and was attempting to finish this course with only one good arm. Without thinking, I sprang into action, swinging towards her, though it was sending me in the opposite direction, back towards the dead-end I had previously encountered. Using all my training and skills, I managed to reach her just in time, grabbing hold of her good arm and helping her gather her bearings.

"Are you all right?" I asked her, staring at her face where she had a deep purple bruise over her left eye.

Had she been hurt while training.

"I...thank you," she said breathlessly, her good arm holding firmly to the rope.

I took in the way she held her injured arm close to her.

"Come, follow me," I directed.

And together we swung towards what I hoped was the correct path. I learned her name was Nora. A few times, Nora lost her grip on the rope and required my assistance, which I gave readily. Many women had already moved ahead, and I was sure we would be the last to reach the end. However, leaving Nora behind did not sit well with me.

I felt as if we had an undue disadvantage. It was not fair that Nora was to fail due to an injury out of her control. Finally, we reached the end of the rope maze, and I pushed myself harder than ever, leading my injured companion through the clearing where traps lay in wait. This part of the obstacle course required a keen eye as under the sand were nets that were waiting to be set off and capture us, preventing us from completing the course. I watched as many of the women who had been ahead got caught up in the nets that lifted them high up over the clearing. Even if they used their daggers to cut themselves out, the jump down was too great.

There was a lesson to be had here. Which was that a keen eye and perceptive thinking was essential to success. More so than brute strength or skills as a fighter. Preventing a fight on the streets, or spotting a dangerous thief was more important than wielding a sword. Because by the time you needed your sword, an innocent civilian had most likely already been harmed in some way.

I was surprised to realize that Nora had a very astute ability to spot the traps. Previously, I had been helping her stay on the ropes. But here, she was aiding me in quite successfully stepping over and around the triggers that lay in wait for us.

Despite her injury, she was not holding me back. Instead, she was helping me get ahead.

Finally, we reached the last stretch of the obstacle course—a wall that needed to be climbed to ring the bell at the top, signifying completion. Nora hesitated, looking up at the daunting height with a flicker of doubt in her eyes.

"Go on," I urged her softly, giving her a reassuring smile. "You have made it this far. You can do it."

With renewed determination, Nora started climbing, using her good arm to pull herself up steadily. I followed closely behind, ready to assist if needed. The other women were gaining behind us and I realized that no one had reached the top yet. We just might be the first.

Hand over hand, foothold by foothold we slowly made our way up. A few women passed us, their speed and agility obviously giving them the upper-hand over Nora.

"You should go," Nora murmured, looking down at me apologetically. "I am slowing you down."

I shook my head.

"We do this together," I replied deftly.

"I do not want to be the reason you fail," she countered.

"If I abandon you, then I have failed regardless."

Nora looked at me with renewed determination and I watched her make her way up with a little more fervor than before.

Nora's determination was palpable as we neared the top of the wall. The bell glinted in the sunlight, a symbol of victory within our reach. I could hear the heavy breathing of the other women below us, some struggling while others moved with grace.

As we climbed higher, Nora's good arm began to tremble with the exertion of pulling her weight for such a lengthy amount of time. I could see the pain etched on her face, but she refused to give up. With each foothold, each pull, she showed a strength that went beyond physicality. It was a strength born out of resilience, out of a fierce will to succeed against all odds.

And then, finally, we reached the top. Both of our hands stretched out together and grasped the rope that held the bell, giving it a resounding chime that echoed through the arena. Cheers erupted from below as we stood there, breathless and triumphant.

Looking at Nora, I saw tears glistening in her eyes. "We did it!" she exclaimed.

I nodded, a smile breaking across my face. "We did," I echoed, feeling a surge of pride for both of us. The Head Trainer approached us, her expression unreadable but a glint of approval in her eyes.

"Well done," she said gruffly, a hint of a smile tugging at the corner of her lips. "You have both shown exceptional teamwork and determination. You have earned your place in the final test." Her eyes went to me, a little misty. "It is an honor to know we are in such compassionate hands." She leaned towards me to whisper in an undertone, "Your majesty."

And then she left to deal with the remaining ten women who had not reached the top in time. Four were stuck in the nets, while six were still struggling to make it up the wall. Nora and I had been the sixth and seventh to finish the course so our place was secure.

"Do you think your arm will be healed by the time we take our final test?" I queried politely.

Nora looked at me and I saw her reddened cheeks. She slowly pulled her arm out of its sling to show me. My eyes widened in surprise. There was a stump where her hand should have been. And the arm itself was smaller than the average arm and seemed almost limp, unused.

"I was born with no bones in my left arm," she admitted. "And my-my-" she revealed hesitantly, her eyes reflecting the heartbreak of her past. "My sire deemed me an abomination. He had me married off at the age of sixteen—"

I gasped in surprise.

"—and my husband calls me worthless because I am unable to have children," she ended morosely. She expelled a breath and squared her shoulders. "But I am here to offer my services to the crown."

I was speechless, my heart heavy with the weight of Nora's struggles. Despite all she had endured, she stood before me with unwavering determination, ready to prove her worth. It did not take much to deduce that the bruises on her face were from her husband. In a land where a woman required male protection, there were vile men who preyed on us. Her resilience and bravery humbled me, and I felt a surge of admiration for her strength of character.

"You are far from worthless, Nora," I said firmly, meeting her gaze with sincerity. "You have shown more courage and skill than many here today. Your past does not define you, and your future is yours to shape."

Nora's eyes glistened with a glimmer of hope in them. She nodded, as if my words had struck a chord within her.

Together, we moved forward to join the other women who had completed the course. The atmosphere was charged with excitement and anticipation for the final test that awaited us. As we gathered around the Head Trainer, she announced the details of the final challenge. But the pit of my stomach dropped when she revealed that the king would personally be present to oversee the final results.

Chapter 26

"You are of perfect health," the physician assured me, packing up his bag.

I looked at him as I sat up in bed. He had not performed any invasive exam, merely performing a routine check-up.

"You did not check to see if I was a virgin," I commented carefully.

The physician tsked.

"I think, judging from the fact that it is common knowledge amongst all that you and His Majesty have been sharing a bed for the last three days, not to mention the whispers amongst the nobility of what goes on in the antechamber, there is no need." He looked at me kindly. "Besides, the true purpose of these checkups is not to check if the queen is untouched. It is to ensure you are healthy enough to bear an heir and a spare for the future of our kingdom. Which you are more than able to do," he assured. "Sooner, rather than later, we will be hearing the happy tidings of an impending royal birth. Of that I am sure."

The kind doctor bid me good-bye and left.

I shook my head. It seemed that I had scaled one mountain only to have another one before me. It is not that I did not desire children. It is that I believed there was more to being a queen than simply birthing heirs. How could I rule by my husband's side, how could I ever bring about the changes I wished to see, if I was constantly with child? Hesitantly, I made my way to King Zayed's chambers, knowing that it was important to bring up the subject again. He might not be happy with my reasonings. But it was my body and my choice. I knew him well enough to know that he would respect my wishes.

But what would happen when months went by and I did not conceive? I snorted in exasperation, wondering if there was a law for beheading a queen who could not or would not conceive. If there was, it was something I would fix.

I entered Zayed's chambers to see him standing on his balcony. Hesitantly, I made my way to him. When he turned to me, the moonlight revealed the harsh angles of his face and illuminated the dark bags under his eyes. It struck me that he had most likely not been sleeping.

"The physician says I am of perfect health to bear strong heirs," I informed him, deciding to broach the topic carefully. I looked at Zayed, trying to ascertain his reaction.

He gave a resigned sigh and moved past me into his room. There he beckoned to me to stand next to him behind his desk

I complied. Reaching into the bottom wooden drawer, he took out a small wooden box. I watched him reach for a small key in a hidden compartment inside his top drawer.

"What are these?" I asked when the box opened to reveal miniscule vials.

"Medicines...poisons...sedatives..." He held up a tiny vial with dark purple powder inside of it. "This is what I utilized to help you sleep on our wedding night," he informed me seriously.

I wrinkled my nose.

"You mean when you drugged me?" I pointed out.

"I did not drug you. Two small teaspoons does not drug anyone. You were quite exhausted. It merely helped you find a dreamless sleep." He set the purple vial back down and I opened my mouth to tell him that it had not been a dreamless sleep. I had had a nightmare about his Lycan form attacking me. But my attention snagged on a clear liquid with a light pink hue to it. I knew what it was. Many women used it. I would have already had it on my person if not for the fact that it would have most likely been treason to acquire it.

"Take three drops in your tea," he explained, handing the vial to me. "It will prevent pregnancy."

My eyes widened in disbelief as my hand closed over the vial. He was...willing to help me?

"You do not want an heir?" I queried.

King Zayed gave me a sad smile.

"I only want what you want," he replied.

"Every monarch wants progeny," I replied in measured tones.

"And what if my heir inherits this curse, Amara?" he ticked out, weary eyes looking at me with sincerity.

I pocketed the vial, realizing he had thought this through quite thoroughly.

I tilted my head to stare at him.

"Your children will inherit the ability to turn into...a Lycan?" I queried.

"All male heirs are born with a Lycan," he corrected gently. "It is what proves their royal birth-line. What equips them to rule, for all shifters bow to the stronger and almighty Lycan."

I chewed my bottom lip, recalling what he had said about his younger brother not possessing the same abilities as he had. Which had then proved that his mother had been unfaithful. His younger brother had not been born with a Lycan.

"Do newborns also turn into Lycans?" I queried.

"We have our first Lycan shift at the age of eighteen," he said seriously. "It is a very painful process. Some do not survive. Hence the imperative reasoning behind giving birth to an heir and a spare," he breathed in deeply, closing his eyes momentarily as he explained everything to me. "However, we possess strength, speed and regenerative abilities that far surpass those of a normal human child. At times, as babies, when we cry and emotions are heightened, our eyes glow red, signaling our beastly side. When those abilities did not manifest in my younger brother..." he trailed off, staring at me.

I reached for him, bringing my arms around him in a comforting embrace. His arms went over my smaller form, holding me to him.

"He did not deserve to die," I murmured. "Your mother did not either."

"She was lonely, even I could see that much," King Zayed admitted, rubbing his chin over the top of my head. "My father, an emotionally closed-off man, saw only one vision: to hold our kingdom together, to cement our legacy as the mightiest monarchs. In contrast, my mother, much younger when they wed, longed for love—a yearning as natural as breath itself."

His hand rubbed up and down my back in a gentle caress as he spoke, lost in memories of his childhood. "She craved the joy of life, while he was consumed by an insatiable desire for power, wealth, and an ever-expanding harem. As her heart ached in the confines of our gilded cage, she found solace in the arms of a young noble, a ward of the crown, closer to her in age and spirit. I caught glimpses of their laughter, their shared moments of unguarded happiness, and–" He paused expelling a resigned breath. "I was too young to understand the implications. Did not know that what she did, put her life at risk. I only wanted my mother to be happy, because that is what we wish for for the people we love. And she was happy."

My breath caught in my throat as I remembered his words.

Go be happy with the man you love.

He had wanted me to be happy.

"What I saw between them...I feared I might never know in a world where I was bound by duty and ambition. Until you came into my life," he admitted, his finger tipping my chin up to capture my lips in a soft kiss.

I kissed him back, my arms going around his neck. However, just as his hands reached for the tie of my robe, a polite knock at the door brought us back crashing down to land from the heavens we had been soaring through together.

Zayed pulled back, regret marring his features as his hands gently roamed over the dips and curves of my body. I noticed they did not rove over my body with urgency like they usually did. Nor were his eyes alight with the primal hunger I often saw in them. Instead he was looking down at me seriously.

"Amara, tonight...Kadin will stand guard outside my room," Zayed explained.

My stomach filled with dread as I realized he meant he would have to shift tonight. I noted the bags under his eyes again.

Guilt consumed me. I had promised myself to find a way to break the curse. Instead, for the last three days, I had been merely enjoying my husband's bed. Of course, I had moved a few laws to be changed. Namely, one where a wet nurse did not have to leave her child behind if she took up a job to nurse a child of the nobility. The nobles were up in arms about it. But Zayed was on my side. And that was all that really mattered. But I should have been working hard to figure out how to break the curse.

I nodded, remorse filling me. Tomorrow. Tomorrow, I would track down Kadin and ask him for more details. And this time, I would not let him avoid giving me a direct answer.

King Zayed bent down, placing a soft kiss on my lips before pulling away from me.

"Enter," he called out and I saw Kadin walk in.

"Thank you for making time tonight, Cousin," Zayed said and I noted how he regarded Kadin with familiarity.

The familiarity that came between siblings. Kadin was the only family Zayed had. And I was glad that in Kadin, Zayed had found a steady dependable friend.

"What else is family for?" Kadin replied with an easygoing smile. He placed a hand on his brow in reverence. "Anything for you, Zayed."

"Will you be all right?" I asked haltingly, looking at Zayed anxiously and recalling the cuffs crusted over with his blood.

Kadin's eyes cut over to me. "My Queen, I can assure you that your husband is in good hands. Besides, it is me you should be more worried for. His Lycan is much stronger than mine."

I gasped in surprise.

"You...are also a Lycan?" I queried.

Kadin smiled wryly. "Though I have more control over my form, yes. Every man born within our family is a Lycan," he informed me.

"Good night, My Queen," Zayed, said, taking my hand and placing a gentle kiss on it. "I will see you on the morrow."

"Be safe," were my final words before I moved away to leave. My final glimpse of Zayed was a light upturn of his lips as Kadin made a joke.

My heart felt a bit lighter seeing a small smile on his face. But I also realized that it was time to get to work. My husband could barely sleep a handful of hours before he turned into a Lycan. It was not fair that I was capable of a full night's rest while he went without. So I made my way to the library, grabbing as many books on curses as I could. However, as I lay nestled in my warm bed with a book propped up on my knees, sleep finally overtook me. Visions of a man cursed to roam as a beast took over my dreams. But he was no longer the evil vicious monster out to kill me. Now he was an ally. A friend. A lover. Someone who needed my help.

"Amaraaaa... Amaraaaa," the voice called out to me, echoing in the darkness and pulling me from my deep slumber.

I awoke, slowly, the hairs on the back of my neck prickling as a shiver paced its way down my spine. Zayed had informed me that tonight Kadin would stand guard in his room while he shifted into his Lycan. It was the first night I was sleeping alone since we had consummated our marriage. Every night, he made love to me, and every morning I was awoken by his gentle kisses. It had been odd, sleeping in my room alone. But it was a stark reminder that I had to find out how to break the curse.

"Come, Amaraaaa."

Fear gripped my heart as I sat up, scanning the room for the source of the eerie voice. There was no one in the room.

Dread enveloped me as I cautiously stepped out of bed, my every movement filled with trepidation. Lighting a candle, I searched the room in the dim glow of the firelight. Ominous shadows danced across the room, taunting me. But there was no one...

"Come to me...."

The haunting voice seemed to grow louder with each passing moment.

"Who is there?" I called out, my voice trembling with a mix of curiosity and fear. Silence was the only response, leaving an unsettling heaviness in the air.

Driven by an unexplainable force that seemed to be tugging me along, I cautiously opened the door to my room. The guard who always stood sentry was not present. Odd. I tiptoed through the dimly lit hallway, my senses heightened and on edge. Something was beckoning to me, leading me deeper into the palace, drawing me towards an unknown destination. Each step felt heavier than the last, as if an invisible hand was pulling me further into the abyss. I was powerless to stop myself. My hand reached for the dagger I always slept with, for even though I had survived thus far, the fear of impending death still lingered.

Finally, I found myself standing before a closed door.

The door was tall and imposing, intricately designed with wrought iron and plated in glimmering gold. The metallic sheen caught the dim light, casting dancing shadows on the floral patterns that weaved and winded over the door like vines. The coppery brass added a warm, almost inviting, touch to the otherwise foreboding entrance.

This was in a wing of the palace I had never ventured into before. It was part of the inner-harem. A harem that Zayed had disbanded when he had become king. My hands closed over the doorknob and the cool, rough texture of the iron against my skin seemed to awaken my senses. I pulled my hand back. Why was I here? Moreso, how had I ended up here? In front of an aged door in a part of an abandoned wing of the palace?

"Amara."

The sharp command called to me. My hand shot out, opening the door upon the command of an unseen force. At once, a musty old smell wafted from the room, dust tickled my nose. Mixed in with this was the faint pungent smell of rotting flowers.

An ominous aura enveloped me, filling me with a sense of foreboding. My hand closed over the dagger sheathed at my side. Whatever was in here was radiating malevolent intent. I could feel it in my bones. I stepped in determinedly, ready to face whatever had called me here. I was no coward. But it was becoming all too obvious that there were unnatural beings that lurked through this palace. Beings that might be the actual reason behind the deaths of innocent women.

I gave myself a moment to adjust to the dark room, cautiously stepping deeper. The door closed behind me with a resolute bang. I did not turn around. Exposing your back to the enemy was foolish.

Something wet hit my cheek. Wet and warm. Wiping it away with the back of my hand, the unmistakable red tint told me all I needed to know. It was blood. Immediately, my head went to the ceiling and what I saw tore a scream from me like no other.

Hanging from the ceiling was a figure of a woman, her body clinging to the ceiling like a spider with her head twisted completely to face her back and stare down at me from an unnatural angle. Her dark eyes, filled with a malevolent glint, locked onto mine, piercing through the darkness. Her yellowed teeth were exposed in a sinister smile, sending a wave of terror crashing over me.

Another blood-curdling scream tore from my throat. The room seemed to spin, and the air became thick with the overpowering stench of all things dead and decaying. The woman's gaze remained fixed on me, her presence suffocating, as if she was reaching into the depths of my soul. She grinned at me, and before I could even blink her form fell to the floor, scampering to me on all fours, head still twisted and staring at me with an evil vicious grin. This was no human. This was no animal. This was something else entirely! Something all my skills could never defeat! I took a step back, intent to run but the demon woman fell upon me, her gray, rotting limbs pinning me beneath her as she cackled.

Her hands were bent at a complete one hundred eighty degrees, holding me down from my shoulder. Yellow rotting teeth closed in on me, putrid breath making me fight down the urge to retch. She was going to kill me. She was the one. She was the one that was killing everyone. I tried to struggle but found myself unable to escape her hold. An iron weight was pushing down on me, making me unable to breath. Unable to move.

But when she opened her mouth, it was not to tear into me. Her rough cackling voice spoke of something much more ominous, much more sinister.

"Each year, one royal bride must fall to your claw,

Or face the wrath of an ancient law.

Should you refuse, your Lycan form will rage,

Bringing death and destruction to your royal stage."

She cackled again, I screamed, trying to struggle but it was futile. It was like an iron band clamped across my body. I was utterly paralyzed by an unseen force..

"The land will wither, consumed by dread,

As a demon rises, hungry and unfed.

Your kingdom shall crumble, devoured by night,

For this curse is eternal, sealing your plight!"

She roared the last line, her voice becoming more and more inhumane. My mouth opened, a gasp of pain eliciting from my lips as I felt her hands twist, nails digging into my skin and drawing blood. What sorcery was this where I was unable to move and only scream?

I stilled, realization flooding me. Without a second thought, I reared my head back and head butted the demon atop me. She stumbled back, the bend of her body unable to withstand the force. The door flew open to the room, flooding everything in light. Dawn. It was dawn.

"Amara!" King Zayed exclaimed breathlessly, reaching me in two purposeful strides.

And just like that, the form before me sank into the shadows, melting and disappearing as if she had appeared out of thin air. As if she had been a figment of my imagination. The iron grip paralyzing my body disappeared right along with her.

"D-did you see that?" I gasped out, gripping his hands as he checked my body for injuries.

"Where was her guard?!" he barked out, his gaze lethal as he stared at Kadin who was still standing in the doorway, shock and disbelief written over his face.

"Zayed," I said sharply, pushing his hands away that had been probing my abdomen to make sure I was not injured. I sat up, looking him in the eye. "Did you see it?"

The hard lines on his face deepened, he looked at me almost...regretfully.

"Yes, Amara. I saw. I can only say you are beyond fortunate to have survived." He looked at me sternly. "You are not allowed to wander the castle at night alone. I have made that clear numerous—"

"Never mind what I am and am not allowed," I cut him off sharply, my eyes narrowing on him. "What is she? What does all of this mean?" I pressed

King Zayed looked at me somberly.

"It means that it has begun," he replied simply, leaving me with nothing but more questions.

Chapter 27

Flashback

"Oh, Liliana, he is just adorable," Mera said, cooing at the three-month-old baby.

Liliana held her son to her bosom and looked towards her son Zayed and nephew Kadin playing together in the courtyard.

"Rowan is no more precious than your son, Kadin," Liliana replied, laughing and adjusting the crown on her head. She looked at Mera and felt happy to have such a good friend in the woman.

"But there is something to be said about a love child, eh?" Mera giggled in an undertone. "A baby that is the product of true love."

Liliana's eyes widened and she looked around frantically, telling Mera to shush with her eyes.

"Oh, it is just us," Mera assured, smoothing the skirts of her dress. "Please, Liliana, you know I am the one that has covered for you many times when you have snuck around. If you get caught, I go down too for being your accomplice."

Liliana's eyes suddenly went to her older son, Zayed, realizing he was standing off to the side listening very intently to everything.

"Come here, son," Liliana said, holding her free arm out for Zayed.

Zayed ran to her. A boy of seven, he loved his mother dearly.

"You want me to tell you a story, my little king?" she whispered, pressing a kiss to Zayed's forehead.

"But it is not bedtime yet," Zayed replied.

"It does not have to be bedtime for stories, my love," Liliana said comfortingly. "I—"

The doors to the courtyard of the harem slammed open and in walked the king. He looked furious. Liliana clutched Zayed in one arm and Rowan in the other, wondering why the king had ventured here. He rarely came to the harem. Often, he would call his concubines to come to his bedchamber. And his visits to his queen were few and far between.

"Seize him!" the king called out to his guards, pointing to Zayed.

Zayed cried out when a guard grabbed him away from his mother.

Dornia ran towards Zayed, immediately trying to take him.

Zayed cried out again, wanting to be free of the guard's rough grasp.

"Let him go!" Liliana screamed as Mera beckoned Kadin over and clutched him to her side.

"Do not touch the future king!" Dornia yelled at the guard.

"Mera!" The king's command was sharp. "I suggest you take your son away from here. You do not need to see this."

Mera whimpered, looking between Liliana and the king before looking at Zayed still struggling against the guard.

She held onto Kadin tightly, her heart pounding in her chest as she felt the tension in the air. Zayed cried out when the guard gave him a particularly harsh jerk to stop struggling.

"Leave him!" Liliana commanded. "That is an order from the queen!"

However the guard merely looked to his king for confirmation. The ruthless king looked at Zayed.

"You watch this, boy. You need to know what happens to unfaithful whores."

Liliana gasped, clutching Rowan even tighter to her. She shook her head.

"Do you deny the fact that you were having an affair with one of my wards?" the king boomed.

Tears fell down Liliana's eyes. But she did not deny anything.

"You were unfaithful to your king! You let another man into your bed! You had his child and tried to play him off as my spare!" Spittle had formed at the edges of the king's mouth as he spoke.

"My King—" Mera began, trying to protect her friend.

"Silence! I order you to leave this place at once, else you will see something you wish you had not! Do you dare deny an order from the king? I do not care if you are my brother's wife. I will punish you too for your disobedience! And your son will also pay the price!" the king snarled, eyes going to Kadin.

Tears falling down her eyes, Mera glanced at Liliana.

"Go," Liliana whispered, trying to force a smile. "I-I will be all right. Go. You must..." Liliana's eyes went to Zayed. She looked at Mera who slowly began to back away. "Take care of my sons," Liliana pleaded, eyes still on Mera.

Mera gave a nod.

"With my life," she vowed before finally exiting the courtyard.

Once Mera had left with Kadin, the king faced his queen, utter contempt written across his face.

"You thought I would not find out the child was not mine? My Lycan has refused to acknowledge him since he was born. His reflexes are not that of a Lycan. They are those of a wolf-shifter! You have sullied yourself by giving that body of yours to another," the king ended with hatred in his eyes.

"We are in love!" Liliana cried out, falling to her knees and throwing herself at the king's feet. "Please...please, My King! Forgive me! Banish me if you must. I am sorr—"

She never finished her sentence because in the time it took her to grasp the hem of the king's silk robes, the king had drawn his sword and in one fell sweep, beheaded the beautiful queen. Liliana's head hit the ground with a heavy thud. Zayed screamed. The baby in the dead queen's arms began to cry as he too hit the floor and landed at the king's feet, splatters of his mother's blood covering his face.

"Where is your lover now?" the king snarled, his eyes holding nothing but contempt. He had killed the mother of his child without even batting an eye. "Hiding away in the mountains. You thought you could join him? Lying, cheating, unfaithful whore. They should all be killed. A cheating heart of a woman cannot be allowed to continue to beat! This is what women like this deserve, Zayed!" the king raged, eyes on his heir who was crying and thrashing against the guard that held him by the shoulders.

Rowan's cries became louder. The king reached down, grabbing the babe into his arms. Dornia was screaming too now, begging the king to stop. The guards restrained her, slapping her across the face in an attempt to get her to stop struggling.

"NO! Please stop!" Dornia yelled loudly, refusing to stop struggling even when blood was spilling from her split lip.

The King of Elamaria paid the wet nurse no heed. He grabbed the tiny baby, his huge hand going over the top of his head and with one deft twist, he snapped the tiny baby's neck. The cries stopped.

Zayed screamed even louder, tears and snot mixing together. Finally he bit down hard on the guard's hand that had a firm grip on his shoulder. Then he ran to his father, throwing himself at the king in a fit of rage.

The king's expression did not change as he dropped the dead baby and grabbed Zayed by the throat, lifting him slowly up to his eye level.

"Your mother chose her desires over her duty. Her choices led to this!" the king boomed, watching Zayed's face turn purple from being unable to breathe. "Do not make the same mistakes as her. You are the future king. But with her gone, I can easily marry another and create more heirs. YOU—ARE—EXPEND-ABLE."

Zayed was then unceremoniously thrown onto the floor where the tiny boy slid a few feet before hitting a stone pillar with a resounding crack. He let out a groan of pain and Dornia, finally free of the guards, ran to him.

She cocooned him in her arms, shushing him and trying to wipe his face with the sleeve of her dress.

"I will be stronger than him one day, Dornia. I will get him back for what he did," Zayed sobbed hysterically into her bosom as Dornia shushed him.

Many hours later, once the guards had left and servants had come in to clean up the mess, the young prince who had lost his mother and brother finally laid eyes on their corpses. With red-rimmed eyes, he asked Dornia to help him bury his family.

The servants helped, agreeing that this was the least they could do for their kind queen. For everyone had known the king's brutality and indifference to the queen.

It had been three days since Zayed's mother had died. The young prince was still haunted by the horrific murder of his mother and brother before his very eyes. Aunt Mera tried to tell him bedtime stories, but it was not the same. He missed his mother. And Rowan. An anger now festered inside of him. One day, he would get his father back for what he had done. Zayed had seen his mother become a happier woman once she met the man she loved. He did not care what society thought was right or wrong. All he cared about was that his mother had started to smile. And that was the most important thing for him. And now, she was gone. Gone because she had tried to be happy.

It was not just or fair. Kings were supposed to be just rulers. Where was the justice in this?

The doors to the courtyard opened where he walked aimlessly with Kadin. Dornia and Aunt Mera were busy preparing his clothes for tomorrow when he was to be presented in court. He would sit on a small throne next to his father and learn how to pass judgements and converse with the nobles. The thought of sitting next to the man who had killed his family made him want to retch. Zayed looked up to see Elvira walk in. Elvira had been his mother's wet nurse. She often visited his mother and the queen would always send Elvira money so the woman could live a comfortable life. Elvira had started off as a peasant woman but by virtue of being the queen's caretaker, the woman was now one of the richest single women in the country. She was also a very powerful witch who had used her magic more than once to protect the future queen of Elamaria.

"This...I sense it...this is where she was killed!" Elvira moaned, falling to her knees in the same spot Liliana had been beheaded. "My little flower..." Elvira sobbed, placing her forehead against the cool stone.

Her eyes suddenly cut to Zayed, anger in her gaze.

"What is the meaning of this! I told them you were not to be allowed inside the castle!" blustered the king, walking in in all his regal finery. His eyes went from Elvira to Zayed and then back to Elvira.

"You!" Elvira snarled, eyes cutting to the king and then to the guards behind him. "You killed my daughter!"

"She was never your daughter, peasant," the king snapped. "I know you are the one who probably helped her hide this affair for as long as she did. Only witchcraft could have been involved to pull a blindfold over my eyes. You should be seized, quartered, and hanged for—"

"A curse upon your bloodline. A curse upon your heir!" she shrieked. "You thought you could hide the truth from the kingdom? They will grow to hate the monarchy as much as I!"

The king's eyes widened in alarm. Elvira withdrew a dagger from her pouch and sliced it clear across her palm. Blood dripped down onto the floor where Liliana had died. The witch's eyes cut to Zayed.

"Each year, one royal bride must fall to your claw,

Or face the wrath of an ancient law.

Should you refuse, your Lycan form will rage,

Bringing death and destruction to your royal stage."

Elvira cackled. Zayed felt a piercing pain sear through his chest and he fell to his knees, a cry of agony leaving his lips.

"Stop this mythical nonsense!" the king screamed, but his voice was tinged with panic. He motioned for his guards to grab Elvira. Meanwhile, the witch kept chanting.

"The land will wither, consumed by dread,

As a demon rises, hungry and unfed.

Your kingdom shall crumble, devoured by night,

For this curse is eternal, sealing your plight!" And just as the guards reached her with their swords drawn, Elvira dug her blade deep into her heart.

Her eyes cut to the king, a sadistic smile on her face.

"You will die, and your bloodline will die with your heir." Blood spilled from her mouth as she gurgled out the words.

A shadow descended from Elvira's form, enveloping the king briefly before dissipating into nothingness. She had poisoned the king with a deadly curse. He would die a slow and painful death, each day feeling a little bit of his life slip from his fingertips. Until one day, he would cease to live. But she had also cursed his son.

Zayed blacked out from the agony he was feeling deep in his heart, as if something fundamental inside of him had been twisted and suddenly taken on a malevolent nature.

Amara's POV

The story still rang in my ears as I sat in Zayed's bedchamber, my face pale and heart thundering against my ribcage.

Kadin and Zayed had relayed the entire story. Their mothers had been best friends. Mera helped Liliana to meet the man she loved.

Elvira had been the wet nurse charged with caring for Zayed's mother. Liliana had been born to a noble household who had been staunch supporters of the king. Upon birth she had been betrothed to the king, who had been nearly twenty years her senior. She was married to the king upon turning sixteen. The thought made my stomach roll in disgust. Liliana had Zayed at seventeen.

Elvira had been employed specifically for her skill in witchcraft.

She was entrusted with the care of the future queen, knowing that only someone with magical abilities could protect the baby from the potential dangers that lurked around her. For many would have wished to see her gone so that they could offer up their own daughters. Liliana's own family did not even know the truth of her death. If they had, it would not have taken long for them to lead a rebellion against the crown. For though Liliana had been of noble birth, she had still been a daughter of Elamaria. Just like me.

And somehow, despite the king spreading tales that his queen and son had died due to some unknown illness, Elvira had found out the truth. Maybe because she had been a witch of great power.

"So...that was the ghost of Elvira? The witch?" I queried, looking at Zayed and Kadin who sat across from me on cushions. Between us was a low-lying table of untouched food.

The mere thought of eating made me want to retch. How could I, after hearing the macabre tale of the curse upon my husband?

My hand tightened over the talisman I now held. It was a striking necklace, crafted from a string of lustrous black pearls, their smooth surfaces catching the faintest glimmers of the morning light. At its center hung an intricate evil eye pendant, the design sharp and captivating. The eye itself was fashioned with a deep, inky-black pupil surrounded by shimmering blue details, as though it could see into one's soul.

The contrast of the dark pearls and the ominous gaze of the eye gave the talisman an aura of mystery and power, warding off unseen dangers while also commanding attention with its dark elegance. I had never been a suspicious sort. But what I had seen...it made me clutch the talisman as if it were a lifeline. Zayed had pressed it into my hand, informing me that by wearing the necklace, adorned with the watchful gaze of the evil eye, the wearer was shielded from harmful influences. Namely, witchcraft and supernatural activity.

"We believe so," Kadin finally said, exchanging a wary look with Zayed. "She wants the curse to be fulfilled one way or another. Her main aim is not the drought or food shortage which will undoubtedly occur—"

"What?" I asked, cutting him off, my eyes going to Zayed. "Drought?" I blinked, recalling the plans for food and water storage.

Zayed glared at Kadin.

"No more secrets, Zayed," I hissed, slamming my palms face down on the table overflowing with food. The cutlery and goblets of water clattered in agreement.

He released a resigned breath.

"I told you...I told you that I tried to fight the curse..." he sighed, running a hand through his hair and motioning to the awful room coated in silver. "I had that built when I turned eighteen. Because I did not wish to kill anyone. I did not wish to become as brutal as my sire," Zayed muttered, closing his eyes in remorse.

"You are not him," I bit out vehemently, aghast that he would even consider it.

The previous king had been a brutal and vile creature whose cruelty knew no bounds. Zayed was anything but. He might be aloof and reserved, but it was only because of the burden placed upon him.

"The famine," I breathed, the horrible memory of emaciated women and starving babies filling my mind.

"The famine," Zayed agreed, inclining his head towards me.

The land will wither, consumed by dread...

As a demon rises hungry and unfed...

"And if he still does not give in," Kadin began, despite Zayed's glares, "the demon of Elvira will rise to devour and destroy everything in her path."

The talisman I had been clutching in my hand fell to the floor as I sat shocked and struck dumb from the full implications of it all.

Chapter 28

"King Farid and Yasmin knew that their adventures had only just begun," I said, pouring a cup of wine for Zayed. My hands shook as I spoke, and I tried to cover up my trepidation by turning my back to him. I cleared my throat. *"They knew that it was of the utmost importance to retrieve the magic carpet from the man who had betrayed Yasmin."* I swallowed, turning to face Zayed who was reclining on my bed and listening to me with intent.

The poignancy of the moment was not lost on me. His mother would tell him stories. For some reason, he liked my stories too. I walked over to him, handing him his golden goblet encrusted with emeralds and rubies with intricate carvings around the rim.

Zayed took the goblet from my hand, our fingers brushing together momentarily. He looked at me warmly, keen eyes roving over my robe-clad form. I could tell from the way his eyes darkened, that he was eager to do much more than listen to the story. I swallowed down the lump of guilt in my throat as I sat down across from him on the bed, careful to maintain an arm's distance. He grinned mischievously.

"You can come closer my little tigress," he teased. "I will not bite, too hard."

My hands clenched at my robe and I did my best to keep my tone stern.

"The story first," I reprimanded.

"Of course." He gestured for me to continue, and the interest in his eyes was not lost on me. He truly did enjoy the stories.

"King Farid discovered the man who tricked Yasmin was a wicked mage, bent on using the carpet to travel to far-off lands and retrieve rare herbs needed for his dark magic. Yasmin, in her naivety, had been tricked." I paused, waiting for Zayed to take a sip of his wine.

He did so, eyes on my form.

"Yasmin could have created a new magic carpet to track down the mage," King Zayed mused.

I gave him a wan smile.

"But it would take far too long, and magic as potent as the kind infused into the first carpet can only be done once," I countered, tightening the tie of my robe.

Zayed drained his goblet, and I watched him like a hawk, careful to keep my expression neutral.

He leaned back against the ornate headboard, his gaze fixed on me. "What happens next, storyteller?" he inquired, his voice smooth like velvet, sending shivers down my spine.

I took a deep breath, feeling the weight of his expectations hanging heavy in the air. And I was about to let him down miserably. I could only hope this would not be construed as a betrayal of the worst kind. That we would be able to overcome what was to happen next. I had spent many hours poring over my options. And I knew what had to be done. What must be done to free my kingdom.

"They set out together to reclaim the magic carpet and put an end to the dark mage's schemes before it was too late," I said calmly.

Zayed's eyes sparkled with intrigue.

"King Farid and Yasmin embarked on their journey across treacherous lands, facing dangers at every turn," I continued the tale, the feeling of my impending betrayal pressing down on my chest. *"Yasmin's heart ached with the knowledge that she had been deceived by the wicked mage, but King Farid's unwavering determination gave her strength. Together, they braved through dark forests haunted by malevolent spirits, crossed raging rivers teeming with deadly creatures, and climbed mountains that seemed to reach the heavens themselves. And through all the trials they endured together, their love for each other grew stronger. Where once they had been foes, they were now bound by an unwavering bond of love and friendship.*

Finally, they were able to track down the wicked mage where he was hiding deep in the mountains in a secluded cave.

The night before their final confrontation, as they sat by a crackling fire under a sky sprinkled with stars, Yasmin felt a heaviness in her heart. She turned to King Farid, his face illuminated by the flickering flames, and reached out to take his hand in hers.

'Farid,' she began, her voice barely above a whisper, 'I fear what lies ahead. But with you by my side, I know we can overcome any obstacle.'"

I paused, noting the droop of Zayed's eyelids. He jerked up, shaking his head.

"I feel—" he began but paused when his words slurred together. And then he looked at me in horror. "Amara!" he barked out as I jumped up from the bed and began retreating towards the balcony. "What-what have...you...done?"

"I am sorry," I whispered, reaching to open the tie of my robe to reveal my Blade-Caller uniform. Two tears trailed down my cheeks and I wiped them away hastily. "It is the only way to break the spell, Zayed," I pleaded, holding up my hand to show him the sedative I had poured into his drink. The very same one he had administered to me my first night here but to him, I had administered it in greater quantity. I had to be sure it was enough to send him into a deep slumber. "To save our kingdom, I must survive one thousand and one nights with your Lycan, I can do it," I stated with a conviction I did not feel.

He looked at me in horror, fighting off the effects of the drug. But it was futile. I walked backwards, closer to the balcony.

"Amara, you—"

Zayed's words were cut off as the sedative took hold of him completely, his body slumping back against the pillows on the bed. I watched him with a heavy heart, knowing that what I had to do next would break both of us. Hopefully, we could build anew from this. Tears welled up in my eyes as I moved swiftly to the balcony, staring out at the moonlit kingdom spread out before me.

I ran across the expanse of the balcony, cool tiles hitting my bare feet. My boots and sword were waiting for me near the balustrade along with a hastily put together makeshift rope hanging from the edge to make my escape quick and effective.

As I reached for my boots, the sound of cracking bones behind me told me he was shifting. I cursed. I had hoped I would have had more of a head start. Maybe the strong sedative had caused the rapid shift instead of allowing him to sleep a few hours.

Zayed's transformation was swift and powerful, echoing through the room. I turned to glance at his figure, briefly watching as it contorted and grew. I did not have much time. Hastily, I slipped on my boots, strapping them tightly over my feet.

The weight of what I had done bore down on me heavily, but there was no turning back now.

With one last glance over my shoulder at the majestic beast Zayed had become, I grabbed my sword and jumped over the balcony, holding steadfast to the rope that would aid my descent.

I knew our kingdom's fate relied on my survival. The famine had been devastating. And I would not let a bitter old witch's curse tear us apart. If I was worth fighting for to him, then surely he was worth fighting for to me as well. We could overcome this curse together. I just had to prove myself to him tonight.

No queen had lasted this long. And the last time Zayed had tried to resist the curse, the effects of drought and food shortage had started within three days. I had a theory that maybe the more days I survived his Lycan form, the more the curse was weakened. I hoped it was the case.

The Lycan King let out a guttural roar from above me on the balcony and my heart pounded in my chest as I quickly maneuvered myself closer to the ground. Closer to land where I could run into the forest. He had transformed quicker than I had anticipated. He was supposed to sleep a few hours before shifting. Had the sedative been too strong? Sending him into such a deep slumber that he immediately shifted?

The moon hung high in the sky, casting an ethereal glow over the land below as I landed on the ground.

I could hear the sounds of commotion behind me, knowing that Zayed would soon give chase in his transformed state. But I had a plan, a desperate gamble in hopes I could survive his transformation night after night.

It was a risky proposition, but I was willing to do whatever it took to see our kingdom prosper. To make sure he could control his Lycan form when the emirs arrived at the end of the week. I would not be his weakness, but his strength.

I turned to look up at my balcony and met the feral red eyes of the Lycan King, and he was looking at me with a primal bloodlust that should have made me tremble in fear. It should have made me scream. Made me want to disappear. But somewhere in there was my husband. The man who would sooner sacrifice all that he held dear to see me alive and well. So I steeled myself for the night ahead and disappeared into the dense forest, making sure he saw me and would give chase.

I would survive one thousand and one nights with the Lycan King and break this curse.

Chapter 29

As I ran through the dense forest, the sound of Zayed's powerful pawsteps behind me urged me to run faster. The moonlight filtered through the thick canopy above, casting eerie shadows on the forest floor as I weaved between trees and leaped over fallen branches. I could hear Zayed's deep, menacing growls growing closer as he pursued me relentlessly.

My heart pounded in my chest, both from the physical exertion and the fear of what Zayed had become. Every instinct within me screamed at me that I was a fool and had zero sense of self-preservation.

Glancing over my shoulder, I caught a glimpse of his massive form charging through the undergrowth, his eyes locked on me with an intensity that sent chills down my spine. His Lycan form was a terrifying sight to behold, a stark contrast to the gentle man I knew. To the man who held me against him so dearly at night, placing tender kisses against my temple as I fell asleep to the calming lull of his heartbeat.

A sudden howl pierced the night air, sending a shiver down my spine. Right now, my husband was the farthest thing from calming. Zayed was closing in on me, his primal instincts driving him forward with relentless determination. I had to find a way to outsmart him, to evade his powerful Lycan form until the cursed night was over. I had a plan however. Hopefully it would work.

Branches whipped at my face as I darted through the forest, trying to put as much distance between Zayed and myself as possible. Despite the fear clawing at my chest, I knew I had to keep moving, keep running, if I wanted any chance of surviving the night.

I pushed myself to run faster, my lungs burning with each gasping breath. The forest seemed endless, the trees a blur as I sprinted through the shadows. I could feel Zayed's presence behind me, his hot breath on the back of my neck as he gained ground.

With a burst of energy, I made a sharp turn, ducking under a low-hanging branch and narrowly avoiding Zayed's clawed grasp. My mind raced with thoughts of how to outwit him, how to survive this night and the many more that were sure to follow.

I veered off the main path, following a narrow game trail that led deeper into the heart of the forest. It was time to enact my plan. I could not outrun him forever, but perhaps I could outsmart him.

The sound of Zayed crashing through the foliage grew louder, closer. But I pressed on, my senses on high alert. My heart hammered in my chest as I ducked behind a thicket of bushes. Settling into my hiding spot, holding my breath, I listened as Zayed thundered forward, his keen senses searching for any trace of me. I stayed perfectly still, the rustling of the leaves and the pounding of my heart the only sounds in the night. I dared not move, dared not make a sound,

Zayed was mere feet away from me, trying to pick up my trail. My breath caught in my throat, and I pressed a hand to my mouth to keep from screaming when I heard him let out a snort and begin to take purposeful steps towards me.

But just as Zayed's growls grew louder and his shadow loomed over me, the successful click went off, signaling that my plan might work. The ground beneath him gave way and a net doused in silver (it was the best I could do at such last minute) sprung up, trapping him in a snare. Zayed let out a deafening howl of pain as the silver-infused trap burned at his flesh, immobilizing him just inches away from where I hid.

Trembling with a mixture of fear and guilt, I cautiously emerged from my hiding spot, taking hesitant steps towards Zayed. His feral red eyes locked onto mine, and a snarl emitted past his lips as he snapped his canines towards me threateningly. The message was clear, he would not spare me once he escaped. The man I loved was buried beneath the snarling beast before me, and it tore at my heart to see him in such a state.

I could not bear to look at the agony on his face, as the silver chaffed against his fur.

"Zayed…" I whispered, my voice barely above a breath as I approached him. His struggles weakened as he regarded me, the flicker of recognition crossing his features briefly before being consumed once more by the animalistic instincts that controlled him.

I reached for my sword, drawing it purposefully.

"I could end you tonight," I whispered, taking aim. "It is what I came for. It is why I volunteered to be your bride. I would end you or end myself trying. But now…" A lone tear made its way down my cheek. "Now to end you means to end a part of myself. It would mean facing a future without the warmth of your embrace." I bit back a sob. "Without the comfort of your touch. You are the Lycan King, capable of protecting our kingdom from those who wish to end the monarchy and wreak destruction upon the realm. You are the vital pulse of the kingdom…and to me, you are the roaring heartbeat fueling my very essence, thundering through my blood and consuming me entirely." I lowered my blade and wiped my tears as the beast snarled at me. It was like talking to an animal. He could not understand me. "I will not give up on you, I will break this curse and we will herald a new era for our people, together." Sheathing my blade, I took a few steps back.

He watched me like a predator watching its prey. My eyes went to the net. It would not hold all night. But it would hold long enough for me to find a suitable hiding spot. It would hold long enough for me to see the first light of dawn.

For a moment, our eyes met, the weight of our shared past and the hope for our future hanging between us.

A low growl escaped his lips as he tried to break free from the trap that bound him, but to no avail.

When I turned my back to him, he let out a bloodthirsty growl.

Under the eerie moonlight, I searched for a spot where I could safely wait out the night. I had seen many hiding spots when scouting the area, but there was one in particular I was looking for.

As I went deeper into the forest, finally, I found it. It was the most beautiful bush laden with jasmine flowers. The sweet scent would hide any traces of myself should Zayed break free. It was directly under an ancient tree that seemed sturdy enough to provide additional cover.

Settling myself behind the bush and under the old tree, I could still hear Zayed's snarls echoing through the forest. The tension in the air was palpable, a thick fog of fear and uncertainty that clung to me like a suffocating cloak.

And the lump of dread increased tenfold in my stomach when I heard a faraway discernible thump followed by a triumphant howl. The Lycan King had freed himself of his restraints much sooner than I had anticipated.

I held my breath, heart pounding in my chest as the realization set in that Zayed was once again on the prowl. Panic threatened to consume me, but I forced myself to focus, to push past the fear and think of how to enact my next plan.

Ashad had taught me well. His words echoed in my mind.

The true warrior is never caught off guard by the chaos of the sands; when the storms strike without warning, they reveal their strength through preparation and adaptability, for survival demands more than skill—it demands foresight.

Minutes felt like hours as I huddled in my hiding spot, the fear of discovery weighing heavily on my mind.

The pale silver moonlight shimmered off twisted tree branches and lit up a mosaic of shadows that could have been anything—a predator, a hideous creature mutated by the curse or simply an innocent deer on its nightly binge.

I nearly screamed when I heard a guttural growl tear through the night, closer than I had anticipated. He was not far.

With bated breath, I peered out from my hiding spot, my eyes scanning the darkness for any sign of movement.

And then I saw him. His back was to me but he was close. Too close.

Zayed prowled through the shadows, his muscles rippling beneath the moonlit dark fur as he moved with a predatory grace. He scanned the area, searching for any trace of me. I held my breath, praying to whatever gods would listen that he would pass by without discovering my hiding place. My next plan depended upon the element of surprise. And time. I needed more time.

Finally, after what felt like an eternity, the sounds of Zayed's pursuit began to fade into the distance. I let out a silent sigh of relief, but I knew that this was only a temporary respite. There was a reason he had stopped so close. He could sense me and no doubt would circle back when he could not find me moving forward.

The scent of jasmine could only cloak my presence for so long. The night was far from over, and I still had many more challenges ahead.

As I cautiously emerged from my hiding spot, I scanned my surroundings for any sign of Zayed. The forest was shrouded in darkness, the moonlight barely able to filter through the dense canopy deep in the forest behind the castle. I was relieved that I had purposefully planned to have this area unpatrolled for tonight.

As I moved silently through the forest, searching for any signs of the bloodthirsty Lycan, I also searched the sky for any signs of dawn. Last time, he had changed back immediately once dawn broke. I was relying heavily on the same incident repeating itself.

My hand tightened around the hilt of my blade, determination fueling my movements. I had to be clever, had to think like the warrior that I was trained to be. Emotions had no place on the battlefield. I ducked behind a cluster of bushes, listening for any sign of Zayed's approach.

Suddenly, his thunderous footsteps halted, and the forest fell eerily silent. I held my breath, waiting for the inevitable moment of confrontation. And then, a low growl rumbled through the stillness, followed by the sound of heavy breathing.

I peered through the foliage, my eyes locking on Zayed's beastly form as he prowled into view looking for me. His massive body cast a menacing shadow in the moonlight, but I refused to let fear paralyze me. I could not run all night. I would have to injure him to slow him down.

With a silent prayer to the goddess for strength and guidance, I moved out of my hiding spot and charged. The Lycan's feral red gaze mirrored his surprise. He was not expecting this sudden onslaught. Good. In a swift motion, I raised my blade. My heart raced with a mixture of fear and determination, knowing that this night would test our wills to the breaking point. But I refused to back down. If I survived, I could only hope he would forgive me.

I brought down my blade in a graceful arc, aiming for his right shoulder, but his claws came up to meet my blade, effectively blocking the attack. Our eyes met. Zayed's Lycan eyes bore into mine with a mix of hunger and recognition, a glimmer of humanity flickering behind the primal veil. I knew that somewhere deep within those primal instincts, my husband still resided.

The tension in the air was blatant as we each measured the other's resolve. Zayed's growls grew louder, reverberating through the forest as he, with a single violent thrust of his claws, exerted pressure on my blade which caused me to stumble back. He let out an angry snarl and prepared to pounce.

As Zayed lunged towards me, his massive form closing in with feral speed, I held my ground, bracing myself for the impact. Everything seemed to move slowly as his clawed hand reached out towards me, his snarling maw mere inches away from my face.

With a swift and calculated movement, I sidestepped his attack, narrowly avoiding his lethal claws. As he stumbled past me, I struck out with my blade, aiming for a vulnerable spot on his side. The blade sunk deep into his fur, drawing a fierce growl of pain from Zayed's lips.

But the pain only seemed to fuel his rage, his eyes glowing with primal fury as he turned to face me once more. I reached for my dagger, knowing that silver was his weakness. I did not want to kill him though, even if I could have. I only wanted to incapacitate him from pursuing me. There were a few hours left until dawn hit. One of the advantages of living in the desert land of Elamaria, nights were not overly long.

We circled each other, the Lycan King limping, as blood trailed down his side.

Zayed's Lycan form lunged at me once more, his claws slashing through the air with deadly intent. I barely dodged in time, feeling the rush of wind as his claws narrowly missed my skin.

With a quick motion, I aimed my silver dagger between the hulking beast's shoulder blades, hoping to incapacitate him long enough for the dawn's arrival. As the blade connected with his back, a pained howl tore through the night, echoing through the forest as Zayed stumbled forward, his movements slowing from the effects of the silver. I watched him fall to the floor in pain, and knew I could not show mercy. Not yet. My blade had not cut deep, he would heal sooner rather than later.

I knelt beside him, my heart aching at the sight of him. But now was not the time for sentimentality. Now was the time for survival. I reached into the camel skin pouch tied at my hip and got out the chains of silver to quickly bind his wrists and ankles.

The effects of the silver chains would not be enough to hold him for long. But it was the best I could do for now. The silver manacles in his silver coated room had been too heavy to carry with me and not even within my access. What I had planned to do, had been planned with the utmost secrecy. Only Sherazi knew my true plan. When I requested Kadin to clear this area for the night, he assumed I wanted to take a leisurely stroll with the king in this area.

With practiced haste, I secured the silver chains around his wrists and ankles, binding him tightly to a sturdy trunk nearby. The Lycan King snarled and thrashed against his restraints, but the silver's touch rendered him weak and powerless. He snapped his jaws perilously close to my neck and I jerked back. I had hoped that somewhere within this beast was my beloved husband...trying to fight against the savage nature that threatened to consume him. But it seemed the bloodlust was too strong. The curse, too powerful.

As I watched him struggle against the chains, a pang of guilt gnawed at my heart. This was not how it was supposed to be. Me trying to survive the night while my husband tried to kill me.

I stood back, my chest heaving with exertion as bitter regret coursed through my veins. I took a few steps back, reaching for my flask of water.

As I drank from my flask, my mind raced with thoughts of what to do next. The chains would only hold him for so long, and I needed to come up with a plan before he broke free. I could not bear the thought of hurting him further, but I had to protect myself.

I watched Zayed writhing in agony against the silver chains, his growls echoing through the forest. Despite the danger he posed, my heart ached at the sight of him in such pain.

The night was far from over, and I needed my strength if I were to survive the challenges that lay ahead. I took a moment to catch my breath, the forest around me eerily silent save for Zayed's low growls and snarls as he struggled against the silver chains. His feral red eyes locked onto mine, a mixture of hatred and something else, maybe longing, swirling in their depths.

As I watched Zayed's struggles, a part of me wanted to believe that he was fighting against the curse, that there was still some humanity left in him. But the reality of his monstrous form and the danger he posed could not be ignored. I slowly began to step away, hoping to get far away from here by the time he broke free. Dawn would be upon us by then. I had done all I could. The rest was up to fate.

The forest seemed to thrum with anticipation as I made my way back towards the castle, every rustle of leaves and snap of twigs amplified in the dead of night. From far away, I heard the distinct roar of the Lycan King followed by the loud clinking of chains. The rending of metal signified that he had broken free. I looked up at the sky, praying for a speedy approach to the dawn. Only once the first light of dawn broke the sky would Zayed revert back to his human form.

The sound of Zayed's enraged roars chased me through the darkness. The forest seemed to close in around me, the gnarled branches reaching out like skeletal fingers, threatening to ensnare me in their grasp.

I quickened my pace, the castle looming in the distance like a beacon of safety. But even as I ran, I could not shake the feeling of eyes watching me from the shadows, unseen malevolent forces waiting to strike.

Just as I reached the clearing where the castle stood, a sudden gust of wind howled through the trees, carrying with it a sense of foreboding. I stumbled on a loose stone and fell to my knees, panic coursing through my veins as I scrambled back to my feet.

I breathed a sigh of relief as the first rays of dawn finally broke through the sky. I turned back in time to watch Zayed break through the forest in his Lycan form. His fur was matted with blood and dirt; his eyes, a feral red, landed on me with angry determination.

I stood there, waiting for him to change back. Wondering if the rays of dawn had to reach him for the transformation to take place.

"Change back," I whispered, taking a few steps back and watching him move forward with purposeful strides.

I shook my head in disbelief as I looked up at the sky, gleaming with the first light of dawn and then looked back at the Lycan King.

He was not changing back. Instead, he was charging towards me, the dawn's light only fueling his determination to kill me.

Chapter 30

I turned, charging towards the palace, wondering all the while where had I gone wrong. He was supposed to change back at dawn. Did the sedative I gave him hinder his ability to shift back into his human form?

Panic surged through me as the realization of what could happen dawned upon me. The Lycan King would rip me to shreds sooner rather than later at this rate. I dared a glance back towards the king and screamed in terror when I saw that he was now gaining on me.

Pushing myself to go faster, I ran with all my might, the sand beneath my feet stinging and making it harder for me to gain any momentum. My lungs felt like they were going to burst, but I refused to let them slow me down.

With a surge of newfound energy borne from the will to stay alive, I pushed forward, my mind racing to find an alternate solution. I could not lead him to the castle where innocent humans might be put in danger, so I circled around to the gardens, hoping against hope that by some miracle, he would change back.

"Kadin!" I screamed, hoping he would hear me. Kadin was a Lycan, as all men in Zayed's family were born Lycans. He could help me. We could overpower Zayed and lock him in the silver-coated room. I felt a part of me break inside, realizing my plan had failed. I had hoped to prove I could survive his Lycan form, and eventually last out the full one thousand and one nights. But now, even the light of dawn could not provide the refuge it had previously.

I screamed, hoping and praying for help.

I pushed myself past the gardens and towards the training grounds where I knew the guards trained. Kadin would be there.

"KADIN!" I yelled again, my voice panic stricken as I heard Zayed's growls from behind.

Up ahead, I saw something that made hope bloom in my chest. Guards. And the Grand Vizier. They stood at the end of the gardens, most likely there to survey something of import.

He stood with a stern expression on his face, which became one of utter shock as he and his men began digesting the scene before them. I, the queen of Elamaria, garbed in a warrior's uniform as the Lycan King chased after me.

I saw the Grand Vizier's eyes glow red and wondered if he would shift into his own Lycan to prevent Zayed from wreaking havoc. But he was an old man, and most likely not strong enough, even in his Lycan form, to overpower the king.

"Get Kadin!" I yelled out desperately, hoping we could somehow restrain Zayed until we figured out what was wrong.

The Grand Vizier's eyes held a mixture of surprise and concern as he took in the sight of the Lycan King gaining on me. With a solemn nod, he raised his hands, and the guards drew their swords.

Zayed's Lycan form gave a guttural roar behind me, and fear gripped my heart. He was going to kill everyone. Unless Kadin arrived here.

I ran with all my might, reaching the guards with a stitch in my side.

"We—need—Kadin!" I gasped out, face red and breathing hard. The Grand Vizier's expression grew even more grave, and he barked an order to one of his men.

But it was not the order I had expected.

"SEIZE HER! Hold her down!"

My world seemed to spin on its axis as the guards turned their swords towards me.

I could see the confusion and indecision in their eyes, but they obeyed nonetheless.

"I am queen!" I gasped out, taking a step back inadvertently closer to the Lycan King who sought to end my life.

"Foolish woman! I told you your days were numbered! The rebel factions are closing in. They infiltrated the palace walls just last night. We do not have the resources to protect the monarchy and prevent a famine. It is time, queen," he spat my title out in derision, "for your reign to end. Long live King Zayed!" The Grand Vizier crowed and gestured for his men to seize me.

I drew my sword, ready to defend myself. Zayed's growls behind me were growing closer and I could hear the clash of swords from the training grounds afar.

I counted ten men closing in on me, ready to grab me and kill me or offer me up to the Lycan King.

The guards advanced, their swords gleaming ominously in the morning light. My options were dwindling, and fast. My eyes darted between the approaching men and the ever-nearing Lycan King. There was no escape, but I would not go down without a fight.

They lunged as one towards me and I dodged, ducking low and swiping my sword at their ankles in a graceful clockwise motion while crouched low on the ground. Half of them stumbled and fell, giving me the opening I needed to escape the ambush created to capture me.

With fear writhing in my veins, I thrust my sword through the air, narrowly missing another guard, his eyes wide with shock at my sudden attack. But there was no time for hesitation, as the remaining guards surged forward, I raised my sword high and aimed to attack.

Desperation fueled me as I parried and danced with my enemies, each blow a gamble of life or death. A sudden swift pain in my side made me cry out, and I jerked back from the blade that had sliced deeply into my left side.

The Lycan King's roar reached my ears. I fell back against the chest of a guard who clamped his hands around my arms.

"Hold her!" the Grand Vizier commanded. "Offer her up to your king. The curse demands a sacrifice. Her time has come!"

The burning pain in my side increased ten-fold as one guard on either side held me firm, my arms spread wide in their relentless grip. The ringing in my ears was growing louder with each passing moment as the time to end my life neared.

I tried to struggle out of their grip and cried out in pain when all it did was widen the gash in my side.

I looked up to see that Zayed was upon us, his eyes reflecting a rage like no other. I looked up at him, his Lycan looking down at me with an inferno of beastly rage in his eyes.

He let out another loud roar that seemed to reverberate through the entire kingdom. Even the guards holding me trembled in fear.

"Zayed," I whispered, my voice barely above a breath as pain lanced through my body. My vision was dimming from the blood loss. "Please, fight ...the....curse," I rasped out. "We can do it... together," I pleaded.

Zayed paused for a moment, his ears twitching as he heard my plea. His angry red eyes softened slightly before he let out another agonizing roar that pierced the air and made the guards tighten their grip on my arms.

I felt my strength slipping away, my blood pooling around me in crimson puddles. I looked up at Zayed once more, desperation etched on my face. "Zayed," I begged him with my eyes raised to meet his gaze. "I love you," I whispered, a tear, filled with my impending heartbreak, making its way down my cheek.

The Lycan King paid me no heed, letting out a triumphant growl when he raised his claw into a high arc, ready to rip into me and end my life. I looked up at him, knowing that now was not the time to cower in fear. I would face death head on. Like the warrior I was. Like the queen I wished to be remembered as. The one who tried to break the curse.

Being brave does not mean the warrior does not fear death; it means that despite your fear, you meet it with eyes wide open, knowing that in the moment of your final breath, you have lived fully and without regret.

Ashad's words echoed in my ears, and I steadied myself.

His claws came down and I braced myself for the impending blow that would mean the unwelcome embrace of death.

Chapter 31

But it never came. The guard next to me gave a yelp of pain and released me. I turned in surprise to see Zayed's claws embedded deep within his chest. Blood pooled in his mouth and fell in torrents down his body as with a swift jerk, the Lycan brought his claws down the length of his victim's body, nearly splitting the man in half.

The guard was still holding my right arm in a vice-like grip.

The Grand Vizier stared at the commotion, transfixed, his eyes wide with shock. Even the guards around me had forgotten their mission of capturing me in the face of the Lycan King's rampage. I took a few steps back, wondering if I should run and then I watched as Zayed turned to the other guard who had been holding me. With a mighty growl that made the ground beneath us shake, he charged towards the man with jaws wide open. I watched in horror as the Lycan King's canines dug deep into the man's neck, severing it off his shoulders with a quick jerk. The snapping of breaking bones and muscle made my stomach churn. The guard's head landed close to my feet, sliced clean off his neck more effectively than a blade slicing through butter.

The remaining guards, realizing the danger they were in, turned their swords towards their king, hoping to fend off his wrath. But Zayed paid them no heed, his angry gaze now on me.

I stumbled and fell to the ground, unable to stay upright. Too much blood loss. My clothes were soaked through due to the gash in my side.

As Zayed approached me, his claws and jaws still dripping with blood, I knew my time was running out. I looked up at him, trying to convey everything I felt within me--my love, my regret, my strength, and my desperation to live. To be with him.

He snarled, lips pulling back to reveal bloody canines. And then he began to shift. My eyes widened in surprise, eyes flitting towards where the sun now hung high in the sky. The curse...had we broken it? Or was he forcing the shift? None of this was making any sense.

Zayed's transformation was quick and intense. The muscles of his face reformed, reshaping as he transitioned from a demonic creature to a human. His eyes lost their feral glow, becoming kind and familiar once more. I watched with a mix of relief and bewilderment as Zayed turned into the man I had fallen in love with, the man who was my husband.

His snarls morphed into the angry grunts of a man, his absolutely furious gaze going to the guards who had been attacking me.

"Hurting the queen is treason," he stated ominously, eyes filled with cold palpable fury, moving towards me brusquely with his body covered in tatters of his fine silk garb soaked in blood.

He bent down, cupping my face in his hands. It was the last thing I remembered as darkness consumed me. The tender look on his face, the gentle grip of his hands cupping my cheeks. The smell of him as he embraced me. I might die from blood loss, but it was better than dying at his hands. To die in his arms was a tolerable way to go.

I awoke in my bed, Zayed's hand smoothing away the hair at my temple.

When he saw my eyes flutter open, he gently leaned forward, bringing me into the comfortable warmth of his arms.

"You are awake," he whispered into my shoulder.

"What happened?" I croaked out, trying to move away from him. I hissed in pain as the burning on my right side reminded me I was injured.

"Careful," he admonished, moving back so I could lay back in bed. "The doctor has stitched your side, but you need to avoid any activity that might pull the stitches open." He motioned to my side that was heavily bandaged.

"The-the curse?" I rasped, my voice barely audible as I paid my injury no mind. The curse was more important.

Zayed's expression tightened, his eyes darkening.

"Never play foolishly with your life again, Amara," he whispered harshly. "You nearly died."

"I survived," I responded.

"If I had not been able to fight off the urge to kill, if I had not been able to wrest control from my Lycan, you would already be dead," he replied angrily, his eyes a furious maelstrom of emotions.

"You controlled your Lycan?" I asked, eyes wide with relief.

"I did," he assented with an incline of his head. "They hurt you. Spilled your blood. And it awakened a part of me I had not known could exist inside my Lycan form. My human side. The side that was your husband, tasked with protecting you." His hand went to rest against the side of my face.

"I do not need protection," I responded evenly. "I am capable of protecting myself."

Zayed sighed, his expression softening as he looked at me. "You are as fierce as the sandstorms that consume whole caravans, Amara. You might not need protection—but I would like to be the calm to your storm, the one who stands by you, shielding you from the harsh elements that would wear you down. Let me protect you, not because I doubt your strength, but because that is what I want to do." He gave me a half-smile, his eyes conveying a mixture of love, concern, and determination. "Because I love you too."

My eyes widened in surprise as he bent down to place a gentle kiss on my lips. He had heard me, even in his Lycan form. I had reached him. Relief poured through me, like warm butter melting inside of me and bringing forth emotions I had never felt before.

When he pulled back, I looked into his eyes and saw the truth in his words. He did care for me. Deeply. And despite the dangers that lurked around us, I felt a sense of safety just being here with him.

"I love you more than life itself, Amara," he whispered, drawing me closer to him in his strong arms. We were so close now that we were breathing the same air. "I promise to fight by your side until our final breath."

"Why did you not shift back when dawn came?" I queried, looking up at him earnestly.

"I do not know the answer," Zayed responded in measured tones, his own confusion evident. "That has never happened before. It might have been the sedative, or something else entirely." He scowled at me, pressing me possessively against his body so that my head went to rest on his shoulder. "This is what I mean when I say we do not know the full complexities of the curse. You took a great risk. One that could have proven fatal."

"We need to break the curse," I whispered brokenly into his shoulder.

Zayed shook his head, pulling back to rest his forehead against mine.

"I can control my Lycan, Amara. Due to what happened earlier today, I am able to remain lucid in my Lycan form. And—" His voice broke, so overcome with emotion was he in that moment. My arms around his shoulders tightened.

"And?" I prodded tentatively.

"It rained. We were blessed with scant rain. The first time since our wedding," he whispered hoarsely, his voice belying a hope and relief that reflected how worried he was for his kingdom.

A gasp of relief escaped my lips. Maybe...just maybe, the curse was weakening. We could see this through. I felt it in my bones.

We clung to each other with a fierce desperation, our bodies pressed together in a desperate attempt to merge into one. The threat still loomed over us, but in this fleeting moment, as I lay battered and bruised in his embrace, the weight of our burden lifted. Here, in the safety of each other's arms, we were just two souls seeking temporary solace from the chaos and danger that surrounded us. But even as we held on tightly, I knew that at any moment it could all come crashing down again.

We stood dressed in expensive clothes made of the softest silk. I was in a light pink skirt with voluminous net petticoats and an embellished pink shirt embroidered with silver sequined floral patterns. Zayed stood next to me in a light gold tunic and trousers, interwoven with gold thread.

We looked out at the emirs and chieftains who had all assembled here for the annual gathering which signified their allegiance to Zayed. My eyes sought out the tribal chieftain of the mountains. Zayed had told me about how shaky the truce was between them. The Grand Vizier, who had been dealt with severely for his part in trying to hold me down for Zayed to kill, suspected that it was the tribes in the mountains funding the rebel factions within our kingdom.

They had a motive. Revenge for what was done to an offspring of their nobles. Namely the nephew of the current chieftain. The bastard son of the chieftain's brother was mercilessly killed by Zayed's father. My eyes tracked the man next to him, his brother. The one who had every reason to hate the crown. Both brothers stood tall and proud, clad in the intricate garb of their mountain tribe. Their hair flowed like a river down their backs, framing faces that bore traits of strong noses and broad faces. Traits passed down through generations. Traits that had probably been evident in Zayed's younger brother.

The chieftain had streaks of gray in his inky-black hair while his brother looked to be no more than forty years of age. He must have been very young when he had been with Zayed's mother. It was not lost on me that the man had not married. Maybe it really had been true love rather than a passing fancy on his end.

My eyes never left the mountain chieftain, who watched us with a mixture of curiosity and caution. We both knew that any misstep could spell disaster for our fragile truce. I sought Zayed's hand and he did not shy away from intertwining our fingers in front of the important dignitaries as if to say, "We are in this together."

It was a bold statement, signifying what I meant to him. And in turn what my true position was within the kingdom. His queen in every sense of the word.

As we stood there, I could feel the weight of all the expectations on us. On Zayed as the ruler of a desert kingdom that was battling a curse and a rebellion, and on me as his queen, who had to be strong enough to support him while navigating through this web of complex politics. But for once, I felt ready. The fear of my impending death that used to grip my heart and paralyze my mind had been replaced with a sense of purpose.

Zayed squeezed my hand gently, a silent promise that he was right there with me, no matter what came our way. I looked up at him, seeing the love and fierce determination in his eyes. We were not just two souls seeking temporary solace, but two people who had found their strength in each other and would do anything to protect their kingdom, their love, and their future together.

"The treaty must be signed today," Kadin's voice rang out from the other end of the throne room. "Then we shall feast to celebrate the renewal of our alliances."

A voice spoke up, it was the chieftain of the mountains.

"King Zayed, our alliance has always been based on mutual trust and beneficial trade. We require the wheat you grow in your oasis, and you require the fruits our valley in the mountains has in abundance. However, my sources have informed me your kingdom is about to experience a food shortage. The majority of your crops have already come up infested by locusts." The chieftain's eyes went briefly to me. "Also, your alliance with the Kingdom of Assar is no doubt severed seeing as you planned to marry their widowed queen and will not be able to follow through."

My hand in Zayed's went slack. This was news to me. My eyes shot to him and he shot me an apologetic look before looking back at the chieftain. "Chieftain Lamar," Zayed said, his voice steady. "There has been a misunderstanding. I can assure you, my alliance with the widowed Queen of Assar did not depend on a union through marriage. However, I fail to understand how that specific alliance would influence your decision?"

"Assar has some of the most fertile lands, an abundance of food, a promise of bountiful yields from acres upon acres of crops. Through our alliance, we could reap the benefits of trade with Assar as well.

Chieftain Lamar's gaze hardened, his voice dropping to a dangerous tone. "And now that you have broken this alliance, what assurances do I have that an alliance with you would be mutually beneficial for my people?"

A hush fell over the gathered dignitaries as they exchanged whispers among themselves. The air thickened with palpable uncertainty. Chieftain Lamar had quite efficiently created doubt in the minds of the Bedouin leaders and emirs (lesser kings) of small tribal pockets scattered across the fringes of the desert.

Zayed's eyes met mine, and I could see the worry in them. He knew as well as I did that the kingdom was on the brink of disaster, and this new development would only make matters worse. But it was not the time to show weakness. We had to be strong, for our people, for our kingdom.

"Rebel factions are on the rise, working to overthrow your reign," Chieftain Lamar continued. "At this time, we believe that an alliance with you might prove unstable at best, catastrophic at worst. I am a leader, and must consider the welfare of my people and of future generations." He paused, scanning the room to make sure he had everyone's attention.

I grit my teeth. Chieftain Lamar was said to be funding the rebel factions, if what the blithering fool of a Grand Vizier said was true.

"It rained the other day," I spoke up finally, unable to hold back my words any longer. "Chieftain Lamar, surely the rains will bring a reliable harvest. How could allying yourself with the most powerful shifter prove to be disadvantageous?" I challenged with a raised eyebrow.

Chieftain Lamar threw his head back and let out a loud booming laugh.

"Powerful shifter? Please child, I am more well-versed than you on the abilities of your husband. As long as you stand before me, he is fair game to be overthrown."

Chieftain Lamar flexed his hand, extending claws from his fingernails. I nearly took a step back in surprise. So all of these leaders standing before me were shifters.

"I might not be a Lycan, but even my wolf could challenge him and take over the kingdom if he remains unstable."

I raised my eyebrows in surprise and looked to Zayed for confirmation.

"If a shifter challenges me and wins in combat, he has a right to the throne," Zayed said in an undertone as he leaned towards me. Then he let my hand go and stepped away from his throne, walking down the steps with purposeful strides.

"Chieftain Lamar, let us dispense with the formalities then." His tone held both allure and danger as his voice rumbled like distant thunder, carrying on a low whisper that permeated with barely concealed raw power. The intensity of his words hung in the air, crackling with energy like an electric storm on the horizon. Every syllable was laced with a primal force that made my skin tingle and my heart race.

Warning bells went off in my mind. He stood before the emirs and chieftains, tall and proud demanding attention and respect, exuding a commanding presence that could not be ignored. And then before my very eyes, his body began to contort, limbs twist and bones breaking as he shifted. His muscles spasmed uncontrollably, the veins beneath his skin darkening and bulging as if they carried molten iron instead of blood. His fingers, trembling and splayed wide, began to elongate, bones cracking and reforming with sickening snaps. The fingernails blackened and stretched into wicked, curved claws, glistening in the firelight.

Zayed's back arched unnaturally, and the sound of his spine rearranging itself echoed loudly—vertebrae popping one by one as they stretched and contorted. The flesh on his back tore in places, revealing sinew and new muscle growing beneath, knitting together stronger and more fearsome than before.

His jaw unhinged, elongating painfully as his teeth were replaced by sharp, glistening fangs that dripped with saliva. That face that looked at me with so much love contorted, the bones beneath his skin shifting with wet, grinding sounds, pushing his nose forward into a snout. Those beautiful green eyes burned with an unholy light, a piercing red that seemed to sear through the darkness, glowing with the predatory power of a Lycan.

Hair erupted from every pore, coarse and dark, spreading across his body in uneven bursts. The skin beneath it stretched and rippled, taut over growing muscle and bone. His chest expanded, his ribs cracking outward, creating a hulking frame that radiated raw power.

He let out a scream that morphed into a beastly roar, his voice caught somewhere between human and feral dominance. As his legs buckled, his knees snapped backward with a sickening crunch, reshaping into digitigrade limbs built for speed and lethal precision. His feet, once human, split and reformed into massive, clawed paws, each step sinking deep into the earth as if even the ground feared his presence.

Blood dripped from his shifting form, steaming in the air around us. Each change seemed to tear him apart before rebuilding him, a process so excruciating it would have shattered a lesser being.

When the transformation finally slowed, the man—no, the beast—stood tall, towering and monstrous. The air around him crackled with energy, a tangible aura of dominance and ancient power. His massive frame was cloaked in fur as black as the void, his muscles rippling with strength that could fell mountains.

The Lycan King raised his head to the heavens, releasing a deafening howl that shook the very foundation of the palace. In that moment, he was no longer man or beast but something greater, something primal, something that commanded submissiveness. And in that moment I understood why the lesser shifters pledged allegiance to him.

The Lycan King was destined to rule.

Chieftain Lamar's eyes widened in shock, disbelief coloring his face as he watched the Lycan King take purposeful calculated strides towards him. This was not a Lycan that had gone half-mad with feral rage.

This was a Lycan in full control of his senses, capable of using every asset at his disposal to fell his prey. And currently, his prey was Chieftain Lamar.

Chapter 32

"The situation called for a swift response," Zayed murmured, leaning back in his chair as Kadin paced in front of him.

"You shifted, practically declaring that anyone who wished to challenge you for the crown could!" Kadin exclaimed agitatedly, pulling at the ends of his hair that brushed against the tops of his shoulders.

He looked visibly upset. Disturbed.

"We might have had an all-out war on our hands," Kadin pointed out, turning to face Zayed. "We are lucky Chieftain Lamar did not rise to your bait and backed down."

Zayed smirked, eyes steady on his cousin.

"He was bound to back down because he knew that his wolf was no match for my Lycan." Zayed shrugged. "The rumours that my Lycan was unstable were also quelled thanks to the shift."

Kadin expelled a breath, running a hand through his dark locks before looking at me.

"The rumors have subsided, but tensions are still high," he said, a frown creeping onto his face as he stressed on the precarious situation we were in. "Rebel factions within the kingdom are still attempting to overthrow our rule. We cannot afford to let our guard down. Not to mention that the news is spreading like wildfire that the Grand Vizier is soon to be stripped of his title after standing trial." Kadin sighed. "Father knows how to keep the nobles happy. Happy nobles means more people of influence on our side." Kadin looked at Zayed pointedly before shooting me an apologetic look. "I am not excusing what he did. But he did it thinking it was for the good of the kingdom." Kadin expelled a breath. "My father has worked his entire life for the kingdom. He knew his role. The second brother...the spare...charged with aiding the king in maintaining peace."

I bit my lip, wondering if maybe the Grand Vizier had grown up to be an utterly jealous man. Perhaps even covetous of the title of king?

"While keeping the nobles happy is important," I cut in swiftly, "It should not be at the cost of the well-being of the common man. After all," I added primly, "they are more in number than the nobles."

I raised a brow and looked at Zayed who was glowering at Kadin.

"You are upset for what I have done to my uncle, your father. But trying to hurt the queen must have consequences. I cannot risk someone trying to do so again."

Kadin stared at Zayed, his gaze full of sincerity.

"If the situation were not as volatile as it currently is, I might have not said anything. But he is deeply remorseful. Especially after the rain fell and he realized the curse is weakening." Kadin shot me a rueful smile. "Contrary to what may be believed, our family does not relish in the murder of innocent young girls. It was a necessity deemed by my father to protect the monarchy and the peace of the kingdom. I have been against it since day one, for the record."

I cleared my throat uncomfortably, not wanting to voice that to an extent, I agreed with the Vizier. If Zayed had not been able to control his Lycan, if my survival meant the ruin of the kingdom, I would be ready to sacrifice myself.

But there was another way. Every curse had a means to break it...loopholes existed in the strongest of magic. And I sincerely hoped we had found one.

"We need to find out who is financing these rebel factions and put a stop to it before things escalate further," I finally said, changing topics. "It is mere speculation that the mountain tribes are behind it. Without concrete proof not much can be done."

Kadin spoke up, his voice firm. "I will investigate the finances of Chieftain Lamar and other key players in these alliances. It may take time, but it needs to be done meticulously."

Zayed nodded in agreement, his eyes fierce as they locked onto mine.

"The rebels must not be allowed to gain any sort of advantage, and we must root out every last one...the rebellion must be subdued. Civil unrest is something we cannot afford currently."

I looked at Zayed and spoke my next words very carefully.

"By subdue you mean to use force on them. The answer is not in violence or suppression. These are our people. Treat them as such. True leaders engage with dissent, understanding that dialogue and compromise strengthen unity. Only tyrants," I spoke with a steady voice, eyes on Zayed, "wield force to silence opposition, believing that subjugation equals control—when in truth, it breeds resentment and division."

Kadin and Zayed exchanged a look. And I knew that my words had struck a chord.

"The rebels cannot be negotiated with, Amara. They are those who are angry because their daughters have either died at the hand of the crown or they are afraid their daughters might be next," Kadin explained gently. "Our king purposefully chose to keep the extent of the curse a secret. For there are many who would wish to manipulate a feral Lycan for their own means. Many kingdoms and enemies who would manipulate the knowledge of the curse to weaken the crown. So King Zayed chose to let the people hate him, for the greater good of the security of our people. There is no negotiating with those who wish to see our king fall."

I looked at Zayed who stared back at me steadily.

"Let them hate me," Zayed finally stated. "If it means they can sleep comfortably in their beds, if it means that they are protected from those who would otherwise plunder and loot the kingdom, let them hate me. They are unaware of the price, for they have never had to pay it."

I attempted to offer words of comfort to him. Words to assure him that we could break the curse and he did not have to remain the hated king.

There was a knock on the study door, however, and I could not even begin to speak.

When the door opened, in walked guards escorting the Grand Vizier who had silver handcuffs around his wrists and silver chains wrapped around his ankles. I gasped. It was a rather cruel display. Zayed showed everyone that even the Grand

Vizier, a man related to him by blood, was not above the law when it came to his queen.

I understood why he felt the need to do it. But seeing the red welts forming on the old man's wrists made my heart twist painfully.

"My King...My Queen," the Grand Vizier murmured, bowing his head low before falling to his knees before me where I sat across from Zayed's desk.

"Forgive me," he sobbed, hands going to the hem of my elaborate pink dress. "Forgive me, child. I thought there was no other way...I thought you had to die...I thought they all had to die..."

I could see the remorse in his eyes, so different from the cruel determination that had always glinted in them. Was this all an act, or was he sincere?

Kadin stepped forward, looking down at his father and placing a hand on his shoulder. "We all make mistakes, Father. Now is the time to atone for them and make amends."

Kadin squeezed his father's shoulder, attempting to pull him into a standing position. The Grand Vizier however stayed kneeling before me, head bowed low to the ground.

"I tried to harm the queen. The one person who is the heart and soul of our kingdom. The one person who is the heart and soul of our king." The Grand Vizier's eyes went to Zayed, filled with remorse. "She is the one you love. And you nearly lost her because of me."

He sounded sincere. In hindsight, I could not blame him. Had I not too offered myself up initially to Zayed for the betterment of the kingdom? What was the death of one peasant girl, if it meant the kingdom could continue to prosper. But now I held value in the eyes of his uncle, because Zayed loved me. The kingdom could not prosper if ruled by a heartbroken king.

I looked at the Grand Vizier, finally reaching down to gently take his trembling hands in mine. "You and I did not see eye to eye from day one," I began, my voice soft but firm. "But tonight, I want you to understand that I, too, have the good of the kingdom...of the people," I amended quickly, "at the forefront of my mind. So perhaps, we can come together on a common ground to work for a prosperous future?"

Kadin looked at me, his eyes full of thankfulness. "You are being kinder than I would be in this situation," he said, his voice low as he too crouched down next to his father.

"I am not doing this for your sake," I continued, meeting the Grand Vizier's gaze. "But for mine. There is no joy in holding grudges or harboring bitterness." I paused, my heart aching for the man who had made such terrible mistakes, yet still held an ounce of remorse within him. And the courage to ask for forgiveness.

"The world is not black and white, and neither are the people in it. Each person has their own story, their own reasons, their own pain." I squeezed the Grand Vizier's hands gently, a small smile forming on my lips. "And it is only when we begin to understand and empathize with each other's struggles that we can truly hope for a better tomorrow."

The Grand Vizier looked up at me, his eyes filled with gratitude for my forgiveness.

"You are a wise queen," he murmured softly. "My daughter-in-law, you have a heart of gold."

Kadin nodded approvingly at the Grand Vizier's words and helped him to his feet. "We cannot keep dwelling on past mistakes, Father. It is how we learn and grow from them that truly matters." He paused, looking thoughtful. "But more importantly, it is how we are able to forgive and move forward together that makes us stronger as a family, and as a kingdom."

Zayed looked at me, his eyes searching for any sign of hesitation or doubt. Seeing none, he too nodded in agreement. "I second that sentiment," he said quietly, his voice filled with sincerity.

The Grand Vizier finally released my hands and turned to Kadin, placing a hand on his son's shoulder. "You were right Kadin in insisting that she should live." He then turned to face Zayed and I. "You have my word that I shall work with you both to make amends for my transgressions. I promise to do everything in my power to help protect the queen and serve this kingdom with honor and integrity."

My gaze then fell upon the guard who held the chains leading to the handcuffs placed around my husbands uncle. "Release him from his restraints," I ordered.

The chains and handcuffs were removed, and the Grand Vizier was left standing before us, humbled and contrite.

"We must use this opportunity to strengthen our bonds, not weaken them," I continued, my voice firm. "It is only through unity and understanding that we can overcome the challenges facing our kingdom."

The Grand Vizier looked as if a great weight had been lifted from his shoulders. He bowed once more before us, and as I watched him closely, I could only hope my words would lead us all on the path to working together.

The aroma of freshly baked bread and honeyed pastries wafted around us. He held my hand in his as we roamed the stalls, a stole thrown over my head and Zayed dressed in a simple cotton garb much like what my father often wore when venturing into the bazaar to purchase necessities for us. We both looked vastly different, him wearing a fake beard while my head covering and veil provided a means to mask my true identity. Although commoners that filled this bazaar, specifically set up as part of the festival that preceded the Blade-Caller trials, probably would not recognise the king as many had only ever seen him from afar, it was still better to be safe than sorry. There were no depictions of the king outside the palace walls. No murals or statues dedicated to him. How could there be? He killed their daughters. Zayed had sacrificed the love of his people, choosing to hide the truth of his curse merely to ensure that no one would use this information against him. Against the kingdom. But I was hopeful that together we could rectify that.

We revelled in the laughter of those around us; people celebrating the festival that would herald the final test to become a Blade-Caller. I stopped briefly, pausing at a stall as a brilliant deep-emerald pendant caught my attention. It was nothing special. A fake trinket. And yet the fact that the color of the pendant was the exact shade as my husband's eyes made me give pause.

"Would the lady like to try it on?" the stall-owner queried, walking forward eagerly.

I shook my head, taking a step back. Baghel nipped at my heels playfully. I laughed, bending to pat his head. Bringing him along had been risky. But we had managed to put him up in a disguise all of his own. His beautiful pristine white coat had been splattered with deep shades of brown. I stood to look at Zayed who was speaking to the peddler who had been trying to sell his trinkets to me. With a smile, Zayed stepped away from him and looked at me, warmth in his gaze.

"Dressing like a commoner and roaming the city of Ilm with you has its merits," Zayed murmured softly, reaching for me and holding me against his side. Leaning down to whisper in my ear he said, "You look beautiful amongst the backdrop of the festivities. And I thoroughly enjoyed dancing with my wife."

I smiled up at him, recalling his firm embrace as we danced together in the middle of the town square under a colorful canopy of silk to shield us from the scorching sun. It was such moments that truly allowed love to flourish. Moments without titles or expectations.

"Here we are, just two people, enjoying a festival," I acknowledged as Zayed stopped at a cart filled with pastries.

I had to hold back the grin on my face when he was reprimanded by the baker for picking up a pastry and not paying.

Zayed dug into the pockets of his trousers, reaching for money with an uncomfortable expression.

It was then that I realized this man had probably never been in such a situation where he had to count out money and pay. He probably had servants and men in the palace charged with such tasks. I watched him, warmth blooming in my chest as he counted out the gold coins, handing them over before placing the pastry into my hands.

"For you...My Queen," he said with a smile.

I took a bite, letting the delicious sweet honeyed flavor dance across my tongue. I held up the pastry for him so he could also take a bite.

The softness of his smile as he enjoyed the confection was all I needed to let my guard down and let our love for each other shine through.

"This is what life is truly about," I whispered into his ear, feeling the warmth of his breath as he listened to my every word. "These small moments, where two souls connect and find joy in something as simple as a sweet bakery item."

The king, dressed as a common man, wrapped his arms around me, pulling me close and pulling me away from the busy crowd.

"I promise you, my love," he began, his eyes gleaming with emerald intensity. "I will do everything within my power to ensure that we never lose sight of these moments."

I looked deep into his eyes and could see the sincerity. It was as if he was vowing to treasure me forever.

Chapter 33

As we continued to roam, we came across a group of street performers. They were an odd bunch, but their talent was undeniable. Zayed pulled me closer, and we watched as the performers twisted and turned in ways I never thought possible. I leaned into Zayed, enjoying the feel of his arm around my waist.

My eyes widened in amazement as a performer held a blazing torch up to his face, expertly manipulating the flames to create the illusion of breathing fire. The heat radiated off of him, warming my skin and adding to the spectacle. The crowd around us gasped and cheered.

And then to my surprise, the performer came towards us, offering up the torch for anyone interested to learn a new trick. I looked at Zayed, my eyes beseeching.

"I would like to try," I informed him, hoping it was safe for me to do so. I would have to remove the veil over my my mouth.

Zayed let out a huff of exasperated laughter.

"Why am I not surprised you wish to try something as dangerous as manipulating fire?" He shook his head and then nodded towards the performer in defeat. "Go on then. Let us see if you can learn a new skill today." Zayed leaned down, lips close to my ear. "We should be fine. No nobles are gathered here and there is no harm in revealing your face for a few moments."

With trepidation, I stepped forward, my hand trembling slightly as I extended it towards the torch. The performer guided the wooden torch gently into my hand, his eyes watching me intently. I could feel the heat radiating off the fire, my heart pounding in my chest.

"It is all in the grip and control," the performer advised, his voice a soothing presence amidst the backdrop of the festival. "Trust your instincts and let the fire be an extension of yourself."

I swallowed hard, taking a deep breath and attempting to steady my nerves. A sudden gust of wind whipped through the crowd, threatening to extinguish the flame.

The flame flickered for a moment before steadying once more.

I lifted the torch towards the sky, manipulating it slowly as the performers had shown me. The flame danced in the air, a bright orange beacon. Slowly I reached for the bottle of spirits, taking a sip. I swished the high-proof, highly flammable alcohol in my mouth, the sharp, biting taste filling my senses. It was a strange feeling, almost like holding fire in my mouth, but I reminded myself that this is the first step.

"No swallowing," my instructor said. "Just hold it, let it sit there."

I complied, fighting the urge to swallow.

I look at the torch flickering in front of me. It was mesmerizing, the way it danced.

The liquid in my mouth felt heavier now.

"One more deep breath through your nose," my instructor advised.

I complied and then I blew.

The alcohol shot from my mouth in a smooth, steady stream, and the moment it hit the flame, I was mesmerized by an explosion of light—a blinding burst of fire erupted in front of me. My breath caught in my throat in a mix of awe and fear, but I held my ground as triumph surged through me. I did it.

The flames twisted and curled in the air, their warmth licking my face, but I did not flinch. My body trembled with excitement. I had learned a new skill today.

"You did it. Do not let the fire control you. You control the fire."

The words said by the performer, who was also my teacher, rang in my ears.

I lowered my hands, taking in the sight of the flame fading back into the air, feeling the heat from the fire and the rush of power that comes with it. It felt almost like a secret connection between me and this wild, untamable force.

The people around me were clapping as the torch was taken from my hand and the performers asked if anyone else would like to learn. I turned to look at Zayed.

Zayed's eyes widened in surprise and admiration. "You are remarkable, my love," he said, his voice tinged with wonder. He pulled me close, his arms wrapping around me protectively as we watched the rest of the performance.

I leaned back against him, letting myself revel in his embrace. For only as a commoner could he embrace me so affectionately in front of so many people.

Revealing how much he truly cared for me was dangerous.

Zayed had told me, in no uncertain terms, that if it ever seemed like I meant too much to him, enemies would seize on that information, using it as leverage to strike against him.

"In this world," he had said, "your value is a weapon—too much of it, and you become a target."

Yet, at the same time, it was vital for everyone to understand that I held some level of importance in his life.

"People need to know you are not just a pawn; you are a piece on the board worth protecting."

It was a precarious balancing act, a tightrope walk between perception and reality. Let them know enough to make them afraid to cross me, but not so much that they would see my value as a means to threaten the king.

"The line between power and peril is thinner than you think," Zayed had warned me the other night, his gaze heavy with the weight of the game we were both caught in.

A game where every move was weighted, every gesture calculated, and every alliance or betrayal echoed across time. In this world, you were not just a player; you were a piece in a centuries-old struggle for control, a struggle that will shape the fates of those who follow.

"You do not just protect the crown. You protect the legacy of those who wore it before you, and those who will wear it when you are gone."

"The stakes are eternal, and the consequences are never truly our own—they ripple outward, for generations to come."

His words from the night before rang true.

But here, in a corner of the city of Ilm, as we watched a caravan of travelers perform tricks, we could forget the weight of the crown on our shoulders. And the curse that loomed over us.

For a moment, we were just two people in love, sharing a simple moment.

I knew that regardless of the danger, our love was worth fighting for. As the performance drew to a close, Zayed led me towards a tavern, away from the noisy crowd. He took my hand in his, and I marveled at how even in this simple gesture, I could feel the strength and security that radiated from him.

As we entered the tavern, the cacophony of noise outside faded away, replaced by the soft murmurs of the patrons and the clink of glasses inside. We were led to a small, intimate booth in the corner.

Zayed took the seat next to me, his hand never leaving mine. He looked at me seriously after we had ordered our drinks.

"Why did you not buy the necklace I saw you observing?" he asked seriously.

I shrugged nonchalantly.

"Growing up a poor man's daughter," I said carefully, "I never had money to buy such things. Trinkets were not important, food was."

His face became solemn and he leaned in close.

"Your mother was a Blade-Caller...your father used to work in the palace..." His brows were furrowed in confusion and I could see him trying to make sense of my words.

"My mother could no longer pursue her career as a Blade-Caller after she gave birth to us," I explained carefully, looking at Zayed. "After conceiving, she had to leave the profession she loved so much. And while the Blade-Callers often welcome women back into their fold once they have finished birthing and rearing children, my mother did not go back. So we had to survive off of my father's salary which was cut in half after he retired from his work at the palace," I ended, hoping Zayed would not push the matter further.

Zayed looked at me, his face tilted as he stared at me.

"Why did she not go back?" he queried.

I cringed, knowing I could not lie to him. I swallowed.

"My mother...was sick. We do not know what ailed her. Only that she often took to her bed, unable to care for me or my sister. It was not an ailment of the body...but of the mind," I explained feebly, looking away. "A good portion of my father's earnings went to buying medicines for her in hopes she would get better. But...she never did," I admitted, staring at a spot on the far wall. I swallowed convulsively. "She loved us. It was not her fault..."

Zayed expelled a breath, his fingers coming to gently cup my chin and force me to look at him. There was no judgement in his eyes. And that made me sigh in relief.

"I am sure she was a wonderful soul," he murmured.

"You...are not afraid I might contract the same ailment?" I queried blankly.

Because many whispers around us had echoed the sentiment. Neighbors had said a weakness of the mind was inherited. That her daughters would be the same. And to be honest, only the future would tell us if what they said was true. But the prospect often loomed in the back of my mind, like a spectre of ill-will waiting to be acknowledged.

Zayed shook his head.

"I do not think ailments of the mind are passed down in that manner. But even if they are...even if you did become like her...I would still love you," he replied honestly. "I love your fierceness, your determination, and your soft side. I would love that side of you as well because we have to learn to accept each other fully. Just like how you have accepted me despite my curse."

I closed my eyes, emotions surging through me.

"Curses can be cured." I swallowed audibly and opened my eyes after speaking the sentence.

"And if they could not, you would still accept me. Just like how I would accept you," he replied deftly, eyes boring into mine.

A fear I had never voiced was admitted here in an obscure shadowy corner of a tavern I had passed many times while traversing the city of Ilm but had never entered. And here, in this corner, I felt as if a burden had been lifted from my shoulders. A fear that had often gripped me in my darkest moments had dissipated into nothing, leaving acceptance in its wake. Is this what it felt like to be loved unconditionally by a partner?

"I have something for you," he whispered, knuckles grazing against my cheek before he reached into his pocket and pulling out a small velvet pouch. Zayed opened it slowly, revealing a single emerald-green gemstone pendant. The very same one I had been observing earlier. It shimmered with a light all its own in the dimly lit room.

"You bought it," I murmured, my eyes rising to meet his.

Zayed smiled. "I did. I could not help but want to purchase it for you."

I smiled shyly, turning so that he could tie the simple leather strand around my neck.

"I adore it," I murmured, cupping the emerald pendant in my palm as I turned to face him once he had clasped it securely. "And I shall never take it off," I proclaimed proudly.

"You...a queen who has access to the most treasured jewels of the kingdom...are treating this trinket as if it is a priceless stone." Zayed chuckled.

I looked at him seriously.

"To me it is priceless because you purchased it for me. And because," I added seriously, "it is the exact same shade as your deep green eyes I often get lost in."

Zayed's smile sobered.

"I have met many women. They all want expensive jewels, the finest of furs, the biggest diamonds. You..." he trailed off looking at me as if I were an enigma. "Do not," he ended, folding his arms together.

"The only thing I want is you," I said seriously. "And for us to rule with kindness and compassion. I wish to be remembered not for the jewels or dresses I wore.

Not for the finery adorned on my person, but for the kindness I showed others. For my prowess on the battlefield, for the victories I brought to my people."

Zayed gazed at me with an intensity that left me breathless. "Your heart is the truest gem of them all. You are the most priceless treasure I could ever hope to possess."

I blushed slightly, glancing away momentarily before returning his loving gaze. "And you are mine," I whispered, feeling a warmth spread through me that had nothing to do with the heat of the sun beating down upon the desert outside.

Zayed bent down, his lips mere inches from mine when the trumpet blew to announce the start of the tests for the Blade-Caller examination. The festival goers would now converge on the training grounds of the Blade-Caller academy to witness the next incoming batch of warriors who would protect the people of Ilm.

And Zayed...Zayed would watch the proceedings as king. Our time as two commoners had come to an end. I watched him pull back, his stoic facade taking over his visage. It was time for my husband to be replaced by the king. And it was time for me to become the warrior I had always strived to be.

Chapter 34

When I stepped into the arena, the ground beneath my feet was hard and un-yielding. The heat of the late-afternoon sun pressed down on me. The crowd had gathered to witness the Blade-Caller trials, an auspicious event that provided entertainment to both commoners and nobles alike. Murmurs rippled through the air, a wave of expectancy that threatened to swallow me whole. Nobody knew that the next contestant was their queen. Yet, the fear of being discovered rattled my nerves. But I kept my head steady, my eyes locked ahead, narrowing the world down to what mattered most—the fight.

The plain cotton of my Blade-Caller outfit clung to my body, simple and un-adorned; no fancy armor to weigh me down. The fabric was worn, faded in places, but it was comfortable, familiar; allowing me to move with a fluidity that heavy armor could never offer. My headwrap was tight, the veil draped over my face, hiding my identity from the crowd and, most importantly, from my enemies who would wish to use my desire to be part of the trials against me. The only thing visible were my eyes—sharp, focused, and determined, as though they alone could speak for me. Could fight for me, perhaps.

I did not need anyone to know who I was. Not then. Not there. Not that day. It was enough for me to know that I had fulfilled the requirements of a warrior. That I was enough, equipped with the skills to be a formidable Blade-Caller. To complete my training was to fulfill an innate determination residing deep within my heart. I wanted to be more than just a queen wearing a crown. I wanted to be a warrior, capable of holding my own in battle, of fighting for what I believed in.

My fingers instinctively curled around the necklace beneath my clothes—the one Zayed had given me. The emerald pendant rested against my chest, a hidden weight I carried with me into the arena. My hand closed around it over the white cotton fabric of my long *kameez*. I gripped it tightly; the coolness of the faux gem grounded me in that moment. I felt the pull of it, a reminder of him, of us.

But I could not afford to think of him then. Not even when his green eyes looked down at me intently, able to spot his queen despite my attempts to remain inconspicuous. Those eyes of his could pick me out in the crowd more efficiently than a hawk identifying its prey in the deepest shadow of the forest—unseen by all, yet never beyond his reach.

The crowd's noise swelled as I walked, a cacophony of voices—from the nobles in their high seats to the common folk gathered along the edges, all eager for a glimpse of the fight, of the strongest warriors who would be tasked with protecting them. Their faces blurred into one mass, but I did not let them distract me. I had trained for that moment, fought in shadows and silence, and that day, I would show them what they never expected.

I felt Zayed's gaze on me from above, perched high on his dais, his presence looming over everything. I could not see his face through the gauzy veil hanging over the canopy to protect him from the sun, but I knew he was watching, his eyes piercing through the veil that hid me. There was always a weight in his gaze, as if he was waiting for me to prove something—not to him, but to the kingdom, to myself.

I raised my chin, my posture tall and sure. There was no room for doubt, no room for hesitation.

The soft thud of my boots was the only sound I focused on as I took my position in the center of the arena. The sun beat down on my back, but I did not flinch. I reached for my blade—simple, unadorned, but deadly in my hands—and drew it in a smooth, fluid motion.

The crowd's cheer grew louder, but I blocked it out, focusing only on the weight of my blade in my grip, the space around me, and the fight that was about to begin.

This was my fight. And I would not falter.

My first opponent stepped forward, her own blade gleaming in the sunlight. We circled each other warily, each of us waiting for the other to make the first move. But I was patient, biding my time, waiting for the perfect opportunity.

She lunged forward, her blade slicing through the air with deadly precision. There was a familiarity in her movements, and I briefly tried to place a face to her style of sword fighting. However, now was not the time to be distracted. I had to focus on the fight.

With a quick flick of my wrist, I deflected her first strike, the metallic clash ringing out into the arena.

And so we began to dance the deadly dance of blades, each strike precise and calculated. Our bodies moved with grace, born from countless hours of practice. The crowd's cheers and gasps were a distinct hum in the background as I focused solely on the fight.

I saw the exact moment when exhaustion began to creep into her eyes, and then the expected split-second hesitation which was all that I needed. With a swift movement, I disarmed her, sending her blade clattering to the ground. But the fight was not over yet. She withdrew her dagger, the silver jagged edge glinting in the sunlight.

With a smirk dancing on my lips, I readied myself as she lunged forward, the dagger aimed at my heart. But I was quicker, sidestepping her attack with a grace that surprised even myself. Using the momentum of her own movement against her, I twisted her arm behind her back, forcing her to drop the dagger with a cry of pain. The crowd erupted in cheers as I stood victorious, my breath coming in quick gasps.

I raised my eyes to look up at where I knew my king sat. And if the gauzy veil that obscured him from view had not been present, I hoped to see a smile on his lips because this was our victory. It occurred to me that Zayed had never truly seen me fight until now. For I had always purposefully kept the extent of my skills a secret from him.

However, in the second moment, my eyebrows snapped together in disbelief as an earth-shattering boom reverberated throughout the arena, sending me to my knees.

I felt my heart sink as I saw great big plumes of smoke rising from the cordoned-off area adorned with colorful silk tents that had been set up for the prominent nobles of the kingdom.

"LONG LIVE THE DAUGHTERS OF ELAMARIA," a voice rang out from somewhere deep in the crowd.

Another boom, bigger this time. Closer.

"NO!" I screamed, looking up at where Zayed sat, the entire dais consumed by bright colorful flames that seemed to dance jeeringly at me. As if to mock me for ever thinking I could have been happy. "ZAYED!" I screamed, ripping my veil from my person to reveal my face as I made a mad dash towards where he was supposed to be. Panic pumped through my veins. He could not be dead. He had to be alive!

In the next moment, I was tackled from behind; the woman I had fought and defeated grabbing me in a desperate attempt to stop me from running towards the inferno that engulfed the dais.

"Stop, it is too late!" she cried, her shockingly familiar voice barely audible over the crackling flames and the chaos erupting around us. But I fought against her hold, my heart racing with panic and disbelief.

"A-Asya?" I croaked out, as I turned to look at her veil-clad face in disbelief.

She looked at me, her eyes full of remorse.

"Amara, the king is dead. You are free. I made a deal with the rebels to let me be here to get you out—"

"My husband," I snarled, twisting in an attempt to free myself from her grasp, "needs me!"

But her grip was too firm, and I was exhausted from exerting myself in the fight. In retrospect, I now realized I had been played. Asya's stamina matched mine. She had purposefully pretended fatigue earlier on in the fight, forcing me to give my all and exhaust myself.

"Let me go!" I shouted, pushing against her with all my strength. But she held on, her grip surprisingly firm despite her earlier defeat. Tears blurred my vision as I struggled against her, my mind unable to comprehend the devastation unfolding before me.

"Amara, we need to go, the rebellion will use the king's death as a means to attack the palace while the monarchy is weak," Asya said frantically, pulling at me. "We must—"

"NO! I WILL NOT LEAVE HIM!" I screamed, wanting to pummel her with my fists until she released me.

I turned to look back at the tent, desperate for any sign of Zayed.

Through the billowing smoke and flames, I could see figures moving frantically, some trying to escape while others seemed to be searching for something—or someone. I prayed for a glimpse of his familiar form emerging unscathed from the fire.

But as the blaze grew fiercer, consuming everything in its path with merciless determination, a sinking feeling settled deep in my chest.

The acrid scent of burning fabric and wood filled my nostrils as I watched in horror. The once majestic dais where Zayed presided now crumbled in on itself, the colorful silks and gauzy veils adorning the dais reduced to ash.

Asya's hold on me tightened, her eyes filled with tears. "Amara, we need to leave now!" she urged, her voice thick with emotion.

But I could not tear my gaze away from the inferno that had taken everything from me.

Chapter 35

Screams erupted from around me as the nobles began to fall one by one. I blinked in confusion, slowly realizing that they were being felled by arrows. This was a massacre of the worst kind. I had told Zayed violence was not the answer. And he had agreed with me. Yet here, the very people I had advocated for were murdering countless people.

Chants filled the air.

"For the daughters of Elamaria."

"For my daughter who rests in the graveyard of the queens!"

"And mine!"

"AND MINE!"

"What is going on?" I asked, my voice hoarse and full of pain.

I had to focus. Even if my heart was breaking in two. I had to focus. Zayed... I could not give in to the dark thoughts. He had to have made it! He could not leave me! We had promised to face everything together! He could not leave me alone!

"The rebellion is taking control," Asya replied firmly. "I am only here to retrieve you and then we leave to live out the rest of our days in peace. Ashad's kingdom will grant us asylum—"

I finally managed to jerk myself free of Asya's grip.

"And what of your betrothed? You expect me to leave my husband—"

"My betrothed has left me for another woman," Asya stated, tilting her chin up a notch defiantly as tears filled her eyes. "He is gone." I watched as a lone tear made its way down her cheek. I stepped forward, trying to bring her into a hug but what she said next made me stop in my tracks. "As is your husband. He is dead. We must leave, NOW."

"My husband is not dead until I see his body," I stated angrily.

He was not dead. He was alive. I turned to look back at the burning dais only to see the fire spreading. Spreading to the civilians still trying to escape the arena.

"And regardless, I am queen. If he is ...gone," I swallowed the painful lump of emotion in my throat, "I will not let his legacy go to waste. I will protect our people." I nodded towards the fire making its way towards the commoners and then the nobles being picked off like flies. In the distance, I could see Kadin attempting, with his guards, to find those responsible for this mess. A handful of guards were trying to ensure a safe evacuation of those trapped inside the arena but it was utter chaos. No one had expected such an attack.

I winced as I saw an arrow hit a young peasant trying to escape.

"Because, to me, it seems like the rebels are too blinded by their hatred for our monarch to think of the common good."

With those words, I took a step back and turned, my eyes tracking the source of the arrows. They settled on the topmost steps of the arena. No, not there....and finally my eyes landed on the food storage edifices still under construction behind the arena. THERE! I recalled the map on Zayed's desk, detailing the construction of these huge granaries and the detailed plan was to create a distribution center nearby.

Warily, I realized only someone who had access to those very same plans could have orchestrated this attack. The screams of my people grew louder, their cries for help piercing through the chaos. Drawing a deep breath, I turned to Asya with a determined gaze. "You have to help me, sister. I—" My voice broke as I tried to voice the words. "I love him."

Asya's eyes widened in surprise and she took a few steps back as if I had physically struck her with my words.

"NO...Amara...he...the Crimson King has killed so many innocent women. You are next on his list!"

I shook my head furtively.

"Sister...all is not as it seems. Please..." I pleaded with her. "Trust me." I looked back at the burning dais. "Help me save my husband and the innocent people trapped in this attack."

From the corner of my eye, I spotted Nora running towards us, her facial veil had fallen away and her head covering was askew. Amidst the chaos, maintaining one's uniform was the last thing on every warrior's mind. Asya turned to look at Nora who stopped in her tracks, her eyes going to me and then to Asya in confusion. I could tell her bewilderment was because she did not recognise Asya as a woman we had trained with. She was a stranger in the arena. For her part, Nora had performed amazingly, winning her trial much to the surprise of everyone who had been watching.

"Nora!" I said quickly. "Gather the rest of the Blade-Callers. it does not matter if they won their trial or not. We need everyone to help evacuate the people to safety. And we need to protect the nobles. Get them to lower ground where they are not easy pickings for the archers."

I pointed to the granaries, huge towering rectangular monuments situated behind the arena. It would take me fifteen minutes, at least, to make it there if I ran as fast as I could.

A sudden barking behind me alerted me to the fact that I would have help.

"Baghel!" I called, watching him run towards me fervently.

I bent down, patting his smooth white coat which had been washed down most likely upon the orders of Zayed.

"Baghel, were you on the dais with Zayed?"

Baghel looked at me with sad eyes before looking at the burning dais. He then looked at me as if to say 'I am sorry'. I held back a sob, holding onto him as if he was my lifeline. Because he was the last thing I had left of Zayed. And though my heart was breaking in two, I knew I had to focus on the task at hand.

"I need to get to the archers. I need to stop them," I said and looked at Asya. "They are going to kill everyone otherwise."

Asya's eyes hardened.

"Then let us go. I will cover you," Asya said with a steely resolve as she took my hand firmly.

We both turned and sprinted towards the chaos, dodging falling debris and weaving through the panicked crowd. I saw a group of Blade-Callers who had been part of the trials today looking around in confusion, unsure what to do.

"Blade-Callers!" my voice boomed out as I moved forward purposefully, lifting my own sword. "PROTECT THE NOBLES AND GET OUR PEOPLE TO SAFETY." I pointed them towards Nora who was directing another group of Blade-Callers who had been gathered on the other side of the arena. I looked back at them, removing my head covering so they could see my features clearly. "That is an order from your queen."

They looked at me in surprise, and I noticed a few who recalled our earlier training together. But I did not have time to further talk with them. Either they would comply, or they would not. I had to keep moving.

So, with those last words, I ran as fast as my feet could carry me, my eyes trained on the archers taking aim and brutally killing those below.

I focused all my energy on reaching the source of the arrows raining down on innocent people. I could hear Nora rallying the other Blade-Callers behind me, their determined footsteps adding to the cacophony of screams and destruction.

I managed to push past the throngs of people, my eyes meeting Kadin's, who helped clear the way for me and Asya.

As we neared the granaries, I saw figures darting among the shadows, their faces obscured by hoods. It struck me then that these were not common rebels seeking justice—they were trained assassins. But I refused to back down. I had a kingdom to protect.

I gripped my sword tightly, ready to face whatever danger lay ahead. But I was taken aback when a few Blade-Callers rushed forward from behind me, Baghel leading the charge.

"We are with you, My Queen," came the whispered response of one of the women as they ran forward to meet the hooded assassins.

I watched as Baghel bit viciously into the leg of one assassin whose sword had been pointed straight at me. His hood fell back and I let out an exclamation of surprise. It was the same man who had instructed me on how to breathe fire.

"The street performers," I breathed out, realizing that they had snuck into the city of Ilm under the guise of performing for the festival.

My stomach twisted in knots. If destroying Zayed had been what they had been after, I had served my husband to them on a silver platter. The words of the Grand Vizier rang in my head as he berated us for being careless. He had been right.

"We have to get to the top," Asya panted next to me, eyes going up to look up towards where arrows were being shot mercilessly.

"Follow me," I murmured, trying to hold onto my emotions which were a hair's breadth away from unraveling and leaving me a blubbering pile on the floor. I blinked back tears and quickly moved towards where I knew a hidden door would reveal a ladder leading to the top.

The sound of clashing metal and cries of pain filled the air as the Blade-Callers engaged in combat with the assassins behind me. Asya expertly deflected an arrow aimed directly at me.

"You were not to harm her!" Asya yelled out, face pointed heavenwards. "The deal was that the queen goes unscathed!"

My heart lurched at the declaration and I looked back to stare at Asya. Exactly what was the true story here? The shrill screams from afar reminded me to stay on task and I quickly pushed open the hidden door, revealing the ladder leading to the top of the granaries.

Without hesitation, Asya and I began our ascent, our muscles burning with every rung we climbed. The commotion below grew distant as we focused on reaching the source of the chaos.

However, the chaos was quickly making its way towards us. A hooded figure appeared, pointing an arrow directly at us. I gulped, looking down only to realize that I would not survive the fall.

As the hooded figure drew back the string of the bow, ready to release the deadly arrow at us, I looked down at Asya, imploring her to finish the task if I died.

"NO!" Asya screamed frantically, grabbing onto me in an attempt to push me out of the way. "NOT HER! WE MADE A DEAL!"

But just as the assassin released the arrow, a blur of white fur appeared behind him and Baghel leaped with a fierce growl, knocking the assassin off balance and causing the arrow to miss its target. The assassin, another man I recognized as one of the street performers, stumbled and fell forward, tumbling down from the great height, passing us and landing with a loud crack against the cool stone floor of the incomplete construction of the granary. I closed my eyes to avoid seeing the gruesome display of his corpse splattered at the bottom.

Breathing heavily, I turned to Asya, who was staring at me wide-eyed and then up at Baghel.

"How did he reach the top so quickly?" Asya queried.

"There must be another way up here," I muttered, my brain searching for answers until it landed upon the most obvious one. "Zayed must have brought him here at some point..." I trailed off realizing that maybe Zayed was protecting me, even in death.

Baghel yelped down at me, as if urging me to hurry. I did not waste any time in resuming my ascent. And as we emerged at the top, we quickly looked around to ensure that there were no adversaries laying in wait. Then slowly, Baghel led us to the door that would lead out to the roof of the rectangular structure which was still incomplete, parts of stone missing along with the lever that would dispense grains to waiting people outside were still under construction.

When we cautiously emerged onto the roof, we were met with a chilling sight—a group of at least ten hooded figures with their bows aimed at the innocent souls below. Their backs were to us, so they were unaware of our arrival.

Asya and I looked at each other, knowing that if our presence had been revealed the assassins would not miss the chance to silence us.

"Stay low," I whispered, my heart pounding in my chest. We sprinted across the rooftop, using the incomplete structure to our advantage as we darted between partial walls and unfinished guard rooms. Once we were close enough to take advantage of the element of surprise, I looked at Asya.

"Now!" I hissed, grabbing Asya's arm and charging towards the group with Baghel at our side. The sword in my hand was shaking, but I steeled myself for the fight ahead. It did not matter if we lost. There were more of them than there were us. But at least the distraction would help save the lives of the nobles below.

Catching them off guard, for it was evident they had expected the man who had attacked us inside the granary to dispose of us, we fought with all our might. Baghel's fangs sank into one of the assassin's arms, causing him to drop his bow in pain. Asya expertly disarmed another with swift movements, leaving him defenseless against my sword.

"Blades have never been my specialty," Asya muttered, overpowering an archer in close quarters by twisting his arm behind his back. He screamed when she twisted and broke his arm. She then bent down to retrieve his bow and sling of arrows. "I can do much more harm with a bow and arrow," she said with a deadly grin, expertly twirling an arrow between her fingers before notching it into the bow. Without blinking, in one fluid motion, she took aim and let the arrow shoot straight into the heart of the man whose blade had come down over me. I had just barely managed to parry his hit. Asya expertly moved back, bringing the assassins within range of her bow and let loose a line of arrows in quick succession. Some missed their mark, but most hit their marks with surprising precision.

"You have been practicing," I commented as if I were talking about the weather, the clash of my blade against my adversaries sword as I blocked an attack clanging in agreement.

"So have you, dear sister," Asya retorted as another arrow of hers sailed by me and into the arm of a man who was attempting to attack me from behind.

I grinned, expertly ducking and delivering a roundhouse kick.

They had been caught off guard, and it was exactly why we were able to fell five of them at first.

I vaguely heard Baghel howling with his own brand of victory before a volley of arrows came hurtling towards us.

As one, Baghel and I quickly moved back, dodging the arrows successfully. They knew now that Baghel and I were formidable in close quarters. Falling back to attack at a distance was their best bet. We quickly moved out of range of the arrows, right until we hit the ledge which would send us to a speedy death. And now, as we stood at the edge of the granary, I felt the first hint of bitter defeat slither through me. Baghel was panting next to me, exhausted from the fight. I too felt as if my lungs were about to burst.

I looked to Asya who was letting arrows fly so quickly, her movements were nearly a blur. Her aim was unerring, her lethal grace serving as a reminder why she was the one who was feared when a bow was put in her hand. But Asya with her arrows, and I, with my deadly blade, and Baghel with his fangs bared, were not enough to completely overpower the dangerous rebels. My heart sank as I counted fourteen of them still standing. I lifted my blade, ready to attack. But I was tired. Exhausted. And I did not know for how much longer I could go on. Looking down below, the bloody sight left me off kilter. Below me were the very same Blade-Callers who had attempted to cover my ascent. But now their bodies were strewn across the desert floor, their white uniforms thoroughly doused in blood. And a stream of hooded men were slowly entering the granary through the hidden door they had seen me enter.

I cursed, turning back to face the archers before me.

"If we die, we die for our people," I said evenly, slicing my blade through the air as a warning.

A battle cry erupted from our trio as we engaged with the assassins, blades clashing and arrows whizzing past.

We charged, my blade finding its rhythm even when the strength in my arms threatened to give out.

Chapter 36

We fought with our backs against the roof's edge, gaining and losing ground in turns. I continued to fight off the onslaught of assassins, parrying their blows with all my might. Determination coursed through me like fire; we needed to keep them distracted until the arena was completely evacuated.

Asya sent her arrows flying, but we both knew more men would be piling out of the hidden door to end our lives. She grabbed one of the arrows from her quiver, aiming it straight at a pile of broken stone close to where the trap door was.

She sent it flying into the pile and I watched as the stones tumbled forward to cover the door. However, we both knew it would only hold the men for so long.

"Baghel," I gasped, dodging one of the archer's arrows. "Over there!" I pointed to the door that was already beginning to tremble under the onslaught of the men pushing against it to reach us.

He obliged, rushing towards the commotion in a sudden burst of speed, howling as he leaped towards another pile of concrete stone nearby, causing the pile to scatter and fall towards the door. I breathed a sigh of relief, knowing he had bought us more time.

Asya and I fought with everything we had left, exchanging powerful blows with our enemies.

Each swing of my blade, each pull of her bowstring, felt like it was slowly sapping our strength away, but we could not afford to falter. I turned briefly to look behind me towards the arena, relieved that the nobles and civilians were being evacuated in an orderly manner. Finally. We needed to hold on just a little bit longer!

Asya let out a cry of defeat and I realized she had exhausted her supply of arrows. But that did not deter her. She swiftly drew her knife and lunged at one of the archers, dropping him to the ground with a murderous slash across his throat. But not before an arrow embedded itself deep in her thigh. I cried out to her but Asya kept fighting, gritting through the pain.

However, my strength was waning; each swing felt heavier than the last.

I felt it in my bones that we were about to be defeated. Though the numbers of our enemies had dwindled faster than a sandstorm disappearing into the horizon, there were still too many. We could not hold them back.

I prayed silently that we had succeeded in buying the innocent people enough time to escape. The hidden door, barred by stones meant to fortify the granaries, cracked and out spilled more adversaries, bloodlust glinting in their eyes.

"Asya," I croaked out, taking a step back and nearing the edge of the roof. "Asya, run. I will hold them off," I whispered.

"I will not leave you, Amara," Asya replied deftly. She held her dagger to her chest, taking a step with me and reaching for my hand. Blood dripped down her thigh. "Not again, sister. We are in this together."

Baghel whined next to me, exhaustion evident on his face. My heart constricted when I saw his pristine white fur matted by blood. He had always been ready to protect me, since the day we had met. I had not expected that loyalty to land him on the edge of death.

"Who is going to save you now, oh great Queen of Elamaria?" taunted one of the men I recognized as one of the street performers. My eyes widened in realization. They had known who I was the moment I had taken off my veil. They had probably been trained to track me and Zayed down. To recognize us instantly.

The tip of his blade came up to rest at my throat, the cool metal resting against my fluttering pulse. I swallowed, looking for an opening. A reprieve. A chance to escape. My eyes met Asya's and I pleaded with her to run now. My eyes flicked to Baghel and then to her. They had a chance. It was me they wanted. Not her. Not Baghel.

"Wait, Darrio. We were not supposed to kill the queen. She is innocent in all of this," came a voice from behind his ranks. "The rebellion only wants the nobles dead."

"SILENCE! She is one of them now!" Darrio spat out, his eyes meeting mine. Eyes full of contempt and loathing. "She might even be carrying his heir in her womb if the rumours amongst the nobles are anything to go by. The king can not keep his hands off her." Darrio leered at me, showing ugly crooked and yellowed teeth. "I might be tempted to see what is so special about her if it were not for the fact that she, and any heir she might be carrying, is better off dead."

The blade moved from my throat and I watched as Darrio prepared to swing it clean across my throat and sever my head from my body. Asya let out a cry of protest, moving to stop him but three men were upon her instantly. Baghel growled and was silenced instantly, a hood thrown over his face as he was man-handled roughly by the men who wished to see us obliterated.

"You promised me she would live!" Asya cried out, struggling against her captors. "I helped you time the fight just so that the king was within the tent when the explosion occurred."

I looked at Asya, realizing the extent of her betrayal. But how had she known I would be in the trials? Did the Head Trainer betray us? Asya caught my sad eyes and looked at me apologetically.

"I am sorry, sister. I did not realize what the king meant to you. Please..forgive me," she gasped out mournfully before swinging her gaze to look at Darrio. "You promised!" she reiterated loudly.

"Promises are meant to be broken," Darrio chuckled, eyes glinting maliciously. "Long live the queen!" he yelled, dark humor oozing from his tone as the blade swung forward at the exact moment that thunder rent through the sky, illuminating everything around us. Immediately I ducked, realizing this was a chance given to me by the divine. I delivered a roundhouse kick to his midsection whilst Darrio was thrown off-kilter due to the unexpected natural phenomena.

"Why you little—" he wheezed, clutching his midsection as his sword fell to the floor. His men rushed forward to overpower me but he held up a hand.

"Do not kill her. She is mine," he hissed, eyes on me. "Restrain her!" he commanded and his men began to close in on me. "It is time to show her what her proper place is. On the ground, with her legs open and submitting to a man!"

Baghel growled, and I narrowed my eyes, reaching for my own dagger. I would kill him before he got a chance. I would slice off his manhood—

Suddenly, like lightning amidst the thunderclouds, a menacing growl reverberated through the roof. I stilled, my heart soaring with joy before my brain told me it must be Kadin.

And when he burst through the hidden trap door right behind where the men had gathered to kill me, the same one Baghel must have used, breaking it clean off its hinges. I let out a cry of relief.

"What is that?!" Darrio exclaimed, turning to stare at the hulking beast taking in the scene before him.

"That," I replied coolly as the beast began to tear into the assassins before him and I realized he had the strength of twenty men, "is my husband."

And then I swiftly raised my dagger, lunging forward and plunging it deep into Darrio's eye, blinding him. His screams of agony were music to my ears. We needed him alive. He was the leader here and would need to be questioned. I moved then, sure the man was incapacitated long enough for me to help free Baghel. I sliced my blade across the neck of one of the men holding back Baghel.

Baghel found his chance and quickly freed himself, twisting and digging his claws into the men who were still holding him captive. Then he pounced on the men who had been holding Asya.

Meanwhile, I readied my blade, looking for Darrio to restrain him only to realize he had escaped. I blinked in surprise. It was almost like he had disappeared into thin air.

"We need some alive!" I called to Asya, realizing we would need to question the underlings now.

My eyes went to Zayed who was tearing into each and every man before him. The Lycan King would not heed my words it seemed.

The screams of terror blared through the air as Zayed, a terrifying beast of vengeance descended upon them with unrelenting force. He ripped their limbs off like they were twigs on a shrub, not bone and muscle. I realized that this was the true extent of the power of the Lycan King. How could anyone ever think to defeat him?

I stared in part-horror and part-awe at the carnage before me.

I glanced at Zayed, his eyes burning with a primal fury, still not done unleashing his wrath on those who dared to threaten us.

"That...is...your husband?" Asya croaked out, her own blade hanging limply in her hand as she looked on in shock as Zayed picked off the last of the men like flies.

I bit my lower lip. This was not the first impression Zayed would have wished to have on my family. And yet...it could not be helped. They already thought him a murderous king.

"Asya, you must not tell anyone of this," I whispered, turning to look at her urgently. "It is a curse...that is the only reason the girls must die and..." I trailed off hesitantly, looking at Zayed ripping off the head of a man with his canines.

"And you love him?" Asya queried, looking at me in disbelief before looking back at Zayed who now stood with blood dripping off the sides of his mouth in his Lycan form.

"I love him," I replied, taking a step forward and reaching out a hand to him. I finally let the tears fall. I finally let myself feel. He was here! He was alive!

Zayed hesitated for a moment, his primal instincts telling him to keep fighting. But looking into my eyes, he saw my fear, my relief, and my love. He knew he had to stop this bloodshed.

With a growl that echoed around us, Zayed slowly shifted back into his human form, his eyes never leaving mine. The once fearsome Lycan King now stood before his wife, covered in blood and sweat, but with a fierce determination in his eyes. And I ran towards him, afraid he might just disappear and that this was nothing but a dream in which he saved me.

But as I folded myself into his arms, his familiar scent engulfing me, he whispered into my ear, "You do not need saving." My lips quirked up as I realized he was recalling what I had told him weeks ago. "But sometimes, even the strongest heroes need help and I will always be your shield, Amara. Through every tempest, every battle, I will be the barrier that keeps you out of harm's path."

His arms, still stained with the blood of the men who tried to hurt me, tightened around my waist.

And I realized, I might not need saving, but I did need Zayed. I would always need him.

And that is when I finally let myself break down into tears, letting myself be weak in front of him and letting him be my shield. Because I had thought I had lost him.

Only when the palm tree's shade slips away does the traveler grasp how much it meant to journey through its refuge. And Zayed....he was my refuge.

Chapter 37

Zayed had not been in the tent when it caught fire. No. He had left the tent to congratulate me on my win. But then, as he made his way down the steps of the arena, he had been waylaid by Kadin who informed him that an attack was imminent by the rebel factions and they were targeting the remaining civilians loitering around the festival grounds. Unfortunately, their sources were wrong. The attack had been on the arena the entire time. Which is why it had taken the guards so long to evacuate the place. Their attention had been fixated on the festival grounds. On the market set up for the festival. By the time Zayed realized he was going in the wrong direction, Kadin informed him that I had already taken off in an attempt to stop the archers.

And that is when all hell had broken loose for Zayed. He had changed into his Lycan form and killed anyone trying to hurt me.

I knew something was amiss. I had a feeling Asya had something to do with the attack. But I knew whatever she had done, she had done for me. So I did not expect Kadin to give orders for Asya's arrest the minute we met him halfway to the arena.

"Stop!" I screamed, moving forward to stop the guards.

Kadin looked at me apologetically.

"She is a person of interest. She helped orchestrate the attack. We have managed to capture a few of the rebels. They have named more than just her..." Kadin trailed off and looked to Zayed and then to me.

Zayed took a step back as if he had been physically hit.

"They are lying," Zayed grit out, hands fisting at his sides.

Kadin sighed heavily, his eyes going to me.

"We should discuss this inside the palace. For now, I must arrest her sister. She will not be harmed," Kadin assured me when I opened my mouth to protest. "It is more for show, My Queen. Too many people have given her name. She was not secretive about the fact that she was your sister." Kadin shook his head. "We must show them she has been arrested. I will order my men to contain her to your rooms. I swear, she will come to no harm under my watch. But we must know the truth." Kadin's eyes went to rest on me hesitantly before signalling for the handcuffs to be clamped around Asya's wrists.

"It is all right, Amara," Asya whispered assuringly. Though her gaze cut to Kadin with hatred. "I will go with you. Let me be your scapegoat for your inefficiency to capture the true perpetrators."

Kadin took a step back, as if he had been physically assaulted, surprised by her vehemence. His lips pressed into a scowl.

Kadin escorted Asya away, her defiant gaze looking straight ahead. Kadin's eyes met mine, pleading for forgiveness but there was something else in them. Wariness? I looked at Zayed, his face one of anguish.

"What is wrong?" I asked.

His eyes went steadily to me.

"Amara...what Kadin said...he meant you were named as one of the inside aides for this attack."

Now it was my turn to take a few steps back as if someone had physically hit me.

"It is all a lie," I stated in my sitting room where Zayed now sat.

After he had told me the truth outside the arena, we came back to the palace. Luckily, most of our people were safe. Those who had not made it would be given a proper burial. And upon my insistence, the peasant families who had lost their breadwinners during the attack would be compensated for life by the crown. Zayed was more than happy to comply, going so far as to state that I helped him see different facets of his citizens' lives. For as a man who had never lived without, he could not fathom the implications of the sole-earner of a family passing away.

Asya was sitting next to me in front of the low-lying table amongst a pile of cushions. The food before us remained untouched.

I studied Zayed closely.

"When Kadin took me aside outside the dais, it was to inform me of exactly that. That you were helping to orchestrate an attack. He did not want to believe it. And neither did I," Zayed admitted, hanging his head.

His eyes went to my sister and I realized it was because of her involvement with the rebel faction that he was more inclined to believe such blatant lies.

"S-someone is spinning defaming falsehoods," I replied in a shaky voice as another thought hit me. "You came to save me...even when you thought I might have betrayed you and our kingdom?"

Zayed reached out a hand, bringing it to rest over mine over the intricately carved wooden table.

"Even if you had betrayed me, I would have still come. It was my duty to protect you. And aside from duty, I love you, My Queen." His gaze held a fierceness that made my heart flutter. "I want to believe you might have come here with intentions to help the rebels, but might have had a change of heart..." He trailed off, and I realized he was waiting for me to admit my deception.

"What makes you think I would have ever helped them?" I asked carefully.

"Why did you volunteer?" he asked steadily.

It was the same question he had asked on my first night here. I had told him the truth, but not the entire truth.

I sighed, looking him dead in the eye.

"I volunteered because I wanted to take my sister's place. Because she was engaged to a man she loved. I did not love Ashad. But yes, there was also another reason I volunteered." I reached for the dagger at my hip, pulling it from its sheath. "I volunteered for a chance to end the life of the king with my own dagger. So I could end the killing of innocent women." I threw my dagger onto the table; it clattered loudly as it hit wood. I looked at Zayed, emotion brimming in my eyes. "I wanted to end the cycle of bloodshed. I thought you were the evil one. A man who held a sick mind and did not deserve to rule. But I was wrong. Your every action has been fueled by a need to keep your people safe. I realize how wrong I was in my first impression of you. But let it be known that I was never involved with any rebels," I ended firmly.

Zayed's hand still rested over mine and he stared down at our hands, before looking up at me.

"You came to kill me?" he queried. "And changed your mind? I truly want to believe you. That you had had nothing to do with any of this. But, Amara, you are one of the few who have access to my desk. To the drawings for the food storage banks and the maps for the festival heralding the Blade-Caller trials. Coupled with the fact that your sister was part of the rebel faction, it would seem you volunteered by order of your superiors within the rebel hierarchy. This is what the nobles now assume. Your disdain for them is no secret, and your affinity for helping the common man seems damning in light of all of this."

I looked down at our hands, the only part of us that remained connected in this moment of turmoil. I felt a sting in my chest as I realized that I was being framed in all of this. But by who?

"And what do you think?" I asked, looking him in the eye. "Do you think I am a traitor? That I orchestrated the attack? I was up there on the roof fighting to keep them from killing the nobles. I nearly died for them and this is what they believe?" I rasped out.

"Nobody saw what you did," Zayed corrected gently. "They did, however, hear your parting order to protect the nobles."

"You were there," I replied curtly.

"I was," Zayed responded, his grip on my hand tightening as his eyes searched mine. "Which is why I assumed you had a change of heart and did not want me to die. Nor did you want to betray me."

I pulled my hand from under his and looked at him with determination. "I am not a traitor," I declared firmly. "I am not with any re—"

His hand came over my lips, silencing me.

"Do not embarrass me by feeling as if you have to continuously voice your innocence. I believe you, Amara. Once was enough. I am simply trying to relay my point of view at the time all of this was happening."

His eyes softened slightly, and I could see the love in his eyes. He believed me. He did not require me to continuously defend myself in front of him.

"What I want to know is, what is the deal your sister made with the rebel factions?"

We both looked at Asya now. She sighed, looking down at her handcuffed wrists.

"I would help them by timing my defeat so that the king would be caught in the explosion on the dais. He was bound to remain seated to watch the queen fight and win. That way, my sister would live, her murderous husband would die, and I could escape with her. But Amara had no part in this!" Asya was quick to add.

"Did you think of the innocent people these factions would harm?" Zayed asked pointedly, his face one of ire. He shook his head in disgust.

"I was not aware of the rest of their plans. The rebellion was only supposed to cause an explosion on your dais. Everyone else was to be left unharmed!" Asya protested.

"So your main intent was simply to murder the king," Zayed ended with crossed arms.

"Yes," Asya responded in measured tones. She looked between Zayed and I. "I thought I was protecting my little sister," she added in a small voice. "Surely...you must know what it is like to want to protect your family."

Something sparked in Zayed's eyes. Something that looked a lot like sadness and regret.

I immediately knew he was thinking of his own little brother.

"You and I have a lot more in common than you know," Zayed finally grunted, reaching past me to break the cuffs that bound her wrists together.

Asya let out a gasp of surprise.

"Tell me what you know about the rebels and who is funding them?" Zayed demanded. "They brutally killed our people. There might be a few members who sincerely might not want to harm innocent people, but the majority seem to be too blinded by hate. Help us bring them down," Zayed stated.

"Most of them are the families of the girls you...that have died as your brides," Asya ended after faltering momentarily.

Zayed's nostrils flared briefly.

"Understandable. What else do you know?"

Asya shrugged helplessly.

"I do not know much. I simply approached them, wishing to join their cause. Wishing for their help in setting my sister free." Asya's eyes went to me. "I wanted to get her away from here, from you."

Zayed bent his head in respect.

"You wanted to save your sister from me, from the man who would eventually kill her," he reasoned. "I can not hate you for wanting to protect her. Especially when that is also my objective."

He reached out a hand to gently loop a stray strand of my hair behind my ear.

"I assume this was planned. They readily enlisted your help and planned to frame Amara. Someone in my palace is feeding the rebel faction information. Someone who would wish to see Amara gone." Zayed's eyebrows furrowed in thought, and he ran a hand through his hair. "We cannot ignore the danger we are in," he continued. "We must find a way to clear your name and uncover the truth behind these attacks."

"Your highness," Asya began carefully.

"I am your brother by marriage, you may call me Zayed," Zayed interrupted gently.

Asya gave a curt nod.

"Zayed," she corrected. "If you allow me to...escape, and make it seem as if I am still on the side of the rebels, I can attempt to find out more? Everyone who saw me fighting with Amara at the top of the granary is dead. I could say I was arrested and my sister helped me escape. I could attempt to gain information for you."

"I think it is dangerous," I said slowly.

"Amara, I will be fine," Asya assured me.

"The idea has merit, but I feel Amara is right about the danger," Zayed muttered. He looked at me. "However, I have my own men on the inside. Men who have not been able to infiltrate the inner-circle due to their background as members of my military. But they can look after Asya and get her out if things go south."

I opened my mouth to further inquire on the effectiveness of getting Asya out should things become dangerous for her, but, in that moment, the knock on my door cut me off.

When the Grand Vizier entered, I was immediately on alert. Was it possible that this man was behind everything? I watched the way his eyes tracked Asya, going to her now unbound wrists.

"My King," the Grand Vizier said, his voice tinged with grief. "Lightning struck our crops, setting everything on fire. We were unable to salvage the harvest and...have lost our food supply for this season."

Zayed sucked in a sharp breath. I felt a lead weight form in the center of my stomach.

"All our resources were focused on the arena. By the time we made it to the farm lands...it was beyond saving. I...I am sorry, My King. Such lightning is unheard of. Almost as if it were aiming specifically for the farmlands. Unfortunately, there will be a food shortage..." He trailed off, looking at me as well with sadness. "Forgive me for being the bearer of bad tidings, Queen Amara. You fought well today and I was loath to bring such sad news to your chambers. But it was imperative to relay this information in a timely manner."

"The curse," I muttered, shaking my head. "This is the work of the curse."

I let my head sink into my hands. Everything was unravelling.

"But, Uncle...it rained! It rained and we thought the curse was weakened," Zayed replied, standing up to look at the Grand Vizier as if the lightning had been the old man's fault.

"I am sorry, My King, I...have no explanation. It might have been a natural phenomena or it might have been the curse. Only time will tell," the Grand Vizier explained with sad eyes.

But I could see the answer on his face. He believed it was the curse.

"Kadin has a theory...that the curse is weakened each night the queen is able to survive your Lycan," the Grand Vizier explained patiently, shaking his head. "However, we all know it is too dangerous to keep trying. Your Lycan might lose control at any moment and try to harm her...it has already been discussed at great length and—"

I jerked in surprise, because, if it had been discussed, it had most definitely not been discussed in front of me. This must have been a meeting solely between Zayed, the Grand Vizier, and Kadin. I clenched my fists under the table and looked at Asya.

I had already explained to her the nature of the curse. It made her all the more determined to find a way to break it. She even suggested finding out more about where the witch Elvira came from or where she had lived. Maybe we could find another way to break the curse by finding out more about her origins. The idea had merit. But I did not want Asya to go alone. I was thankful that Asya made sure Baba was in hiding. With danger lurking so close, it was a relief that he was safe.

I turned to look at the Grand Vizier and Zayed who were still discussing how to tackle the food shortage.

"We will buy grains from the Kingdom of Assar," Zayed muttered. "I must meet with their queen."

That got my attention. This was not the first time I had heard of her.

"We must meet with her," Zayed corrected hastily, eyeing me and the way I was observing him.

"We need to make plans and formulate a strategy to overcome these obstacles," I muttered.

I looked at Asya.

Asya nodded, understanding the gravity of the situation. "I will do what I can to help from the outside," she promised, her eyes flashing with determination.

"Failing to gather more information could result in catastrophic consequences for the kingdom. I will help, not because I have any allegiance to the king...but for my sister." Asya's gaze went to me, love and protection shining in her eyes.

I reached to hug her.

"We will safely smuggle her out tonight, and make it seem as if she escaped. I will inform Kadin," the Grand Vizier assured us.

I looked at him, not willing to trust him yet. Because someone who had access to Zayed's records was part of this. But who?

As if he had been conjured by the mere mention of his name, Kadin himself strolled through the doors and into my room.

I did not miss the disdain on Asya's face the minute Kadin walked in. She did not like him. I wondered why. Kadin gave Asya a good-natured smile before greeting me and Zayed.

"I merely wanted to inquire after the health of my king, queen, and the queen's sister," Kadin said politely.

I heard Asya huff in exasperation next to me. Since the first time they had met, Asya seemed to find him bothersome. I would try to rectify this rift but at a later time.

Quickly, we informed him what was to be done in regards to Asya. He readily agreed, even leaving momentarily to direct his men on what was to be done.

"Now, My King, I know it is late, and you are tired, but you must write a letter to the Queen of Assar at once and send it post haste," the Grand Vizier beseeched.

Zayed sighed, getting to his feet but not before glancing at me. I knew he did not want to leave. But we both had our part to play as pillars of the kingdom. My eyes went to Kadin who had re-entered and was now ready to follow Zayed out again.

"Kadin, please stay, I would like to discuss a few things with you," I commanded quietly and Kadin paused on the threshold of my room, turning back instead of following his king.

"I am at your service, My Queen," Kadin replied with a respectful incline of his head.

Asya snorted next to me. I shot her a look. I did not know why she found him annoying. But right now was not the time for silly feuds.

"You have a theory, a theory that each time I survive one night of Zayed in his Lycan form, the curse weakens," I stated, gesturing for him to come sit at the table and partake in the food before us.

Kadin sat down, reaching for the pot of tea, choosing to forego the food.

"That is nothing but a mere theory," he said dismissively, pouring himself tea and then reaching for the sugar. "It is too dangerous. Zayed has already said he is not going to risk his Lycan going volatile."

"But if you were there," I urged and watched as he jerked in surprise, spilling the teaspoon of sugar across the table top instead of pouring it into his teacup, "in your Lycan form, maybe you could help keep him under control. And we could help weaken the curse."

Kadin ran an agitated hand through his hair.

"It might work. But..." He expelled a breath. "Zayed's Lycan is strong. Probably stronger than mine. We would have a better chance of him maintaining control if you were to become a Lycan and—" He clamped his lips shut, eyes widening at the same time that I let out a gasp of surprise.

"Is that possible?" I asked eagerly, leaning forward at the same time that he let his head sink into his hands.

"I should not have spoken," he moaned into his hands, head still buried in them.

I reached out, latching onto his wrists and pulling his hands down so that he had no choice but to look at me.

"Tell me," I implored him. "Please. If it can help the kingdom, I need to know."

"It is all speculation and too dangerous!" Kadin said abruptly, jerking his wrists from my grasp. "It is madness to try something so risky as a turn."

"A turn..." I trailed off, looking at the grains of wood on the table.

The clattering of Kadin's teaspoon as he stirred in his sugar was the only sound echoing in the deadly silent room as I went over his words. Turn. I could be turned. Into a Lycan.

"Please stop thinking about it. Asya, make your sister see reason," Kadin implored.

"You are a complete fool for opening your big mouth," Asya spat at him.

I felt her hand on my shoulder.

"Amara, he is an idiot. Do not try anything so risky. We will manage to find a way to break the curse without risking your well-being," she assured me.

I opened my mouth to argue but the sudden clattering of the teacup against the ground as it fractured into a million pieces made me look towards Kadin only to see him clutching his chest as he gasped for air, eyes bulging as he tried to take in great big gulps of air.

"P-poi—son," he rasped out before falling to the floor in a dead faint.

Chapter 38

Someone had tried to poison the King and Queen of Elamaria. The royal tasters had not been affected when they drank the tea before sending it to my room. However, it was not the tea that had been poisoned. The poison had been in the sugar. Someone had known the sugar was often overlooked by the royal tasters. My blood chilled at the realization that enemies lurked closer than I had ever thought. And they were getting bold if they were now infiltrating the kitchens as well.

"Kadin will survive. Luckily, his Lycan healing abilities were able to stave off the spread of the poison," Zayed whispered as I stood on the balcony attached to my room.

His hands came around me from behind, wrapping around my waist as his warmth settled over me like a comforting blanket, making me feel secure. However, his next words were anything but meant to comfort me.

"Amara, there is a possibility that you were the actual target. The sugar meant for your rooms was the one that was poisoned. If there is a spy amongst our inner-ranks, they also must know my Lycan abilities would prevent me from dying."

I leaned back into his embrace, my eyes going to the full moon above as my head rested on his chest.

"We need to send Asya," I murmured, realizing that was the only plan we could come up with currently. "I am scared, Zayed," I admitted, feeling the truth of the words spilling from me like a river breaking free of its banks. The fear that had been gnawing at me since I entered this palace was now too much to bear alone. "I am scared of always teetering on the cusp of an inevitable death."

I turned in his arms, looking up at him with beseeching eyes, letting my hands now rest palms flat on his chest.

"I will never let any harm come to you," he vowed, looking down at me with his green eyes flecked with gold. He lifted a hand to cup my cheek.

"I want to be able to protect myself," I argued. "And I want to help break the curse. Only then can the Grim Reaper constantly hovering over my person truly be gone. We do not know the motives for the attempted poisoning. It might have been a disgruntled noble, it might have been someone who wished to see us both incapacitated, or it might have been someone who knows of the curse and would wish to see me dead for the betterment of the kingdom," I ended decidedly.

He looked down at me, startled, and began to rub soothing circles on my back.

"I can see you are agitated due to everything—"

"I am not agitated," I cut him off brusquely, eyes hardening as I levelled him with a look. "I am determined. Determined to do something other than stand here and wait idly for our enemies to make their next move."

Zayed's nostrils flared and his arms dropped from around me.

"Is that what you truly believe I am doing?"

I lifted my chin a notch defiantly. "No. But it is what I am doing," I replied deftly.

Zayed expelled a breath, running a hand through his hair in agitation. "No, it is not. Because we are a team. And I need you to support me in my endeavors. I have a plan in place. A meeting set with the chieftain of the mountains to form a union between Kadin and one of his daughters which will help bring stability. The Queen of Assar is on her way as we speak to broker a trade deal with our kingdom to prevent a food shortage from ravaging our people. And if it were not for the fact that it maintains great effort to control my Lycan from succumbing to the bloodlust spurred by this catastrophic curse, I would have already strategized on how to deal with the rebel faction. When I removed my uncle from his duties as Grand Vizier as punishment for what he did to you, his duties were dispersed amongst my trusted men. Even after he gained your forgiveness, I have not fully reinstated him because...because he might have your forgiveness but he can never have the extent of his full powers back. He exercised them wrongly when he ordered the guards to hold you down. And he will forever pay for that decision. Resultantly, his duties have been substantially withdrawn from him. Kadin was the one charged with keeping an eye on the rebel activities. Something Uncle had been doing."

Zayed expressed a frustrated breath. "I realize now that Kadin was not doing an adequate job."

I breathed deeply, back straight and head held high.

"Regardless, there is one more thing we can do. Something our enemies would never expect," I stated.

Zayed's eyes met mine; his curiosity piqued.

"And if you truly believe me to be your equal, you will agree. So that I really can be your equal, in every way," I stressed the last three words. I watched the storm brew in his eyes as he realized exactly what I was going to say next.

"Turn me into a Lycan."

His jaw clenched and his entire being rebelled instantly. I could see it in his body language, in his visage as his body became as tensely strung as a bow. He opened his mouth to most likely reject the statement but I spoke, preventing him from voicing any objection.

"It will enable me to protect myself against your Lycan, to survive the nights that lay ahead, to fight for our kingdom and walk hand in hand with you into battle. Being a Lycan Queen will grant me the empowerment I desire," I insisted, my conviction unwavering.

Zayed shook his head furiously, swallowing convulsively as he stared at me with equal parts frustration and imploration.

"It is too dangerous!" he thundered. "The transformation can be uncontrollable. It could consume you. Try to understand, changing someone who was not born with the ability can have severe repercussions. If it were so manageable, everyone would have attempted to become a Lycan. You might not survive."

Frustration bubbled inside me, and I stepped closer, desperation lacing my words. "The rewards far outweigh the risks, Zayed. I am not asking for permission. I would no longer be vulnerable and the strength I could wield—"

"I do not care about your strength. I care for your safety!" His eyes were no longer hard, but now tinged with panic. His voice was laced with desperation. "There is not a glorious transformation. It is excruciatingly painful. And if you manage to survive, you would face a constant struggle between your humanity and the beast within. It can lead to madness if not managed well. This is not a simple spell. It is a biological procedure which changes you forever!"

I took a deep breath, grounding myself. "I am willing to accept that burden!" I declared, my voice rising with conviction. "I refuse to live in fear of what I could become. Rather, I embrace the power to shape my own destiny, step into the unknown with courage, and become the person I choose to be—an unapologetically fearless queen with the potential to rule by your side. Not just a vessel for bearing heirs," I ended.

Zayed looked at me, his face now red from anger.

"Is that what you truly believe I view you as?" he asked quietly.

My stance softened.

"No...never you," I whispered. "But you are attempting to dictate my decisions, which makes me give pause." I haltingly reached for his hand. "Trust in me, Zayed," I whispered, raising his hand to my cheek. "Trust in us and our love. It has the power to overcome all obstacles. And respect my decision to want to become like you. To better help you rule. To better protect myself against our enemies. If we truly are equals, you will help me in this endeavor, not try to dominate me."

He gently cupped my cheek, the pad of his thumb grazing across my cheekbone. "What if I lose you to the beast?"

My voice lowered to a softer tone as I clutched his hand that still rested against the side of my face. "I know my heart. I will not let the beast take over. Let me prove that I can harness this power."

His other hand came up to also cup my cheek and then he was cradling my face in his hands.

"I cannot lose you, Amara. What if we fail?" he whispered.

His eyes betrayed a deep well of fear and vulnerability, mirroring the cautious hope of a weary traveler who, after endless miles of struggle across a merciless desert, spots an oasis glimmering on the horizon. Every flicker of light and shadow in his gaze spoke of the fragile hope that it was not a mirage, that this moment, that our time together, was not too good to be true, that salvation was not just an illusion dancing on the horizon.

I had never had another person look at me as if I were their everything. As if I were their hopes, their wishes, and their dreams personified.

I smiled gently, hoping my eyes mirrored my own unwavering belief that we would see it through. "But what if we succeed?" A lone tear slipped from my eye, so overwhelmed was I by the emotions that flickered across my husband's visage.

"I wish I were not king," he revealed, expressing the sentiment on a long slow exhale. "I wish...we were just two people, a husband and his wife...and this burden to maintain peace and prosperity was someone else's to bear."

I gave him a watery smile. This is why I loved him.

"It is because you want peace, not war, that you are the best man to bear this burden," I murmured, turning my face to kiss the palm of his hand. "A true king chooses unity over division, understanding over conquest, and compassion over destruction." I looked back up at him. "Let me help you bear this burden. Let me help you rule. As your Lycan Queen."

Zayed sighed, his forehead meeting mine. He closed his eyes in defeat.

"I will explain the procedure to you first....and if you still truly believe it is what you want...we can consider it?"

I nodded, grateful that he was willing to further discuss it with me.

"If you go through with this, promise me," he breathed, his breath hot on my face. "Promise me that you will never forget who you are and who you love."

I wrapped my arms around his waist as he held my face close to his, our foreheads touching and eyes closed as we basked in each other's presence.

"I promise."

And so we stood under the moonlight in the very same position for only the goddess knew how long. We both knew that change was coming, but united in our determination to face everything together, we would rise stronger than before.

It had been three days since Zayed and I had argued about turning me. Three days since Kadin had been poisoned. He was doing better now, but still resting. He had instructed his most trusted men to smuggle Asya out of the castle. The nobles assumed she had escaped. And I was the culprit in their eyes. However, I could not care less at this point what the nobles thought.

Zayed had relayed to them how I had fought for their lives on the roof of the granaries. If that was not enough to make them loyal to me, then nothing would be.

I walked with purposeful strides to where I knew the Queen of Assar was in a private meeting with my husband. I had heard the rumours. Her beauty was incomparable. She had hair the color of gold, eyes as blue as the deepest sea, and skin so white, it was as if it had never known the touch of the sun.

And I might have been petty for paying more attention than usual to myself as I prepared to meet her. Which is why I was late.

In a long flowy dress of tea pink, for pink often suited my coloring best, I pushed open the doors to the meeting room. And for a moment I stood frozen in shock. I saw a woman whose beauty had been no exaggeration. She was fragile, pale, and petite. Her features were dainty, with big expressive eyes and a tiny button nose. She was the exact opposite of me with my toned warrior's body and patrician nose.

"Ah, this is your queen," she commented lightly, looking to my husband who stood at the windows of the meeting room. I stepped through, letting the guards close the double doors behind me. I watched her closely, her eyes going to my husband. "We had a deal, Your Majesty. And you have broken your part of the bargain. Why should I think to trade with you?"

"I have explained everything to you, Queen Seraphina. Our betrothal can no longer go through," Zayed sighed, turning to face her with a scowl. My eyes narrowed. So there had been a betrothal agreement in the works which Zayed had not informed me of. My husband's eyes reverted to me apologetically. "Forgive me, Amara, for not sharing the truth with you earlier. Queen Seraphina and I had an agreement of mutually beneficial nature. There is no love lost between us," he clarified. "But it is best to keep this just between us three, for there is much she wishes to keep secret until the time comes to reveal everything to...the right person," he finally ended carefully.

I blinked, not fully understanding what Zayed meant. Reveal what? And to whom?

Queen Seraphina gave a disdainful snort. Somehow, she even made that seem regal and graceful. One delicate strand of her long golden hair, which was tied in an intricate bun behind her head, came loose. I stepped forward, unable to keep my eyes off the strand of molten gold that unfurled and nearly reached the ground.

"The entire reason we had the agreement was so I could keep everything a secret. What am I supposed to do now? And for what? Because you fell in love?!" she stated loudly, her cheeks turning red as she looked at my husband in anger. "I should leave! I should not have come here in the first place. But I wanted to give you a chance to explain why you have tossed me to the jackals without a second glance."

"I am willing to help you in any way you deem appropriate," came Zayed's sharp reply. "I will protect you from the King of Shadowfell—"

Queen Seraphna cut him off with a dark laugh.

"I do not need protection. I need to figure out what to do about this!" With huff of anger she stood, her voluminous ice-blue robes swallowing her form. But in the next moment she reached for the tie on her robes, letting the outer covering fall away to reveal her form in nothing but soft blue silk. And outlined through the silky fabric was a noticeable bump, evidence that she was pregnant. "This is all your fault!" she stated, hands going to her protruding belly as she looked at Zayed accusingly.

Chapter 39

My mouth ran dry as I stared at Queen Seraphina holding her belly protectively with fire in her eyes. No. It could not be...Zayed would have surely told me if he were about to become a father. My eyes went to my husband who was staring at Queen Seraphina in ire.

Queen Seraphina was beautiful. Could I fault Zayed for entering into a betrothal with her and going farther than deemed necessary? We had not been together then. That much even I was sure of. But envy and jealousy were wrapping around me, constricting my heart in a vice-like grip over the thought of him with another woman. A cold shard of ice pierced my heart, damaging my resolve and rending the sturdiness of my love for Zayed. But I steeled myself, knowing that I could not let this destroy me.

"Stop with the theatrics. It is not my fault you choose to keep your child a secret from the father," Zayed snapped.

I expelled a relieved breath. Zayed had not kept secrets from me. He was not thinking of abandoning a woman he had gotten pregnant.

Zayed's eyes tracked mine and the light of realization entered his eyes.

"Do not tell me you thought that I was involved with Queen Seraphina," he implored, walking to me quickly. His hand reached for mine.

"Often when a pregnant woman says 'this is your fault' while holding her protruding belly, the aforementioned man is usually responsible for the pregnancy," I croaked out weakly, letting myself lean into him for support.

My heart was still beating faster than a sparrow's wings and my mind was still a whirlwind of emotions. It would take a few minutes to make sense of everything going around me.

Zayed shot Queen Serpahina an angry look.

"I agreed to claim your child as mine because you did not want the 'Dread Sovereign' to find out about the child you two had created. For me, it was the perfect opportunity to unite our two neighboring kingdoms. This child would rule over my kingdom while your elder son ruled over Assar. The people of my kingdom would flourish with free trade with Assar, a land which possesses fertile lands and green meadows. Impending droughts or famines would no longer be a problem. You would gain my protection from the biological father of the child. However, things have changed, Seraphina. I explained everything to you when I last visited. Please understand that I will help you in any way...any way but marriage," he corrected, eyes going to me.

Queen Seraphina stared back at Zayed with a mix of resentment and acceptance in her eyes. I could tell she knew that there was no turning back now. The fragile alliance they had planned was crumbling before her very eyes, and with it, her own hopes and dreams. Her hand unconsciously moved to caress her belly.

"How could you claim the child as yours?" I finally uttered, looking at Zayed. "Would not everyone have found out when he did not possess...the same traits?" I ventured hesitantly.

King Zayed grinned.

"The child is a Lycan. Because his father is a Lycan." Zayed looked at Queen Seraphina. "I think it is a sign for you to reveal to King Silas—"

Queen Seraphina cut him off with a dark laugh.

"Yes, reveal to him that I am about to have his child so that he will attack my kingdom and burn everything to the ground in an attempt to have his heir." Queen Seraphina shook her head. "Silas betrayed me. He never loved me." My heart ached for the beautiful queen who stood before us with tears filling her eyes. "I was just a warm body to him. Nothing else. And I will not let him have my son to corrupt in the same way that he has become corrupted. King Silas is evil. He seduced me, lied to me, and betrayed me! A man who spins false tales for power should not be allowed to raise any child."

Zayed expelled a breath and I could tell he had had this argument with Queen Seraphina many times.

"Queen Seraphina, though you are older than me by five years, I still view you as a close friend. You have shared your thoughts on the matter with me. I will not argue with your decision. But there are always two sides to a story. He is not called 'the Dread Sovereign' for nothing. So I assume his heinous proclivities have earned him such a reputation. But I also have a reputation as a bloodthirsty killer. They call me the Crimson King."

I jerked in surprise, not having expected Zayed to know what his subjects called him.

"Yet I am anything but that. I would sooner end my life than kill an innocent citizen of my land. But, as you know, I do not want to risk the curse adversely impacting my people. So here I am...stuck in a cycle of vicious killings."

"And yet you did not kill her," Queen Seraphina mused, eyes going to me.

"I did not," Zayed agreed with an incline of his head. He turned to look at me. "Every night I told myself I would let her live to see only one more dawn. I would listen to her beautiful voice only one last time as it spun fanciful stories. And every dawn...I could not bring myself to end her. And then...I fell in love with her. With her fire and resilience...she found her way into my heart, a quiet thief of my very soul. And I would sooner forsake all that I hold dear—every dream, every valuable item I possess, every tether to this world—than ever witness the light of life dim from her eyes, for that would be the end of all I am."

I felt my heart swell with emotion as Zayed's words etched themselves into my very being. The depth of his love for me, despite all the darkness that surrounded us, was a beacon of hope in the midst of turmoil.

Queen Seraphina's shoulders sagged as she held back a sob.

"That was beautiful!" Queen Seraphina murmured, wiping tears from her eyes.

Though Queen Seraphina tried to maintain her facade of strength, there was a vulnerability in her eyes that I had not seen before. Her gaze was one of bitter longing. But it was not Zayed she longed for... that much was clear. She looked like a woman torn, her heart heavy with the weight of her past choices that had lead to a devastating heartbreak.

Zayed watched Queen Seraphina tentatively, his expression soft.

"Queen Seraphina, you know that I will always be here for you, as a friend and ally. But our paths have diverged, and we must each follow our own destinies now."

"I...I cannot fault you for being loyal to the woman you love," Queen Seraphina finally admitted, her tiny shoulders drooping forward. She expelled a breath and reached for her robes. "Very well. You shall have your trade agreement. But—" She raised her chin and looked straight at Zayed. "One day, you will owe me a favor. And when the time comes for me to call in that favor, you. Will. Honor. It." Every syllable dripped with intent; a slow, inevitable thread of menace, weaving a tapestry of calculated threat. "Or else I have no qualms letting the famine overtake your kingdom."

The words hung in the air, sharp and cold, like an assassin's blade poised just out of sight.

"As you wish, Queen Seraphina," Zayed replied evenly, his voice unwavering. "I will honor any favor you ask of me when the time comes." His words were laced with a subtle warning of his own, a silent reminder that he, too, held influence and resources that could be brought to bear if needed.

Queen Seraphina's lips curled into a small, sardonic smile as she nodded in acknowledgment.

It seemed we had reached a truce. Finally. The famine would not ravage our people. Not this time.

"I would rather not remove it," I murmured, clasping the green pendant nestled between my breasts as I looked at Sherazi.

She had drawn a bath for me and I stood before her in my thin chemise and the necklace Zayed had given me strung around my neck.

Sherazi smiled benignly.

"It seems that the king has gifted this to his queen," Sherazi mused, moving back demurely with her hands clasped in front of her.

It was then that I noticed a dark grayish mark on the back of her hand. It looked like some type of skin condition. The edges of the rash were jagged, as though torn from beneath the surface. It looked angry, inflamed, and unyielding, a grotesque map of irritation and fungus against the pale canvas of the skin.

"What happened?" I queried.

Sherazi's smile dropped and she followed my gaze.

"I have developed an odd rash," she revealed in a small voice, biting her lower lip.

Her eyes went to Baghel who was prancing around the room. He paused, sniffing the air momentarily and then his gaze went to Sherazi.

"What happened? You should get it checked by the doctor," I said kindly.

Sherazi expelled a breath.

"It is nothing. I will get it checked. I just have not had the time," she revealed slowly.

I looked at her sympathetically. The fact that she was my personal maid and that no other servant was allowed in my rooms without her presence was taking a toll on her.

"Take the next few days off," I offered with a congenial smile as I turned towards my bath.

"Thank you, Your Majesty," Sherazi said, bowing demurely. "I just need to purify the room and hang new protection talismans to ensure your safety."

I sank into the fragrant water, closing my eyes and waving her away.

"Go rest, Sherazi and get your hand looked at."

"But," she protested, the agitation in her voice prominent. Despite my closed eyes, I could tell her visage was marred with urgency. "The talismans. New evil eyes must be strung up and blessed water sprayed on the walls."

I sank deeper into the water, waving her away carelessly.

"First, have yourself seen by the doctor. It can wait another day. There has not been any suspicious activity of late."

Truthfully, with everything else going on, a demon trying to kill me was the least of my worries.

"At least let me hang up the talismans," Sherazi murmured, reaching for a bag of flowers with the evil eye pendant strung up between each jasmine flower. "Then I will leave."

I let her have her way, and hummed to myself as I slowly began to wash myself.

I was not aware when Zayed entered the room. Or when Sherazi left. It was his strong hands on my shoulders, gently trailing down to cup my breasts that made me realize he was here and Sherazi was gone.

I turned whilst still sitting in the tub, looking up at him with a smile.

"Are you well, my love?" Zayed's voice was tender, filled with genuine concern. I leaned into him, enjoying his arms around me as he kneeled next to the tub. It did not seem to bother him that my wet form was causing the front of his silk shirt to become soaking wet.

I lifted my eyes to meet his gaze, finding comfort in his presence. "I am...fine. But I worry for my maid," I admitted softly. "She has developed a strange rash on her hand. It looked... unnatural."

Zayed looked at me with furrowed brows.

"Unnatural? How so?" Zayed inquired, his voice tinged with curiosity and a hint of caution. His fingers brushed over the pendant he had gifted me, a subtle reminder of our time together at the carnival. Of what life could be like if we were two normal people.

I described the rash on Sherazi's hand, the jagged edges and inflamed appearance that seemed almost otherworldly. As I spoke, a shadow crossed Zayed's face, his expression darkening with concern. His hands fell away from my body, all thoughts of enjoying our time together gone for now.

"There are sinister forces at play," Zayed murmured, his eyes narrowing as he contemplated the implications of Sherazi's affliction. He sighed heavily. "I fear the famine is just the beginning, Amara. The plague will come next. And this might be an indication that it is starting sooner than we anticipated."

Zayed ran a hand over his brow. "When I first tried to resist the curse, the plague came after the famine. And Elvira's demon began to wreak havoc across the palace. People dear to me began to end up dead. Kadin's mother was one of them, for she had cared for me like I was her own son after my mother's passing. My servants also began ending up dead, and they all had one key characteristic in common on their bodies...ugly brown patches of skin."

I sucked in a breath, wondering if those servants closest to me were next. And the closest to me no doubt was Sherazi.

"So we might have stopped the famine, but all it means is that the plague and killings will start sooner," I realized slowly.

Zayed nodded gravely, his gaze fixed on a distant point as he spoke. "Yes, the curse is insidious and relentless. Which is why I was previously keen on marrying the Queen of Asser. I thought that if I managed to name an heir, not of my bloodline, the curse would weaken. And even if I could not fight the urges of my Lycan to kill, I could be contained while Queen Seraphina ruled until her son was of age. But now we must figure out a new strategy. The curse will not rest until it has claimed its due."

"Until it has claimed me," I corrected, getting out of my bath to towel off.

Zayed quickly stood and grabbed the towel from my hands.

"Let me," he murmured, drying my naked body with a tenderness in his touch that belied the gravity of our conversation.

"The king wishes to do the work of a maid for me?" I teased.

Zayed laughed.

"Taking up that role has its perks." His hand landed firmly on my backside.

I turned to face him, a mischievous glint in my eyes as I playfully swatted at his hand. "Oh, does it now?" I retorted, a playful smirk dancing on my lips. Despite the weight of our conversation, Zayed's touch and humor brought a sense of lightness to the moment.

His eyes flitted to the pendant on my neck, allowing his fingers to run over the smooth surface.

I blushed as I admitted, "I am loath to remove it from my person."

His expression grew thoughtful as he absorbed the significance of my statement. And then he got a mischievous glint in his eye as he went to cup my breasts in his hands.

A smile tugged at my lips despite the weight of our earlier conversation. "Behave, King Zayed," I chided, though the warmth in my eyes betrayed my amusement.

"Who, me? Behave?" Zayed countered with a devilish smile, his hands not budging from their place on my body.

"Do you wish for me to give you privacy to change?" he teased.

I laughed, recalling how, at the start of our marriage, I always asked him to step out while I changed before we sparred. It made me realize how far we had come in two short months.

Now, his touch ignited a fire within me that burned brighter by the second.

"I would rather you stay," I whispered huskily, leaning further into his touch. "Maybe, you can help me dress?"

Zayed smiled. "I rather like you like this my beautiful wife—naked and in my arms. Let us enjoy this time together, Amara. And we will tackle the challenges that lie ahead in the morning."

As his lips met mine in a passionate kiss, I melted into the moment, savoring the warmth of his touch and the intensity of our connection. He picked me up gently in his arms and laid me on my bed. My arms went around his neck.

Zayed's touch sent shivers of delight down my spine as he explored every inch of my body, arms gently trailing up and down my sides, over my stomach, my thighs, and sending waves of desire crashing through me.

Our bodies moved in perfect harmony, each touch and kiss fueling the growing hunger between us. In that moment, there was no curse, no impending doom, only the raw, sincere love we held for each other. The need to be closer and join our bodies together bound us together in this moment.

"I am still angry at you for not agreeing to turn me," I panted as he nipped my earlobe. His one hand trailed over my thigh and began to tease the area between my legs. I gasped, my legs falling open of their own accord.

"And I am still angry at you for wanting to turn," he replied evenly, his thumb rubbing at a particular spot that sent waves of pleasure coursing through me. "But that does not mean that I love you any less. Or that I do not want you."

I groaned, tilting my hips in need, my hand going to his trousers to pull them down. He was still completely clothed while I lay under him a naked and writhing mass of want.

"Patience, my love," he whispered huskily, his fingers moving over my folds with expert precision. "Bringing you pleasure is not a decision to be taken lightly."

I tugged at his shirt, still damp from when I had been resting against him in the tub earlier, telling him I wanted it off.

"Can not have you ripping more of my shirts," he chuckled, moving back and turning away from me to remove it from his person.

My arms wrapped around his body from behind and my lips kissed his bare shoulder, making a trail down to a scar under his left shoulder blade.

"What happened here?" I murmured, running my tongue gently along the jagged scar before placing a kiss there.

He exhaled and spoke seriously. "You tried to kill me."

My hands that had been gently making their way down his abdomen from behind, in an attempt to grab the evidence of his arousal, stilled. I pulled back in surprise, realizing this was the evidence of the wound I had given him on my first night here in the palace. Had it really been deep enough to leave such a scar?

"I would say sorry, but I was defending myself," I replied seriously, wondering if he hated the fact that a woman had inflicted these scars on his body.

He turned to face me, lips pulled up in a smile.

"My little tigress, I wear these wounds with pride. For no man has ever been able to best my Lycan. This warrior queen of mine however..." He got a mischievous glint in his eyes and grabbed me by the waist. "I wanted you from the very first moment you struck out at me, in a whirlwind of fury and flowers, a tempest of rose petals and jasmine swirling around you. I had never seen a more beautiful sight. You were like a vengeful goddess, draped in gold silk and fragrant blooms, a vision so divine it made the world itself hold its breath."

It took me a moment to realize he was referring to our wedding night. I blinked, momentarily disconcerted that while I had thought he wanted to murder me, he wanted...to do *this*.

His lips met mine with an intensity that matched the flames within me, our tongues dueling for dominance. I kissed him back, allowing him to push me back onto the bed. I wriggled beneath him, needing him to take control and bring me to the brink of ecstasy.

"Zayed," I pleaded, my voice breathy and urgent. "Please."

I arched my back, a soft moan escaping my lips as his touch intensified, one hand massaging my breast. I was the only one who could successfully get the best of him in combat, and he was the only one who could ignite a fiery passion within me I had never thought myself capable of feeling before.

Ashad's kisses I had tolerated. Zayed's kisses I consumed like a woman parched in the desert finally obtaining water.

His lips trailed down my neck, nibbling gently as he whispered sweet nothings in my ear, adding to the euphoria coursing through my veins. I felt his hardness pressing against me and moved my hips impatiently, signaling what I wanted from him.

"I love you, Amara," he whispered, his voice thick with emotion.

I wrapped my arms around him, pulling him closer.

He adjusted his length against me and thrust inside in one swift move. A cry escaped my lips as he entered me fully, our bodies moving in perfect harmony. His hands gripped my hips as we moved together, our passion building to a fever pitch.

"Oh, Zayed," I cried out, nearing the edge of the precipice. "Zayed, I love you too!"

His rhythm intensified, our flesh slapping together with each thrust, and I gripped onto his shoulders, feeling my body being taken over by waves of intense pleasure.

"Tell me, do you like it when I am deep inside you?" he grunted as he moved inside of me at a punishingly fast pace.

My eyes rolled upwards, and I could not even form a coherent sentence due to the pleasure this man was making me feel. His thrusts stuttered to an agonizingly slow pace.

"I asked you a question, Amara," he whispered, pulling out of me completely, his cock teasingly circling at my entrance.

"Yes, oh yes!" I cried out, my body arching off the bed as I attempted to take him inside me again.

He complied with my wishes, resuming the pace he had set before. A hiss of satisfaction escaped my lips.

This man knew how to bring me to new heights of ecstasy. He had taken the time to learn my body. And now I was nothing but a writhing mass of want in his arms.

Waves of pleasure washed over me and I felt my toes curl.

"I-I am close," I breathed out.

"Good," he grunted, and I could see the telltale tremor in his body that told me he was holding himself back. Waiting for me to find my release first.

His lips met mine once again, our bodies entwined as we reached for our climax. The room was filled with the sound of our heavy breathing and our moans of pleasure.

I screamed his name when I came and with a guttural groan emitted from his lips, I felt him finally let go and come inside me.

Our bodies remained joined and we rode out the waves of ecstasy together.

Finally, as the intensity of our pleasure began to subside, Zayed pulled away his eyes meeting mine. I could see an eternity of warmth and love reflected in them. Along with a hint of fear. I understood his fear all too well. We were playing with fire, the curse hovering over us like a dark storm, waiting to break. In this bed, we could steal a fleeting moment of peace, forgetting, if only for a breath, that a kingdom's fate rested on our shoulders. But that brief illusion would shatter, as it always did, after our coupling.

He sighed, gathering me in his arms and placing soft kisses along my forehead before moving down to my cheek.

He whispered softly into my ear, "Promise me, Amara, that no matter how dark the night may seem...we will find the dawn together."

"I promise," I replied, my body completely sated as my eyes dropped shut. "I promise you, Zayed, we will...find the dawn together," I murmured in a yawn.

My eyes dropped shut and I felt him kiss my lips briefly.

"Sleep, My Queen. Tonight I have matters to attend to regarding the spies I have installed within the rebel faction. And each moment I am away from you, my beautiful wife, I will be picturing you in my mind's eye."

As I drifted off into a contented slumber, the weight of our earlier conversation and the impending dangers subsided, replaced by the warmth of Zayed's love. For in that moment, I felt as if we really could conquer everything.

Unfortunately, when my eyes snapped open to the sound of sinister laughter, I realized that Elvira's curse would constantly threaten to tear us apart. For above me, on the ceiling of my room, hung the wicked demon witch laughing as she looked down at me with her sinister red eyes.

"One bride per year. The curse demands human flesh. My curse demands revenge!" she cried, throwing herself straight through the gauzy curtains of my bed.

Chapter 40

I screamed, jumping out of bed just in time to escape her.

My eyes went to the doors of my veranda only to see Baghel through the lattice work of the doors butting his head against them as he attempted to get in. The doors were locked.

I reached for my silver dagger on the side table.

"Curse you!" I spat at the demon twisted up in the sheets as she attempted to gain purchase.

Elvira lunged towards me, quicker than I could even blink. I sliced my dagger in an attempt to protect myself. She could be harmed. I hoped. But she dodged my attack as her eyes blazed with malice and she fell upon me. The smell of rotting flowers nearly overwhelmed me.

But I was not about to go down without a fight. With every ounce of strength I had, I pushed back against her, determined to protect myself and those I loved from her malevolent intentions.

"You will not break us!" I shouted, my voice trembling with defiance and fear.

Elvira's furious red gaze locked onto mine, a sinister smile curling on her twisted lips. With a swift movement, she reached out a clawed hand towards me, a dark energy crackling around her fingertips.

"I already have!" she cackled, and her clawed hands sliced through the air. I managed to twist my body so that instead of my throat, they dug deep in my left arm. Searing, burning pain exploded in my arm.

I yelled in agony. Baghel's barking grew louder and more frantic.

With a fierce battle cry, I plunged the silver dagger deep into Elvira's shadowy form. Warm blood spilled over my hand holding the dagger as her deafening shriek filled the room. It was like nails grating against a chalkboard. She was in pain from my attack but did not let up her hold on me.

I screamed again when she pulled my hair roughly, clumps came out in her hands.

"You are going to die tonight, Queen," Elvira cackled. And I watched in horror as her jaw opened wide. Wider than any normal being could open. "It is time for me to feast," she spoke, though her voice was echoing around me rather than coming from inside of her.

A sharp, searing pain shot through my body as Elvira's monstrous form pressed against me. I pulled the dagger from her shoulder, preparing to aim for her heart, or where one should have been. But tendrils of black smoke, cold and leathery, wrapped around my arm, keeping me from attacking her again. She could not paralyze my body like before, for the evil eye talisman was sewn onto my clothes, hidden in the folds of my outfits. But the black magic of hers was physically restraining me using shadows.

The demon witch's mouth stretched wide open, the edges of her lips pulled back to reveal rows of razor-sharp teeth—a grotesque sight that sent waves of nausea and fear washing over me. I could feel the bile rising in my throat as she continued to inch her mouth closer, her breath hot and putrid on my skin.

The stench of decay and death intensified with each passing moment as her mouth stretched ever wider, morphing into a gaping maw, black tendrils of smoke pouring out of the depths of her mouth.

I bucked beneath her but she was strong. Much stronger than I with her demonic strength and I felt the tendrils of smoke wrapping around the rest of my body, curling around my throat to hold me in place. I gasped, unable to breathe. The dagger I had been clutching fell to the floor with a clatter.

Baghel's frantic barking roared in my ears as I heard the doors to my veranda rattle.

I looked up at the demon, her eyes bulging with anticipation as she positioned her mouth over me. She really was going to eat me. To feast on me. Black spots danced across my vision as I felt myself slowly suffocating. Her lower teeth pressed against my throat as her mouth came over my head, shrouding me in complete darkness. I debated on whether to simply allow myself to pass out to avoid the pain of being eaten alive.

There was a deafening crack as the doors to my veranda splintered.

I heard Baghel burst through, snarling and barking at the same time that the doors to my room also broke open.

"Be gone, vile witch!" Zayed roared.

Light from a torch of fire spilled forth from the flames, visible even from the depths of her mouth and an ear-splitting shriek filled the room as the demon over me dissipated into a cloud of malevolent energy, leaving nothing behind but the scent of putrid burning flesh.

My dimming vision returned, and I took in gratifying gulps of air as the pressure was lifted from my throat. I looked to see the sheets she had been tangled in on fire.

Baghel was barking up at the ceiling as if Elvira was still floating somewhere above us.

Strong arms wrapped around me, and I was pulled into the comfort and security of Zayed's chest. He smoothed back the hair on my face, hands searching for wounds.

"She needs to be moved," murmured Dornia's familiar voice. "This room was not properly purified which is why Elvira was able to enter here."

The room was filled with the smell of smoke and charred fabric.

"Dornia, I almost lost her," came Zayed's mournful voice.

I finally spoke, my vocal chords aching after being constricted so harshly.

"But you did not," I rasped out, and I watched tears welling up in Zayed's eyes as he held me tightly.

His lips pressed firmly against the crown of my head. Zayed's arms around me felt like a lifeline, grounding me in reality amidst the chaos that had just unfolded.

Dornia approached us, her expression grim yet determined as she began to assess the damage done by Elvira's presence.

"We need to act swiftly to cleanse this room and protect you from any further attacks," Dornia stated, her voice steady and sure.

She called for water to bless and spray across the walls. Meanwhile, Zayed lifted me in his arms, preparing to take me to his room.

I looked back at her briefly before the doors closed behind us and then I looked at Zayed who was placing kisses across my brow as he carried me.

"I should have never let you out of my sight," he murmured.

I kept quiet, wondering if Dornia's assistance would hinder Elvira or help her. But I did not share my thoughts with Zayed. For it was clear he adored the old woman who had been like a mother to him.

I fell asleep in my husband's bed, in his arms and the last words I heard from him were "I am sorry, Amara, forgive me. My Queen...this is all my fault."

But I had to wonder what there was to forgive. None of this was his fault. However, I was too exhausted. The minute I had reached Zayed's rooms, he had called for a doctor who checked me over and then administered medicine to help calm my nerves. It made me drowsy. So before I could speak to him, I had already nodded off to sleep.

"We must be more vigilant," Zayed said, his voice determined. "Elvira will not stop until she sees her curse fulfilled."

I woke up to hear Zayed's voice outside his room. He was speaking to someone outside the room but the door was open a crack, allowing his voice to waft through.

"Do not worry, Zayed, we will increase the number of guards outside her room and station a few outside on her veranda. We are lucky you were taking a walk with Dornia and heard Baghel's panicked growls. Otherwise...I shudder to think what would have happened."

It was the Grand Vizier.

I slowly sat up, the silken sheets falling away from my form, and I clutched my head. I tried to swallow and winced in pain. My throat hurt; it felt as if someone had taken a thousand sharp knives to it.

"If I had not shown up..." Zayed trailed off. "Uncle...I must equip her with the means to protect herself. I think...I think I should give in to her request."

The Grand Vizier was silent for a beat before speaking.

"Then tell no one what you plan to do. We will inform everyone that she is unwell. Because her shift will be something our enemies do not expect. She will be able to defend herself against any future attacks. Against Elvira as well. Her demon haunts these walls, Zayed. And she must eavesdrop on conversations. Walls have ears, especially within the palace. You and I will care for her during her shift. No one else."

"Thank you...Uncle."

"Zayed, I promised my father I would protect the crown and our kingdom. I would do whatever it took to ensure that my brother and his heirs stayed on the throne. Somewhere along the way, I became obsessed with fulfilling that promise, so much so that I forgot to be the uncle you so dearly need. I see it all more clearly now however. I am your uncle first and must look out for your interests before looking out for the monarchy. Your happiness is more important to me," the Grand Vizier spoke with a voice brimming with regret.

"In many ways...you were always more of a father to me than my real father," Zayed whispered.

I watched their shadows move through the crack in the door which showed me they were embracing.

And then Zayed's shadow moved and the door opened fully. He paused at the sight of me sitting up.

"How are you feeling?" he asked gently as he came to sit down beside me and brush a stray strand of hair away from my face.

I tried to speak but winced, the pain in my throat still raw and throbbing.

"My throat feels as if it is on fire," I whispered hoarsely.

Zayed's brows furrowed in worry as he reached for a glass of medicine on the bedside table, helping me take small sips to soothe my throat.

"I assume you heard everything," he said somberly, setting the glass back on the bedside table.

I nodded, unable to voice my thoughts.

"But I need to tell you what it entails. You need to know the full extent of what you are agreeing to," Zayed said seriously. "For me to successfully turn you, my Lycan needs to bite you under the full moon. Long enough for my venom to seep into your bloodstream. It will render you paralyzed until the turn is complete." Zayed swallowed hard. "Very rarely have my kind turned our partners. It is because the turn is painful. Your very body undergoes extreme biological changes, organs shifting and your brain essentially cleaving into two to create the consciousness of a beast to live inside of you."

"Will it culminate in a shift?" I asked.

"It will, but not immediately," Zayed said gently. "Not until your body accepts the drastic change inside of you. It could take days...or weeks. It is different for everyone, Amara. But it will be painful. Very. Some do not survive. But I think...I know you will," he corrected. Zayed cupped his hands around my face. "I will be there with you every step of the way. And my Lycan will be there for yours."

"Zayed, I trust you," I whispered, reaching up to touch his face. "As long as you are there, I will be fine. Thank you for agreeing to this."

"The demon witch is strong and has otherworldly strength and speed. The only way you can defend yourself properly is if you can match her skills. And there is only one way to ensure that." He looked at me resignedly. "Sometimes," he moved a strand of hair gently away from my face, "I feel that you might have been better off without me. You should have gone with Ashad. Far away from this kingdom with its curse hanging over it like a shroud. There, he would have kept you safe."

I shook my head. "You are my strength. My happiness." I leaned forward and pressed a gentle kiss to his lips. "No more regrets, Zayed. This is our home, and we will protect it. We will surpass Elvira's curse."

I felt the weight of our shared destiny resting upon our shoulders as he held me in his arms.

The days that followed were a blur of anticipation and fear as Zayed prepared me for the upcoming transformation. We spent hours poring over books, gleaning them for each and every bit of information regarding a human turning into a Lycan.

We also spent countless hours in physical training, as Zayed pushed me to my limits and beyond. He insisted that strength and endurance would be vital in surviving the shift. During my spare time, I tried to figure out a way to contain plagues. Because Sherazi was not the only servant who began to develop patches of scaly gray skin. Anyone with such a symptom was being quarantined in an attempt to slow down the plague created by the curse. I had barely seen her since my attack. She was too afraid of the king to enter his personal chambers. And by the time Zayed felt comfortable letting me go back to my room, the quarantine for anyone possessing the skin condition had already been ordered.

And finally, when the full moon loomed over us, it was time.

The night of the full moon arrived, its bright glow casting an eerie light over the palace. It seemed to mock us, daring us to confront our fate.

Chapter 41

Zayed held my hand tightly as we stood on the balcony, staring up at the moon. The fear pulsated in his touch, he was afraid for what was to happen next.

This was our shared destiny now, entwined with the rhythms of the wild moon.

He exhaled on a deep resigned sigh and brought my hand to his lips, kissing my knuckles before letting my hand drop from his.

Then he breathed in deeply and I watched as he slowly began to transform. Muscles bulged, bones cracked and dark fur sprouted from his skin like a second layer. His eyes took on that otherworldly reddish gleam and I took a step back as the untamed hunger in them became apparent. There was a chance his Lycan might just kill me. We both knew this. But I had told him I wanted his Lycan to be the one to turn me.

I closed my eyes and took a deep breath, mustering all the courage I could find within me. The time was coming for me to embrace my own transformation into a creature of the shadows.

The beast looked at me, a low growl emitting from deep within him. And then he stepped forward. I forced myself to meet his gaze and to stand firm. I would not cower. I was not his prey.

He raised a clawed hand, reaching for me. For a moment, I was back in the forest, on the first night I had spent in the palace. Fear skittered through me as I recalled the feral hunger in his eyes that night.

But his eyes were different now. They glowed an ominous red but looked at me intently. Carefully. His claws grazed my wrist lightly as his humanoid pawed hands clamped around my forearms, pulling me to him. He was so soft, I realized as my body settled against his, my head burying into his chest.

How could something so dangerous, feel so warm and comforting? This beast was cursed to kill me. I could feel him shaking, perhaps fighting his more bloodthirsty urges.

"I trust you," I whispered, my arms slowly trailing up his fur-matted chest, before entwining around his neck. I had to stand on my toes to be able to successfully reach so high.

The Lycan before me let out a low hum. Almost like a purr.

"You are enjoying our proximity," I murmured, laying my cheek against his chest. I sighed in content and closed my eyes. This was not the first time I was encountering his Lycan. We had practiced before. But each time, he required a concentrated effort to hold back the effects of the curse.

His snout went to nuzzle the crook of my neck. Another content sigh escaped my lips. It was no wonder I had slept so peacefully next to his Lycan form after our first time. The Lycan King was a lethal predator, a force of nature capable of shattering my bones, but he was also my husband. And in his embrace, I found not just safety, but a fierce, unshakable sense of belonging

I felt his tongue lave over my skin and breathed deeply, trying to relax against him. He would never hurt me. Then I felt the points of his razor-sharp canines as they settled over my pulse point. He stilled, hesitating.

"Zayed," I breathed, my cheeks red as I arched my neck, giving him better access. I pushed myself more firmly against him. "Please."

His teeth sank into my neck under the full moon's glow and I let out a gasp of part-pain and part-pleasure. He held me against his body, canines embedded deep inside of me and I felt the flow of his venom slowly begin to pump into my veins. It started slowly, a vague burning sensation that seemed to increase as the moments passed. As he held me to his body under the full moon shining down upon us on my veranda, slowly, that vague burning sensation became a searing pain radiating from where his canines were attached to spread across the rest of my body.

The pain became unbearable, a raging fire that tormented every inch of my body right down to the tips of my fingers and my toes.

But I knew it was necessary for the transformation to begin.

I recalled Zayed's words in my mind; him promising to be there for me. Promising that our Lycans would run together in the woods and that his beast would help mine. I focused on the memory of his comforting voice as I felt pain exploding inside my veins, like fire racing through my blood wanting to burn me from the inside out.

I screamed in pain, my knees buckling. The pain was no longer just inside me. Now it also felt as if my skin was on fire. Strong fur-matted arms wrapped tighter around me, and the Lycan lifted me into his arms, canines still attached to my neck. But it did not hurt there anymore. Or rather, everything hurt and I was unable to focus on any one singular pain. It was excruciating. As if every nerve, every internal organ, was burning and twisting inside of me.

A wet sensation on my face told me I was crying. I opened my mouth in a silent scream, because I was unable to speak. My vocal chords had been paralyzed. It made sense, since those were the organs inside my neck. The venom was slowly starting to change my organs to accommodate that of a Lycan counterpart.

I felt as if I was moving and realized that he was moving me into the room. Soft sheets beneath my skin told me I had been gently laid down on the bed. My world spun around me as the transformation progressed and a splitting pain erupted in my skull. I heard Baghel whining, worried about his mistress.

I choked, trying to scream in utter agony again. But nothing came out. I felt my muscles slowly tearing and mending anew, leaving me a ragged mess.

As the night wore on and bursts of pain seemed to ebb and flow through my entire body, I felt the comforting kiss of Zayed's lips on my forehead. The brush of his gentle hands against my skin. It dulled the pain, but only momentarily.

And through the fogged haze of pain, I registered a new voice.

"The turn is going slower than anticipated. It will take her another day."

It was the Grand Vizier.

"What am I to do, Uncle?" Zayed's suffocated, guilt-ridden voice, because of the pain I was going through, was evident.

I tried to open my mouth to speak, to lift my head. To even open my eyes. But it was all futile. I could not move. I could not speak. I could only feel the pain of a thousand suns as my skin felt as if it was bubbling and blistering from the invisible fire licking its way outside and inside my body.

"Zayed, the chieftains demand the contract to be signed. You must meet them on neutral territory as agreed upon and sign the betrothal contract for Kadin. It is merely a three-hour ride from here. You will be back in time. It has been two days, it will take at least another for the transformation to be complete."

"I cannot leave her vulnerable like this!" Zayed stated vehemently.

"She will not be vulnerable. I swear on my own life, I will protect her. Everyone believes the queen to be sick. I will inform Kadin to increase the guards outside her door, and if need be, I will inform him of Amara's predicament," the Grand Vizier assured him. "I swear on the goddess, Zayed, I will not let anything happen to the woman you love."

Zayed expelled a frustrated breath. A cool liquid was passed down my throat and I realized that it was a nourishing broth.

"If I leave now, I can be back before the morrow's dawn," he muttered and then I heard the closing of the door.

I did not like the Grand Vizier. But Zayed trusted him. And I would place my faith in Zayed's good judgement. Slowly, I sank down into the deep oblivion of pain I had been sinking in and out of. A cool towel was pressed against my forehead.

"Fight it out, Queen Amara. For our kingdom needs you more than ever right now," came the encouraging words of the Grand Vizier.

"I have more cold water," said the voice of a maid I did not recognize.

Vaguely, I wondered where Sherazi was and then I recalled how she was in quarantine. It had been ordered to keep this entire turn a secret so she had no idea what I was going through. But I wished she was here. If the curse succeeded, she might not be alive much longer. All because I was granted the chance to live. I heard Baghel's worried yelps next to me, and then a pressure on my hand that seemed like my little protector was nuzzling his nose against the palm of my hand. But I was in too much pain to feel any other sensation.

As the hours ticked by, I felt myself drifting in and out of consciousness, my body wracked with pain that threatened to consume me. Every so often, I would feel the touch of the Grand Vizier on my forehead, his gentle reassurances that I would make it through this ordeal. He seemed almost fatherly. So unlike the man I had thought him to be. He loved his nephew and by extension, he cared for me too. Asya had been bent upon killing Zayed, until she learned I loved him.

I did not know the exact time, but at some point my eyes flew wide open as unprecedented torturous crippling pain ripped through my body. It was dark outside. The Grand Vizier was pacing the length of the room. I tried to lift my head but could not. I tried to cry out for water, but could not. I was still completely paralyzed as pain coursed through me, and I felt as if my very skull was slowly being pried apart by a cold steel blade. My vision swam, the room a distortion of ripples before me.

But I registered, with my head turned to the side, through the slightly parted curtains, the opening of the door and Kadin stepping in.

The Grand Vizier halted, turning to look at his son. My vision dimmed and came back as a jolt of pain shot through my skull.

"What are you doing here?" the Grand Vizier queried sharply.

"I heard the queen was unwell and thought to check in on her." I heard Kadin's voice rather than saw him. When my vision returned, he was standing next to his father. "No doubt, the ink on my betrothal contract is still wet as the king rushes back home."

"I know you did not wish to marry—"

Kadin's sharp bark of laughter cut him off.

"I wished for very many things, Father. But you never took heed of my desires because the crown comes first."

"It is our legacy," the Grand Vizier replied smoothly. "And our duty to protect the heirs."

"No, Father, no more. I will not be shoved into a corner and expected to do your bidding any longer. Mother wanted me to be happy. You only ever want what is good for the crown. For Zayed. Not for your son."

My heart constricted for Kadin, even in the throes of pain. Did he love someone else? Was he being forced into this? All for peace? I tried to speak up. To tell him I could help find another way, but I was completely immobile due to the turn.

I watched the Grand Vizier lift a hand to place on his son's shoulder. Kadin jerked back angrily, refusing comfort. The door behind Kadin opened again and in walked Sherazi.

Was it possible that they were together?

"Is everything ready?" Kadin queried.

Sherazi nodded, her eyes on the Grand Vizier and her head held high. Her head was not bent over demurely. She did not look like the meek servant who was always afraid of even her own shadow.

"Is this the plan? You are going to run away with some peasant girl who reeks?" the Grand Vizier snarled.

Kadin let out another sharp, humorless laugh.

"Sherazi, please tell the guards on the queen's veranda that they have been dismissed for tonight."

Sherazi murmured her assent and moved away. I heard the door to the veranda opening and closing as Sherazi moved to instruct the guards to leave. They were not allowed to exit through my rooms. So they would use a rope to slide down to the ground.

"I take it this peasant girl is the reason for your anger," the Grand Vizier began placatingly but Kadin cut him off with an exasperated sigh.

"You really are an imbecile."

I watched Kadin then deftly pull out his sword and, within a blink of an eye, bury it to the hilt within his own father's chest. The Grand Vizier had not even had time to react. His eyes were wide in surprise, unable to believe his own child would turn on him.

Chapter 42

The Grand Vizier stood there, blood pooling from the wound in his chest where his son's sword was buried.

"Wh-whyyyy?" the old man rasped out as he stared at his son in shock.

"Because I should be the next king. My mother was not content to let me play the role of Zayed's lackey. We have planned for far too long to let you, old man, get in the way." Kadin's voice lowered an octave as he leaned in to speak into his father's ear. But it was not so low that I could not hear his next words. Words were no longer garbled to my ears but louder and much clearer than before. Which meant I had developed the hearing ability of a Lycan. My turn was nearly complete! Kadin's next words however, sent my mind reeling in utter shock.

"It was my mother who informed the late king that his queen had been unfaithful. She had hoped to incite a war upon the queen's murder and death of the bastard son of the chieftain's brother. A war in which I would rise as the next king."

Disbelief slammed through me. The woman who had pretended to be the queen's best friend was the one who had betrayed her?

Kadin was talking still and he showed no remorse as he pulled his sword out and watched his father fall to the ground in a pool of his own blood.

"She is also the one who told Elvira that the previous king murdered his wife. But Elvira did not kill the king's line like Mother hoped. Instead, she cursed the future king. No matter. This curse will destroy Zayed. Destroy his rule. And I will be there to take up the mantle of responsibility. I have not been funding these rebel factions just for you and a mere slip of a girl who thinks she is now queen to ruin it all. I kill her now and Zayed will think she died at the hands of the rebels. He will lose control of his Lycan and rage. Since Amara did not die by his hand, the requirements of the curse will remain unfulfilled. An unstable ruler can be overthrown."

I wanted to yell, to scream, to stand up and fight.

My mind raced as I tried to process all of this information. How could I have been so blind?

But there was no time for self-pity and regret. Kadin had just killed his own father and was now planning on killing me too. I needed to act fast if I wanted to survive. But I could not move!

I heard the opening of the doors to the veranda and wondered what Sherazi was here to do. Was she working with Kadin? Or would she help me?

"It is done, Sherazi!" Kadin called out, stepping over his father's body twitching as the life ebbed from him.

Sherazi stepped forward, eyes on Kadin's father. Slowly, she sank to her knees where the Grand Vizier now lay dead.

"I....it has been so long..." she rasped, tilting her head down.

And as Sherazi lifted her head again, her eyes were no longer filled with tenderness. They glowed with a fierce red light that sent shivers down my spine. The air around us seemed to grow colder as the stench of rotting flowers and decay filled the room. NO!

I watched in horror as Sherazi's features contorted and shifted before my eyes. Her once delicate hands grew sharp claws, tearing through the fine silk of her gown. Dark scales emerged on her skin like cracks forming on obsidian stone under intense heat. A pair of twisted horns sprouted from atop her head, curling wickedly towards the ceiling like blackened tendrils seeking prey.

With a primal snarl that reverberated through the chamber, Sherazi transformed into a demon right before me—a grotesque creature straight out of nightmares made flesh.

I could scarcely believe that this was unfolding so rapidly. Had the haze of pain pulled me under a hallucinogenic state? Like a mirage in the desert? This could not be!

But one instance reverberated through my brain, reminding me that I had been a fool.

"I know the names of all the servants within my palace," said Zayed.

But he had not known Sherazi. Back then, I had thought he was an insufferable arrogant king, lying to me. But now, in retrospect, I realized he had not known Sherazi because she had never been a servant in the first place. She had been planted here by Kadin....

But what was she?

Before my eyes could fully comprehend what was happening, Sherazi grotesquely opened her mouth wide and began tearing into the flesh of the Grand Vizier with voracious hunger. The sickening sounds of ripping sinew and crunching bones filled the chamber as blood sprayed around her in macabre arcs.

"It must taste better than the corpses of the dead brides you feast on after the Lycan King kills them," Kadin muttered off-handedly, as if he had not just killed his own father and let some demon eat his corpse.

Sherazi paid him no mind, digging in voraciously and I could do nothing but watch helplessly through the curtains as she pulled out his intestines and tore into them with her sharp gleaming teeth.

"Much... better..." Slurping noises punctured her words as she feasted. "The organs are still warm," she grunted through a mouth full of blood and entrails.

"While you indulge, I must go do what we planned to do all along. What you failed to do numerous times," Kadin admonished, turning his back to the woman eating his father's flesh. "We could have done this sooner had we not had to wait for the protection charms against you to wear off. Dornia was altogether too thorough in her work. You were unable to sneak in and harm her until now. No matter. All is well that ends well. It is so much more satisfying this way. Guilt will eat Zayed alive that he is to blame for the rebel factions killing his precious queen. He should not have left her alone while she was unwell. I had originally planned that he would agree to turn her and we could kill her then, and let the guilt consume Zayed. But this will get me what I want. A war on the horizon that will make people unhappy with the king for we will whisper into the right ears that he is the one who killed Amara. It will be all too easy to take over now. Elvira, it has been a pleasure working with you. "

Kadin purposefully began to walk towards me and I realized what exactly he meant.

Sherazi...was Elvira. And she had been placing fake protection charms around the room. When Dornia did it after the last time I had been attacked, Elvira had not been able to enter my rooms. That is why I had not seen her for so very long. Because she could not physically enter due to Dornia's charms. She had not been in quarantine. I had been such a fool. How many people in this castle were under Kadin's thumb? Most of the army no doubt. And servants too, for a servant had told me Sherazi was in quarantine.

Bile rose up in my throat as I realized that Kadin had been playing us all this entire time. He had slowly been amassing power and allies. I had thought he was our friend, that he was trustworthy...

But the truth was far worse. Far darker.

Kadin's eyes gleamed with a twisted satisfaction as he walked towards me, his lips curled into a sadistic grin. And for a moment I recalled the cold cruel man who had tried to kill Asya back in the market. I had gotten a brief glimpse of the evil beneath but had not been able to put the pieces together. Neither had Zayed. Because he loved Kadin like a true brother. We had trusted the wrong man.

I felt a hand brush against my cheek and revulsion mixed with the agony flowing through my limbs.

"That stupid cousin of mine, always thinking he could trust me. The foolish king did not realize he was playing right into my hands when he agreed to meet the chieftains to sign the betrothal contract. My back-up plan was always to murder my own wife and pin it on Zayed. A war is exactly what I need to weaken the crown. Ah, it is all coming together now. Finally. Your death will further anger the rebels and commoners."

My heart raced as I tried to comprehend the full extent of these revelations. Kadin, the man I had trusted implicitly, was nothing more than a cunning mastermind who had been manipulating everyone around him for his own gain because he wanted to be king. And Sherazi, the beloved servant girl who had been my companion, was a demon in human form, feeding on the dead bodies of those who had fallen to the curse!

Zayed probably never stayed after his Lycan felled his brides. It was Sherazi, feasting on the corpses that always left behind a macabre sight.

Kadin had placed her here, close to me. Close to all the other queens. Nobody would question if the Army General brought in a head maid. But Sherazi had never, not even once, appeared before Zayed. Because he knew all the servants. He would have realized something was amiss.

I tried to move but it was futile. I caught the glint of a dagger from the corner of my eye and realized Kadin was about to swipe it across my throat. A low growl suddenly gave him pause and then a blur of white crashed into him.

BAGHEL!

The sounds of a scuffle ensued as Kadin was thrown off his feet and Baghel pinned him to the floor. My head pounded, a sensation akin to someone cleaving into it with an axe made my vision dim again and another silent scream tore from my throat.

"I commend...your...loyalty," Kadin panted out and let out a grunt of pain as Baghel gave a particularly loud snarl.

I could not see. I could only hear. The air was filled with the sound of blows being exchanged. Baghel's vicious growls reverberating off the walls. Suddenly, I heard a loud painful whine followed by dead silence.

"But your loyalty will not save your mistress. It will only land you in the grave."

There was a thump and a grunt of pain from Kadin. Baghel let out a feeble yelp of pain.

"Stupid mutt," Kadin muttered and I heard him rise to his feet. "Elvira, if you wish to feast on a dead dog, I have more food for you right here."

My vision swam and rippled, giving way to Kadin standing over me with bloodied hands. If I could have cried, I would have. But my body was still immobile. Dead. Baghel was dead.

A feeling of utter despair and hopelessness consumed me, and I could not help but utter a soft, mournful cry that echoed throughout the chamber. The pain of his loss, releasing my body momentarily from its immobile state. Tears began to trickle down my cheeks as I attempted to move to defend myself. Kadin had orchestrated all of this, a twisted game for his own twisted desire.

My mind raced in a desperate search for a way out of this nightmare. If only I could move!

Kadin chuckled darkly, the scent of death clinging to him as he moved closer to me. His eyes glowed with an insatiable hunger for power that chilled me to the bone.

He reached out a bloodied hand and I was sure he was about to choke the life from me. Instead, his fingers brushed against my collarbone and then snagged onto the rope of the necklace Zayed had gifted me. He gave a hard tug and it broke away from my neck, the green pendant twinkling mockingly in his hand.

"Maybe I will give this to Zayed as a keepsake of your memory," Kadin sneered, pocketing the pendant.

I opened my mouth, wanting to scream. But I could not.

"Being unwell has its merits. You are unable to speak or move due to the high fever," he chuckled. "Oh, this does take away the fun of the chase. But so much more efficient this way. Good-bye...Your Highness," Kadin snarled, lifting the dagger over his head to plunge it deep into my heart.

"Not while I am still alive," came a new voice followed by a whirring sound.

An arrow shot straight to Kadin's hand holding the dagger, piercing through his palm. The dagger fell to the floor with a loud clattering sound.

Elvira, face buried in the Grand Vizier's body, looked up. But she was soon taken care of when an arrow went straight into her left eye and she began to scream in pain, her own blood now mixing with the blood of Kadin's father on her face.

Kadin's eyes widened in shock and fury, but before he could react, another arrow whizzed past his ear and lodged itself in the wall. Then another hit his shoulder.

"Guards!" Kadin bellowed.

At once ten men stormed into my room at the same time that Asya reached me.

"We need to get out of here, Amara," she whispered into my ear. "His men tried to kill me rather than deliver me to the rebel faction. I knew something was amiss with that man. The army is filled with his followers. It is too risky to stay here. Live to fight another day, sister."

She hauled me up worriedly.

My vision was blurry, but I could see Asya's determined face as she helped me to my feet. I stumbled, and she caught me, her muscles tense as she whispered urgently, "We must go now!"

Kadin was roaring out orders to his men, and I heard Elvira shrieking in the background. A volley of arrows came through my balcony.

"I have back up. We have been waiting in the shadows. The guards previously on your balcony were ordered to leave and it gave us the opening we had been waiting for," Asya supplied, pulling me along. "Leave this to the king to clean up and then you may return. Too many of Kadin's men have infiltrated the palace. You are not safe. Even I was able to gather that much during my time here. It is quite easy to eavesdrop on conversations when people think a person of no consequence is nearby. Especially a person being held within the jail cells." Asya grimaced.

I gasped as a sharp shock of pain thundered through my body and I felt as if my skull might crack open from the force of it.

"Come, you are unwell. We must hurry," Asya whispered, dragging me out to the edge of my balcony. I looked around to see men garbed in the rebel faction's black with silver trim. They were here to help me or kill me? Even I did not know.

"The men on the granary roof were all Kadin's men trying to kill innocent people. It was nothing but a show put on for us," Asya informed me. "The rebel faction did not attack the arena. We were all being made fools of. It is only when Kadin's men tried to kill me on my way to meet the rebel leaders that I realized you and the king were being tricked."

She grabbed onto one of the makeshift ropes hanging from the balustrade.

"Follow them, Elvira!" I heard Kadin command. "Shed this form and take your true one!"

A blistering heat against my back told me my room had somehow caught fire.

Suddenly we jumped, and I was airborne as the roaring flames engulfing my room surged closer. I looked back to see bright red flames, their hunger devouring the air as billowing clouds of smoke choked the room. Torrents of fire raged through the darkness, crackling and spitting, as if the very walls were screaming in agony.

Asya held me tightly, her heart pounding against my back. The rebels below scrambled to help us as we plummeted to the ground.

Landing was a jarring impact, but my sister was quick to shield me from harm.

"We have to get to Zayed," I murmured weakly.

"We will," she assured. "He must be told of the truth."

And that is when I finally gave into oblivion because the pain overwhelming me was too great to bear. My last glimpse was of the palace, the place which had been my home, as flames obliterated the side where my quarters were.

Danger had been closer than we had originally thought, and a new journey was about to begin now. One where Zayed and I would need to rely on each other more than ever. For our list of trustworthy allies had diminished significantly.

Epilogue

Kadin's POV

That stupid wench. I should have killed her when I spotted her in the market after leaving Baghel at the veterinary clinic. I had known Amara's sister would be trouble. I just had not expected her to be this much trouble. And yet...she was Amara's sister. I really should have expected it.

Now Amara had escaped and my plan was in danger of falling to pieces.

I ran my still injured hand through my hair in an attempt to calm myself down. Stupid bitch got my shoulder too. I was lucky she had used arrows owned by the rebel faction. I could still do this. No matter if Amara got away. Improvising was my specialty. As I stood in the Queen's quarters, Elvira was already hot on Amara's trail. She would find the two sisters and kill them. I stood over the body now burnt to a crisp, the green pendant around its neck. Luckily, Elvira was able to shed her human form so we could burn it. This body was not the same stature as Amara's but after being burned so badly, down to the bones, no one would notice. And the pendant hanging around the neck of this skeleton would be enough proof. Elvira had told me Amara was partial to it, loath to remove it from her form. Zayed would believe this corpse belonged to his wife.

I would pin it on the rebels and whisper into Zayed's ear that the Chieftains also had something to do with this. It could have been a joint effort. I would tell Zayed I had risked my life to try to save Amara, suffering injuries on my hand and shoulder in the process.

Zayed would be quick to believe that the chieftains worked to lure the king away while the rebels burned his queen alive. He trusted me implicitly because I was his cousin. Because we grew up together. Because after the death of his younger brother, he latched onto me as his only brother. Foolish king. He thought I was content to follow orders. That was the problem with Zayed. Thought everyone was his enemy except for his own blood. Oh how wrong he was.

Elvira and my mother had been working together. Elvira wanted the king's line gone for what he had done to Zayed's mother. She did not know it was my own mother who was to blame for the late queen's murder.

When the opportunity had presented itself, I had implanted Elvira as the daughter of a previous servant into the retinue of maids reserved for the queen fated to die. But we had to be careful because if she ever appeared in front of Zayed, he would have become suspicious.

That smell of decay never truly left her demonic form no matter how many perfumes and oils she doused herself in. Human noses were not as sensitive as a Lycan's. Zayed would have realized immediately. And so, I bided my time. Waiting in the shadows as the rebel faction gained strength and momentum with each queen that passed away. Secretly, I funded them and helped them with a slew of my own men on the inside making sure to guide the faction to work in a specific way.

Until the attack took place during the Blade-Caller trials. Now there was dissent and the rebels had fractured into two groups. One that agreed with the attack, my own men, and one that condemned the attack, those who wished for peace and merely to put an end to the murder of innocent daughters. I knew it was only a matter of time before Father caught on to my involvement. Poisoning myself was the best way to deflect suspicion. And to spur on Zayed to turn Amara. For when he turned her, I had planned to stage her death in hopes that it would cause the king to go mad.

No matter. I achieved my goals. The Grand Vizier was dead. Stupid old man. It was his fault I was nothing but a lackey to the king. If he had been even half as ambitious as my mother I would already be king. Mother groomed me from a young age, guiding me on how best to plot and plan to become king one day. And that day was nearing. I could almost taste victory on my tongue.

I turned, passing by Blade-Callers gathered around the queen's rooms. If there was one group I could not infiltrate, it was these Blade-Callers. Stupid women with their high-ground morals. Once I became king, they would know their place: on their knees before a man, sucking his cock.

"The king has arrived," intoned one of my men.

A smile curled my lips.

It was time to put my plan into motion.

"Fortify the silver chains. We will need to restrain him once the news breaks," I directed, turning in the direction I knew my fool cousin would be rushing in from. I took a deep breath, wiping away the smirk from my face and putting up the mask I had so carefully cultivated through the years. The mask of a dutiful and loyal cousin, the mask of a man who truly cared for his family. I need to appear genuinely heartbroken at the news of the queen being burned to death, even though in reality...I was the one who had orchestrated everything. I let a grimace of pain mar my features and purposefully kept my injured hand in front of me, within everyone's line of sight.

My plan was risky, but if it succeeded, it would give me the power I needed to claim the throne and remake this kingdom according to my own desires.

Zayed battered through the double doors of the palace, his gaze frantic and searching as desperation etched itself across every inch of his face.

This was going to be all too easy.

"Where is she?" Zayed demanded, moving past me.

"I..." I choked out, fake tears gathering at the corners of my eyes. Zayed turned to look at me and then again towards the hallway that would lead him to his queen. "I tried, Cousin...I was too late..." I let out a mournful pained cry. "They killed Father too."

It had been necessary to kill the old man. Zayed would have been immediately suspicious otherwise. Besides, Father would have never condoned my plan. He had lived a good long life. He was going to die soon anyway from old age. Better that his death serve to further my purposes.

"Too?" Zayed turned to look at me shaking his head incredulously, eyes wide. His eyes went to my injuries.

"I tried to save them." I took a step forward, exaggerating a wince over my injuries. "I was...too late..."

Zayed took a step back. "NO! Tell me it is not so, Cousin!"

It was all I could do to keep from laughing. I swallowed hard, wiping the imaginary tears from my face. Weakly, I motioned to the bodies now being carried towards Zayed. Three bodies, burned so that their wounds were not discernible, laid out before him. One of the foolish dog, another of the Grand Vizier and lastly...

Zayed let out a cry of pain and bitter disbelief. A shaking hand reached for the charred necklace around the corpse of his queen. Another hand reached out to my uncle and then the useless mutt.

Zayed looked so vulnerable, so lost. It was almost enough to make me feel guilty for what I was doing. Almost. But then I reminded myself of all the sacrifices I had made for this very moment. The countless nights spent plotting and scheming, the times I had to watch my father grow weaker and more supportive of Zayed. I knew my father would never support my own goals.

As Zayed crumpled to his knees, I stepped forward, placing a hand on his shoulder.

"No, no, no...my queen...my family...my love..." he murmured, repeating the words over and over again. "MY WIFE!" he cried out in agony, clutching the pendant to his chest and shaking as if in physical pain.

"I am sorry, Cousin," I whispered, my voice flickering with empathy.

Zayed looked up at me, his eyes wild with grief and anger. I had never seen my cousin this distraught.

This was the final act of the play, the end of a long-drawn strife for power. If I faltered now, there would be no one left to rule. No one to complete my mother's dream. I must be ruthless.

Zayed was trembling, shaking his head as he mumbled "No, no, no" repeatedly. And then his body began to shake and his eyes lit up with fire.

He opened his mouth, letting out an anguished scream that slowly morphed into a pained howl.

The corner of my lips tilted upward. I knew this would happen. And with Elvira hot on Amara's trail, the queen would be dead soon enough anyway.

"AMARA!" he howled out, his back arching as he bent over into a transformation.

And then the Lycan King stood in all his glory, sniffing the air mercilessly for his next kill. I let him have it, for killing a few innocent servants who had brought the bodies out would be a good enough precedent to shackle him in his silver cell.

I raised a hand, signaling at my men to let the darts filled with sedatives fly. Unfortunately, the Lycan King was fast. He dodged the attacks, ripping into the men taking aim at him.

His eyes flashed with rage as he looked around the room, searching for any threat. The room was still, the only sound the faint dripping of blood from his claws. More men arrived to contain him. And he felled them one by one.

As the chaos ensued, I calmly retreated to the shadows, my eyes never leaving the scene before me. The Lycan King was a thing of beauty and danger all in one. I could never think to overpower him in my own Lycan form. His ferocity was matched only by his strength. But he was distracted. Unaware of the traps I had carefully laid out for him.

In my mind's eye, I could see Zayed losing everything he had ever known—his family, his precious hunting dog, his kingdom, his wife. And all because of me. I bit my lip in satisfaction at the thought of Zayed's downfall. He had always been first. My father loved him more because he believed it was his duty to nurture the young king. Everyone in the palace gave him importance. Everyone except my mother. She taught me how to put on a facade in front of everyone. I had learned from the best.

As the Lycan King tore through my men, I smirked behind my cloak of shadows. They had underestimated the danger at hand, and it was with a sadistic delight that I watched their ranks dwindle. With each one that fell, it was another pillar added to the foundation of my own impending rule. The king had become bloodthirsty and too possessed by his beast to rule.

It was a delicate dance, this game of power and manipulation. My mother had taught me well—to be subtle, ruthless, and always two steps ahead.

I allowed myself a small smile as I noticed the silver chains dangling from the ceiling, hidden in plain sight among the ornate chandeliers. The bait was set, and now it was just a matter of time before Zayed fell for it, just as I had planned.

As the last of my men fell to the ground, I stepped out of the shadows, my smile growing wider. The chaos I had orchestrated had played out perfectly. I raised my hand, signaling to my remaining men to approach the Lycan King with caution.

With a roar of fury, Zayed spotted me and lunged towards me. His eyes were wild red, his muscles straining with the effort of maintaining his feral form. But I had anticipated this move as well. He was too far gone in bloodlust with nothing left to ground him. Amara had grounded him and was gone now. I gave the signal and the silver chains fell from above, but he was fast, dodging them effortlessly. My eyes widened as I tensed, ready to shift and try to defend myself. But Zayed jumped over me and towards the double doors faster than anyone could blink. He took off, ready to run amuck across the kingdom.

"Find him and capture him, he is dangerous and unstable. Who knows what he might do to the innocent citizens," I ordered my men.

Immediately they moved to do my bidding. I rolled my shoulders and prepared to call the nobles and king's cabinet for an emergency meeting.

It was not until we were all gathered in the throne room and I had briefed everyone on the situation that one of the nobles close to my father finally said what I knew was inevitable. Because he too was one of my allies now. Especially after Amara had ruled against him in the wet nurse case.

"Then by right of succession, you are the next heir to the throne. You, Your Highness, must take up the mantle of king lest our kingdom spiral into chaos!" Lord Arin's voice rang out loud and clear.

I bent my head demurely.

"I am not worthy. The title belongs to my cousin."

"Your cousin is no longer fit to rule. His queen is dead, along with any potential heirs she may have carried. You are the true king now!"

I hid a smile.

"I am not equipped to deal with the complex matters of this kingdom," I replied humbly.

"You have been in charge of the soldiers and often helped the king on important matters of security. You are more than capable of taking up the responsibility," spoke up another noble.

A few remained quiet and pensive, but most were nodding along in agreement.

"Long live King Kadin!" the nobles around me yelled, their fists going up into the air in triumph.

I let out a breath of relief. It was done.

Finally. Now I would show them what a true king was capable of.

"Then as my first task as king, I declare we go to war to avenge the attack on our dead queen! We will crush the rebels and the chieftains in the mountains for attempting to destabilize our kingdom!" I declared, raising my own fist into the air.

A war would keep everyone preoccupied. By the time the debris cleared, further questions on the queen's untimely demise would be forgotten. Our people needed something to divert their attention, and a war was the perfect solution. I would lose good soldiers, and the kingdom was not in a position economically to sustain a war. But it was the only option for now until my rule had become solidified.

I smiled humbly, preening internally as chants of "Long live King Kadin of Elamaria!" resounded around me.

To be continued...

Rise of the Lycan Queen

COMING SOON

If this is your first rodeo with me, yes my plot twists are brutal. I am sorry (sort of). But for what it is worth, Amara and Zayed meet up fairly quickly in book two and they get to develop their relationship without intrigues of court surrounding them. It will be interesting to explore a new dynamic between them.

Follow me on my socials to stay updated regarding book two as well as proceeding books which will all be fairytale retellings. Queen Seraphina is part of my Rapunzel retelling.

1. <u>Rubyk12author (IG)</u>

2. <u>Ruby's Reading Room</u> (Facebook reader group)

Acknowledgements

I did not think anyone would be interested in an Arabian Nights retelling. This story was something I worked on during writer's block for my wolf shifter stories. My plan was to actually write the story of Queen Seraphina as a widowed Rapunzel.

However, my wonderful author friends Jaylie Wright and Tember Sapphire motivated me to put the story out there and publish it. Thank you ladies for all of your encouragement.

I also want to thank my husband, my lycan king, for always supporting me in my endeavours and not complaining when I was ignoring him to meet my deadlines.

Thank you to my volunteer proofreaders/beta readers. Alyson, Candi, Jo, Lechelle, and Faith really helped me comb through this story and fix it up. We were always popping in and out of the #1001nights discord chat, screaming over the twists. Let's not forget our favorite mantra—KEEP READING. Get ready for book 2! Thank you, Emily, for proofreading/editing this story.

Last but not least, thank you to all of my readers who were following along via subscriptions. It is because you believed in me that I had the courage to believe in myself. Your belief in me kept me from actually signing my rights away to predatory serialized reading apps so I could own my work and self-publish. I cannot thank you enough for your enthusiastic response to this story!

A Note from the Author

Within this story, I explored some complex societal constructs that were deemed perfectly normal in the past: Wet Nurses and Marital Rape. In many societies, the role of wet nurses in the past was both vital and complex, reflecting the intricate social, economic, and cultural dynamics of their time. These women provided essential nourishment to infants whose biological mothers could not breastfeed due to various circumstances—often prioritizing social obligations, facing health challenges, or being pressured into weaning one child so more children could be born. However, this practice was not without its ethical dilemmas.

Many wet nurses had endured profound personal tragedy, having lost their own children to illness, malnutrition, or the harsh realities of life in impoverished conditions. Driven by desperation, they often took on the role of wet nurses as a means of survival, nurturing another woman's child while mourning their own. Others frequently left their children in care homes, where infant mortality rate was startlingly high. The children left behind did not often survive. This painful irony added emotional complexity to their work. The psychological toll was significant; they often formed strong attachments to the infants they nursed, amplifying the grief for their own lost children. Society imposed expectations on motherhood, compelling these women to fulfill nurturing roles while grappling with the deep emotional scars of personal loss. Their stories serve as poignant reminders of the sacrifices made and the silent heartaches endured. I knew I wanted to highlight this issue (which has often been swept under the rug), within my story in a setting where wet nurses were common. Thankfully, those dark times are behind us. Unfortunately, the same cannot be said about marital rape.

Historically, many legal systems and societal norms have viewed marriage as a contract that grants unconditional sexual access to one's partner, effectively rendering the concept of marital rape invisible. This issue is compounded by various factors, including cultural beliefs, power dynamics, and social stigmas. In many societies, there is a pervasive myth that marriage inherently implies consent, leading victims to feel isolated and unsupported when they seek help or speak out. Survivors may experience a range of psychological effects, including depression, anxiety, post-traumatic stress disorder (PTSD), and feelings of worthlessness. Marital rape is sexual assault. In the United States, about 25% of rape cases are marital rape cases and approximately **10%-14%** of married women are raped by their partners. That is a startlingly high number, especially when it is illegal in 50 states. Even more startling is that it was not made illegal until 1993.

Here is a link to a resource if you or someone you know needs help.

(For those reading the print version, you can go to rainn.org)

ARTBYHAADI
ON INSTAGRAM

www.ingramcontent.com/pod-product-compliance
Lightning Source LLC
Chambersburg PA
CBHW022148010726
47493CB00002B/397